LORD OF THE SEA

BY

DANELLE HARMON

PUBLISHED BY:
Danelle Harmon

LORD OF THE SEA
Copyright © 2013 by Danelle Harmon
ISBN: 0989233065
ISBN: 9780989233064

COPYRIGHTS:

_ Book Cover Design by Seductive Designs
_ Stock Image copyrights (man): © Taria Reed/ The Reed Files
_ Stock Image copyrights (hair) © Jenn LeBlanc/Illustrated Romance
_ Stock Image copyrights (barrels) © ksushsh
_ Stock Image copyrights (large ship) © jgroup
_ Stock Image copyrights (sea landscape) © tortoon
_ Stock Image copyrights (ship): © Gerald Todd

$\mathcal{D}$EDICATION

No book writes itself, and there are many whom I wish to thank when it comes to this one—my beloved family for their uncomplaining patience and understanding while I worked so hard to finish it; my talented editor Christine Zikas, with whom it was wonderful to be working again after all these years; and my sweet and treasured ReaderFriends, all of whom "feed" and inspire me every single day. All of these people deserve my gratitude, but it is to my dear friend Nancy Fields that *Lord Of The Sea* is dedicated. It was Nancy who came up with the idea of putting Connor and Rhiannon together; it was Nancy who encouraged me when I didn't think I had it in me to write another full length novel after a decade spent away from publishing; and it was Nancy who spent many a late night on Facebook with me, talking about the book and inspiring me in ways she could never imagine. Thank you, Nancy, for all your help, enthusiasm and encouragement—but thank you, most of all, for your friendship.

They that go down to the sea in ships, that do business in great waters; these see the works of the Lord, and his wonders in the deep.

Psalms 107:23-24

CHAPTER 1

... Somewhere in the Caribbean Sea, 1813

He was intimately familiar with clouds. High, cirrus clouds wisping across the zenith. Thick, billowing cumulus. And deadly black thunderheads, squalls that could knock down a ship in minutes.

These were black squalls.

A prudent mariner would have taken one look at that unpredictable monster swarming up on the horizon, brought in the schooner *Kestrel*'s big square topsail and sent down its yard, stood by to reef the mainsail and then turned tail and run. But Captain Connor Merrick was a Yankee privateer, and there, a mile away off the larboard bows, were the fat, bloated sails of a British merchantman, ripe for the picking.

From across the water, rolling like the echoes of distant thunder, came the sound of guns as the big ship was attacked by the pirates who had found her first.

"Your orders, Captain?"

Connor stood at the weather rail, watching the squall approaching off to windward. Already the sea was starting to grow restless, throwing scud up over the bows and great sheets of water sluicing through the scuppers and along the deck as the schooner shouldered each swell that paraded toward them.

His every instinct told him to get the devil out of there.

But there was the matter of that merchantman. . . .

He plucked a telescope from the rack and put it to his eye, steadying the instrument in the crook of his elbow with the ease of long practice. Into the spherical field swam the merchantman, bluff-bowed and tubby, wallowing in the seas, and far off under her lee, a hostile coast swarming with pirates that were loyal to no nation.

"Hmph," Connor said, half to himself.

His lieutenant, who was also his first cousin, raised a brow. "Hmph?"

"Seems we have a choice to make, Nathan," he said, glancing yet again at the approaching squall. "Yonder merchantman is flying British colors and trying to defend herself against a horde of pirates in small boats. She cannot, of course. They'll slaughter everyone aboard, and then take the ship. So, do we do the gallant thing and sweep in to her rescue? Or do the safe thing, and hightail it out of here before the storm puts us on our beam ends?"

"Hmph," said Nathan, imitating his cousin. "You never do the safe thing."

Connor grinned. "And taking her as prize after saving her, is certainly not the gallant thing. But it's what I intend to do. Fetch Toby, would you? I need him on deck."

Moments later, Nathan's fourteen-year-old brother, red haired, freckled, and eager to please the cousin and captain he idolized, was on deck. He took one look at the squall looming up on the weather horizon, the foam beginning to blow like chaff from off the waves, and paled.

"Toby, lad. I've a mind to outrun a storm as well as take a prize. Douse the galley fire, call the hands to quarters, and load up both broadsides with grape and chain." Already, the wind was strengthening, beginning to gust ominously. "Send down the kites and let's ease the main and fore a bit. Time to see what our wild black mare can do with her reins out to the buckle."

It would be a hair-raising gallop indeed down onto the British merchantman, but Connor had a sharp crew, a fast ship, and the devil's own luck. "Put the helm up," he said, and the chase was on.

"Pirates," said Alannah Falconer Cox as she and the young woman she was chaperoning were both frantically herded belowdeck. Alannah, widowed fifteen months before and only recently out of mourning clothes, was the younger sister of Sir Graham Falconer, the famous British admiral currently stationed in Barbados—the ultimate destination of the merchant ship *Porpoise*.

A destination that looked, at the moment, as though it would never be reached.

Her companion listened to the footsteps pounding on the deck above, the frantic, shouted orders of the captain and his officers, and the sudden report of gunfire from somewhere close.

"We're going to die," said Rhiannon Evans, who really wanted to see more of life than her mere eighteen years had granted her.

"Stop it! Don't talk like that!"

"Well it's true! You heard the captain, we were doomed from the moment we lost touch with the rest of the convoy after that storm three days ago. That's it, I'm going topside. If I'm going to die, it's not going to be down here."

"No, Rhiannon, it's too dangerous up on deck!"

"It's no less so down here, because we'll be trapped here when those pirates board!"

"If you go topside, they'll kill you—or worse!"

"If I stay here, they'll sink the ship, and us with it!"

"Rhiannon, *no!*"

But the younger woman, grabbing the hem of her gown, was already bounding up the companionway and as she emerged back on deck, unnoticed and ignored in the melee, her dread turned to downright horror.

Three small boats surrounded the ship, and already, a horde of savage, screaming men brandishing pistols, cutlasses and knives were swarming over the rail and onto the deck.

Rhiannon screamed.

Shots rang out, and suddenly one of the brigands turned and saw her.

Rhiannon ran for the hatch—and at that moment, the shattering roar of a cannon from somewhere off to starboard nearly deafened her.

Her head jerked up, and in an instant she saw it—another ship, giant black storm clouds swelling up behind her, sweeping down on them with the spray breaking from her bows and smoke already rolling across the water from the gun she had just fired. The pirates took one look at her, pointed and began yelling, and some began leaping back over the sides and down into their boats. But those that remained weren't about to go down without a fight, and three of them ran to the merchantman's small starboard cannon and, shoving aside the cowering crew, began to load it. Another savage boom echoed over the water as the approaching ship bore down on them, firing once more, and as she swept past, all sleek black hull and sharply back-swept masts, Rhiannon saw men in her rigging and cross-trees, firing down on the pirates with muskets and long rifles.

"*Rhiannon!*"

Alannah was there, grabbing her arm, crying out as one of the merchantman's crew suddenly staggered and pitched to the deck, clutching his throat. Rhiannon stood paralyzed, unable to move, and then Alannah was hauling her back toward the hatch, down it, both of them tripping on their hems and tumbling the last few feet to the deck below, Alannah landing on open palms, Rhiannon on one foot that twisted beneath her.

"My ankle!" she cried. "You go, save yourself!"

"I'm not leaving you!"

Above, thunder roared again, and this time the mer-chantman shuddered as iron found her hull but Rhiannon had no time to scream, for Alannah had all but dragged her aft into the captain's cabin. She slammed the door shut, threw the latch, and together, sobbing in terror, they hauled the captain's heavy sea chest up against the door.

"What else can we barricade it with?" Rhiannon cried.

"I don't know, everything else is bolted to the deck!"

Another deafening crash from above, thuds, bumps, screams and shots, and then the sound of men yelling in a frenzied war cry, more screams, and footsteps pounding on the deck just above their heads.

The two women threw themselves against the door and wrapped their arms around each other, crying in fear.

Suddenly the guns stopped booming, and all went quiet on the deck above.

Rhiannon lifted her head, and heard only the frantic hammering of her own heart. Cold sweat ran down her spine, and hesitantly, she and Alannah drew back.

And then they heard it.

Footsteps, coming toward them.

"Dear God," Alannah breathed.

Rhiannon rose, her ankle shrieking in agony. There was nothing in the cabin with which to defend themselves, but on the captain's desk lay a pair of brass nautical dividers, V-shaped and needle-pointed, which the master used to chart a course. She grabbed them and turned to face the door as a fist pounded against it once, twice, three times.

She glanced at Alannah and the other woman ran toward her, trying in vain to find a weapon.

Suddenly, the door crashed open beneath the force of a powerful male shoulder, shoving the heavy sea chest out of the way with it, and both women screamed.

A man stood there. In the gloom, he was lean and lanky and so tall that he filled the doorway. He wore a short blue pea coat with brass buttons, canvas trousers, and a straw hat. In his hand was a pistol, which, upon seeing the two women, he lowered.

"Well, well," he said, and with an elegant bow removed the hat, revealing carelessly tousled chestnut hair that was thick and curling and fashionably cut. His was a face of hard planes, translucent green eyes, and a recklessly smiling mouth. Entering the cabin, he calmly plucked the dividers from Rhiannon's nerveless hand. "I am Captain Merrick of the American privateer schooner *Kestrel*, and it would appear that we've found a most lucrative prize, indeed."

ℭHAPTER 2

Well, well, indeed, Connor thought, tossing the dividers to a nearby table.

Rum. Sugar. Molasses. Spices. Exotic fruits. Even, God forbid, slaves. Those were the sort of things one normally found when they took a ship in these latitudes, but this was an altogether different sort of cargo, indeed.

Women. Two of them. One dark-haired with flashing blue eyes and a vaguely familiar look about her. She was fair enough, though he suspected she'd like to retrieve the dividers and stab them straight into his heart. The other one . . . .

Keep to the business at hand.

Oh, the other one. . . .

That one, Connor thought as her huge, long-lashed green eyes lifted to his, was surely the most beautiful creature he'd ever seen in his life. She was young and willowy, with fiery red-gold hair set off by clear, flawless skin, mischievous eyes, and lips that made him want to trace their bow, their perfect shape, with his finger. His tongue.

Something stirred in his groin.

This could be a problem.

Ignore her.

He turned away just as the dark-haired one found her voice.

"Privateer? You're nothing but a pirate! This is an English ship, and I demand that you release us immediately!"

The beauty grabbed the dark-haired one's elbow. "Alannah, he just saved our lives!"

"Only to rob us! Oh, just wait until my brother hears of this!"

"Better to be robbed than *dead*!"

"He may well kill us yet! Or God forbid, ravish us!"

Connor shot a glance at the sunset-haired beauty. *Don't give me any ideas,* he wanted to say, because she had spunk as well as loveliness and she was looking at him the way any damsel in distress might just gaze upon her rescuer, looking at him in a way that made him want to pull himself up a little more and puff out his chest and slay a dragon for her. Though, come to think of it, maybe he just had. At any other time, her worshipful gaze and that impish smile would have been all he needed to follow his baser instincts. At any other time, he might take great delight in further pursuing that coy, unspoken invitation—preferably in a place that involved a mattress, sheets, and an hour or two of free time. But he had business to conduct here, there were squalls bearing down on them, and he couldn't let himself be distracted.

Papers. He had to get the ship's papers.

The other one was still harping on him. "Furthermore, I'll have you know right now Captain Merrick, that I object most highly to the way you forced yourself into this cabin like some barbarian! Just what do you think you're doing?"

Ignoring her, Connor sent a conspiring grin the way of her companion, went to the captain's desk and yanking open a drawer, began searching for the merchant ship's papers.

"Did you hear me? What do you think you're doing?

Ignore her.

Easy enough.

Ignore the other one, too.

Not so easy. . . .

Rhiannon, feeling her heartbeat skipping, somersaulting and tripping over itself as she watched the Yankee privateer rifling through the desk, had caught that covert, amused glance he'd thrown her and couldn't take her eyes off him. Footsteps echoed outside and now another man entered the cabin, a sword in his hand. Though not as tall or lean as the captain, he too was handsomely made, with thick, tawny hair that was bleached by the sun, steady brown eyes, a quiet demeanor and a look of solidness and strength about him. He glanced at her and Alannah, then turned toward the mahogany-haired god who was cheerfully pulling out a sealed oilskin packet from the desk.

"Captain, there are five from this tub who reckon they want to sign aboard with us; the rest, including the master, have resisted, and we've got three remaining pirates a'begging for mercy."

"Begging for mercy, are they? Hmph. Given that they showed this crew none, I'm not inclined to oblige them." The privateer slammed the drawer shut. "Secure the prisoners in the fo'c'sle, with the pirates separate from the crew so they don't add to the slaughter. How's that squall tracking?"

It was then that she remembered his introduction.

Merrick . . . Kestrel . . . *Merrick* . . . .

"Veering off, sir, heading north by west. I think it'll miss us."

"The devil's own luck, that," the American said, slitting open the leather pouch with a small knife and beginning to scan its contents.

"What are you going to do with us?"

The American ignored Alannah.

"I *demand* to know what will become of us!"

"Do be quiet, madam, I'm trying to think," the captain snapped, handing the papers to the newcomer with a sound of annoyance. "Read this, would you, Nathan? I don't have time to sit here and make sense of it."

"Aye." The one named Nathan said, looking at the papers. "She's out of Southampton, bound for Barbados, carrying fine English linens, china, beer, various foodstuffs, and muskets."

"Muskets! How provident." The captain reclaimed the papers and stuffed them back into the leather pouch. "Muster a prize crew for this tub. We'll send her into Mobile, as it's the closest port from which to auction her off. Jenkins can command her. Ladies, collect your belongings."

He tossed the pouch to a nearby table, and it suddenly hit Rhiannon just who this handsome god was.

"You're Captain Merrick!" she exclaimed excitedly. "Of the schooner *Kestrel*!"

He just looked at her as though she were daft. "Aye, that's what I just said."

"From Portsmouth, England?"

"No, ma'm, from Newburyport, Massachusetts." He began to stalk toward the door.

"But you were in Portsmouth this past spring! I know you were!"

The American turned, and something glinted in his clear, pale green eyes, something that wasn't quite amusement, something that belied a memory, perhaps, that he had no wish to recall, before one corner of his mouth—his very firm, very sensual mouth, Rhiannon thought—turned up in the faintest of grins.

"And how might you know that, Miss . . . ?"

"Evans. Rhiannon Evans. You don't know me, but I'm Gwyneth's sister!"

He lifted a brow. "Gwyneth's sister."

"Yes! We rented a house in Portsmouth together, and it was *you* who was rescuing French and American prisoners from the hulk *Surrey*, *you* who risked your life for them time and time again as the elusive Black Wolf, *you* who saved my brother-in-law, the marquess of Morninghall, from certain death by snatching him right out from under the guns of a firing squad with this very ship! It was you, wasn't it? Connor Merrick! You're the Black Wolf!"

Even the other man had paused to stare at Rhiannon. "Well, this certainly complicates matters, Connor," he said, his brown eyes amused.

"Only if we let it." And then, frowning: "What the blazes are you doing all the way out here? You're a long way from England."

"My friend Alannah here invited me to accompany her to Barbados, and since I wanted an adventure, I came along. Oh, I can't wait to write to Gwyneth and tell her all about what you just did for us; you saved our lives, Captain Merrick! Thank you!" It was all Rhiannon could do not to fling her arms around his neck in relief and gratitude. "Oh, thank you!"

The American's green eyes crinkled with humor.

And Alannah, seeing the unspoken connection between Rhiannon and this man who had so audaciously taken their ship, and was now looking just a little too long, and with a little too much interest—the *wrong* kind of interest—at the girl she was charged to protect, wasn't so forgiving. Especially since there was something disturbingly familiar about him.

"I don't care who you are, or what you did in Portsmouth, but I will say this," she spat. "I demand that you return this ship to her rightful captain and allow us to continue on our way to Barbados. Because if you do not, I can guarantee you that this will be the last ship you and that—that piratical-looking vessel of yours out there will ever take as a prize."

"Oh? And by what authority do you make such a threat, ma'm?"

"By the authority vested in my brother! Vice Admiral Sir Graham Falconer!"

If that proclamation was intended to intimidate, impress or cow the two men, it had a completely opposite effect. The Yankee privateer turned and looked at his companion, and suddenly both of them began laughing.

"Thought she looked familiar," Captain Merrick said as an aside to his lieutenant, before the two started laughing all over again.

"You think this is funny, do you?!" Alannah cried, stamping one small foot. "When my brother hears of what you've done, he'll string you up to his flagship's yardarm and hang you by the neck until you're dead!"

At this, Captain Merrick only laughed all the harder, until finally taking pity on the bristling Alannah.

"Sir Graham will do no such thing," he said. "Your pretty young companion here recognized me without ever having seen me, but you, madam, met me eight years ago when your brother married my sister Maeve. I'm surprised you don't remember me. Must be the hat, eh, Nathan?"

"Aye, Con. Must be the hat."

Alannah's mouth fell open and she paled in dawning realization and horror.

"Dear God in heaven," she breathed, staring at him. "I thought your surname sounded familiar. My brother . . . your sister. . . ."

"Yes, and stringing me up to the yardarm with a noose 'round my neck would, shall we say, complicate things in their marriage. Nathan? What do you think? Shall we make for Barbados and deliver these two ladies to the admiral in person? Pay Sir Graham and Lady Falconer a little social call?"

Alannah recovered herself. "You can't just sail into Barbados, this is a Yankee privateer and our countries are at war!"

"So they are," Captain Merrick said blithely. "And far be it from me to do anything but take full advantage of that fact, because wars like this make people like me, rich. Now, ladies, say goodbye to this leaky old tub. Your passage to Barbados is about to get a whole lot faster."

Alannah just stood there, gaping and at a loss for words.

But Rhiannon's eyes were sparkling with anticipation and delight. All her life, she had longed for adventure such as her sisters had had. She had watched as Morganna had found love in the arms of a handsome suitor, and then as Gwyneth got swept away by her dark and dangerous marquess. And now here she was, rescued in the nick of time from bloodthirsty pirates and about to be put aboard a Yankee privateer captained by none other than the most admired, elusive, talked-about, and yes, hunted man in Portsmouth–the audacious, recklessly brave, startlingly handsome Black Wolf. He'd outsmarted the Royal Navy and made the pulse of every woman in that city beat a little faster. And now he was making Rhiannon's pulse beat a whole *lot* faster.

Nathan left to do his captain's bidding, Alannah stormed out in a huff, and Rhiannon took a step and sucked in her breath in pain.

Captain Merrick's easy smile faded, and his sharp green gaze went to her feet.

"What ails you, madam?"

"I fell going down the hatch," Rhiannon said, her cheeks going hot. "Twisted my ankle."

"I see." Then, before she could protest, he stepped forward and swung her easily up into his arms, grinning as Alannah, marching back into the cabin to see what was taking Rhiannon so long, began to sputter.

"Put her down!" she snapped. "That is most ungentlemanly of you, sir!"

"On the contrary, ma'm, only a cad would make a lady walk on a twisted ankle. Now do make haste. We've got squalls out yonder, the seas are building beneath our feet and I'd like to get this business underway." He shifted Rhiannon's weight in his arms and began to walk with businesslike authority from the cabin, easily negotiating the growing pitch and roll of the ship. She could feel the solid strength of his chest against her arm, caught his scent of bay rum and salt spray, and thought, quite happily, that she had never experienced anything quite so heady and wonderful as the sensation of being carried in a handsome man's arms as though she weighed no more than chaff on the wind. Oh, sweet Lord, this was going to be one exciting adventure indeed.

"Wind's picking up, sir. More squalls approaching from the southeast."

Captain Merrick, pressing her face against the hard wall of his chest so she wouldn't see the carnage on the deck above, had carried her like some prize of war from the merchantman onto the low, racy deck of his privateer, hove to with sails banging and slatting against the wind, the man at the tiller looking nervously off at the dark clouds that boiled up on the horizon and cast an eerie green glow over the sea. Now, the schooner, its long bowsprit and jib-boom angling far up and out over the swells parading relentlessly toward them, swung into action as orders were hastily given and carried out.

"Reef the main right down, double lash the guns, and get another headsail on her," Captain Merrick said, with a quick glance up at the pennant snapping like gunshots in the wind so far above. He set Rhiannon down. "We'll stay on the sta'b'd tack and head northeast straight toward Barbados. I want to be well clear of that lee shore when this thing hits."

"Aye, sir."

Rhiannon, standing beside an uncharacteristically quiet Alannah, heard the low murmurs of the seamen around her.

"*Barbados*?"

"That's a British naval port!"

"He's crazy," muttered a nearby sailor, with an admiring grin.

"Isn't he always?"

"Aye, but ye can't say it won't be a fast passage."

Captain Merrick ignored them all. "Toby, lad! Take these two ladies below and see that they're comfortable. Mind Miss Evans's ankle. Handily, now!"

Rhiannon clung to the weather shrouds as the deck began to buck like a horse beneath her. She looked at the merchantman that had brought them from England, already moving away under the command of the prize crew Captain Merrick had put aboard her. Farther off, the small boats carrying the pirates bobbed in the building seas as they sped back toward the safety of their lair, and Captain Merrick, who seemed to orchestrate the nervous chaos around him like some maestro in a Mozart symphony, was precise, calm, self-assured, and anything but worried as he glanced once more at the squall, coming in fast and hard.

Someone was tugging at Rhiannon's elbow. Tearing her gaze from the captain, she saw a young lad standing there beside her. He had a face full of freckles, salt-smeared spectacles, and a shock of curling red hair blowing wildly from out beneath his round hat.

"Captain says you need to follow me," he yelled above the wind, now beginning to whistle and scream through lines and shrouds. "It's safer below."

Alannah found her voice. "It won't be if we capsize!"

"We won't capsize. My uncle Brendan designed this grand old lady, my grandpa built her, and the most competent and capable master in the world commands her. But the seas are already washing through the scuppers, ma'm, and none of us'll be able to save you if ye get swept overboard."

"Toby, damn you, make haste!" roared Captain Merrick.

"Aye, Captain!" The boy offered one elbow to Rhiannon, the other to an increasingly green-looking Alannah and, bracing himself against the schooner's roll as she began to heel over hard in the wind, hurried them toward the nearest hatch, Rhiannon limping and holding on to the young man for dear life.

They managed to get below, and Toby guided them aft. An unlit tin lantern swung wildly from a hook bolted to the deck beams above, and the only illumination in the small, darkening cabin came from an overhead skylight and the stern windows, which the lad ran to double latch against the mountainous waves that reared and broke like things possessed just beyond.

"This is Con's cabin," the lad said. "You'll be safe enough here, but we'll be closing the hatches as soon as I'm back topside to prevent flooding below. Hang on tight, and I'll be back as soon as we're through the worst of it."

He touched his hat to them and was gone.

And as the eerie, black-green squall began to fill the view of the windows behind them, Rhiannon, clinging once again to Alannah, had never felt more frightened in her life.

"I'm sorry, Rhiannon. Spared from slaughter, only to die in a storm at sea . . . I should never have invited you along with me to spend the winter in Barbados with my brother and his family, it was selfish of me, madness—"

"Oh, stop, Alannah, it'll be an adventure."

"How can you be so calm? We're going to die. . . ."

"Captain Merrick is *not* going to let us die."

"Captain Merrick might look and act like a Greek god, but he has no more power to command the wind and waves than you or I."

"No, but he *does* command this ship, and I'm quite certain he knows what he's doing up there."

The other woman had made her unsteady way to the neatly-made-up bunk and there, sank to her knees on the deck flooring, her arms on the coverlet, her head buried in them as though in prayer. The schooner heeled over even further, shuddering as the full force of the wind slammed into her, and Rhiannon fought down an involuntary sense of panic as she heard shouted commands from the deck above. On the table nearby a pewter tankard began to slide, and she grabbed it before it could tumble off and hit the deck flooring.

"Besides, Alannah, if we were all going to die, I daresay Captain Merrick would look a lot more worried than he did when we last saw him. Did he look scared? Worried, alarmed, or upset? No, he looked like he was actually enjoying this, that it was a challenge to him."

"I can't believe I didn't recognize him . . . we were both at that wedding between our siblings all those years ago . . . . Ohhhhh, I feel so *sick*. . . ."

Alannah was getting greener by the moment.

"Lie down, Alannah. Get in the bunk and close your eyes. Hold my hand. Think of someplace else . . . such as . . . such as how excited you'll be when we reach Barbados and you get to see your little nephew and nieces!"

"We'll never reach Barbados. . . ."

"Yes we will, just . . . faster than we expected."

Alannah, pale and sweating, only moaned, and with Rhiannon's help managed to get into the bunk. Quickly, Rhiannon cast her gaze around the storm-darkened cabin, looking for a bucket, a pail, anything, before her friend succumbed to the *mal de mer* brought on by the motion of the ship. She managed to grab a bowl and stagger back to Alannah just as the other woman sat up and began retching. Rhiannon sat beside her, rubbing her back, trying her best to soothe her in her misery.

"Fine admiral's sister I make," Alannah said weakly, lying back in the bunk.

"Don't be so hard on yourself. Even Lord Nelson got seasick."

"And how is it that you're not, Rhiannon?"

"I don't know. I guess some people are more vulnerable to it than others." She took her friend's cold, clammy hand. "I know you don't think highly of him for capturing our ship, Alannah, but he *did* just save our lives."

"Not yet he hasn't. Besides, I don't like the way he was looking at you."

"Was he? Looking at me?"

Alannah made a noise of despair and put the back of her forearm over her eyes. "Lord Morninghall trusted me to watch over you until we can get to Barbados, where my brother can assume your guardianship . . . he's not for you, Rhiannon. Forget what I just said."

"But was he? Really looking at me?"

"Of course he was. But pay him no heed. Men like Captain Merrick are in the business of breaking hearts. He'll take yours and snap it over his knee like there was no tomorrow."

"You know nothing about him, Alannah!"

"I know what I see, and what I see is a charming rogue who knows very well how women react to him. He'll ruin you, if you let him. And now, I don't want to talk anymore . . . not about Captain Merrick, not about anything . . . dear God, Rhiannon, I think I'm going to be sick again."

Rhiannon grabbed the bowl once more. Outside, the storm intensified, the noise of the wind now so loud that both women felt like they were in the very maelstrom of hell. The schooner rose on each towering crest, quivered beneath them as it bravely fought through wind and rain and furious seas, then smashed down into the troughs with an action that had Alannah soon huddled in a sweating, moaning, sobbing ball of misery on the bunk. Outside, rain slashed against the stern windows, and daring to look out, Rhiannon saw angry green seas beyond the glass in one instant, then black horizon in the next before it was obscured, once more, by the heaving swells.

The storm seemed to last for hours, though Rhiannon knew it couldn't have been more than thirty minutes before they were through the worst of it. Eventually, the cabin seemed to lighten, and beyond the stern windows the sky began to show wedges of blue as the squall moved off. The heavy, laboring motion of the schooner began to ease, and Rhiannon realized that the unholy screaming of the wind through the rigging had lessened in pitch and now had subsided to a few strong, brief gusts.

She stroked her friend's arm and let out a long, relieved breath. "I think it's over."

There was a discreet cough just outside the door before it was pushed hesitantly open. Young Toby stood there dripping rain or seawater or both, and blushing a bit as his gaze found Rhiannon. He bowed, trying hard to be gallant and gentlemanly despite his tender age.

"Captain's respects, ladies, and he inquires about your welfare. The squall has passed."

"We're fine . . . a little shaken up, but fine."

"He also says there's something topside that he thought ye might enjoy seeing. If you'd both come with me?"

"You go," Alannah said weakly. "I'm not quite recovered enough to go up on deck."

The youngster looked at her appraisingly. "Beggin' your pardon, ma'm, but you might feel better with some fresh air and the sight of the horizon."

"I'll be up in a little while . . . for now, take Rhiannon."

Rhiannon hesitantly tried her ankle, and though it still hurt, it was able to bear weight. Together, she and Toby ascended the hatch and emerged on a wet, still heeling deck under a sky that was blinding white with sunlight. After the darkness below, she stood blinking as rain dripped down from the rigging and sails above. Far off to leeward now, the squall was moving away; the horizon in all other directions was hard and bright and clear, the sea a deep cerulean blue.

"Miss Evans." The captain came forward, looking wet and disheveled and virile, as though he had enjoyed the life-or-death experience they'd just been through. "You survived."

"Were we ever in any danger?"

"The business of any ship is to stay on that small bit of space between the sky and the bottom of the sea, otherwise known as the surface. The fact that we remain in that small bit of space is always cause for a prayer or two of thanksgiving."

"So we were in danger."

Grinning, he unbuttoned his pea coat. "If we were, we aren't now."

His warm gaze remained on her as he peeled the wet jacket from his body and tossed it over a nearby cannon— *no, not cannon,* Rhiannon thought; *a cannon is called a gun when it's aboard a ship*—and Rhiannon, blushing, wondered if that same look was what Alannah had so objected to. Thank goodness her friend was below. It put a little quiver in her belly to have a man like Connor Merrick looking at her like that, and she felt a sudden, swift tingle in her breasts.

I could get used to having him look at me like that.

And then:

I wonder what it would be like to have him . . . kiss me.

She glanced down, afraid that he could read her thoughts, and found herself staring at his wet canvas trousers and bare feet. Bare feet! Had she ever seen a man's bare feet before? Muscled thighs, strong ankles, and a sparse covering of hair from his knees on down drew her eye; her blood suddenly seemed too warm, and she realized that she was staring. She looked up and boldly met his smiling gaze. "You have something to show me, Captain?"

Besides your bare feet?

The corner of his mouth was twitching; he was obviously well aware that his bare legs had unsettled her. He offered his arm. "Aye. Come forward with me."

As they moved past the schooner's two sharply raked-back masts and up into the plunging bow of this sleek and beautiful craft, Rhiannon looked up and saw it—a rainbow, arcing clear across the zenith and filling the sky with dazzling bands of color. She clapped her hands in delight.

"Oh, Captain Merrick, look!"

His grin came easily. But it was not just the rainbow that he had brought her forward to see. Firmly holding her elbow and steadying her against the sharply angled deck, he inclined his head, and it was then that Rhiannon suddenly heard a strange buzzing sound, saw a silvery flash, and jumped back as, a second later, something landed, flopping, at her feet.

"A flying fish!"

Another buzz, another fish, and then something furry streaked past her ankle, pounced on the fish and, clenching it in its jaws, darted quickly aft.

"Was that a cat?"

"Yes, Billy, I think. Or maybe it was Tuck. We have two on the ship, and I can't tell them apart." He smiled. "Well, at least I won't have to feed them, tonight!"

Rhiannon watched in delight as more of the strange fish leaped through the air, buzzing and flashing silver. The beautiful arc of the rainbow was spread out and up before them. In that moment she had never felt more alive and, raising her face to the wind, she looked out over the schooner's long, plunging bowsprit as it smashed down on each swell that paraded toward them, foam hissing out around it. The wind was brisk, blowing the tops off the incoming waves and flinging spray and foam against her face and clothes. On an impulse, she reached up, untied the strings of her bonnet and yanked it off, letting the wind rip the pins from her hair and rejoicing in the girlish exhilaration of feeling it streaming out around her.

Laughing for the sheer joy of the moment, she looked over at Captain Merrick—and the sound caught in her throat. *That look again.* Only this time, he was staring down at her with an almost predatory intensity and though he was still smiling, his eyes had darkened in some small but not insignificant way that she couldn't identify.

"I beg your pardon, Captain," she said, smiling. "You must think my shameless display of free spirit dreadfully uncouth."

"On the contrary, ma'am." His eyes seemed suddenly greener. "I find it quite charming."

"Oh!" Flustered, she looked out once more over the plunging bowsprit and long, long jib-boom, all too aware now of the captain's gaze still upon her. She suddenly felt too hot beneath her clothes, and hastily tried to stuff her hair back into her bonnet.

"Don't," he said, catching her hand. "Your hair is too pretty to hide beneath a hat. And I enjoy watching you delight in the feel of the wind."

He stepped a bit closer, a little *too* close, and her heart suddenly began to pound. *Oh, dear, what do I say to* that? Rhiannon thought, all too aware of his height, his nearness, his very *presence*. She pulled her hand from his, took a safe step back, and crumpled the bonnet in her palm, trying to think of something, anything, to say. . . .

"Will we make Barbados soon?"

His gaze remained on her. "With this wind, we'll raise Bridgetown by tomorrow."

"Your ship seems very . . . uh, very fast."

Oh, he was standing close. She was having trouble breathing, let alone thinking.

"She is, indeed. She can outrun anything the British send after her."

Rhiannon, unsettled by that keen, direct gaze, turned away to look out over the water. "Why is she so fast?"

"My father designed her back during the last war. She was a legend then, and I intend to make her a legend now."

"That doesn't explain her speed."

"No, I'm afraid it doesn't. My *Dadaí* often tried to teach me about ship design, but I have no head for it. When he'd explain to me why a raked mast added speed, or how a certain amount of steeve in the hull allows a ship to slip that much quicker through the water, my mind would wander onto other things. So while I know this ship is fast, Miss Evans, I'm the last person who could ever tell you why."

"And yet you have no fear, taking her into a British port?"

"There are certain advantages to having an English admiral for one's brother-in-law. But I won't tarry there. Wouldn't do to wear out my welcome."

"If you won't stay long . . . where will you go?"

"'A' privateering, ma'm."

She looked over at him. He was grinning down at her again, and the thought of him dropping her and Alannah in Barbados and then sailing off, probably never to see him again, made her feel sad. In his own way, he was a connection to her sister back in England whom she missed desperately, but it was more than that. He was Connor Merrick, for heaven's sake—the Black Wolf—and had there ever been such a romantic figure?

And here she was, standing beside him.

Talking with him.

Wondering once again what it would be like if he kissed her. . . .

She looked out again over the endless waves filing toward them, and *Kestrel*'s long, long jib-boom pointing the way. She sensed a restlessness in the man beside her, as though he'd indulged her long enough and was eager to send her back below so he could return to the business of his ship, but oh, she didn't want to be stuffed safely belowdecks; she wanted to be up here with Connor Merrick, enjoying the wind in her hair and the salt spray on her cheeks and the heady breathlessness of being next to him and having him notice her, talk to her, give her his attention.

This magical moment might not last forever, but she would gratefully take even a few more seconds.

He was offering his arm. "I should take you below now, ma'm."

"Yes . . . you have a ship to run."

"Duty before pleasure, I'm afraid."

She planted her feet, hoping for just those few more seconds before she was relegated to the safety of his cabin once more. "I wish I weren't afraid of heights," she said suddenly.

"Are you?"

"Yes. When I was a little girl, I climbed a tree and got stuck up there for hours. I was afraid to come down . . . it's easy enough to climb up, but once you get up there and then look down, it's only then that you realize how high up you are and how terrified you are of falling. My sister Gwyneth finally found me, and it was she who came up and rescued me. Funny how something like that stays with a person."

"That is a pity. There's no better view in the world, than from up high."

"I see your men climbing up in the rigging with not a care in the world. I could never do that." Her gaze went once more to the schooner's long jib-boom, surging up and down as it pointed the way out over the swells. "But to go out there along that long spar—the jib-boom, I believe it's called?— and feel it plunging and dipping beneath me like a racehorse in full flight?" She sighed wistfully. "Now, *that* would be fun."

"It can be a wild ride," he allowed, looking at her once again with that same interest he'd shown when she had taken off her bonnet. "Perhaps when the seas quiet down a bit, I'll take you."

"Oh, I don't think I should. I don't know how to swim."

"Well, far be it from me to force a lady to do something she doesn't want to do. But if you change your mind. . . ."

"I shall keep that in mind." She clawed the hair out of her eyes and, knowing it was time to relinquish him to his duties, put out her hand. He took it in his large, callused one, dwarfing her ungloved fingers within her own as their gazes met. "You saved our lives today, Captain. Not just once, but twice." She smiled up at him. "I can't thank you enough."

His eyes had that wolfish hunger in them again. "All in a day's work, ma'm," he said, grinning. "All in a day's work."

CHAPTER 3

All in a day's work indeed, Connor thought, as he gave the delectable Miss Rhiannon Evans into the care of a blushing, tongue-tied Toby to escort below, and went aft to take the tiller from Nathan.

He couldn't get the memory of that beautiful hair of hers flying around her face, the delighted sparkle in her eyes, the way the wind had molded her gown up against her slim curves and long legs, out of his mind. But it was more than that. She had pluck, and he liked that. Liked it very much indeed. It was too bad she was so young and innocent. Or maybe it was just as well—she was a good girl, sweet and untouched despite her spirit, and certainly not the sort of woman with whom he'd indulge in a dalliance, despite the cravings she ignited in his blood. Aye, it was a good thing his father had designed *Kestrel* to be fast, because Rhiannon Evans was a dangerous bit of fluff, and had already claimed more of his attention than he was willing to give. Furthermore, he'd have to be as blind as the bats in the hayloft of his mother's barn not to notice that she was completely infatuated with him. He couldn't wait to make Barbados.

"Shall I shake the reef out of the main?" Nathan asked.

"Eh?"

"The mainsail, Con. The squalls have passed. There's still a reef in it." His cousin's mouth curved in a knowing smirk. "In case you haven't noticed?"

"Oh, yes of course," he said, distractedly.

"She's a fetching piece."

"What?"

"Miss Evans."

"Stow it, Nathan. I don't have time to be chasing skirts."

"Probably just as well. She'd be a distraction."

"Aye, that she would."

"Still, I think she fancies you."

"She's just a girl. Too young to know what she wants." Connor took the tiller and tried to ignore his cousin, but as usual he had trouble focusing his thoughts on one thing when there were six and a half dozen other things competing for his attention, and he was unable to parry Nathan's amused taunts while his mind was still occupied with Rhiannon Evans and the feel of her soft, pretty hand within his own, let alone consider what sails were best set to speed them to Barbados all the faster.

He dropped his forehead to his hand, kneading his temples, trying to think. "Why don't we hoist the fore topsail back up," he said, his mind finally settling, and quite happily at that, on the memory of Miss Evans's lustrous, red-gold hair flying out around her in the wind. . . .

"Of course, it's about time you settled down, Con."

kled, her tongue coming out to taste the salt on her lips as

"I think it's time to tack," he heard himself say. "Why

don't you go see to it, Nathan. Oh, damnation, here comes

Jacques, grinning like a damned fool."

The Frenchman, one of several crewmembers that

Connor had rescued from the prison hulk *Surrey* back in

Portsmouth in his guise as the Black Wolf, was the most

singularly ugly man he'd ever met. But despite his pointed,

jutting ears—one larger than the other, and both sunburned

to the color of boiled lobster—, a face marked by pox scars,

and a lower lip split nearly in two by a long-ago knife

wound, Jacques fancied himself to be quite the ladies' man.

Unfortunately, he'd caught the tail end of whatever

conversation Connor had been trying to keep from having

with Nathan.

"Got your eye on that *petite fille, Capitain*?" he asked,

with a leering grin.

"She's got hers on him," Nathan put in.

Connor glanced at the compass. "Don't you two have

anything better to do?"

"Actually, no."

"Then find something." He looked up at the pennant

above, gauging the wind, then made a slight correction to

the schooner's course. "Such as another fat merchantman

or something."

Toby was back, looking discomfited.

"What is it, Toby?" Connor asked, feeling more and

more irritated.

"I was just wondering where the ladies should sleep

tonight."

The ladies again.

"They can have my cabin. I'll sleep on deck."

Not that I think I'll get any sleep, knowing that girl is so close.

"Mrs. Cox might be a bit of trouble, Con," said Toby, shifting his weight from one foot to the other.

"Not as much as the other one."

"You know, *Capitaine*," Jacques put in, still with that leering grin, "I bet you could win her heart like that"—he snapped his fingers—"if only you put your mind to it."

"My mind is occupied with enough other things at the moment. There's no room in it for the pursuit or thoughts of a young and innocent girl, no matter how pretty she is. We need to find a place to get *Kestrel* careened. And the stores we took out of that merchantman won't last forever. I'm worried that that prize we just sent off to Mobile will get retaken by either the British or Lafitte's gang, I'm worried that that mend in the foresail isn't going to hold under this wind, and I'm worried that I'm going to get stuck in Bridgetown having to endure a long visit with my sister and her family for the sake of being polite when I have a million other things I've got to get done, including getting the hull careened."

"Why don't we just careen in Bridgetown?"

"Oh, and you think Sir Graham is going to allow that? He may be my brother-in-law, but he's fighting for the other side, and he'll not lift a finger to aid us in our own endeavors, I can assure you." Connor glanced up at the pennants, saw that the wind was veering, and now blowing strong from over the starboard quarter. "Ease the main and fore," he muttered. "And now that we've got a stiff breeze abaft, get the t'gallant and studding sails on her. I've a mind to get to Bridgetown as soon as possible, and then hightail it the hell out of there."

Many hours later and some two thousand miles to the north in the bustling seaside town of Newburyport, Massachusetts, the two people who were responsible for Connor Merrick's existence lay together in bed, holding hands and listening to the cold November winds moaning around the eaves of their stately Georgian home.

Another New England winter, on its way.

Already, the fire in the hearth was having trouble pushing its heat out into the well-appointed bedroom.

She was petite and pretty and her hair, a deep chocolate color threaded with gray, was still thick and long, still straight as a board, and tonight, caught in a loose braid. He was an older version of the lean, laughing man who had so set Rhiannon Evans's heart a'flutter. Some thirty-odd years before, he had designed and drawn up the drafts for the same schooner that his son was currently using to wreak havoc on British shipping. He, Captain Brendan Jay Merrick, had become a legend during the American War of Independence, earning widespread acclaim with which he had never really been comfortable. After the war ended he had partnered with his brother-in-law, Matthew Ashton, and the two of them had taken over old Ephraim Ashton's shipyards on the mighty Merrimack River. Matthew Ashton and Brendan Merrick had turned out many ships over the years, all of them sound, well-designed, stoutly-built creations that had helped further New England commerce, and made the shipyard famous.

But none of those many ships had ever been the equal of Brendan's legendary masterpiece, the lean, predatory, widely-acclaimed topsail schooner, *Kestrel*.

"Another winter on its way, *Moyrrra*," he said, his musical Irish brogue with its Connemaran cadences still thick after nearly forty years spent living in New England. "Listen to that wind out there, tonight."

"Everyone's sayin' it's gonna to be a bad one, this year. Lots of snow, bitter-cold temperatures, starting early and goin' on forever."

"They say that every year."

"And every year, they're usually right."

She snuggled closer to him beneath the mound of blankets, molding herself against his ribs, resting her hand atop his chest, and laying her head in the beloved and familiar cup of his shoulder. He had never gone to seed, as so many other men seemed to do in their later years, but retained the lean, wiry, strength he'd had when she'd first met him thirty-five years before. She knew, and loved, every part of him . . . from his curling chestnut hair, getting greyer every year but as thick and lustrous now as it was when she'd met him, to his laughing, honey-colored eyes, to the lines carved around his mouth and fanning out from the corners of his eyes when he smiled, which he did often, for he was a man with a happy, playful heart, and always had been. Her fingers found the little knot of scar tissue where once, a long time ago, the evil Richard Crichton had tried to kill him with a shot from a pistol.

Crichton was many years gone, but the memory of him was enough to make Mira shudder.

"Cold, *stóirín*?"

"No, just thinking . . . ."

Danelle Harmon

His hand came up to gently stroke her upper arm through the cotton shift in which she slept, and she knew that in a few minutes, her body would be warm enough that she wouldn't be needing the blankets, the shift, nor even the fire flickering in its grate.

But that still left the prospect of heading into yet another interminably long, cold, New England winter, squarely in the offing.

"Brendan?"

"Aye, love?"

"Wouldn't it be nice to get out of Massachusetts for the winter?"

"It would, indeed." His fingers strayed toward the edge of her breast, gently rubbing it through the cotton until Mira, growing too warm indeed, kicked off the blankets. "Why, what do you have in mind?"

"Barbados."

"Barbados?"

"It's been three years since we last visited Maeve and Sir Graham. We're not gettin' any younger, you know, and I'd like to see our grandchildren."

"Faith, there's a war going on, *Moyrrra*."

"And since when has that stopped you in the past?"

He laughed. "I can't think of a single time it ever has, actually."

"Can we go to Barbados, Brendan? Spend the winter there with our daughter, with our grandchildren, and in warmth? Away from this bleedin' cold? We can even ask Liam to go with us. It'll be good for his rheumatism."

"What about Matt? The shipyard?"

"Matt can manage without us for a few months."

"I don't know, *stóirín*. We're not getting any younger."

"Which is precisely the reason we *should* go. We can even take the new sloop, the one you designed and built for Kieran, see how she handles, see how fast she is, and heaven knows she'll *need* to be fast to get us past the British blockade—"

"I don't know—"

"Come now, it'll be fun. For that matter, Kieran can go, too, as he hasn't seen his sister since her wedding to Sir Graham and that was what, eight years ago now?"

"If Kieran goes, he'll be itching to take every British merchant ship that hoves into sight."

"Not if you captain her."

He smiled, his fingers moving ever closer to Mira's nipple, and she turned within his arms, cradling his dear, handsome face within her hands as she gazed down into his warm and laughing eyes.

"Please, Brendan?"

The corner of his mouth turned up into a helpless smile, for he had never been able to deny her anything in the past, and he certainly wasn't able to do so now.

"Barbados it is, then," he murmured, and set about the business of making her so warm that the wind howling outside, the cold drafts seeping beneath the window casements, were soon forgotten.

CHAPTER 4

❦

"For heaven's sake, Rhiannon, there are other things to look at besides Connor Merrick," Alannah Cox said with a mixture of both exasperation and worry as she followed the direction of her companion's gaze. "I'm beginning to think I'd have been wiser to leave you back in England."

"Oh, come now. We're having an adventure."

"An adventure I'll be glad to see reach its end."

Throughout the previous afternoon and all through the night, the Yankee schooner had cut through the long ocean swells like a knife through butter, raising Barbados as dawn had painted the sea in glorious colors of salmon, pink and silver. Under a flag of truce, Captain Merrick had brazenly sailed her into the turquoise waters of Carlisle Bay and dropped anchor amongst the British men of war there, almost within the shadow of Vice Admiral Sir Graham Falconer's mighty flagship, *Orion*.

Alannah was gazing down into the sparkling waters, so clear and crystalline a blue that they could see the anchor resting on the sea floor seven fathoms below.

"Look at the fish down there, Rhiannon," she said, shading her eyes against the sun as she peered down at the colorful marine life darting just beneath the surface.

Rhiannon didn't answer, and Alannah glanced up to see her charge still staring at the Yankee privateer.

"Rhiannon!" she said sharply.

"I'm sorry, what was that?"

"Stop looking at him!"

"But he's taken his shirt off. I can't *help* but look."

"He's a damned pirate!"

"Privateer."

"Same difference. It's men like him who are capturing our merchant ships and driving up insurance so high that England is likely to go bankrupt before this war even ends. Why my brother even tolerates one in his waters, let alone right here under his nose in a British port is beyond my understanding."

"I am sure he's caught in the middle, being married to Captain Merrick's sister. One must keep the peace at home, you know."

Rhiannon's gaze slid back to Connor Merrick, who, standing barefoot on the deck and clad in nothing but belted pantaloons cut off at the knee, was munching an apple while he directed the furling of the sails. He seemed not in the least bit concerned that he'd placed an American privateer squarely in the midst of the Royal Navy's Caribbean fleet.

If seeing his bare feet and calves the previous day had stolen her words, seeing so much more of him bare now was stealing the very breath from her lungs. In the strong tropical sunshine his hair was a burnished red-chestnut, thick and curling and just touching wide, powerful shoulders that were bronzed and glowing with the faintest hint of sunburn. Hard-muscled arms, a lean and tapered torso laddered with muscle, and long, long legs completed a picture of perfection that, had the day not already been as hot as it was, would have elevated the temperature of Rhiannon's Welsh blood considerably.

And she'd thought his bare legs and feet were distracting?

Compared to *this*?

As though feeling her admiring gaze upon him, he glanced over, grinned, and saluted her with his apple before returning his attention to his task.

Rhiannon swallowed hard and wondered yet again what it would be like if he kissed her.

What it would be like to have him look at her the way he'd done when she'd taken off her bonnet to the wind.

Her mouth went dry, and she wished she could touch those bare arms just to see if the muscles beneath were as hard and powerful as they looked. . . .

There was movement from shore. Already, a flurry of boats were coming out to meet them carrying customs officials, painted doxies, dark-skinned vendors selling fruit, and God only knew what else.

"I hope we're not stuck here too much longer," Alannah said, trying to get Rhiannon's attention on something other than the American. "I don't know about you, but I'm just dying for a cup of tea and the chance to see my little nieces and nephew."

The captain, still munching his apple, walked toward them. "They're my little nieces and nephew, too," he said.

"So what does that make us when it comes to relations, Mrs. Cox? Aunt and uncle-in-laws?"

She just shot him a quelling glance. "We are *not* related."

He laughed and winked at Rhiannon, whose own lips began to twitch in response. Out of the corner of her eye she caught movement, and turned her head.

"Oh, look," she said, pointing out over the water. "There's another boat, and that one sure doesn't look like it's carrying fruit!"

Captain Merrick followed her gaze. "I'd beg to differ," he said wryly.

Amidst the small flotilla making their way toward them this one stood out for what it was, a British naval vessel. Smartly dressed tars in striped shirts and round hats managed each stroke of the oars with perfect precision and in the stern was an officer, his blue coat tightly buttoned, his gold epaulets blinding in the sun, his face in shadow beneath his oversized hat.

"Well, would you look at that," Alannah said proudly. "My dear brother has sent not only a smartly turned out boat and crew, but an actual officer to meet us!"

"Who doesn't have the sense to strip down in this heat," Captain Merrick quipped, taking another bite of his apple.

Alannah glared at him, but he merely shrugged, one corner of his mouth lifted in a teasing grin as he chewed.

"Would you stop baiting her?" Rhiannon scolded playfully. "Make her angry enough and she could have that same officer take you off in chains."

He laughed. "Oh, I have all kinds of ways of making Mrs. Cox angry," he said, and as though to prove his point, let his fingers brush Rhiannon's shoulder; Rhiannon blushed, Alannah started sputtering, and at the moment, the Royal Navy boat was hailed.

Soon enough, the officer, resplendent in his blue and white uniform with its blinding gold accents, was aboard the ship and striding purposefully toward them. He was tall, with cool gray eyes that, with the sunlight bouncing off the waves and striking light into the irises, looked almost amethyst. Upon seeing the women, he respectfully removed his hat, revealing curly black hair that was drawn severely back from his face and caught in a short queue. His shoulders filled out his uniform in a way that cut through Alannah's sourness and brought a little smile to her lips, but it was clear, as far as Rhiannon was concerned, that he was a dull stick indeed; his mannerisms were older than his years, and he had a tightly reined-in air about him, one that did not invite conversation, familiarity, or even idle chit-chat about the weather.

He looked at the shirtless Yankee captain with faint disgust, thinned his lips, and snapped, "Don't they issue clothes in America, Connor? One would think you'd don some in the presence of two ladies, but then, your manners are as barbaric as the country that spawned you."

"And yours haven't improved despite the fact you're now Sir Graham's flag captain." Captain Merrick bit into his apple. "Heat getting to you, Delmore?"

Alannah raised her brows. "You two know each other?"

"We're cousins," said Connor Merrick, grinning.

"Don't remind me," muttered the Englishman.

"How many cousins do you *have*, Captain Merrick?" asked Rhiannon, looking from one to the other and trying to find a resemblance.

"Nathan and Toby are the sons of my Uncle Matt and Aunt Eveleen in Newburyport. Captain Lord here is from the English side of my family. His mother is first cousin to my father, so I guess that makes us second cousins?"

"Your manners, Merrick," said the Englishman, tightly.

"Yes, of course. Miss Evans, Mrs. Cox, this is Captain Lord of His Britannic Majesty's Royal Navy."

Mollified, the naval captain bowed stiffly, formally, and with military precision to them both. "It is a pleasure to make your acquaintances, ladies. May I be the first to welcome you to Barbados."

"Just so you know, Del, Mrs. Cox is Sir G's sister. I'm sure he's expecting her? They were traveling aboard the merchantman *Porpoise*, but got attacked by pirates," Captain Merrick said, offhandedly.

Alannah drew herself up. "And then attacked by *you*."

"Come now, Alannah, he didn't attack us," Rhiannon insisted. "He rescued us."

"After he attacked us!"

Captain Merrick grinned, and his gaze met Rhiannon's.

The Englishman, whose irritation had increased at the American's deliberately casual use of his and his admiral's names, stiffened. "And where is the merchantman?"

"On her way to a prize court in Mobile," returned Captain Merrick. "Ought to fetch me a good price at auction there, I reckon."

"You will *not* practice your privateering in Sir Graham's waters, or I'll have something to say about it!"

"Say it, then, and be done with it. It won't affect my actions and you know it." Captain Merrick took a last bite of his apple and pitched it casually over the rail. "And now, can we get this tedious business underway? Perhaps you're comfortable, buttoned up to the chin in that uniform, Del, but me? I'm restless, hot, and fancy a swim."

CHAPTER 5

Shortly afterward, Rhiannon and Alannah were safely aboard the boat and being rowed away from Captain Merrick's sleek black schooner.

Rhiannon looked back with longing. Already she felt bereft, being away from him. His restless energy and high spirits had buoyed her and in their absence, she felt suddenly empty in a way she couldn't fathom. He was likable and fun and had taken great delight, it seemed, in recklessly tormenting his stiff and starchy English cousin.

She would have liked to have stayed and watched him have his swim. . . .

Oh, yes. She would have liked that very much indeed.

She was aware of that same English cousin sitting in the stern sheets and studying her from beneath the shadow of his hat. His gray eyes narrowed, and the faintest of lines appeared between his brows as he noted the direction of her gaze.

"I see that that notorious rogue has caught your attention," he said tightly. "A pity that his sister married my admiral and that he enjoys the protection of that worthy man here in British waters as long as he behaves himself. Personally, I hope he doesn't. Behave himself, that is, for I would take great delight in blowing that schooner right out from under him for all the damage he's caused to British shipping."

Rhiannon raised her brows in surprise. Perhaps the naval captain had some fire in him after all.

"I take it there is no love lost between you and your cousin?"

"Oh, we get on just fine," the officer said tersely, but his face had gone a little darker and there was now a thin sheen of perspiration forming on his skin, not surprising given that every button of his uniform was done up, a starched white neck cloth was all but choking him, and he had to be close to dying, dressed as he was in that long-sleeved coat, tight breeches, and buckled shoes. He pulled out a perfectly folded handkerchief and dabbed at his upper lip, then, with a smile that never reached his eyes, looked out over the water, courteous and rigidly in control of his emotions once more. "I'm sure you'll see more of that lamentable rogue at Sir Graham's dinner table tonight."

I can hardly wait, Rhiannon thought with a private smile, her gaze going once more to the schooner growing smaller and smaller behind them.

Rhiannon had met the charismatic Admiral Sir Graham Falconer some months earlier when he had come to Portsmouth on leave with his wife and family. In the small drawing room of their rented house in that seaport

Danelle Harmon

city, the admiral had been woefully out of place with his black hair, piratical hoop of gold in one ear, and commanding presence, but here in his spacious house on Barbados he seemed right at home.

"And how are your sister and Lord Morninghall doing?" he asked, ushering them all toward the back of the house where a beautiful veranda, bathed in sunshine and swept by the warm trade winds, ran the length of the house and commanded a stunning view of Carlisle Bay. Coconut palms rustled in the breeze, and the scent of flowers filled the air. "Quite a scandal, that. I'm glad it's all over with. All's well that ends well, I suppose."

"Yes, and thanks to Captain Merrick for his part in saving Lord Morninghall," Rhiannon said, hoping that she could smooth the way for the American based on the animosity she already sensed toward him from Captain Lord. "If it weren't for his letter to the Prince Regent confessing himself to be the Black Wolf, I'm not sure Lord Morninghall would have been pardoned and allowed to return to England."

Beside her, Alannah shook her head and rolled her eyes. "It would seem, Gray, that my young friend here is hopelessly smitten with your brother-in-law. I tried to dissuade her, I really did, but it was a losing battle."

"And I'm supposed to assume your guardianship while you're here, am I?" asked the admiral, a twinkle coming into his blue eyes as he took the letter the marquess had sent along to him in the care of his sister. He quickly scanned the contents. "Sounds like I'm going to have my hands full, keeping the men away from you."

Across the table, Captain Lord suddenly blushed beneath his hat and hurriedly looked down.

Rhiannon laughed. "Surely you exaggerate, Sir Graham!"

"Surely I don't." He smiled and folding the letter, put it down on the table. "You are most welcome to stay as long as you like, Rhiannon, and when Maeve gets back from her walk with the children I'm sure she'll be delighted to see you—as am I—but I must confess, I'm a bit surprised that you're here. I thought your sister was in the family way?"

"She is, but the baby's not due until spring. She and Lord Morninghall are very much in love, and I wanted to give them some private time after all they went through, and besides, I . . . well, I wanted an adventure. Gwyneth, my other sister Morganna, even the women in the books I love to read . . . everyone has had an adventure, except me. So when Alannah and I formed a friendship at a house party at Morninghall Abbey, and she said she was going to come here to get away from the damp English winter and asked if I'd like to go along, I jumped at the chance. I'm sure I'll be home in time for the birth of my little niece or nephew."

"Did I hear my name mentioned?"

At that moment, Maeve, Lady Falconer, swept into the room with a twin toddler on each arm and her oldest son trailing behind her. Now that she'd met the brother, Rhiannon could see the resemblance between the two siblings—both had rich, lustrous hair of mahogany, though Maeve's had more red in it and, unlike her brother's, was as straight as a board; both were tall and lean and had the same lines to their cheeks and chins, but where Captain Merrick's eyes were a startlingly clear green, his sister's were gold, like the glowing eyes of a tiger.

She bent down and hugged Rhiannon, then Alannah, as greetings were exchanged and her young son flew into Alannah's wide-open arms.

"Auntie!"

"Ned! My, how you've grown!"

"Auntie, I'm so glad you're here! Did you know that Papa and Mama are going to give me another little brother or sister soon? At this rate, they're going to run out of pirate names to give us!"

"That is right, you are Edward after the infamous Blackbeard, and your little twin sisters are Anne and Mary, after Anne Bonney and Mary Read. Really, Gray, can't you come up with a decent and respectable English name?"

"Sounds decent and respectable enough to me," he said a bit sheepishly.

"My second name is Horatio," young Ned said, sticking out his chin. "After Papa's famous friend, Lord Nelson."

Maeve, however, was standing at the railing and looking out over the glittering turquoise waters of Carlisle Bay. Absently, she put the two toddlers down and plucked a telescope from a nearby rack.

"Damn if that's not *Kestrel*," she said softly. "What brings my brother to Bridgetown?"

"Us," said Rhiannon.

"Yes, he took the ship we were on as a prize just as brazen as you please, sent her off to Mobile, and brought us here himself."

"I hope he's planning on giving me my schooner back," Maeve said, still holding the glass to her eye. "I miss her."

Rhiannon, studying the ex-Pirate Queen's frowning countenance, decided to keep to herself her suspicions that

Connor Merrick would not be parting with the schooner any time soon.

The rest of the afternoon passed with catching up between the families, news from back home in England, and laughter over the antics of the children. Eventually, Rhiannon pleaded fatigue and was brought to a spare bedroom by a servant and there, spent the hot afternoon napping, and dreaming of being carried off in the arms of *Kestrel's* half-naked captain.

Rhiannon awoke feeling as though she hadn't slept a wink. Still basking in the memories of her strange dreams, she accepted the assistance of one of Maeve's housemaids to tidy herself up and, peeking out over Sir Graham's magnificent veranda just outside, saw that the sun was well on its way down to the horizon, casting long shadows and a bright orange glow over everything.

It was a beautiful sight. There was the town of Bridgetown on one side, and on the other, framed by potted bougainvillea and palm trees through which the trades never seemed to stop sighing, the beautiful turquoise expanse of Carlisle Bay where ships and boats rocked gently in the harbor. Dominating this forest of masts and spars was Sir Graham's massive flagship, *Orion*.

She moved closer to the open window. What a beautiful place, Barbados. She looked forward to exploring it. But where was Captain Merrick's schooner? The singularly beautiful ship with the black hull and the white stripe down its side, and the distinctly raked masts that made it look like no other vessel Rhiannon had ever seen?

A sudden prickle of dread went through her.

Had the handsome American already left Barbados?

From outside she heard voices, laughter, and the sounds of conversation, and hurriedly made her way out of her room, down the hall, and out through the big doors that swung open onto the verandah. She hoped she wasn't too late, and if she was, that it hadn't held up the dinner. But it proved to be an informal gathering. The meal had not yet been served, and Sir Graham sat relaxing at the head of the table, his beautiful wife on one side and his flag captain, still dressed in full uniform, on the other. Alannah was already there, bouncing the giggling twins on her lap as they squealed with laughter, and the boy Ned stood leaning over the railing, looking out over the harbor. As Rhiannon appeared, both the admiral and his flag captain got to their feet, bowing, and Captain Lord hurried forward to pull out a chair for her.

"Thank you, Captain," she said, and felt a stab of disappointment that Connor Merrick had not chosen to join them after all. She had not seen his schooner when she'd taken that cursory look out the window from her room. Had he already weighed anchor and sailed away? Had he come and visited his sister and her family while she'd napped, then departed without saying good bye? And why would he bother? She meant nothing to him. Still, her gaze wandered to the harbor over which Ned was gazing, checking for the distinctive rake of the masts that marked the sleek, fast, Yankee privateer. And oh, there it was! Rhiannon's heart settled happily in her breast, and a moment later its captain himself came sauntering in, larger than life.

"Uncle Connor!" cried Ned, running across the room and into his uncle's embrace. "I thought you weren't coming!"

"And miss the chance to see my favorite nephew? You sorely misjudge me, young man!"

Rhiannon swallowed hard, feeling her heart begin to twitter like a songbird as he looked up over the child's head and purposely caught her eye.

There it was again. That *look*.

Beside her, Alannah let out an audible groan.

"When are you going to take me sailing, Uncle Con?" the boy asked, excitedly. "Can I be your midshipman?"

"That all depends on whether the Royal Navy can spare you," Captain Merrick said, grinning as he reached into his pocket and produced a bit of scrimshaw. "I understand you're quite the credit to your father's crew! Here you go, lad. A little souvenir I picked up in my travels to add to your collection."

"Thank you, Uncle Con!" The boy ran to the balcony railing to study the scrimshaw in the burnished evening light, a huge smile lighting his face.

Captain Merrick, dressed in clean canvas pantaloons, a loose shirt rolled up at the sleeves, and sandals, began making the rounds of the table. He looked casual, fresh-scrubbed and utterly gorgeous, and Rhiannon couldn't take her eyes off him.

She blushed and shoved her hands together beneath the table cloth, pinning them between her suddenly clenched knees to stop their shaking. Across the table, Maeve smiled and rose to accept her brother's embrace, Sir Graham shook his hand and murmured some words of welcome, and Captain Lord inclined his head with a resigned formality that bordered on coldness.

At last he came to the ladies, and to Rhiannon, it felt as if his smile was made just for her.

"Good evening, Mrs. Cox. Miss Evans." He bowed over each of their hands, then plucked a glass of rum from the tray of a passing servant and drained it with the same casual recklessness with which he seemed to do everything else. "I trust you're happy to be back on dry land again after so long at sea?"

"I most certainly am," said Alannah. "If I don't see another ship for the next two months I'll count myself blessed."

"And you, Miss Evans?"

"Well, I thought it was all rather exciting," she said, looking up at him through her lashes and smiling. Only she knew of her suddenly damp palms, her racing heart.

His eyes warmed. "Did you, now?"

"I did. And unlike Alannah, I quite like ships. Especially yours. She's pretty."

He raised a brow, amused, and setting his glass down on the table, pulled out the chair beside her. There were plenty of empty seats around the table and he could have chosen any one of them but no, he was going to sit right next to *her*. Rhiannon's heart began to pound as he casually settled his long, lean frame into it with an easy, detached grace. *Oh, my goodness*, she thought, in a combination of panic and excitement at his very nearness. She caught the scent of his shaving soap, bay rum, perhaps, or some other exotic island scent, as he sat back in the chair, one arm slung casually over its back, the picture of lordly repose save for his sandaled foot, tapping a bit restlessly against the tiled floor.

Some people, she thought, had the energy of gunpowder sitting in the desert sun; this man, with his charisma, his presence, his barely-contained restlessness, was one of them. He was affecting her, and affecting her quite noticeably, and he most certainly had to know it.

"Well then, since you haven't had enough of ships, Miss Evans, maybe I'll take you for a sail around the island before I leave."

Her eyes glowed with sudden excitement. "I would love that, Captain!"

Down the table Maeve, unaware of the exchange between them, interrupted. "I'm glad you've decided to join us for supper, Connor. Where are Nathan and Toby?"

"Still aboard *Kestrel*. They'll be along in the morning, I'm sure."

"They'd better be, or they'll have me to answer to."

Sir Graham poured rum for the gentlemen and frowned as he glanced over at Captain Lord. "You know, Delmore, we don't stand on ceremony here, of all places. For heaven's sake, no need to be dressed in full rig in this wretched heat. Why don't you remove your coat, get comfortable like the rest of us?"

"I am quite comfortable, sir," said the younger man, somewhat stiffly.

"Well, just because you're my new flag captain, don't think you need to impress me. I'm far more interested in your seamanship than your fashion sense. More rum, Connor?"

"Much obliged," said Captain Merrick, pushing his glass down the table toward his host.

Rhiannon concentrated on taking deep breaths to try and calm her racing heart. His leg was just inches from her own. Oh, she could fall in love with this man. God help her, she could. He had chosen to sit next to her. He was looking at her the same way she had often seen Lord Morninghall looking at her sister. And he'd said he'd take her on a sail. . . .

Oh, she was having the *best* adventure, already!

"I'm glad to hear my cousins will be along soon enough, then," Maeve was saying. "And you, Connor? What have you been up to? The last I saw of you, you'd just deposited Lord and Lady Morninghall on the decks of my husband's flagship, taken *Kestrel*, and sailed off to the east to adventures unknown. Are you taking good care of my ship?"

"*Your* ship?" He grinned and reached for a mango from a bowl set in the middle of the table. "My ship, now."

The ex-Pirate Queen's gaze met and locked with her younger brother's. "I've a mind to take her back."

"When I'm done with her."

"What are you doing with her?"

"What do you *think* I'm doing with her?"

"Probably privateering."

"Probably."

Maeve's eyes narrowed. "You already lost one ship, Connor. *Dadaí* designed and built *Merrimack* just for you, and you managed to lose her in a battle you never should have been reckless and stupid enough to fight in the first place. Will it be *Kestrel* next?"

A sudden hush fell over the table.

"*Will it?*"

Quietly, Sir Graham reached out and laid a restraining hand on his wife's wrist. "That's enough, Maeve."

"I know, you think that just because I'm once again in the family way that I'm not in control of my emotions." She turned once more to her brother, who had gone very silent, his mouth tight, his entire posture one of stiffness and anger. "But Connor, you're reckless, you take risks you shouldn't, you seek one thrill after another with little thought for the consequences. Maybe I'm concerned about you. Maybe I don't want to see you end up rotting in another prison hulk in some British port. Maybe I don't want to see you *die*."

"All of us have to die sometime." His jaw hard, he looked down, took a paring knife to the mango, and did not meet his sister's eyes though Rhiannon saw that his knuckles had gone white and his green eyes, so easily given to laughter, were now sullen and hard. "At least when my death comes, it'll be in service to my country. There's no shame in that."

"It's a stupid war, this one," his sister retorted. "Madison's war. You ought to stay out of it."

"Too late for that."

"*Kestrel* is old. She can't stand up to the sort of punishment you'll encounter if you find yourself in a fight with a Royal Navy frigate."

"Old, yes, but fast. There's not a ship afloat that can catch her."

"Damn you, Connor—"

Ned, alarmed, had turned from the railing. "Uncle Connor's not going to die, is he, Papa?"

"Uncle Connor's not going to die," Sir Graham put in, with a concerned glance between the two siblings.

"I don't want Uncle Connor to die," Ned began, his eyes going glassy with tears and his lower lip beginning to tremble. "He's my favorite uncle."

"Now see, you've upset the children!" Maeve cried unreasonably, and slamming down her napkin, rushed from the room, leaving an uncomfortable silence in her wake.

Captain Lord and the admiral exchanged glances. Alannah picked up the toddlers, took Ned by the hand

and quietly hurried after Maeve. And Connor Merrick remained staring down at his plate, cutting up the fruit into smaller and smaller pieces that, Rhiannon suspected, he no longer had any intention of eating.

She didn't know he'd lost a ship.

But she did know that having his sister embarrass him like that in front of not only her and Alannah, but Captain Lord—with whom he appeared to have some sort of rivalry—had to sting.

She reached out and quietly touched his forearm in silent support. The muscles beneath his fine lawn shirt were coiled, hard and tense. He glanced over at her, gave a fleeting smile, and suddenly putting the knife down, began to rise.

"I shouldn't have come."

The admiral raised a staying hand. "Sit down, Connor. She gets like this every time she's expecting. Pregnancy is hard on her."

"Must be even harder on you," Captain Merrick muttered. "Makes me glad I'm single and intend to stay that way."

"I wouldn't trade my marriage to your sister for all the tea in China. She's the best thing that's ever happened to me. Someday, should you take a wife, you'll understand. And you'll take the good with the bad, as anyone does in any successful union."

Captain Merrick only tightened his mouth, but beneath the table Rhiannon noticed that he was dangling his sandal by one toe and making rapid and agitated circles with his foot.

"Besides," Sir Graham continued, reaching for the rum bottle and topping up his glass, "she's got the Sight, you know. It makes it all the more difficult for her, especially as it's often correct."

Captain Merrick finally leaned back in his chair, took a deep and visible breath, and let it out, the puff of air lifting a lock of damp, curling hair that had fallen over his forehead. "That damnable Irish gift that came down through our Da's side. What, has she had some Vision of my impending demise?"

"If she has, she hasn't shared it. But you know she loves you, and she loves that ship. That schooner is part of your childhoods."

"I'll give her back to her when the war's over. Though rightfully, she belongs to our father."

"Have a care, Connor. I'm fond of you, and you're my brother-in-law, but I can't and won't protect you should you decide to start raiding shipping here in my waters."

"Are they your waters, Sir Graham?" the American asked, with false innocence and unmistakable challenge.

This time, the admiral was the one to draw a deep, steadying breath. "I mean it, Connor. You're welcome to stay here as long as you like, but I demand that you cease your privateering while here. That you . . . behave yourself."

The American's lips quirked in a smile. "Behave myself."

Down the table, Captain Lord just eyed his cousin quietly, not saying a word. At that moment, servants began to bring out bowls and plates and the sudden tense moment was broken. From somewhere, Rhiannon caught the tantalizing smell of roasting meat. In response, her stomach gave a long growl and she hurriedly clapped a hand over it, mortified.

But the chestnut-haired god at her left elbow, though he had to have heard it, gallantly chose to ignore it.

"So, Miss Evans," he said, spearing a chunk of mango with a small wooden skewer and popping it into his mouth, "What do you think of Barbados? Sure beats an English winter, does it not?"

"If Paradise exists on earth, then surely this is it," Rhiannon replied happily. "I can't wait to see more of it!"

"Perhaps I'll take you on a little tour of the island tomorrow instead of a sail. There's a newly-erected statue to Lord Nelson in town that I'd love to show you. It's a great likeness, wouldn't you say, Sir Graham?"

"Impeccable."

"*You* met Lord Nelson?" asked Rhiannon, intrigued.

"Aye, eight years ago, when my sister and Sir Graham got married. The admiral was a great friend of theirs, and offered his home for the wedding. Seems like ages ago now, doesn't it, Gray?"

"Aye. Time passes," said the admiral, quietly.

"You are both fortunate to have known him," said Captain Lord, finally adding to the conversation. "As was my brother, Colin, who was Sir Graham's flag captain at the time." He ran his thumb along the top of his glass. "Alas, I was born several years too late."

Captain Merrick looked suddenly bored.

"How long have you been Sir Graham's flag captain, Captain Lord?" Rhiannon asked, trying to include the other man in the conversation.

"Long enough, madam, to count myself fortunate to have been chosen for such an honor."

Captain Merrick slid a sideways glance full of humor to Rhiannon, quietly mocking his cousin's heavy seriousness, and immediately set about reclaiming Rhiannon's attention.

"You know, Miss Evans, it's a pity that you and I never made each other's acquaintance when I was still in England." He grinned and popped the fruit into his mouth, his eyes teasing, though she didn't know whether the target of his pointed attention was herself or the irritation of his stuffy English cousin, whose expression had gone stony once more. "It would have made my time in Portsmouth that much more enjoyable."

Rhiannon's heartbeat kicked up.

"Yours, too," he whispered recklessly, and for her ears alone.

As Rhiannon blushed furiously, she was dimly aware of Sir Graham asking about affairs back in England, and even more aware that Captain Merrick had moved his foot, now minus the sandal he'd kicked off, right up alongside hers beneath the table, and that he was letting his toes tickle her ankle.

She swallowed hard, and with her hand, began fanning her face. "I'm sorry, what was that, Sir Graham?"

The admiral was looking at her oddly, unaware that his brother-in-law was making a mess of her composure and that her body was responding to that foot against her ankle in ways that made her unable to think. She heard herself sputtering and answering some inane question, saw the Yankee privateer looking at her with high amusement, and realized that her mouth seemed to be running independent of her brain, which was still busy trying to calm her racing heartbeat, and she wasn't altogether sure just what she said.

"Besides, what was there for me in England?" she continued, unable to stop her runaway mouth. "I'm not nobly-born, I'm never going to have a Season or be presented at Court, and surely, my sister and Lord Morninghall deserved to have their home to themselves without me being constantly underfoot, that is, if it's even possible to be underfoot in a residence as large as the marquess's ancestral home!"

She moved her foot away from Captain Merrick's.

Eyes twinkling, he moved his back up against hers.

She shot him a look all her own.

Maeve returned looking pinched and still somewhat angry, Alannah, holding Ned's hand, by her side. A servant brought out a plate mounded with raisin cakes and cheese and offered some to each guest. Rhiannon looked down, pretending an interest in a fold of her skirts while her mind went over and over what she'd just said, or what she *thought* she'd just said, dissecting it for anything foolish or stupid. She was *not* going to move her foot again. This was *her* space beneath the table and she wasn't going to give it up by letting the roguish Captain Merrick tease her into relinquishing it.

Besides, it was rather wicked to let his bare toes be touching her ankles.

And if truth be told, she was rather liking it. Even if it was wicked. Even if she wasn't supposed to be liking it. And even if his actions were making her unable to think of anything but *him*.

I'm having an adventure. And I'm enjoying it.

Captain Merrick was selecting another piece of fruit, the name of which Rhiannon would have been hard-pressed to identify, but instead of putting it on his own plate, he leaned over and gallantly put it on hers.

She looked at it dubiously. "And what is this?"

"Pawpaw, Miss Evans."

"I . . . see."

She had no idea how to eat it.

Captain Merrick was watching her.

She glanced in panic around the table; Sir Graham was conversing with his flag captain, Maeve was talking to Alannah, and Rhiannon was on her own, trapped here with a strange piece of fruit she had no idea how to go about eating.

Now what?

"Have you never tried pawpaw before, Miss Evans?"

She looked up into those amused green eyes and hoped the blush that was heating her blood wasn't showing up on her face. What a ninny he must think her!

"I confess, Captain Merrick, that I have not."

Smiling, he stood up and then, leaning down right next to and somewhat over her, so near that his clean, faintly exotic scent filled her nostrils, picked up the small paring knife next to her plate, his arm—decently clad in a loose white shirt now but oh, she knew, God help her, she *knew* what the muscles under that shirt looked like after seeing him earlier!—just inches from her cheek. Rhiannon looked down at his long, suntanned fingers, deftly cutting the fruit in half, and took a deep and trembling breath. How on earth was she going to get through this meal, let alone the rest of the evening, with such a distraction as Connor Merrick sitting right next to her?

Forget him. He probably has a lady friend. He probably has lots *of lady friends—*

"There," he said, and looking down, Rhiannon saw that he'd cut up the fruit and arranged its seeds on her plate in the shape of a smile.

She felt her lips quivering in laughter. He had a sense of humor, and she liked that.

"Thank you, Captain," she said, but not before he reached down, plucked the nose from the middle of his little design, and popped it into his mouth, watching her in high amusement the whole time.

"My pleasure, madam."

She had no idea what to say to him, and knew that anything she attempted was going to come out sounding foolish. But she tried, anyhow.

"Did you go swimming after we left?" she blurted.

Yes, it definitely had come out sounding foolish.

"Aye, that I did."

Rhiannon looked down at her plate, eager to try the fruit but not quite wanting to change, destroy or rearrange the design that *he* had made. "I wish I knew how to swim."

"You don't know what you're missing."

"And what am I missing, Captain?"

"Beautiful fish, seen up close. Coral reefs. The occasional shark—"

"Shark!"

He leaned close, too close, and murmured, for her ears alone, "I could teach you to swim, you know."

Rhiannon's mouth dropped open and her blood was suddenly too hot for the confinement of her veins. Once again she wished, desperately, for a fan.

Connor Merrick simply looked at her, one brow raised, smiling a wicked little smile.

With a trembling hand, she reached for her spoon. "And where did you learn how to swim, Captain?"

"My siblings and I grew up in Newburyport, Massachusetts, on the Merrimack River," he said. "My father, even though he came up through the Royal Navy where sailors aren't encouraged to learn the art, is a fine swimmer himself and insisted that the three of us learn to swim, and to swim well."

"Your father is Royal Navy?"

Captain Merrick gave a little laugh. "My father was the most famous privateer of the Revolution," he said, proudly. "For the American side."

"But you just said—"

"He started out in the Royal Navy, aye, but one thing led to another and he ended up fighting for the Yankees," he said, wickedly plucking the eyebrow from Rhiannon's design of fruit and popping it into his mouth. "I was raised on tales of his derring-do, acts of daring, and triumphs."

"They weren't tales, Uncle Connor!" said young Ned, who had gotten up and come around the table to be with the uncle he idolized. "Mama says that they are true, every one of them."

"And so they are, lad," said Connor, lifting the child to sit on his lap. "And if your grandpapa was the most famous privateer of the last war, your uncle Connor here is going to be the most famous privateer of the current one, you just watch and see."

"Not in my waters you won't be," warned Sir Graham once again, from down the table.

Captain Merrick just laughed. "Blind eyes are wonderfully useful, especially when turned the other way."

"I turned a blind enough eye, Connor, to your doings while back in Portsmouth, but my patience goes only so far, especially here. Don't think I won't move to have that schooner seized and given back to your sister if you don't behave yourself."

"I always behave myself. Until, of course, it behooves me not to."

Sir Graham had been wearing a tolerant smile; now, it faded in the face of the younger man's blithe challenge. From down the table, the perfectly-composed Captain Lord raised a dark brow, eyed his American cousin with a disdainful, barely perceptible shake of his head, and turned his attention back to his meal.

Rhiannon thought it time to intervene. "I think, Captain Merrick," she said, feeling a bit wicked and certainly scandalous, "that I would very much like to learn how to swim. When can we start?"

The American speared another piece of fruit on his little wooden skewer, put it into his mouth, and gave her a look that made her feel like a rabbit being sized up by a wolf. "Any time you'd like."

CHAPTER 6

Well, well, Connor thought to himself as he bowed over the hand of the lovely Miss Evans, bade his sister and brother-in-law goodnight, and gave a parting shot to his too-stuffy-for-his-own-good English cousin, *that* had certainly been a most interesting evening.

He didn't know what he'd been thinking, deliberately choosing the seat next to the girl and allowing himself to respond to her in ways he'd been determined to defy. What in tarnation was wrong with him? She was young and unspoiled, and he'd have had to be blind not to notice that she had been hanging on his every word, sliding covert glances at him when she thought he wasn't looking, and that her bright green eyes had been sparkling like stars on a cold winter night every time he turned to talk to her. He knew better than to encourage such an impressionable young girl. He *knew* better. But he had gone and done it anyhow.

It was just an innocent flirtation, his conscience told him.

But no, it wasn't. He was old enough to know that, and he shouldn't be encouraging her down a road he had no intention of joining her on. But he hadn't been any more immune to her closeness than she'd been to his, had been unable to stop his own impulsive reactions to her, and a big part of him had basked in the looks of infatuation, the coy glances from beneath her long lashes, the way her lips had twitched when he'd baited Sir Graham.

You shouldn't have paid her so much attention. She fancies you, and you know it. But you don't have time to be chasing skirts. You're a Yankee privateer, and there's no room in your life for a romance or, God forbid, a wife.

Nothing good or possible could come of this. Nothing.

And if he knew any better, he'd take *Kestrel* out of Carlisle Bay as soon as he collected his crew from Bridgetown's taverns and houses of ill repute, and get back to work.

Work.

Just the thing he ought to be doing to take his mind off certain young Welsh beauties.

He had no intention of "behaving himself," as Sir Graham had put it, in "his" waters. The admiral might be his brother-in-law but he was British, and it had been the British that had made most of the past year of Connor's life a living, excruciating hell with his incarceration aboard the prison hulk *Surrey* in Portsmouth Harbor following the humiliating loss of *Merrimack*. Though he didn't consider himself a vengeful or unforgiving man, he had seen such unspeakable things and witnessed such suffering that the idea of taking as many British prizes as possible and sending them back into American ports did not plague his conscience.

Already, insurance rates on British shipping were rumored to be three times higher than normal, thanks to the actions of American privateers. The cost of goods in England had skyrocketed, and it was Connor's fervent hope that it would rise even more before the cries of protest from the English populace would convince its government to abandon this war against Britain's former colonies.

But not until he and others like him could profit from it. There were slower ways for a man to find his fortune than hitting it lucky as a privateer.

And he knew he had more than just luck on his side. His father, the one man in the world that Connor idolized and looked up to, had designed and built the schooner *Kestrel* back in 1778 as a privateer for the American side in that decisive and patriotic war between England and her soon-to-be former colonies. Back then the schooner had been considered a vessel ahead of its time, with her low freeboard and lean, predatory lines, her rapine, sharply raked masts, her distinctive square topsail and her jib-boom that went on forever. His father had made *Kestrel*, and *Kestrel* had made his father, and it was time, Connor reckoned, that *Kestrel* made him.

No, he had no intention of honoring British admiral Sir Graham's requests.

He thought again of Miss Evans, and how the candlelight had made her lively eyes all the more enchanting. He thought of the fresh, lemony scent of her hair, the forbidden valley between her high, firm breasts that he couldn't help seeing, didn't want to help seeing, when he'd leaned over her and helped her with the pawpaw. It had been all he could do not to lean in a little closer and whisper something suggestive in her pretty little ear to see if he could pull another blush out of her.

Thank God he'd managed *some* semblance of control.

Ah, well. He'd stay another day for the benefit of his sister's family, especially little Ned. He'd be polite to Miss Evans and he wouldn't encourage her any more than he'd already foolishly done. He'd be the perfect gentleman privateer, and then he'd make sail and hightail it out of here before things got too complicated. In short, he would. . . .

Behave himself.

His sense of balance restored, Connor's mood brightened considerably. He had left one of *Kestrel's* two boats pulled up on the beach and now he pushed it out into the surf, climbed in and took up the oars and, tipping his head back to look at the thousands of stars scattered across the inverted black bowl of the night sky, whistled jauntily as he rowed himself back to the schooner.

Funny, how resolve could restore good spirits.

"Ahoy, there, *Kestrel*!"

A face appeared over the rail, dimly lit by the glow of a lantern hung in the shrouds. It was Jacques, standing the midnight watch. "Welcome back, *Capitaine*. I trust your dinner with the admiral and your sister went well?"

"Well enough, Jacques."

Another form melted out of the darkness as Connor hauled himself over the rail.

"You're back early."

"And you're up late, Nathan. I hope Toby hasn't turned in for the night . . . I owe him a chess match."

"He's in your cabin with the board all laid out and ready." And then, in a quieter voice, "Thanks for not keeping him waiting . . . you know he hangs on your ever word, Con."

Connor smiled. He was tired, and he might have sought his own bunk after a day in the hot tropical sun, but he knew his young cousin all but idolized him and he would not disappoint him. The lad was only fourteen, thin and freckled and sensitive in nature, though there were flashes of his father Matthew's Yankee scrappiness in the youngster's temperament that pleased Connor to no end. Though Toby served as *Kestrel*'s midshipman, Connor had always thought he was better suited to study law or medicine, but he was an Ashton and determined to measure up to his brother and Merrick cousins as best he could.

Forward, the bell rang out, signaling the end of the watch. Jacques saluted his captain and then Nathan, who had come up to relieve him of the deck, and headed off below.

"I suppose you charmed the stockings off the poor girl," Nathan murmured, leaning his elbows on the rail and gazing out into the night where boats, small craft and large vessels, all of them dwarfed by Sir Graham's big flagship, were beginning to turn in the tide.

"She's too young for me. But I confess, she's caught my eye in a way I wish she hadn't."

"Don't think she's the one for you, Con. You ought to find yourself a good Yankee lass, not an Englishwoman whose country we're at war with."

"She's not English, she's Welsh."

"Doesn't change the fact we're still at war with her country."

"No, it does not, but you and I both know nothing will come of it, Nathan. I don't have time for a dalliance. We'll only stay here long enough to scrape the weed from the old lady's bottom, get her provisioned for a short cruise, and then we're off. A man isn't going to get rich sitting around in the harbor."

"Nay, he won't. But don't break her heart, Con."

"We won't be here long enough for that to happen. And oh, speaking of getting rich, did you find out anything about that convoy?"

"Aye. A good two dozen ships are already harboring in St. Vincent and getting ready to make sail back to England. Carrying quite a cargo between them, too. They'll be well armed, Con."

"I'm not worried about it. Don't tell me that you are, either."

"Just saying."

"Right. Maybe a short cruise westward is in order within the next day or so. And now, I'm off . . . far be it from me to keep your little brother waiting."

Unable to sleep, Rhiannon was also still up at that late hour.

The verandah ran along the entire rear of the second floor of Sir Graham's beautiful island home, and her bedroom opened out onto this lovely place at which to sit, sip a glass of punch, and gaze up at what had to be a million stars above her head. Down in the harbor she could see the twinkling lights of ships at anchor, and wished she knew which one of them was *his* ship.

Connor Merrick.

Just whispering his name made her blood glow with warmth and she smiled softly to herself, remembering again his sense of humor as he'd arranged the fruit on her plate in a little smiling face, and how his very nearness had made her feel inside: all hot and gushy and nervous and *alive*.

She wondered if he was thinking of her, as she was of him—or if he had cast her out of his mind the minute he'd bid her good night and taken his leave. She wondered if he had gone back to his beautiful ship, or if he had some kept woman, here in port. She wondered if she would see him again on the morrow.

And she wondered if he really intended to teach her how to swim.

Maybe Connor Merrick wasn't actually serious, after all.

Maybe he'd just said that in order to make conversation, and be just a little bit of a rogue at the same time.

And then she remembered the way he had looked at her. *Maybe not.*

She wished her sister Gwyneth was here to guide her.

On the other hand, perhaps it was best that she was not.

Early the next morning, Rhiannon opened her eyes to morning sunshine and a deliciously mild breeze that swept in through the windows, through the mosquito netting of her bed of polished Barbadian mahogany, and across her pillow.

Her night had been a restless one, filled with dreams that left her body hot and wanting, and her first thoughts were of Connor Merrick.

She was instantly awake.

She lay there for a moment wondering if the rest of the household was up yet, but the hour was early, and she could hear nothing beyond the swish and crackle of the coconut palms just outside her window.

She thought about summoning the servant that Lady Falconer had assigned her last night, but she didn't want to disturb the girl if she, too, were still abed, and she had a sudden urge to explore a little before her time was no longer her own.

She performed her morning ablutions, tied her hair back with a piece of ribbon, and choosing a simple pastel blue gown of sprigged cotton and a broad-brimmed hat to shade her face from the sun, crept quietly downstairs.

There was a small figure sitting there on the bottom step, an oversized and old-fashioned cocked hat on his dark head and a toy sword in his hand.

Smiling, Rhiannon sat down beside the would-be pirate.

"Good morning, Ned," she murmured, to Sir Graham's and Lady Falconer's eldest.

"Good morning, Miss Evans," the boy said sullenly.

"Are we the first ones up?"

"Aye. Papa told me he'd take me down to the beach today to look for pirate treasure. But I'm so excited that I couldn't sleep."

"Is there truly pirate treasure in these waters, Ned?"

"Papa thinks so. But it will be hours yet before he rises, finishes his breakfast and morning paperwork, meets with Captain Lord as he does every morning, and brings me down to the beach."

"I see," said Rhiannon, thinking. And then: "Do you think your papa would be terribly upset if you and I were to go down to the beach together right now, and perhaps we could look for pirate treasure ourselves?"

The boy instantly brightened. "I don't think he would mind at all, Miss Evans."

"Please, call me Rhiannon. But I think you should certainly ask your papa if he would mind. I would not like to draw the ire of a man who is both my host and one of the most famous admirals in the Royal Navy!"

"Sir Graham will not mind at all," said a voice, and glancing up, Rhiannon found herself looking into the striking gold eyes of the admiral's wife. Maeve, looking fresh, rested, and much improved in mood from the previous evening, was beautiful and alluring despite the fact that her belly was heavy with child. She leaned down to kiss the brow of her gangly, dark-haired, son. "In fact, Ned, why don't you take the little rowboat out into the harbor and see if you can catch us something for dinner tonight?" She gave Rhiannon a secretive wink. "Maybe, while waiting for a fish to bite your hook, you might spy some pirate treasure just sitting on the bottom."

"But I promised Miss Evans that I would spend the morning with her!" the boy said loyally, though Rhiannon could see that he was itching to take his mother up on her offer.

"Perhaps Miss Evans would like to join you if you give her a few moments to have some breakfast, first."

"Me?" Rhiannon gulped, thinking of being alone in a boat with a seven-year-old and not knowing how to swim.

"Oh, Miss Evans—I mean, Rhiannon—would you go with me? I can show you around the harbor if you'd like, while we look for a place to drop our lines."

"Um . . . uh. . . ."

Maeve, who could not know of Rhiannon's concerns, misinterpreted at least part of the reason for her houseguest's hesitation. "Oh, don't worry about Ned and his ability to get around in a small rowboat," she said cheerfully. "I know he's young in years, but the education of any child of ours would be sorely lacking if he or she did not know how to tie a reef or hoist a sail or manage a boat by the age of five. You will be perfectly safe with our Captain Ned, I can assure you."

The boy drew himself up to his full height, his excited grin already lighting up his little face.

"So what do you say, Rhiannon? Would you like to come with me?"

Far be it from her to break his dear heart. She extended her hand so that he might raise her from her seat on the step. "It would be my honor, Captain Falconer."

CHAPTER 7

Maeve had not overestimated her son's abilities.

Even so, it did little to soothe Rhiannon's nervousness as she took off her shoes and, holding them in one hand and the hem of her gown in the other, waded a few feet into the gentle surf and following the boy's direction while he held the bow steady, climbed into the little boat.

It was one thing to be out on the water with the size and security of an actual ship around her; it was quite another to be in a tiny, tippy boat with a seven-year-old when one didn't know how to swim. Rhiannon sat stiffly on the thwart as the boy, with a staggering amount of self-confidence and competence in one so young, tossed his fishing gear into the boat, waded into the surf, pushed the craft backwards out into the water and with the agility of a monkey, leaped aboard. The boat tipped from side to side for one frightening moment, but Ned knew what he was about and, picking up the oars, fastened them in their locks and turned to face her.

"You look scared, Miss Evans."

"I am, a little."

"Mama's right, you know. I won't let anything happen to you."

"I know you won't, Ned," she said, reaching out to pat his arm. "But you see, I cannot swim, and these little boats make me nervous."

"You don't need to know how to swim. We won't capsize." The boy's azure eyes were bright beneath the shadow of the oversize hat. "Would you like to row? It might take your mind off your worries."

But Rhiannon, who had lifted her head to gaze out over the peaceful sight of the ships in the anchorage, had just spied something that took her mind off her worries far more than any other distraction ever could.

The schooner *Kestrel*.

There she stood at anchor, the bright pinks and golds of the early morning sun casting her sharply backswept masts in silhouette. The pennant at her masthead floated in the breeze, appearing almost orange in the burnished light. Rhiannon could hear laughter and jeers coming from the sleek vessel as a group of men gathered on her deck and a few more clustered in the rigging of her mainmast.

"I wouldn't mind rowing if you should wish me to be of service to you, Ned, but perhaps you might explain to me just what it is your Uncle Connor's men are doing out there on their schooner so early in the morning?"

The boy twisted around to follow Rhiannon's gaze and grinned. "Mama says not to be concerned with what Uncle Connor is up to. She's worried that he's going to make Papa cross by going privateering." The boy's eyes flashed to hers and took on a secretive gleam. "And if he does go, I'm going with him."

"I don't think your father would like that."

"And do you know what *I* think?" Ned's eyes sparkled with mischief. "I think that we should go find out what my uncle is doing."

Yes, Rhiannon thought. Watching Connor Merrick was far preferable to wondering how many feet of water lay beneath her feet planted on the seemingly fragile hull and the sandy, sparkling bottom so far below.

Grinning, the boy put his skinny arms to the task of rowing, and the little boat picked up speed as it knifed across the water toward the anchored schooner.

Rhiannon's heart began to pound, and it had nothing to do with fear.

"Now *that* is one crazy bastard!"

The laughter and raucous shouts grew louder as Ned rowed them closer to the schooner, and shading her eyes, Rhiannon tried to discern just what was happening aboard Connor Merrick's sleek and dangerous-looking vessel.

The voices grew louder as they approached.

"A dollar says he won't do it."

"A quarter-eagle says he will."

"I'll raise ye to a half-eagle. He'll do it."

"A half eagle? Is that all you think my courage is worth?" called a deep, familiar voice, and looking up as they drew closer to the schooner, Rhiannon saw its captain climbing the shrouds that supported *Kestrel*'s sharply raked mainmast. The schooner's mainsail had been raised about halfway and now swung somewhat uncertainly out over the water in the light breeze, taking both gaff and long boom, which stuck out far astern of the trim little ship, with it.

Connor Merrick, barefoot, bare-chested, and garbed once more in his cut-off canvas pantaloons, was now walking with confident balance out along the gaff, that great spar that angled up and out from the mainmast and from which the schooner's huge mainsail was hung.

Rhiannon's heart caught in her throat.

Though the mainsail had only been raised about half the height she knew it was capable of attaining, it looked awfully high, up there out over the water. . . .

"Ned, what are they doing?" she asked urgently.

More laughter came from the ship.

"I don't know, but it looks like fun. But then, it always is—fun, that is—where Uncle Connor's concerned."

The boy rowed them closer, and one or two of the seamen on the privateer's decks gave them a cursory, dismissive glance before cranking their heads back once more to watch their commander, who had reached the peak of the gaff and now stood there holding on to a stay and grinning.

"Connor, you're insane," called up one of the men on deck, and Rhiannon recognized his cousin, Nathan. "If you end up killing yourself, don't blame me."

"Anyone want to up Jacques's bet to an eagle?" returned their captain, from high above.

"Aye, I'll do it!"

"Fifteen!"

More laughter—and at that moment, *Kestrel*'s captain let go of the stay, bent his knees, and threw himself out into space.

Rhiannon screamed.

Connor was fully aware of the woman in the little row-boat, though it wasn't until she screamed and he saw, out of the corner of his eye as his body was plunging, knifelike and upside down toward the sparkling blue waters of the harbor, that that woman was none other than Miss Rhiannon Evans.

The rushing thrill of the fall, the *whoosh* of the wind past his ears, the delicious fear of the dive—it all paled in those seconds of free-fall beneath the excitement that *she* was here, that *she* was watching him, and that *he* had the opportunity to either make a complete idiot of himself, or, impress the stockings off her.

Connor knew he had his faults, not least of which was the fact that he was, as Nathan was so fond of reminding him, a show-off, but there were times when a man couldn't help himself.

He ducked his head between his outthrust arms, drew his legs together, pointed his toes toward the sky and hit the water.

It was a heady way to start the morning and one that he enjoyed mightily; the warm waters and gentle breezes of the Caribbean were a far cry from New England's cold Atlantic at this time of the year. Swimming easily, he angled his body up and broke the surface right next to Ned's boat.

"Uncle Connor!" the boy cried in delight.

On the thwart behind him, Miss Rhiannon Evans was looking about as pale as a fillet of cod.

Despite himself, Connor gave her his most dazzling grin. "Mornin', ma'm," he said, treading water and wiping his wet hair out of his eyes. "Here for your swimming lesson?"

Her mouth opened, then shut, and then she seemed to straighten up a little bit and, despite the faint twitching at the corner of her mouth that betrayed a certain delight at the spectacle he'd just made of himself, looked him straight in the eye.

"Captain Merrick, you are shameless, and a show-off, beside."

He laughed. "Just having fun, Miss Evans. Gotta live a little, you know. Why don't you and young master Ned here hook on to our chains and come aboard to watch?"

"Oh, I couldn't. . . ."

"Why not?"

"Well, for one thing, it is hardly proper for me to come aboard a ship full of grinning, leering men, and without a chaperone at that."

"I'll chaperone you, Miss Evans!" cried Ned, happily.

"I still don't think—"

"Oh, please, Miss Evans?" the boy begged, tugging at her arm. "Please? And you, Uncle Connor—just what is it you're doing? Can I join you?"

Connor, still treading water and looking up at the pair, thought about resting his hands on the gunwale of the little boat, but everything about her stiffened posture, white knuckles, and inability to relax from her bird-perch on the thwart decided him against it. The poor girl was scared enough as it was without fearing that he'd capsize them all into the drink.

But giving her a swimming lesson? Though he'd only been in jest last night, the idea was looking more and more appealing. . . .

I really must *leave Barbados.*
Immediately.

"Uncle Connor?"

"Aye, lad?"

"I asked what you were doing. Are you going to tell me?"

"Well, Ned, what we're doing is gambling, and you shouldn't be a part of it. Your father would skin me alive."

"He's going to skin you alive anyhow, Uncle Connor, when you start taking prizes in the Caribbean."

"Well, he'll have to catch me at it, first," Connor said blithely. He winked at his young nephew, let himself sink down below the surface and with a strong kick, propelled himself beneath the little boat and came back up on the other side. Rhiannon Evans gasped as he broke the surface. "So will you?"

"Will I what?"

"Come aboard."

"Captain Merrick, you are a rogue. The idea of visiting your schooner without Alannah or Maeve as a suitable chaperone fills me with misgivings. If you knew anything about women, you'd know that I shouldn't even consider it. "

"On the contrary, Miss Evans." He winked. "I know a lot about women."

Her jaw came unhinged.

Damnation, here he was doing it again, making her blush, making her eyes sparkle all the brighter, making her all the more infatuated with him.

He couldn't seem to help himself.

Oh, the hell with it. Just . . . the hell with it.

"And I think you *should* consider it," he said. "After all, didn't you want an adventure?" He saw her gaze slide helplessly to his bare chest and upper arms as he tread water beside the boat. "You sure won't find one in my brother-in-law's mansion."

"Please?" Ned cried in excitement. "Can we, Rhiannon?"

"Well . . . given that you've got the courage to be diving into the sea from the heights of your rigging, I suppose I should display equal bottom by accepting your kind offer, Captain Merrick. I will come aboard."

Connor gave a wolfish grin.

His morning had just gotten a hell of a lot more interesting.

A hell of a lot more interesting, indeed.

I know this is wrong, I know I shouldn't be doing this, I know I am courting trouble, Rhiannon thought to herself as she allowed Ned to show her how to sit in the sling of ropes that was lowered to her from the deck of the schooner, *but I am going to do it, and that is that.*

It was just as well that Gwyneth wasn't here. Her older sister would not have approved of her going aboard a ship full of grinning tars.

And surely young Master Edward Horatio Falconer was, at seven years old, hardly an acceptable chaperone.

Chaperones be damned. She was going aboard.

She held onto that same youngster's hand as she rose unsteadily in the boat, following his direction to stand in the middle, to hold this line, to not be afraid because he was watching out for her and so was his Uncle Connor and cousins Nathan and Toby, and nothing was going to happen to her.

"Just don't look down," called Captain Merrick, whose handsome grinning face had appeared at the schooner's rail above her head. He was still dripping wet, and Rhiannon found it immensely reassuring that it was the American privateer's strong hands—and even stronger-looking arms—that were holding the thick ropes of her perilous little "chair." She settled herself into the rope contraption, gripped it in determined hands, and felt those very strong muscles she'd so recently been admiring begin to haul her up the schooner's side.

No worries, Captain Merrick. I have no intention of looking down.

Not when looking *up* yielded such a spectacular view of wet, half-naked, male flesh.

With the schooner's low freeboard it didn't take long for its captain, whistling a sea chantey with each haul on the rope, to have her up the side. As she ascended, she glanced at the black hull-planking with its distinctive white stripe running from bow to stern and through which the sun-baked muzzles of several cannon—guns, she reminded herself—poked from their open ports, reminding her that *Kestrel* was no pleasure or merchant craft, that Connor Merrick was no friend to Britain, and that no matter what on earth its captain and crew had been doing up there in the rigging when she and Ned had happened upon the scene, this lithe and elegant vessel was a warship.

He took her hand as he brought her securely over the varnished rail. "Welcome aboard, Miss Evans," he said, bowing over it with an elegance more suited to a London drawing room than the decks of a Yankee warship. She smiled and he held her hand for a moment longer, his lips warm against her knuckles, his clear green eyes look-ing up at her through long, dark lashes that were still wet from his swim. He turned to glance at his crew, all lined up behind him; many of them had quickly donned shirts and now doffed their hats at her appearance, though Captain Merrick did not seem inclined to do the same, and that suited Rhiannon, looking at the droplets of seawater poised on the hard, bulging muscles of his upper arms and shoulders, just fine.

You wanted an adventure, Rhiannon. In a few days he's going to sail away and you'll have forever lost your chance to have with this man what your sisters have found with theirs. He probably thinks you're too young for him. And maybe you are. But he's got that look in his eyes again, and that has got to mean something. You have the chance at love. Are you going to throw it all away?

No.

Her fingers itched to reach up and flick away those tantalizing drops of water that stood atop his shoulders, and especially, the one that was trickling down his cheek from out of the rich whorls of his wet hair.

She smiled a bit impishly. "Don't your men believe in getting their captain a towel, sir?"

Someone snickered.

"This is a warship, ma'm," he said, his eyes warming in response. "People get wet on ships."

"Under normal means, perhaps."

"*Capitaine*, I'll get a towel for you," said a man standing nearby whose split, scarred lip was curved in a leer. "But I won't dry you off!"

More laughter, free and easy and infectious, and Rhiannon joined in. Behind her Ned had also come up over the side, disdaining both the bosun's chair that had brought Rhiannon aboard and the help of freckled, red-haired Toby Ashton, who had stepped forward to lend him a hand. The boy hurried to stand beside Rhiannon, grinning in excitement from ear to ear.

"I say, Captain! Can't have us a Brit aboard, now can we?" said one of the crew, tousling Ned's dark hair. "This young scallywag here'll turn us in!"

The boy lifted his chin. "Behave yourself, as my father says, and I shall keep your confidence," he said importantly.

Laughter erupted from behind him, and even Captain Merrick's grin flashed white in his handsome, tanned face. "Leave young Mr. Falconer alone, you lot," he said cheerfully. "He's as much an American as he is British. Besides, if we have one Briton aboard, then we shall have two," he added, with a pointed look at Rhiannon. He reached down to pick up one of the two cats sunning itself on the deck. "Would you care for some punch, Miss Evans? Lemonade?"

"I would love a glass of lemonade," she said, smiling in delight as he placed the cat in her lap. "Hello, Billy! Have you dined on any more flying fish?"

"I do believe this one's Tuck. Can't tell 'em apart. Toby! Fetch Miss Evans some lemonade, would you?"

Rhiannon stroked the cat, which curled itself onto her lap and began to purr. Toby, blushing faintly through his freckles, was quickly back, and she accepted the lemonade that he eagerly pressed into her hand.

"Can I get you anything else, Miss Evans?"

"I'm quite fine, thank you, Toby. This lemonade is wonderful."

"I put sugar in it. Figured you'd like it that way."

Rhiannon smiled at him, recognizing a young boy's infatuation when she saw it, then turned her attention to the sail above.

"So, Captain," she said, taking a sip of the lemonade, "just what *were* you doing up there? I know your plunge into the sea wasn't an accidental one."

One of the crew guffawed, someone else thrust a clandestine elbow into a neighbor's ribs, and Nathan, carrying a plate of what looked to be eggs, came aft, an old round hat covering his tawny, careless curls. He took a bite out of a piece of toast and gestured with it toward his captain. "Really, Connor, where are your manners?"

"Gasping, speechless and love-struck at the young lady's feet," Captain Merrick returned smoothly, with a sideways wink at the suddenly blushing Rhiannon. "What have I done wrong this time?"

"Failed to offer her and young Ned here some breakfast, for one thing."

"I'll get her some! Ned, too!" Toby gushed, and headed below.

"Oh, don't let us keep you from whatever it is you're doing." Rhiannon gave a little wave of her hand. Dear Lord, hadn't these men ever seen a woman before? The way they were all hanging on her words and falling all over themselves to please her made her feel like a queen in her court. "Whatever it was that you *were* doing, that is. . . ."

"Just having a little contest," said Captain Merrick. He reached out and neatly snared his cousin's toast, took a bite, and tossed it back onto the plate before Nathan, turning back to look in puzzlement down at the half-eaten bread, even knew what he was about.

"It looked to me as if you were trying to find creative ways in which to kill yourselves," Rhiannon said.

"You could say that." Captain Merrick found an empty wooden cask, hefted it in his strong arms—*show off,*

Rhiannon thought again, but with a flush of appreciation and delight—and set it down before her. "Have a seat my dear. We're about to crown a winner for our little competition here. After we're done, I'll take you for a tour of the schooner *Kestrel*."

"If you survive, you damned fool," muttered Nathan. "So sorry, ma'm," he murmured, taking off his hat. "I forget myself."

"Uncle Connor!" It was the admiral's young son, ever conscious of his self-prescribed duties as Rhiannon's chaperone, who had followed them to the shade of the awning. "Are you continuing your game, now? I should like to watch, and have a try myself."

"You may watch, but your father will geld me, young man, should I let you have a try."

"No he won't, but my mother might. Therefore, we simply won't tell her."

"And if you end up flat as a Shrove Tuesday pancake upon the surface of the deep blue sea?"

"You don't give me enough credit, Uncle Connor."

Toby had returned with two plates of eggs and toast; he presented one to Rhiannon, the other to Ned, and with a glance at Captain Merrick, rescued his commander from the boy's persistence. "Tell ye what, Ned. Why don't we let your Uncle Connor finish this contest he has going with Jacques and One-Eye, and then you and I can have our own little competition from off the transom?" He leaned close to the boy and gave Rhiannon a conspiring wink. "Why, the captain says there might be pirate treasure down there. What do you say?"

"I would like that very much," Ned said, and came to stand importantly beside Rhiannon, his pride and dignity restored.

She watched Captain Merrick as he looked up at the big wooden boom's fifty-foot length, now swinging in a bit as the breeze backed a point. She could sense the same eager restlessness in him that she had perceived last night at dinner, the itch to be moving, the inability to stand still for long. That he was a man of action, she had no doubt.

"Right, so, I made the last jump," he said, standing next to Rhiannon and leaning a little too close to her as he looked up into the rigging. "So it is now your turn, Bobbs. Ten shillings says you don't have the guts to try it at thirty feet."

"Twelve shillings says I'll make the dive at thirty-five feet."

"I'll raise you to forty."

"Forty-five."

Bobbs started to look dubious, and a flicker of worry came into his eyes. "Forty five, then." He cocked his head and squinted at his grinning captain. "But if I make the jump at forty-five, sir, I expect you to do it at fifty."

"Very well. One-Eye? You in?"

The other man, who actually possessed two eyes, but of differing colors with one being blue, the other being brown, just smiled and shook his head. "Nay, I'll fold."

"Jacques?"

"*Non*, but I'll throw another two dollars into the pot if you both go forty-five."

"Very well, then. After you, Bobbs."

The two men walked purposely over to the larboard shrouds and were soon climbing easily up into the rigging.

Toby, noting the pleat between Rhiannon's brows as she tipped her head back and tried to discern what this was all about, came to stand beside her. "Bet you're wondering what they're doing, ma'm."

"I am indeed."

"It's a contest. Do you see these two long, long spars, the shorter one on the top, the longer one on the bottom? The ones that lead aft from the mainmast, between which the sail is hung?" He cleared his throat importantly. "The one on the top that angles up and out like this—" he motioned with his hands—"is called a gaff, and it gets hauled aloft, carrying the sail with it. The one on the bottom, running horizontally out over our heads and all the way out over the stern, is called the boom. You'll see a bunch of men heading over to the sheet—in layman's terms, ma'm, that rope, there—which is currently cleated to hold the sail in place. In a moment, they'll uncleat it, start hauling on it, and you'll see the gaff, with the sail suspended from it, begin to go higher. They'll raise it to their best estimate of forty-five feet, then cleat it, and the contest will continue."

Rhiannon had a pretty good idea of what this "contest" entailed, and it seemed like madness. But she was compelled to ask, anyhow.

"And then what?"

"Then, the contestants walk out and up the gaff spar and dive off. Whoever manages to dare the most height, wins all the money in the pot." He grinned. "We started with ten who were willing to play, and one by one they've quit. Only Connor and Aaron Bobbs here are left."

"Fools," his older brother Nathan said again, but he had his hands folded across his chest and was leaning back with a little smile, chewing a last bite of egg and watching as a group of grinning seamen did exactly what Toby said they would do. The great mainsail began to climb even higher, its mast hoops spacing out along the mast and the huge boom over their heads swinging out a bit in the faint breeze.

Bobbs moved, monkey-like and barefoot out along the gaff so high above their heads, while Captain Merrick waited in the shrouds.

"Does your captain do this sort of thing often?" Rhiannon asked the older Ashton, not knowing whether to be impressed, shocked, or flattered if Connor Merrick was performing this feat of reckless bravery solely for her sake.

"Let's just say, ma'm, that he lives for excitement and thrills."

Toby was trying to get a better view. "And he likes to keep things interesting."

"I wish I could try that," piped up young Ned, wistfully.

"Boat approaching off to sta'b'd," muttered One-Eye. "Uh-oh. The King's man, himself."

"Yeah, and if Humpty Dumpty falls off the wall, all the King's men in the world won't be able to put him back together again," muttered Nathan.

"It's Dull-more."

Someone snickered; there was a familiar, impeccably dressed naval officer in the boat and the vessel was, indeed, cutting through the gentle swell with smart precision and headed straight for the schooner.

Someone shouted from above and Aaron Bobbs, with a howl of half-terror, half-excitement, came flailing down, tumbling through space and managing, at the last moment, a clumsy dive into the blue water. Everyone rushed to the rail to see if he had survived the impact. Rhiannon held her breath, waiting, and a moment or two later the young man's head broke the surface.

"Thunderation," he panted, and swam weakly toward the Jacob's ladder. "That one hurt."

The naval boat was getting closer, and a look of annoyance pinned itself firmly on young Ned's face. "Damn," he muttered. "I bet Papa sent him for me."

"We'll have none of that language in front of a lady, now," chided Nathan, who went to the rail as the schooner was hailed.

"Permission for Captain Lord to come aboard!" shouted the British coxswain.

"Now what?" said Toby. "He's not expecting us to pipe him aboard as a captain, is he?"

"Probably, but he's the damned enemy," muttered Nathan. He walked a little distance away, peered up through the great network of sails, stays and lines, and cupped his hands around his mouth. "Connor! Ye've got company!"

Rhiannon looked up and saw that Captain Merrick was standing nonchalantly, confidently, on the gaff some forty or fifty feet above her head. Terror for his safety prickled through her, making even the roots of her hair tingle.

"I'll be right down," he yelled back, walked a few more feet up and out on the gaff, and launched himself far out into the air.

Rhiannon saw it all. His form bunched up and falling through so much space . . . his men gasping and running for the rail . . . Ned's gape-jawed horror, beside her . . . and in the boat, Captain Lord's stiff, thinly veiled contempt as *Kestrel*'s daring, thrill-seeking captain unrolled himself from the tucked ball he'd assumed, did a half-somersault in the air until he was facing downward, stretched out his body with arms and hands pointed out over his head in a perfect, knifing V, and entered the water with barely a splash.

The men at the rail waited.

Danelle Harmon

And waited.

Rhiannon felt a flare of terror and glanced nervously at Nathan. "Oh, my God," she breathed.

But the lieutenant just shook his head, rolled his eyes, and went to the side to receive Captain Lord.

No matter. His captain had already surfaced a few feet from the British officer's boat and, affording him a half-mocking, half-jaunty salute, called up, "Care to join us, Captain Lord?"

CHAPTER 8

"Not on your damned life," the Englishman snapped. "Thank God you're not in our Navy, I'd have you keel-hauled for such a display."

"I had the chance to join your navy when your colleagues blew *Merrimack* out from under me, declined it, and chose internment on a prison hulk instead. A move I've never regretted."

"I daresay our Navy was well served by your refusal to join it."

"As was America," Toby proudly piped up.

Connor Merrick, swimming with long, easy strokes, kept pace with the Royal Navy boat as it drew steadily closer to *Kestrel*. He was not even breathing hard. "Haven't you ever tried diving from aloft, Delmore? It's great fun, I can assure you."

"I have other ways of finding my entertainment."

"Really? I'd not have known. As for me, I'm bored," Captain Merrick said, turning over to float on his back, "and since your admiral has forbidden me to go a'privateering in his waters"—the word *his* was delivered with no small degree of mockery—"we must find something to amuse us. You should try it yourself sometime. Learn how to have fun, Del. *Live* a little."

The other captain allowed the tightest of smiles. "That's Captain Lord to you, sir."

"Come aboard, Del," said Connor, propelling himself smoothly through the water and managing to avoid getting clipped by one of his cousin's men's oars. "There are only two of us left willing to make the dive at this height, so the day's excitement is almost over."

"Pray God you're one of them," Captain Lord said, with faint acidity. "I'd rather see you done in by your own reck-lessness than to have to blow you out of the water when you defy Sir Graham's wishes to—what was it he said?—"

"Behave myself."

"Yes, behave yourself, as I'm sure you have every inten-tion of not doing."

"Ah, we may not know each other well, Delmore, but you have me pegged," said Connor, and he swam toward the rope hanging over the side, as at home, Rhiannon thought, as a fish in the blue, blue sea.

And Captain Lord — did he really mean what he said about wanting to sink the American privateer?

Worse, did Connor Merrick mean what *he* said? Was he serious about going privateering, and right under his British brother-in-law's nose?

Oh, dear.

And she had thought diving into the sea from high aloft was dangerous and foolhardy. . . .

A few moments later, Captain Merrick was back aboard the schooner, shirtless, dripping wet, and standing in a growing puddle as Toby handed him a towel. He vigorously toweled his hair then tossed the towel over a nearby cannon. "Pipe the captain aboard, Nathan," he said good-naturedly. "Don't want it said that we Yanks aren't courteous."

Rhiannon heard the shrillness of a bosun's whistle, and the schooner's rag-tag, casually dressed officers lined up at the rail to receive the impeccably uniformed British captain.

"I don't know why you delight in baiting him so," Nathan muttered.

"Aye, not very sporting of me is it?" Captain Merrick said blithely, with a sideways glance at Rhiannon. He watched his English cousin coming up the Jacob's ladder. "I'll break that stuffiness of his before I'm done and show him how to live a bit. You just see if I don't."

"You should leave well enough alone, Con."

Captain Merrick just grinned.

The Englishman came aboard. His cool gray eyes held an expression of contempt, impatience, and even a bit of envy.

But for what?

The beauty of his American cousin's sleek, lithe, command?

Or the freedom that Connor Merrick, unfettered by rules, protocol, and expectations, enjoyed?

Still dripping wet, Captain Merrick came over to stand possessively near Rhiannon, tiny droplets of water running through the sparse hair of his lower legs, down his ankles and to his bare feet. The English captain's expression went stony.

"So what brings you aboard, Delmore?" Captain Merrick was saying. "Oh, but wait. Let me guess. Sir G would really like to see me leave so as not to make his situation any more complicated. Is that it, Del?"

"Sir *Graham* would like his son back. He had planned to take him fishing this morning. I've come to retrieve him."

"Why'd he send you? You're a flag captain for heaven's sake, not a lowly mid."

Captain Lord's eyes flickered momentarily to Rhiannon, and the faintest bit of color lodged itself, briefly, beneath his cheekbones. "I volunteered."

"Ah." Connor Merrick had, Rhiannon saw, noted the tell-tale slide of his cousin's gaze to her, and his eyes began to take on a hard glitter. "So I see."

Was Captain Merrick actually *jealous*? Good heavens, women must be in short supply here in Barbados if the two of them were competing for *her* attentions. It was a heady feeling to be sure, but oh, dear, what was she to do? Both were undeniably handsome men, yes. One proper, civilized and suitable, the other . . . not so much. One, a rising and respectable officer in the Royal Navy, the other, little more than a legalized pirate.

Ned was protesting.

"Uncle Connor, I cannot go back with Captain Lord; I have a duty to chaperone Miss Evans, and cousin Toby said we could have a diving contest off the transom! Surely Papa can wait!"

"Your father does *not* like to be kept waiting," Captain Lord snapped.

Ned was undeterred. "Well, I am not leaving until Uncle Connor finishes his contest with Mr. Bobbs."

"Contest?"

Captain Merrick folded his arms across his chest. "Aye, whoever makes the last, highest jump from aloft, wins. Care to toss a coin or two into the pot, Del?"

The British officer's nostrils flared. "Not in your life, Merrick. Collect your things, Edward. I will not risk your father's ire."

"What, are you not a gambling man?"

"I will not compromise the dignity of my navy by aiding and abetting such nonsense."

"Well then, why don't you prove your Navy's courage by participating in it?"

"*What?!*"

Young Ned saw immediately what his uncle was up to and his face lit up with sudden understanding. "Yes, Uncle Con's right! Why don't you get into the contest too, Captain Lord? You can represent the Royal Navy!"

Kestrel's crew seized upon the idea.

"Aye, Royal Navy versus an American privateer!"

"Now *there's* a contest with a predetermined outcome, ha ha ha!"

Laughter and guffaws echoed all around.

Captain Merrick grinned. "What's the matter, Del, don't you know how to have fun?"

"This is an outrage!"

"Guess you don't mind, then, if you leave my men thinking that we Yanks have more courage than a captain in His Majesty's Royal Navy. But never mind, Delmore. Another time, eh?"

Around them came the sounds of snickering from *Kestrel*'s crew. The proud Englishman was well and truly trapped. Rhiannon saw him forget himself for the briefest of moments, looking up to regard the gaff swinging so high above his head before he quickly drew himself up and turned to the American privateer to give him a stinging rebuke.

She decided it was time to step in before things got out of hand. "Actually, I think I should have Captain Lord take me back to shore," she said, taking pity on the man. "I feel a bit of a headache coming on with all this morning sunlight in my eyes, and it would be rude indeed to keep Sir Graham from his own son." She gave an apologetic smile to Connor Merrick, who had his arms folded across his bare, dripping, incredibly manly chest and was regarding her with one brow raised; the man might be reckless but he was no fool, and Rhiannon saw immediately that he knew exactly what she was up to and in his own way, respected her for it. "Master Ned? Will you chaperone me?"

The boy looked at her uncertainly for a moment, confused about this veiled exchange between his uncle and his father's flag captain. But there was nothing, really, for him to do but bow, smile, and agree to accompany her and Captain Lord back to shore.

CHAPTER 9

Connor stood at the rail, carefully overseeing the departure of Miss Evans from the ship, his hands sure and steady upon the rope that eased her, safely seated in the bosun's sling, down toward the damned Royal Navy boat in which Delmore waited to receive her.

Connor was smiling, but inside, his guts were twisting with frustration and something he identified as jealousy. He thought he was quite adept at hiding his dismay but his cousin knew him well.

"Ain't sitting well with you, is it?" Nathan asked, lifting his hat to Miss Evans as she looked up at them both and offered an apologetic smile.

"It damn well isn't," Connor growled, thinking of the sweet smile she'd bestowed upon Deadly Dull-more. "But no matter. I shouldn't even be thinking about her. She's not for me."

"Aye, and *we* should be thinking of pulling up the hook and getting the hell out of here, Con. Not making any money sitting here in Carlisle Bay when there's an ocean of prizes just plying the Caribbean."

Connor said nothing as he let his precious burden down another few inches.

"Of course," Nathan added thoughtfully, "It's not like you to give something up without a fight. She's enamored of you already. Wouldn't take much to win her."

"And what the devil would I do with a wife? And a British one at that?"

"I can think of a lot of things one can do with a wife, British or not."

Connor let the rope down a few more inches and with every bit of distance that increased between himself and Miss Rhiannon, he felt his ire growing. He wanted her, that sunset-haired beauty that Delmore was about to take away from him. Wanted her with a grinding ache that was firing every part of his body. "You're entirely correct," he muttered. "This was supposed to be a quick, in-and-out visit, drop the women off and get the hell out of here. We should have weighed anchor last night."

"So why not make the best of the situation?"

"Eh?"

"Since we're here, let's scrape the weed from the old lady's bottom, get her speed back up to where it should be with a good, clean hull, and while we're doing that, you can pay court to the beautiful Miss Evans." Nathan offered a rare grin. "Ain't getting any younger, Connor, and you know it. You gonna sit by and let Delmore have her?"

"I'll be thirty later this year."

"Precisely my point."

"I can't commit to any one woman. I get bored too easily and end up breaking hearts. I don't want to break hers, Nathan."

"You won't get bored with that one."

"She's too young for me."

"A younger woman will tolerate your foolishness better than a mature one."

"She's too good for me."

"She's perfect for you. Not many would put up with your restlessness, Con. That one?" He nodded toward the woman below. "She's got mischief in her eyes. She'd be more than a wife. She'd be a partner in crime."

The rope slackened as Miss Evans's feet landed gently in the Royal Navy boat. Connor watched his impeccably dressed cousin take her hand and help her get seated. Saw the radiant smile she gave the British captain and felt something tighten in his gut. The tars at the oars were trying, unsuccessfully, to keep their eyes off her, and between it all, he felt a sudden uncontrollable urge to do something violent.

Nathan made a *hmph*ing sound. "See what I mean?"

"For God's sake, Nathan, I'm a privateer in service to our country. I don't have the time or luxury for a romance, let alone a wife."

"I'm sure your mother and Da would like more grandchildren. American ones, that don't live one or two thousand miles away."

"Oh, just stow it, would you, Nathan?" With a bitter sigh, Connor yanked the rope contraption, now slack and painfully empty, back up the side and flung it to the deck. "We'll stay here, but for no longer than it takes to get *Kestrel*'s bottom scraped as best we can without being granted use of the Careenage. In the meantime, I'll remain here aboard the ship. There's nothing awaiting me on shore but trouble."

He turned away then and thus, missed Nathan's knowing grin.

There was nothing, of course, that drew Connor Merrick in faster, than "trouble."

"Trouble" came some hours later when Connor impulsively accepted his sister's invitation to dine with the Falconers. He and his crew had spent the day scraping the weed from *Kestrel*'s hull as best they could without totally hauling her out and careening her, and by the time the shadows were long across the schooner's decks he was bored, restless, and ready for a change of scenery.

He knew Rhiannon Evans would be there.

He knew it was the last place he ought to be.

And against his better judgment, he accepted anyhow.

Tired from spending the day in the sun, nursing a burn on his shoulders and back and a deep cut on his arm from an encounter with a barnacle, Connor arrived on the veranda (late as usual), only to find the seat beside the beautiful Miss Evans already occupied by none other than Captain Delmore Lord.

He saw red, and his earlier proclamations to Nathan were promptly forgotten.

No, he didn't have room in his life for a romance, and he was plenty aware of his numerous shortcomings. But he damn well wasn't going to give up the only woman to have ever caught his interest hook, line and sinker, to his stuffy prig of a cousin, either.

And now Delmore was telling sea tales.

And Miss Evans was staring at him, fascinated and attentive.

Connor's fist, buried under the tablecloth, itched to connect with Delmore's sudden smile as Miss Evans widened her eyes and put a pretty little hand to her high, firm bosom.

"You were very brave to do that, Captain Lord! And to a French man of war, besides! No wonder Sir Graham made you his flag captain!"

"Oh, it was a most decisive engagement, Miss Evans," Dull-more was saying. He sat up a bit straighter in his already stiff dress uniform, obviously enjoying the attention. "But far be it from me to trouble your gentle ears with the details of the battle. Suffice it to say, we won the day and sent the French ships packing."

"But I would love to hear the details, Captain Lord!"

Connor rolled his eyes. "Aye, so would I."

Delmore tightened his lips. "Accounts of battle and the complicated strategies of naval engagements are not appropriate conversation in genteel company. You should know that, Connor."

"Naval engagements, eh? Ah, let me guess. You were a hero of Trafalgar along with every other mariner the Royal Navy ever bred."

"I was not at Trafalgar," Dull-more said tersely.

"So!" Alannah interjected cheerfully, with a worried look between the two captains. "What did you all think of that lovely conch soup we had for supper this evening? Marvelous, was it not?"

"Indeed," Connor bit out, his eyes narrowing as his English cousin refilled Rhiannon's lemonade glass. He had never been in a position of having to compete for a woman's favors before, and the unfamiliar bite of jealousy twisted in his gut. He felt a muscle tic in his jaw and thought about how attractive the dashing Captain Lord would look with his teeth sprinkled all over Sir Graham's floor after a chance meeting with his fist.

"And what of you, Captain Merrick?" Alannah Cox continued, a little too brightly. "Do you have any good battle stories?"

"Plenty, ma'm. But I concur with my cousin. Such tales are not appropriate for a lady's ears."

Connor reached for more rum. Dull-more droned on expansively about the beauty of the Barbados flora, the Hampshire downs where he'd spent his childhood, the mysterious and wonderful things he'd seen in his years at sea. Connor pointedly yawned. Rhiannon laughed at something the Englishman said, and Connor's heel started to tap, tap, tap against the floor beneath the table. He wondered if there was a way to get up, seize Rhiannon by the arm, and haul her out of here without looking like a complete boor.

She's mine, he thought savagely. *Mine.*

He was glad when the ladies repaired to inside the house, leaving the three men alone out on the verandah.

The admiral wasted no time. "So when are you leaving, Connor?" he asked, point-blank.

Connor raised his head and looked flatly at his brother-in-law. Did Sir Graham want him out of here so as not to upset Maeve? Or so that the oh-so-perfect Deadly Dull-more could have free rein to pursue Miss Evans without competition? Of course, Sir Graham would never discourage Delmore from courting the girl. Delmore was a choir boy compared to himself. And Delmore had surely not gotten himself thrown out of school after numerous canings, beatings and whippings had failed to stop him from fighting, disturbing the other children, and staring moodily out the window when he was bored.

Delmore, he knew, wasn't stupid, as he had been.

As he still was.

For a fleeting moment, he saw again a long-ago street in Newburyport, heard again the mocking taunts of the other children.

Connor! Connor! You're stupid and have no hon-or!

The other boys had been easily silenced with his fist, but no matter how successful he was as a privateer, no matter how much he drove himself to prove his worth by taking one rich prize after another, the self-doubt remained. . . .

"Connor?" the admiral persisted.

Connor grinned but he was angry, and the grin didn't reach his eyes. "Eager to be rid of me, Sir G?"

"Your presence here requires no small degree of tact and maneuvering on my part to keep things on an even keel. Any one of my officers would, I daresay, be quite happy to remember that you are an American privateer." The admiral reached for his glass of rum. "Nothing personal of course, but it does put me in a bit of a spot."

"I understand. And I know the only reason you haven't seized *Kestrel* and thrown the lot of us into some forgotten prison is because I'm 'family.'"

"Look, don't make it any harder than it already is. War is ugly, and this one in particular leaves a bad taste in my mouth." He looked out over the riding lights of the ships anchored in the bay. "I'd rather be battling the French than you Yankees. Remember that."

Across the table, Delmore Lord quietly helped himself to a glass of punch from one of the two bowls that didn't have a gallon or two of rum dumped into it. Connor frowned. Did the man practice temperance along with all his other constraining habits?

What a dead bore.

He splashed a hefty dose of rum into his own mug and unflinchingly met the admiral's blue gaze. Beneath the table, his foot was making restless circles, moving faster and faster as his agitation increased. "Well, I shan't trouble you with my presence past the end of the week, Sir Graham. After all, I have *work* to do, and it's not going to get done sitting in Carlisle Bay."

"If you intend to hoist the Stars and Stripes and take that schooner privateering—"

"That's exactly what I intend."

A muscle twitched in the admiral's jaw. "You're a damned nuisance, Connor."

"I try to be."

"Your sister's about to have a baby. She's already upset enough, worrying about you. She's been dreaming about death. Yours, or that of someone she loves. For God's sake, why do you insist on doing things that upset people so?"

"Now that's a fine sentiment, given the source."

"Your penchant for thrills and living dangerously is unfair to those who care about you."

"As you said, Sir Graham, war is ugly. This one started because Britain was stomping all over the rights of American seamen, and it will end because those same American seamen will prove to be your superior. Mark me on that. Despite the might of ships like *Constitution* and *United States*, our navy is small and so it falls to men like me—America's privateers—to take up the slack." He took another swallow of rum, looked the admiral straight in the eye and, wondering how much further he could push his brother-in-law before he lost his temper, recklessly set about trying to find that tipping point. "Why, even you must admit that we're doing a damned fine job of it."

Captain Lord sipped his punch. "Honorable men do not become privateers. They join their country's navy, instead."

Connor set down his mug. "Dare you call me a dishonorable man, Delmore?"

"Stop it, both of you," Sir Graham snapped. "I'll not have a duel between you."

"And I'll not stand to be insulted so."

"You two are cousins, for God's sake. But this isn't about who's in what navy, is it? Or who has the most honor?" The admiral's blue eyes narrowed. "Don't think I haven't noticed the two of you circling Miss Evans like a couple of curs over a bone. And I'll tell you right now, I won't have it. The girl is eighteen, and I'm charged with her guardianship while she's here. She arrived here as an innocent, and when I send her back to her sister and Lord Morninghall in six weeks' time, I intend her to still be an innocent."

Connor just looked at the admiral, a tiny hint of a smile playing with one corner of his mouth as he lifted his mug, took a long swallow, and gave his cousin a challenging stare over the rim.

Captain Lord drew himself up a little straighter in his chair and said nothing, in rigid control of himself once more.

Sir Graham looked at them both. "And now, that's enough of that. I hear the ladies returning, and I don't want anything upsetting Maeve any more than it already has."

Rhiannon had returned to the veranda with the ladies only to find a tension in the air that was as charged and heavy as an impending storm. Something had transpired out here in their absence and by the looks of things, it wasn't anything good. Captain Lord was even stiffer than usual, Sir Graham was pretending a lightning bolt wasn't going to crack down out of the ceiling at any moment, and Connor Merrick was hard-eyed, agitated, and drumming his long, handsome fingers against the table; at a cross look from his sister at this lapse in manners, he'd resorted to tapping his foot against the floor in a way that betrayed his restlessness, and Rhiannon wasn't at all surprised when he made his excuses as soon as it was polite to do so, stood up, and bade them all a good night.

As he bowed over her hand, his green eyes met hers from over her knuckle; there was something hard and angry in them, but he quickly smiled, making little crinkles fan out from the corners of his eyes and transforming his face into one of careless good humor, and the moment was lost. Perhaps she'd only imagined his anger; he seemed too much of a free spirit to harbor such an emotion. But all too soon, he was striding toward the big glass doors, broad-backed, lean and handsome, the lantern light falling softly on his tousled chestnut curls. A moment later he was gone, taking his larger-than-life presence with him.

Small talk ensued. But Rhiannon's gaze kept going to the empty chair where Captain Merrick had been sitting, and she was painfully aware of his absence.

And so she passed the rest of the evening feeling much lower than she let on, speaking when she was spoken to, smiling when she was supposed to smile, and being kind to the naval captain whom, she feared, was fostering an interest in her that she probably shouldn't encourage. Captain Lord was a good man, a noble one, entirely suitable but altogether wrong for her. She would break his heart, and she knew it. Captain Merrick, on the other hand, was entirely unsuitable but altogether *right* for her. He made her heart beat a hundred times faster and her blood to race and her thoughts to turn to wicked, imagined things that couples did in the darkness.

She went to her room as soon as it was polite to make her excuses, and from somewhere off in Bridgetown, the strains of lively music came wafting through the warm night. The breeze moved gently into the room and Rhiannon, wishing for tiredness but unable to turn off her thoughts, her mind, her memory of the brave, half-naked Captain Merrick leaping fearlessly from the rigging earlier that day, could not sleep.

She pulled the lantern close and picked up a book, but the words filed before her, empty of meaning, and she found herself going over the same paragraph over and over again without remembering what she had read.

She got up and paced, finally stopping at the open window and looking down into the harbor where the riding lights of the British fleet, merchant ships, trade vessels, and somewhere, the American privateer schooner *Kestrel*, winked in the darkness.

Connor Merrick was out there somewhere.

Connor Merrick, who leaped with fearless abandon from high in the rigging . . . who had saved her beloved sister from drowning back in Portsmouth . . . who had rescued her and Alannah from bloodthirsty pirates, brought them safely through a terrible storm at sea, and delivered them without incident to Barbados; Connor Merrick, who made her blood thrum and her knees weak and a strange, restless ache to gather between her legs.

She would not sleep this night.

Frustrated, Rhiannon turned from the window, moved across the room, and decided that a walk in the warm night air might soothe her enough to find the rest she sought.

For her, as it was for Captain Merrick, trouble was waiting.

Connor had not gone back to *Kestrel*.

He needed exercise, the release of moving his body, and there wasn't room enough on the schooner's eighty-foot deck for the hard walk that his muscles, let alone his temper, craved. Instead, he stalked angrily away from the house and down the lawn toward the water, even the balmy trades against his skin unable to soothe his anger.

Damn Sir Graham. Damn Delmore Lord. Damn everyone, damn everything, and damn himself for letting himself get hooked by Miss Rhiannon Evans when he'd known all along, when he'd told himself all along, to walk away.

If he were a smart man, he'd sail out of here tonight and leave her to Delmore. But he was a proud man, not a smart one, and there was no way on God's green earth he was going anywhere.

Not now, when Sir Graham had all but thrown down the gauntlet.

Not now, when Delmore had set his own eye on the woman that he, Connor, had found first.

Not now, when his insides felt like someone had twisted them into a knot and set them on fire.

Oh, he had his pride all right. Rhiannon Evans was *his*.

Ahead, the moon was poised above the western horizon and lighting up the sea. He reached the water's edge and reaching down, picked up a stone and flung it, hard, out over the water, trying to get it to skim and skip the surface as he and his siblings had so often done as children.

What are you going to do, Connor?

Yes, what was he going to do?

He picked up another rock. Sent it flying out over the surface.

She was just a young girl. Too young to appreciate him for anything more than the careless daredevil she knew him to be, too young to want him for the real man he actually was. A man who couldn't stop striving to be all that his father had been before him. A man who wasn't, in some respects, quite as confident as he would have others believe. A man who had a secret so shameful that she would surely pity him, maybe even laugh at him, if she were to ever find out about it.

So what are you going to do, Connor?

The hell with pride. He would be smart, just this once. He was going to go back to *Kestrel*, that's what he was going to do. And he was going to stay there until every last man of his crew returned and then, he was getting the devil out of Barbados and going back to work.

He pitched one last stone and headed back up the beach.

Rhiannon had intended to just spend a few moments outside, but the night was quiet, the front gardens deserted, and a gibbous moon was just setting over the western horizon, lighting a serene path of gold out over the water and seemingly into forever.

Above her head, the trades whispered through the palms and in the near distance, Rhiannon could hear the gentle, timeless rhythm of surf against the beach.

She headed toward the sound, thinking to find a place to sit and watch the moon setting over the sea, and to think.

"Connor Merrick."

There, she'd said it. Breathed life into the name and, in so doing, made this strange, exciting, shivery feeling of infatuation, real. But was it infatuation? Or was it something more?

Was it possible for a woman to fall in love at first sight?

Of course it is. He saved your life.

And, your sister's.

She'd had infatuations before, of course. What young woman didn't? But she had been younger then, and there was a big difference between the shy, pimply, insecure youths she'd known back in the little Welsh village where she'd grown up, and a confident and virile man like Connor Merrick.

What would Gwyneth—who had raised her and Morganna after their parents had died so many years before, who had taken a position in the local public house so the three of them would have enough to eat, who had married the elderly Lord Simms in order to give her little sisters a better life— have to say about her obsession with Connor Merrick?

Ahead, the beach glowed pale in the light of the moon. Sighing, Rhiannon moved closer to the waves breaking gently against this protected western shore, kicked off her shoes and, arranging her skirts around her, sat down, curling her toes in the warm sand. She folded her arms across her knees and, resting her chin on her wrists, gazed morosely out over the path of moonlight that led out over the sea and to the horizon.

Down here, the riding lights of the ships anchored in the harbor were brighter, glowing like stars from rigging and tops alike, casting their own tiny reflections over the water.

"Connor Merrick," she said again.

And sensed movement behind her, and a presence.

She knew who it was before she even turned and saw his tall, lean form leaning against a palm tree a short distance away.

"How long have you been standing there?" she asked, mortified—and grateful that the night hid the sudden, hot blush that filled her cheeks.

"Long enough to hear my name uttered." He bowed, and she could see that he was smiling. "At your service, ma'm."

"Were you spying on me?"

"Actually, I was on my way back to my schooner when I noticed you sitting there. My curiosity was aroused. Forgive me."

"You *were* spying on me."

"Very well then, I was spying on you. And thinking of a million ways to send Deadly Dull-more to hell and back for the fact that he had the good fortune to be sitting next to you tonight, and I did not. Pardon my language, ma'm."

"Why, Captain Merrick . . . if I didn't know better, I'd think you were jealous!"

"Hmph. Of that starched up prig? Hardly."

He came forward, and her heart began to pound.

"I should go inside, this is not proper."

"Proper? What, Miss Evans, about the world is?"

"I beg your pardon?"

"Our president Madison declared war against your country when he should've declared it against the French, who were guilty of many of the same insults that offended us in the first place. I'm an American privateer supping with a British admiral who only tolerates my presence here because he's married to my sister. My nephew and nieces speak with an English accent, my normally fierce sister is an emotional, weepy mess, and my dead-bore of a cousin claimed the seat at the dinner table tonight next to the most beautiful woman in Barbados." He gave a little grin, acknowledging her blush. "And you speak to me about 'proper?' The world is a strange and confusing place, Miss Evans. I should think that two people enjoying the beauty of a tropical moonlit night might count it as one of the only things in this world that *is* proper, given the upside down state of affairs in which we find ourselves." He smiled. "Would you care to walk?"

"I think you should take me back to the house. If anyone discovers us out here alone, it would be disastrous."

"Who would care, here in Barbados? You're not in a London drawing room."

"I—"

"Do you *wish* to go for a walk, Miss Evans?" His smile turned roguish. "Or better yet, that swim?"

Her eyes widened. "You were serious, then? About teaching me?"

"Indeed I was, ma'm."

"Well, I confess the idea makes me rather nervous . . . it's dark out. There might be sharks. I lack the courage you display in hurling yourself out of the rigging, you know. But if you vow to keep me safe. . . ."

"Courage isn't defined by doing things you aren't afraid to do, no matter how terrifying anyone else finds them. Courage is about doing the things you *are* afraid to do, no matter how *un*-terrifying anyone else finds them. Even so, d'you think I wasn't just a little bit afraid, when I jumped out of the rigging like that?"

She laughed. "No, I do not think you were afraid at all, Captain Merrick, but having the time of your life."

"Then you sadly overestimate the few qualities of my character, Miss Evans."

"You were only doing that to impress me, weren't you? Because you had a female aboard?"

"Oh, no. Though I do confess that knowing you were watching did compel me to jump all the higher. Come, let us walk. I know a quiet cove just south of here. The water is shallow, gentle, and warm."

He reached down and, having no choice, Rhiannon slid her fingers into that broad, strong hand, picked up her shoes, and allowed him to raise her to her feet.

He was a tall presence beside her, one that made her feel both safe and protected and in great danger all at the same time, and she felt all the blood in her veins beginning to turn to steam.

I should not be doing this! How do I get myself out of this situation?

And then: *Do you* want *to get yourself out of this situation?*

No. Oh, absolutely, positively, not. She was having an adventure, she was with the devastatingly handsome Black Wolf, and he was jealous that another man had shown her attention.

She had nothing to lose.

And everything to gain.

He's going to teach me how to swim!

She tucked her hand into the crook of his elbow, her heartbeat beginning to thunder in her ears. Oh, this was deliciously wicked to be out here alone with him. Forbidden, sinful, by every rule of society. But oh, if he could "live a little," as he seemed to say so often, then so could she.

I wonder what it would be like if he were to kiss me . . .

The sand, still warm from the heat of the day, scrunched under her bare feet as she allowed him to lead her down to the beach, the lights of Sir Graham's mansion receding into the trees behind them.

"So, what compelled you to become a privateer, Captain Merrick?"

"The money," he said, with a half-apologetic smile.

"No overwhelming sense of patriotism or pride?"

"No." He shook his head. "This war's different from the one we fought thirty years ago. It's not about independence this time. And to be fair, there are many of us in New England who were against it. Jefferson's Embargo Act squeezed most of us such that the economy was in ruins. We could have done without another war, but since one was declared, might as well profit from it."

"And so here you are."

"Here I am. Destined, it seems, to ply the same course my *Dadaí* did back in the old war, and with the same ship, as well."

"Your father was a privateer, too?

She leaned a little closer to him as they continued along, her hand tucked safely in the crook of his elbow, hearing his words through a strange, delighted thrumming of excitement at the fact that she was out here all alone with him in the dark.

Wicked.

Scandalous.

Forbidden.

Alone.

"Yes, and a good one. I grew up hearing the stories about him," he continued, his voice fond with admiration, perhaps even awe. "He was a rising officer in the Royal Navy, but defected to the American side shortly after the war began and made a name for himself as one of the most legendary privateers of the Revolution. From the time I could remember, I heard the stories, told to me by my mother, by my aunt and uncle, by the townspeople of Newburyport, by everyone, really, except my father himself . . . stories of how he outsmarted the British by pretending to be in shallows when *Kestrel* was in deep ocean water . . . stories of the outrageous numbers of prizes that he and my Uncle Matthew brought back into Newburyport, making them both rich beyond imagining . . . stories of how he managed to save *Kestrel* when the British admiral blocked the American fleet in Penobscot Bay by cleverly setting a prize ship afire and using it to blast a hole through the British ships so he could escape . . . stories of Irish luck and miraculous survival, breathtaking feats of seamanship and daring. . . " He looked up and out over the sea, his gaze far away, a little smile playing with the corner of his mouth. "I used to think that they were just stories, those tales of my father's daring feats, but they were not."

"What does your father say about them?"

"Oh, he's a humble, self-effacing man. He doesn't talk much about the old war, and is content these days to run his shipyard with my Uncle Matt, designing and building ships, investing in trade, timber, that sort of thing. He became quite wealthy during the last war and invested wisely; it is my intention to follow in his footsteps, and—" here, he grinned—"surpass his exploits, to the extent that I can."

"Like father, like son?"

"Indeed."

"And now you are here."

"And now I am here. With you. Which, until I weigh anchor and go seek my own fortunes, is exactly where I want to be."

"Are you serious, or just an accomplished flatterer?"

"Both."

She couldn't help it; she laughed, and so did he, and something connected between them.

"What about you, Miss Evans? Tell me about yourself."

"Oh, I'm not all that fascinating. I'm just a simple country girl from Wales who likes to read, and who wishes her own life had a little more excitement."

"I could give you that, you know."

"Give me what?"

He grinned, the charming rogue once more. "That excitement."

"You've rescued me from bloodthirsty pirates, shown me flying fish and rainbows, and you're about to teach me how to swim. I don't know how you could make things any *more* exciting, Captain!"

"Have you ever been courted before?"

"Not by anyone whose attentions I particularly sought."

"Did you leave behind any broken hearts in England?"

"Only my dog Mattie's. I'm sure he's missing me."

"Have you ever been kissed?"

"Captain Merrick!"

"Well, have you?"

"That's rather a personal question, don't you think?"

"Indeed it is." His eyes were laughing, and she was glad it was dark out so she couldn't see how unsettled—and excited—such a probing question was making her. "Are you going to answer it?"

"All right, Captain Merrick. No, I have never been kissed."

"I could give you that, too, you know." He leaned down, close to her ear. "That first kiss."

She couldn't help a little gasp. How on earth was she supposed to respond to *that*?

He mistook her confusion for shock.

"I'm sorry. I have many flaws, Miss Evans, and one of them is a certain impulsiveness of thought that, all too often I fear, finds its way onto my tongue. You're a pretty girl. It's been a long time since someone's turned my head and commandeered my thoughts the way that you have, and I'm just being honest."

"Honest?" she squeaked.

"Aye, honest. I've been wanting to kiss you from the moment we stood together in *Kestrel*'s bows, and you took your bonnet off and let your hair free to fly in the wind."

She just looked at him, not knowing what to say.

He paused and turned her to face him. "Live a little, Miss Evans," he said, and then, before she could know what he was about, he put a finger beneath her chin, tilted her face up to his, and lowered his lips to hers.

She was unprepared. For the feel of rough male jaw-bristle against her tender skin. For the forcefulness of his mouth, the drive of his lips against her own, and then, the insistent pressing of his tongue against the seam of her lips until she opened to him. She tasted rum and felt his heat and hunger, the whisper of his breath against her cheek, the press of his fingers against her jawbone. She sighed and shut her eyes, her own hand coming up to hesitantly touch his shoulder, the base of his neck, and to push upward into his thick, loosely curling hair.

And then, suddenly, she realized what she was doing and pulled away. Wide-eyed, her hand went up to cover her mouth, and she licked her lips, tasting him.

"Oh," she said, simply.

"Oh?"

She touched her fingers to her lips. They were tingling, and she felt a strange yearning deep in the pit of her belly, centering between her legs. This could get out of control if she wasn't careful. She was playing with fire, and people who played with fire inevitably got burned.

"Perhaps I should take you back to the house," he said, reaching out to touch her hair.

No!

"It would . . . it would probably be smart."

"Nobody has ever accused me of being smart, Miss Evans."

"And nobody has ever accused *me* of being reckless."

They continued walking, slower this time, both think-ing about the kiss, neither of them willing to actually end their time together but both knowing that a decision lay before them and once made, there was no turning back.

"So what is it to be, Miss Evans? Are you feeling reckless? Or should I take you back to the house?"

If I let you take me back to the house, my adventure will end here and now. And I'll forever wonder what might have been, if only I'd followed it through.

She boldly met his gaze. "You did promise me a swimming lesson, Captain."

"Aye, that I did."

"So, let us be about it, then."

They had reached a clearing and there, ahead, was a small cove, with surf that lapped gently at the beach. Each tiny, curling wave sparkled like diamonds in the moonlight as it broke against the pale coral sand, then hissed and foamed as it retreated into the sea. Rhiannon trembled inside. She had just had her first kiss, given to her by none other than Captain Connor Merrick himself, and he was now about to teach her to swim beneath the stars of a Caribbean night . . . did life get any more magical than this?

Her heart gave a little flutter.

There would be no lamenting lost chances, no wondering what might have been when this night was over.

None.

She was going to do this. No matter how dark that water out there looked, no matter how many sharks might be lurking beneath the surface, no matter how conflicted she suddenly felt when she realized just what she was doing, and with whom.

He led her down to the little beach and there, reached down and took off his sandals.

"You're nervous, aren't you?" he asked, looking over at her.

"I'd be lying if I said I wasn't."

"Admitting a fear is the first step to conquering it."

"Maybe some fears should be respected, not conquered. Maybe . . . maybe we could just sit here on the sand and talk. I am not sure there's any real need for me to learn how to swim."

He yanked his shirt free of his waistband, and pulled it over his head. "No, there is not."

"It's an utterly useless skill, really . . . not something that a person in my position has much need of."

"Yes, utterly useless."

"*Are* you courting me, Captain Merrick?"

His gaze warmed. "Aye, Miss Evans. I am."

She fought to find her breath. "Then in that case, perhaps we should be proper about this. . . ."

"Proper?"

"That is, I, uh . . . think you should take me back."

He tossed the shirt to the sand, crossed his strong, hard arms over his chest and regarded her with a little smile, the moonlight glinting off his teeth, his tousled hair, the tops of his wide and powerful shoulders.

"I can if you wish," he said, regarding her with that long, warm gaze that she had come to think of as *the look*. The one that made her heart bounce around in her chest and her breathing to become unsteady and her palms to go damp. "But is that what you really want?"

"What I really want, and what I really ought to do, are two different things."

He leaned close, humor and challenge lighting his eyes. "Live a little, Miss Evans."

"You say that a lot."

"Words to live by. Besides, I promise to keep you safe."

Of course he would. Her resolve restored, Rhiannon gathered the hem of her skirts in one hand and, placing the other in the crook of his elbow once more, allowed him to lead her toward the water. The waves swirled around her ankles, as warm and delicious as a bath.

From far away in the night, she heard revelry coming from somewhere in Bridgetown, and from several ships anchored out in the harbor, the clang of bells as the watch ended.

And suddenly Rhiannon realized that to learn how to swim she would have to get wet, and if she got wet, her thin muslin gown and shift beneath would be plastered to her body and Captain Merrick would see everything she owned.

The idea was strangely titillating.

Wicked.

But it is dark outside, a little voice inside her head countered. *What, really, can he see?*

What, indeed.

She took a step further into the surf until she was up to her knees. If they went any deeper, her modesty would be compromised.

She hesitated.

This is my adventure. One that I could only have dreamed about. It is happening to me right here, right now. And I'm going to enjoy it.

Boldly, she let go of her skirts as he led her in even deeper, until the surf moved with gentle stealth around her knees. Her thighs.

There, Captain Merrick stopped, turned her gently around to face him, and took both her hands in his own.

"Do you trust me?" he asked, his voice deep and gentle, the stars so far above his head suddenly very, very bright in their vast expanse of night.

"I trust you."

He let a moment go by, and then, still holding her hands, he lowered them until both his hands and hers were under the water. There they both stood, face to face, her face tilted up to regard his, he looking down at her with an expression in his eyes that was deeper than the vastness of the night beyond his head. And then he raised a hand from the water and placed it, dripping and wet, alongside the line of her jaw, his thumb gently stroking the hollow beneath her cheek.

"I don't make it a habit of ravishing beautiful young ladies," he said softly.

"Of course you don't. . . ."

"So if you change your mind, I would advise that you give me a hard and decisive slap across the cheek, and perhaps it will knock some sense into my poor befuddled head."

"I don't want to . . . to discourage you, Captain. Let alone harm you."

He lifted his other hand from the water and laid it alongside her other cheek, raising her head so that her eyes looked steadily into his own. "Then never let it be said, Miss Evans, that a Yankee privateer is anything but a gentleman," he murmured, and bending his head, claimed her lips with a gentle firmness that rocked her to her core.

Rhiannon melted. Every single cell in her body, every bit of bone and blood and muscle and nerve, suddenly felt as though the strength had been stripped from them as she tilted her head back and allowed him to deepen the kiss, to increase the pressure, to claim her willing, eager lips with his own. Of their own accord her hands came out of the water, roved up his strong, hard arms, and up through the tousled curls that just touched his nape. She stood on tip-toe, inhaling the scent of him—bay rum, sea salt, and trade winds—obediently opening her mouth when she felt his tongue pressing against her lips. Her nipples fired, and the strange ache between her legs became pressing, persistent, and stronger by the second. Her knees began to buckle, and as though sensing it, he slowly drew back, gazing down at her with a look of hunger, admiration, and longing.

"Well," he said, as she reluctantly let her own hand slip from the back of his head. "I suppose . . . we should get started."

Her heart was pounding. "Yes, you did promise to t-teach me to swim."

"Though if I were smart, I would take you back to the house."

"But you know that you will not."

"I desire you, Miss Evans. That should be obvious. But that doesn't mean I can't behave myself."

She couldn't prevent a little grin. "Poor you," she said. "There's that phrase again. First you must 'behave yourself' for Sir Graham, now you must behave yourself for me. No wonder you're eager to put Barbados far behind you."

"Perhaps," he countered, "I'm not so eager, after all."

He gazed down at her, his eyes very dark and intense in the faint light. Rhiannon shivered with desire. How she wanted this man, wanted the feel of his hands against her skin, his strong arms lifting her, his handsome, wry, mouth against her own once more. But she sensed that he was indeed a gentleman no matter how roguish his words, no matter how passionate his kiss, and that he was indeed going to take her back to the house, make his way back to *Kestrel*—

And sail out of her life forever.

He was already turning, heading back toward the shore.

"Teach me to swim," she said, impetuously.

He paused, the water lapping against his hips and sparkling in the moonlight. For several moments he just stood there, a tall, dark presence against the starlit sky that spread out into forever over his head.

And then he turned and looked at her.

Just looked at her.

Rhiannon's throat went dry. She lifted her hand and held it wordlessly out to him, desperate to keep him here, desperate to make this magical night last, to keep this compelling, reckless, fascinating man with her just a little longer even if it did mean doing something terribly scandalous, and altogether forbidden.

He came back to her, fitted his strong hands around her waist and lifted her straight off the sea floor, holding her there and letting her get the feel of what it was like to not have her feet on the bottom.

Rhiannon flung her arms out to the sides to keep her balance.

"Relax," he said quietly.

Relax? When his hands were spanning her waist, holding her suspended in the sea while his mouth, that beautiful, sinful, sensuous mouth, was only a few inches from her own?

"I am going to put my hand on your belly," he said. "I want you to tip forward, and lie against my hand. I'll hold you up."

He set her back down, letting her feet anchor themselves once more in the sand and yes, his hand was against her once more, intimate, broad and flat and warm against her abdomen through the layers of wet muslin, the tips of his fingers perilously close to her most private regions.

The feeling was wickedly sensual, and the ache between Rhiannon's legs became a slow burn.

"Lean forward," he instructed, his voice sounding a little hoarse.

"I am afraid."

"I've got you." *Oh, how warm and wonderful that hand. . . .* "Trust me."

She trusted him. With her life. But she didn't know how to do as he asked, and when she hesitated further, he put his other hand against the small of her back, lifted her once more off the sea floor and tilted her, slowly, until she was all but lying on her belly in the water.

Fear rose in her throat and she began to breathe hard, her arms shooting out, trying to find purchase in a medium that offered none.

"Relax," he said again, holding her. "Take a deep breath, let it out, and relax. I've got you, Miss Evans."

"I'm afraid."

"I know."

"I mean, really, *really* afraid."

"Of what?"

"Drowning."

He smiled then, supporting her easily with one hand under her belly, his other gently rubbing the small of her back, encouraging her to relax. To trust him. "I did not let your sister drown in the cold waters of Portsmouth, and I'm not about to let *you* drown here in Carlisle Bay."

Rhiannon began to shake as the reality of this situation began to overwhelm her.

"Are you ready?" he asked.

"I'm ready."

He began to walk, slowly, and Rhiannon, still lying on her stomach with his hands supporting her, felt water moving against her collarbone, streaming along her body.

"Lower your head. Let your chin rest in the water."

She froze, afraid all over again.

"I have you, Miss Evans."

She stiffened but did as he instructed, and felt the water come alarmingly up to the level of her ears, swirling around her jaw, her chin and the back of her head as though wanting to swallow her.

Trust him.

"Put your arms out," he instructed. "Pretend you're flying. I won't let you go."

She did so, and suddenly felt the sea dragging against her arms as he pivoted her around him in a small circle, allowing her to get the feel of the water.

But Rhiannon wasn't thinking about the water.

She was thinking of those two kisses, and the way his hands against her skin were making her feel, and the fact that he'd said he was courting her. Every cell in her body was aware of one thing only, and that was Connor Merrick.

"I am going to take my hand off your back," he said.

"No!"

"And leave my other hand under your belly and ribs."

"Don't let me go!"

'Pon my life, ma'm, I will not. Do you still trust me?"

"I still trust you."

He took his hand away from her back, balancing her, now, on the one hand he still had beneath her belly. His thumb was close to the underside of her breasts.

And his little finger, to her navel.

She wondered what it would feel like if he spread his fingers and touched her in those most intimate of places.

"Now, I want you to make reaching motions with your arms . . . put your hands together as if you were praying, reach forward, then stroke back, as though you're trying to push the water behind you. And while you're doing that, I'm still going to hold you."

"All right."

She did as he asked, her mind torn between fear and desire and the dizzy, heady exhilaration of being freed from gravity, of the ocean bottom, of. . . .

Flying.

"Now, as I walk with you, and you stroke with your arms, I want you to gently kick your legs. Again, I will not let you go."

"Promise?"

"Promise."

She tried, but she was too tense, too scared, too *aware* of this man beside her, and she grew confused, unable to stroke with her arms and kick with her legs in any sort of meaningful rhythm.

He paused, allowing her to collect her courage.

"Still afraid?" he asked.

"Terrified."

"You're doing fine."

"I bet you say that to every girl you teach to swim."

"On the contrary, Miss Evans. You are the first." He paused. "Now, I want you to stand up and find the bottom.

I'll keep my hand here, on your belly, and then I will take your hand, as we're a little deeper than we were and I don't wish you to be startled. Are you ready?"

"Ready."

He gently helped her to find her feet and she stood up, trembling with excitement and desire and triumph. Her hand was still caught securely within his own and he looked down at her, smiled, and gently released her, walking a few steps backward away from her while the water made a swirling wake around his hips.

He continued to move backward until he was six or seven feet away from her. There he stopped and, extending his hands toward her, smiled.

"Now, I want you to swim to me, Rhiannon."

Rhiannon.

"I did not give you permission to use my given name, Captain."

"No, you did not. So come here and do something about it."

"I don't know what you want me to do!"

"Push off from the bottom, bring your arms up and let yourself fall, and at the same time that you do this, slice the water with your arms to break your fall," he said, motioning with his own arms to illustrate. "As you feel yourself starting to sink just a little bit, pull the water back as you were doing just a moment ago, and kick with your feet. You only have to reach me. Throw yourself toward me, and then use your arms to keep yourself afloat."

"And if I do that, Captain? Will you end this lesson, bring me back to the house, and leave on the morrow, never to return?"

"If I knew what was good for me, that is precisely what I would do."

"Given your actions in the short time since I've met you, I'm not convinced you know what is good for you."

"And you would be right. Now try it, Miss Evans. If you can traverse the several feet that separates us, you'll be able to call yourself a swimmer."

She nodded and took a deep, steadying breath, suddenly afraid all over again.

He stood there, silhouetted and unmoving against the night sky, his arms stretched encouragingly toward her . . . .

So close.

With a little gasp, Rhiannon half-fell, half-threw herself forward, felt the sea close around her, trying to come up over her head—and panicked. Water sloshed into her eyes and up her nose, burning her sinuses, and suddenly his hands were there beneath her, holding her once more, supporting her, as she splashed and panted in fear and tried to get her pounding heart back under control.

"I sank," she cried, in despair. "I am not made to swim!"

"You sank because you panicked," he said with quiet firmness. "You must try it again, Miss Evans, otherwise you'll never find the courage to make another attempt, and that would be a pity."

"Oh," she said, trying to quell her rising hysteria. "Oh, I don't think that I can."

"Really? I think that you can. And I think that you *will*."

She would have protested further but he had set her back down again, retreated a little ways closer into shore, and once again had his hands outstretched, beckoning, encouraging her forward.

To trust him.

Once again, Rhiannon took a deep breath, let herself fall, and this time her hands came up to automatically break her fall—

"Stroke!" he urged, with a grin splitting his handsome face, and suddenly it all came together and Rhiannon, propelled by the momentum of her frightened plunge toward him, held afloat by her desperate arms, was swimming.

Swimming.

It was only a couple of feet but she did it on her own, and suddenly he had caught her arms and pulled her joyously out of the water, laughing in delight at her triumph.

"You did it!"

"I did it!"

"I'm proud of you, Miss Evans!"

"I'm proud of me, too! Thank you, Captain! Oh, God help me, I swam! I *swam*!"

He laughed, still holding her by both arms, and then the sudden, frenzied triumph stilled in her blood and she was aware of only his eyes, the sudden fading of his smile, the height and strength and feel of his big, wet body in the moonlight.

Time stilled for both of them.

"You're going to kiss me again," she breathed.

He merely smiled.

"Aren't you?"

He didn't answer, but just drew her forward by her arms, pulled her up and off the sea floor, and raising his leg, set her down atop his bare, wet thigh so that she straddled it, the hard muscle pushing against that burning area between her legs. *Oh, dear God!* Her suddenly desperate arms groped blindly for something to hold onto, and found only his wet torso as his mouth came down on hers once more.

CHAPTER 10

Ned Falconer was unable to sleep.

It wasn't often that Uncle Connor came to visit and the boy, lying awake in his bed while the mosquito netting moved gently in the breeze around him, couldn't get the memory of him leaping from the main gaff out of his mind. Again and again he saw his uncle plunging down, down, down with fearless abandon, only to execute a perfect dive into the sea.

Nobody else on Uncle Con's schooner had dared to jump from such a height. Even Captain Lord had not dared to do such a thing and he was Papa's flag captain.

Oh, what must it feel like to soar through the air like a bird, to plunge like a knife into the turquoise waters of Carlisle Bay while everyone cheered and threw money into a pot celebrating your bravery?

Ned wanted to do the same thing.

He tossed and turned, and tossed and turned some more, and as he lay there staring up at the darkened ceiling, he heard voices coming from down near the beach.

He sat up in bed, listening.

One of those voices sounded like Miss Evans's.

Ned parted the mosquito netting, swung out of bed, and went to the window.

The figures were small with distance, and the gently waving palm fronds obscured any clear view of whomever was down there on the beach.

Suddenly, the voice that sounded like Miss Evans's let out a short, terrified scream, and worried now, the little boy jumped out of bed and ran to get his parents.

Through the haze of sensation that was enveloping her body, centering in her nipples and in that suddenly raw and aching spot between her legs against which Captain Merrick's hard, wet thigh was pressed, Rhiannon was aware of his voice, lowered to a whisper as he quietly broke the kiss, lowered the leg on which she was perched and, framing her hips with his hands, gently set her away from him.

"I am going to take you back to the house now, Miss Evans."

It took her a moment to realize what he'd said, and the confusion and disappointment must have shown clearly on her face.

"But . . . why?"

"Because if we stay out here any longer it will end up as more than just a kiss, and far more than a swim lesson. You're a good girl. I'd like to ensure you stay that way."

"But—"

"Shhh." He took her hand and together they trudged from the warm waters, Rhiannon aching with a longing she did not understand, her lips tingling from the kiss, her skin on fire where he, with his big, warm, strong hands, had touched it.

They emerged, dripping, onto the beach. There, he bent to pick up his shirt. Shaking the sand from it, he gently placed it around her shoulders in an attempt to restore a bit of her modesty, and it was then that she saw a large bulge at the front of his wet, cut-off trousers.

Her eyes widened.

He noted the direction of her gaze. "I did not, shall we say, 'behave myself' tonight, Miss Evans. Please accept my apologies." He grinned. "You make me forget myself, ma'm."

He offered his arm and there was something hurried about him now, something that spoke of restlessness and regret and an eagerness to rush her back to the house and be done with her. Rhiannon, trying not to glance at his trousers, felt her confusion mounting. She felt hot and cold and dizzy and faint from a million different sensations she could not identify. She wanted to laugh. She wanted to cry. She didn't know what she wanted, really, except to find a way back into his arms, and to feel his lips against her own once more. . . .

They had just reached the edge of the trees when Captain Merrick suddenly halted and, in one swift motion, put her behind him.

There was the frightening sound of a pistol being cocked. "Who goes there, by God?" a voice of authority demanded.

Rhiannon froze, and a sensation of pure horror shot from the base of her spine, up into her throat, and stole the breath from her lungs. Oh, dear God above. It was Sir Graham, and he stood not ten feet away, a pistol aimed straight at Captain Merrick's heart, with his wife—brandishing a cutlass—at his side.

"It is I. Connor. I was merely enjoying a late night swim following the day's heat, and I'd be much obliged, Sir Graham, if you'd lower the pistol."

"Ned just came to me to tell me he heard a woman cry out. That it sounded like Miss Evans."

"It was probably just a night bird, nothing more."

Rhiannon didn't dare to move, and the iron-grip that the American captain had on her arm warned her against it. He was trying to keep her hidden behind his own body, to protect her reputation, to try and salvage this situation as best he could. But then there was movement and noise in the undergrowth behind the admiral and Alannah appeared, holding a lantern.

Sir Graham took the lamp and held it high.

"Whom do you have with you, Connor?"

"With all due respect, Admiral, though you may be my brother-in-law, you are certainly not my keeper, my father, or for that matter, my commanding officer."

But the admiral had shoved his pistol into his waistband and frowning, was coming closer, his eyes, dark in the shadows cast by the lantern, going hard.

Still hiding behind her protector, Rhiannon took a deep and shuddering breath. The game was up and she knew it. She stepped out from behind the protection of Captain Merrick's broad back, her face flaming, her arms coming up to shield her dripping body, knowing that the water had made her shift and thin muslin gown cling to her like a second skin. She was mortified. But to let Captain Merrick take the blame was unfair. She was as much responsible for the awful, scandalous mess in which they both found themselves as he was.

Perhaps even more.

"Oh, my God," breathed Alannah.

Sir Graham's face went even darker, and beside him Maeve moved to take his arm.

"Don't blame Captain Merrick for this," Rhiannon said with more courage than she felt. She raised her chin and steadily met the admiral's hard glare. "I asked him to give me a swimming lesson."

"A *what*?"

"A swimming lesson, Admiral. Nothing more."

"I daresay it was a lot more than a swimming lesson, girl!"

Sir Graham turned his full, frightening fury on Connor Merrick. "Do you realize that Lord Morninghall sent the girl to me trusting that I would protect and guard her while she was under my care? *Do you*? She's only eighteen years old, and if you weren't my wife's brother I'd have you shot where you stand."

"Sir Graham, if you would let me speak—"

"Let you speak?" The admiral's voice was icy with barely-suppressed rage. "You're trouble, Connor. *Trouble.* You're reckless, proud, over-confident, swaggering, and nothing like the father you seek to emulate, a man for whom I have the highest degree of admiration. So help me God, if he were standing here instead of me he couldn't be more ashamed of you than I am right now. Miss Evans, you will accompany Lady Falconer and Alannah back to the house."

Rhiannon, however, dared not let go of Captain Merrick's arm which, despite his relaxed stance, had gone very tense beneath her fingers. She did not quite believe that her host wouldn't shoot him, for she had never seen the normally affable Sir Graham in such a state of rage, and she was suddenly afraid for the American captain.

"Sir Graham, we did nothing wrong—"

"I *said*, you will accompany my wife back to the house. And you will do it *now*."

"*Wait.*"

Captain Merrick, who had been content to let Sir Graham give vent to his blistering fury, finally spoke.

"You're right in that I should have known better than to plunge a young lady into the situation in which she was discovered tonight." His voice hardened, and the charming, smiling man that Rhiannon had thus known him to be was suddenly gone, to be replaced by someone every inch as forbidding and dangerous as the admiral himself . . . maybe even more so. "But you are wrong, *dead wrong*, sir, when you say I am nothing like my father."

"Your father is a decent and honorable man!"

"And you do me a grave injustice, Sir Graham, by implying that I am not. Don't think I'm not willing to meet you at dawn for such an insult."

"Enough, both of you!" Maeve said sharply, moving between the two of them. "I'll have none of this!"

"And neither will I!" Rhiannon cried, suddenly alarmed.

But the British admiral was looking at the American privateer with a cunning, contemplative eye. "And just how do you intend to prove to me, Connor, that you've inherited a shred of your father's goodness of character?"

"I have nothing to prove to you. And no obligation to. But I know my duty, and I'll marry the girl. You may think the worst of me, Admiral, and you're free to do so, but let no man say I'm not decent or honorable. I am my father's son, and if Miss Evans will have me, I request your permission, as her guardian in Lord Morninghall's absence, to make her my wife."

In the sudden silence, nobody spoke.

Captain Merrick stood waiting, a proud and noble figure despite the fact he was barefoot and clad in nothing but wet trousers.

And Rhiannon's heart stopped beating in her chest.

"My apologies, Connor," the admiral finally said, with a tight, grudging smile. "It seems as though I've misjudged your character, after all." He turned to Rhiannon, his face grave. "And you, Miss Evans? Have you an opinion on this?"

Had she an opinion on this?

Her head spinning, the situation growing more surreal by the moment, and feeling perilously close to fainting, Rhiannon took a step closer to Captain Merrick. She inhaled deeply, trying to control her shaking. Her numbness. There were worse things than being married. There were worse things than being married to a Yankee privateer.

And there were certainly worse things than being married to the noble, daring, heroic man who had rescued so many hapless souls from the atrocities of the British prison hulks, who had rescued Lord Morninghall from a firing squad and helped secure his royal pardon, who had rescued her sister from drowning, who had rescued herself and Alannah from pirates, and now, had rescued her reputation from what could have been a terrible scandal.

Sir Graham had been wrong.

Connor Merrick was a good and decent man.

She took a deep and steadying breath. "I would be honored to have him, Sir Graham."

CHAPTER 11

A s he made his way back to *Kestrel*, that same noble,
daring, heroic man who had rescued so many hapless souls was feeling anything but noble, daring, or heroic,
and he realized, quite desperately, that the one who needed
rescuing this time was none other than himself.

Marriage. *Marriage.* To a girl who wasn't even past the
age of guardianship, a girl he barely knew, a girl who was
already half in love with him—a girl who would turn away
in pity if she were ever to discern the truth about him.

Nobody has ever accused me of being smart, Miss Evans.

His earlier comment to her had not been in jest.

Oh, God help me.

He wiped a shaky hand over his face and felt his heartbeat kicking up in his chest. Fear prickled his spine and
he stepped up his pace, determined to escape the land and
reach the solace of his ship.

Three weeks for the banns to be read, and he would be
a married man.

Three weeks for him to figure out what in tarnation he was going to do.

The boat was waiting on the beach where he'd left it, and he pushed it out into the surf, wading in until the little hull was floating free before stepping inside. He picked up the oars and began to row, the boat knifing across the still, night-blackened harbor.

He would marry her, of course. It was the gentlemanly thing to do, and it was the least he owed her. But he would keep her at arm's length, refuse to let her get too close to him, ensure that their marriage was distant, perhaps even platonic if it would keep her from falling in love with him, even if he had to keep himself off to sea and away from her as much as possible; if he didn't let her into his heart, her girlish infatuation would never become love, and she, at least, would never discover the secret that only he, Nathan, and the closest members of his family shared.

For Connor knew he was defective. The wonderful, loving relationship that his father and mother had enjoyed for so many years was not something he was destined to have for himself.

And no woman would have him, if only she knew.

Nobody has ever accused me of being smart, Miss Evans.

Through the darkness ahead he could just see the white stripe that marked *Kestrel*'s wale, and never had his little ship felt so welcoming.

The schooner stood quietly above her anchor, a lantern hung in the larboard shrouds of her foremast casting a rippling finger of light over the water toward him. Her figurehead was the small, predatory hawk for which she'd been named, and it stood out clearly against the starlit horizon as Connor rowed toward her. In the darkness, he could just see Jacques standing the watch, his pipe glowing. Connor hailed him and hooked onto the schooner's main chains. Moments later, he was up the side and standing on the deck.

"*Bonsoir, Capitaine,*" said the Frenchman, taking off his hat in salute.

Connor merely nodded and headed forward.

"Have you lost your shirt, sir?"

"No, I know precisely where it is."

Jacques trailed him, grinning as though he knew some big secret to which the rest of the world was not privy.

"Did you get to see *mademoiselle*?"

"None of your blasted business. Go to bed. You're relieved."

"She's a pretty little *fille*, that one. You know, *Capitaine*, I have a suggestion for you. I know women, I do. And the best way to a woman's heart is through extravagant complements, flowers, beautiful—"

"I said go to bed, Jacques. That is an order."

"Trust me, *Capitaine*, you listen to me and you'll have *mademoiselle* eating out of your hand."

Connor turned and stared hard at the Frenchman who, surely, couldn't know the first thing about how to go about winning a woman's attention.

"Jacques, if you do not go below this instant and leave me to my thoughts, I swear I'm going to throw you over the side."

"As you wish, *Capitaine*. Just trying to help." Again, he raised his hat, replaced it, and with a grinning leer that made the knife-scar that split his bottom lip all the more ghastly, finally went below.

Connor paid him no further heed. He had a hard enough time keeping his thoughts aligned and on course without additional distraction, and right now he needed to think, needed to be alone, and needed to cool down. Sir Graham's words had stung and he was still angry, not only with the admiral but with himself. There was only one place in the world where he would find the solitude and clarity of mind that he sought.

One place in the world that was open, free, and, at the moment, entirely his.

He went to the rail, began to climb, and a few minutes later was safely perched in the crosstrees, the gently swaying foremast stretching down to the deck far below, the topmast, with its crossed yards and a black hemisphere twinkling with a thousand stars, above him.

There he remained, high above the quiet waters of Carlisle Bay, looking out at the riding lights of the ships around him, feeling the warm trades caressing his cheek and playing with his hair and making the pennant tickle the sky above his head.

He did not have the intimate relationship with ships in general, and this one in particular, that his father enjoyed, though on nights like this Connor fancied he could feel the schooner's very soul around him. She had been part of his earliest memories, when his father had taken him, Maeve and young Kieran, often joined by their cousins Nathan and Toby, out sailing in her. Da had taught them all how to set the sails to get the best trim, how to reef and steer and tie a knot, how to go aloft without fear, how to read the compass and take a noon sighting and interpret the signs in the clouds and in the wind and in the seas themselves warning of impending weather. Occasionally, Da would let them fire off one of *Kestrel*'s guns, though it was their mother who taught them how to aim it with deadly precision.

Eventually, Connor knew, he would have to return *Kestrel* to his father. It was to his *Dadaí* that the schooner rightfully belonged, and perhaps he'd get in one more privateering cruise before collecting his young bride and setting a course for New England, two thousand miles away.

And perhaps, since the ship was fully provisioned, he'd begin that cruise tomorrow.

I would like that, *Kestrel* seemed to say around him, and Connor smiled at last.

Maybe he shared more of his Da's intimate relationship with the schooner than he'd thought.

Alone out on the veranda of Sir Graham's beautiful island home, Rhiannon was also sitting beneath the stars, her thoughts her own.

She was miserable.

Oh, how had this evening ended up so badly? How had it gone so terribly wrong?

The admiral was furious with Captain Merrick, and he didn't seem much happier with her either, having slammed into his study the moment they'd all returned to the house with orders that he was not to be disturbed. Maeve, however, had been far more understanding.

"You must forgive Sir Graham," she said, coming out onto the veranda and pressing a glass of lemonade into Rhiannon's hand. "He may be angry with my brother, but I can assure you he's far angrier with himself. He feels as though he failed you, as well as Lord Morninghall's trust in him."

"It all seemed so innocent," Rhiannon had said quietly, and put her head into her hands, trying not to cry.

"These sort of things usually do—at first." Maeve pulled out the chair beside Rhiannon, her hand on the small of her back before easing herself down. The swelling of her belly was readily apparent beneath her simple gown of sprigged cotton. "Sir Graham behaved no better than my brother did in the days leading up to our marriage, and perhaps even worse, so don't let him fool you into thinking he's some paragon of virtue. He was an incurable rogue. And he'd be the first to say that it takes one to know one."

Rhiannon had taken a deep, steadying breath. "Everyone always blames the man. I was as responsible for this as Captain Merrick. And yet he's the one to have a pistol aimed at his heart and forced to do something he may not have been willing to do if his own sense of honor had not demanded it."

Maeve had let out an unladylike hoot of laughter. "My dear, don't disillusion yourself. My brother cannot be forced to do anything he doesn't want to do. He offered for you tonight because he *wanted* to."

"I suspect he's the most unhappy man in the world right now," Rhiannon said sadly. "And I blame myself for that."

"Unhappy? Connor?" Maeve guffawed. "I guess you didn't notice the way he was watching you all through dinner these last two nights. No, Rhiannon, I suspect that once he gets over the initial shock of it all, he'll find himself happier than he could ever imagine."

"But I let a lot of people down tonight. . . ."

"Nonsense. Connor needs someone like you to anchor him. To steady him. He's a ship in a full-force gale, restless, unable to sit still, constantly in motion and headed for certain trouble unless someone can find a way to rein him in. He's gotten cocky and overconfident in his desperation to prove himself, and that'll be his undoing. I worry about him." She reached out and touched Rhiannon's hand. "You'll be good for each other."

"I wish I could be so sure."

Maeve smiled. "I have the Irish gift of the Sight," she said. "And I have the feeling that you will be the saving of my wild and reckless brother, in more ways than one."

Without a word to anyone except his betrothed, to whom he sent a brief note saying he'd be back in a fortnight, Connor had taken the schooner *Kestrel* out of Bridgetown that very night and in the two weeks that followed, made himself such a complete nuisance to shipping between Africa and the West Indies that a desperate appeal was finally made to Vice Admiral Sir Graham Falconer in Barbados asking the Royal Navy to do more to protect British ships from "a mysterious American privateer that swoops down out of the clouds, takes our merchantmen, and is off before our own guard ships can do anything to protect us."

His natural recklessness, stoked to a derring-do that had even Nathan and those who knew him well, worried, stood him in good stead: in those two weeks that Connor allowed his frustrations free rein, *Kestrel* cut five fat merchant ships out of a Jamaican-bound convoy and sent them back to Mobile for auction: destroyed three coastal sloops that were supplying the British with goods that Connor decided his enemy didn't need: eluded a Royal Navy frigate that gave chase one long afternoon before finally being shaken off under cover of darkness: and finally slipped back into Carlisle Bay and innocently dropped anchor in the wee hours of the morning several days before the scheduled wedding. He woke an hour later and lay tossing and turning in bed, staring up in the darkness, his stomach in knots and cold dread washing through him. For a few moments, he allowed himself to wonder what it would be like to make love to his young bride. She was surely a virgin, and the idea of being someone's first—and only—was wildly exciting. And then he remembered the upcoming wedding and his certain pre-destined failure as a husband, and his excitement faded and became a deep and abiding depression.

Dawn was just breathing light into the eastern horizon when he was awakened by a hand on his shoulder.

He opened bleary eyes and saw Nathan's face in the early-morning gloom above him.

"Come topside, Con," his cousin said, and there was something in his face that spoke of barely restrained excitement. "There's something you need to see."

"What?"

Nathan just gave him a rare grin, turned, and left him to his confusion.

Connor swung out of the bunk, pushed a hand through his hair, and knuckling the sleep from his eyes, trudged up through the hatch and onto *Kestrel*'s deck, now glowing a pale pink as the sky to the east began to catch fire with the approach of the coming sun.

There his cousins, their backs to him, stood at the rail, young Toby pointing excitedly toward a ship that had also slipped into the harbor sometime overnight and lay quietly at anchor nearby.

She was a sloop, lithe, predatory and like *Kestrel*, sporting a gleaming, low-slung black hull that seemed to be born of the water itself. She had one single, sharply raked mast and a bowsprit and jib-boom that went on forever, designed to carry a magnificent press of sail and now pointed toward the rising sun whose light was already starting to gleam upon the upper reaches of her topmast and pennants. She was beautifully designed, beautifully made, and beautiful to see, for the name on her counter read *Sandpiper* . . . and beneath that, was a single word.

Newburyport.

Connor stood staring, his melancholy forgotten, for there was a lone figure standing at the rail, a figure who was tall and lanky like himself, a figure who, with the rising sun behind him, was still in silhouette.

Perhaps it was a shift in the tide that caused *Kestrel* to subtly swing her bowsprit toward the newly arrived ship, but Connor knew it wasn't the ship itself that his own vessel was straining so eagerly toward.

It was the man standing at her rail.

The man who had created and loved her.

The man who now grinned and touched two fingers to his hat in an amused salute.

And as the sun's blood-orange disc finally pushed itself up over the horizon, lighting up the harbor and the man himself, Connor could restrain himself no longer.

"*Dada!*" he cried in pure joy, and without a second thought threw himself over the side, arcing in a perfect dive into the newly-awakened waters of Carlisle Bay.

CHAPTER 12

"Faith, laddie, I would have sent a boat across," said Captain Brendan Jay Merrick, laughing as he reached down to help his son aboard. "No need to get wet!"

"Da!" Connor shook his father's hand, and then allowed him to yank him forward and enfold him in his embrace for a long moment. His head was reeling, his father's familiar Irish brogue the most welcome, blessed sound in a world that had gone totally mad. "What are you doing here in Barbados? How did you get past the blockades the British have of the eastern seaboard? How did you get past Sir Graham's ships? And where is Mother?"

"She's around," Brendan said cheerfully. "We arrived late last night, and really, lad, you should know better than to wonder about how easy it is for your dear old Da to get past a simple blockade." He spread his arm to indicate the sloop on whose decks they stood. "Especially in something like this." He grinned, his eyes crinkling with a teasing good humor. "Is she not the prettiest little lassie you've ever seen?

Fast as a thoroughbred filly, but not the racehorse that one there is," he added, nodding toward *Kestrel*. "How is the wild black mare?"

"She's made me rich," Connor returned. "Took twelve prizes in the last month alone. The pickings in the Indies, Da, are plentiful. We can work together, now that you're here."

His father laughed. "No, laddie, my privateering days are behind me. I'm too old for that sort of thing, and Madison's War is one I never supported to begin with. You know how it is in New England, with the Federalists at the helm and too many people out of work, starving and in desperate straits. This is not a popular conflict back home."

"I can't believe I'm speaking to the man who was the most audacious privateer of the last war; listen to yourself!"

"That was a different war, and I was a younger man. Besides, my son-in-law is a British admiral and my little grandchildren are being raised English. No, Connor, this war is not one for me to fight."

"You're getting old, Da."

"Aye, Con. That I am." He reached out and clapped Connor's shoulder. "But don't think for one moment that I couldn't give the Lion's tail a good tweaking if I'd a mind to, laddie. Would you care for some coffee?"

"I would love a cup."

"Good, because Liam is brewing some." And then, a bit sheepishly and in a lowered voice, "I thought it better that *he* make it, rather than your mother."

They laughed, for everyone knew that cooking was a skill that Mira Merrick had never mastered, and even a pot of coffee was surely asking for trouble.

"So Liam is here, too," Connor said, his spirits rising even more as he anticipated seeing his father's oldest and best friend, who was like an uncle to him and his siblings. "Maeve will be thrilled. By God, I still can't believe you're here!"

"Your mother talked me into it," his father admitted, with a wry grin. "Neither one of us felt like riding out another Massachusetts winter when we could be down here in the tropics spoiling our grandchildren."

"Yes, and Maeve wrote to tell us she's expectin' again," said a woman's voice, and looking up, Connor saw his mother sitting astride the main boom, her eyes sparkling. "I wouldn't want to miss the birth of my next grandchild!"

"Mother!"

"Hello, Connor. I was wonderin' how long it was gonna take you to realize I was sitting here. Cripes, your manners are worse than my own."

Connor strode over to the boom, which lay atop the stern rail and then out over the water, and deftly plucked his petite mother from her perch and set her down on the deck. His powerful arms went around her, and then he picked her up and swung her around until both were laughing and her cheeks were flushed like a schoolgirl's.

"My manners are indeed atrocious, Mother, and I'm afraid they've gotten me into an awful lot of trouble," he said, sobering.

Both his parents and now broad, beamy Liam, coming up from below with a tray on which stood a coffee pot and several pewter mugs, looked at him in expectation.

Connor took a deep breath. "I have news for you," he said. "I'm getting married."

"*Married?!*"

"Yes, Mother," Connor said a bit sheepishly, and proceeded to tell his parents, Liam, and now his youngest sibling Kieran, who had come up on deck looking sleepy and rumpled, about the events that had transpired over the last few weeks.

"Faith, laddie," said his father, sitting on the sloop's rail and shaking his head, but he was grinning from ear to ear, making no effort to conceal his delight and even less to judge the circumstances that had landed his eldest son in such a mess. "So it appears we're to get not only a new grandchild, but a new daughter as well! And what do you think of that, *Moyrrra*?"

Connor grinned. His father's Irish brogue was as pronounced as ever and even now, after some three and a half decades of marriage, he still spoke his mother's name with a certain awe. "What do I think? That I can't wait to meet her!"

"God almighty, I never thought I'd see the day," said Liam, shaking his head as he set the tray on the deckhouse a few feet away. "'Tis about time ye found someone to settle ye down, young man."

Nobody can settle me down, Connor thought, and again felt that prickle of despair and foreboding. Instead, he murmured, "I doubt Sir Graham will even let me near her until the knot is tied. In fact, I should probably make good use of my last few days as a free man, because there's no money to be made for a privateer who's sitting in port, and a British one at that."

"Cool your heels, laddie," said his father. "We haven't seen you in many a month, it would be nice to visit for a while." He got to his feet and poured a mug of coffee, carefully testing it with his hands to make sure the pewter vessel wasn't too hot before handing it to his wife. "Coffee, Liam? Connor?"

"Aye."

"Well, with three children and another on the way, the poor man probably has his hands full without having the guardianship of a young woman thrust on him," Mira said. "How *is* your sister, Connor?"

"Pregnant, emotional, unstable and unpredictable."

"I'm glad to hear that. I was too, when I was carrying each of ye. Brendan, dearest, are you almost done with that coffee? I'm itchin' to see Annie, Mary, and little Ned."

"Ned isn't so little anymore, Mother," Connor said.

Brendan drained his coffee and gazed across the water at *Kestrel*, and as he did so a fond smile came over his face—one that was almost, but not quite, as gentle and reverent as the one he saved for Connor's mother.

Along with his wife and children, the schooner was the other great love of his father's life.

"How's her planking holding up, Con?" he asked conversationally, but Connor had noted the slight frown on his father's face, the fleeting something that told him his Da knew and saw more than he was letting on.

"Serviceable, but she'll need dockyard attention before much longer."

Brendan was still looking thoughtfully at the schooner, saying less than he was thinking. "Seems to me, laddie, that a privateer needs to be constantly maintained in order to remain on her toes."

Connor tensed. "I know, Father."

"She may be the swiftest thing afloat, but if she can't outrun a British frigate she's no good to you."

"It's not as though Sir Graham is going to let me careen her here and tend to what needs tending."

"No, I can't imagine that he would, given that he knows you'll turn right around and use her against the shipping he's obliged to protect. Your mother and I plan to stay here until the birth of Maeve's child, but after that I think it would be wise to let us sail her home to Newburyport. Get her up in dry dock, give her old frames and planking the attention they deserve." He smiled ruefully. "It's not easy getting old, you know. We ancients need a little more care and coddling than you youngsters." He stood up then, noting his wife's restlessness, and with the sun now a hot white ball rising ever higher from the eastern horizon and making the sea sparkle like diamonds, it was time to pay a call on the Falconers.

But as they all got down into *Sandpiper*'s boat and Kieran rowed them steadily toward shore, Connor couldn't help but notice that his father's gaze moved quietly to the grand old schooner and remained on her for a long time.

He had made good on his word, then.

He had not sailed away like the scoundrel Sir Graham had implied him to be.

Rhiannon, who had spotted *Kestrel*'s distinctive raked masts when she'd looked out over Carlisle Bay that morning, was just sitting down to breakfast with the Falconers and hoping that Captain Merrick would forego his pride and pay a call on the admiral's household, when a servant came quietly out onto the veranda and leaned down to speak in Sir Graham's ear.

Smiling broadly, the admiral pushed his chair back and, with toddler twins Mary on one arm, Anne on the other, got to his feet just as another servant led a small group of people into the room.

"Merrick, by God! What an unexpected surprise and a damned pleasant one at that! Come in, come in!"

Everything erupted into chaos as Maeve, with a squeal of joy, lunged out of her chair and threw herself into the arms of the tall, lanky man who dominated the doorway. Ned let out a scream of delight and was swept up by the petite woman who had appeared next to him. Introductions were made, more hugs were exchanged, and one of the twins spit up porridge all down the front of the admiral's clean white shirt.

Standing a bit uncertainly behind this group was Connor Merrick. His smiling gaze took in this happy reunion for a moment then fell upon Rhiannon and stilled.

The humor in his clear, sea-green eyes faded, and something hungry, intense and wanting took its place.

Rhiannon's world stopped. She remembered his hot kisses under the moonlit sky that fateful night, the wicked sensation of his wet, hard-muscled thigh against her womanly parts there in the warm waters of the bay, and wild excitement swept through her blood. And then he allowed a smile once more and, stepping forward, raised her from her chair with a gallant bow and a kiss on the back of her hand, and turned her to face the newcomers, pride evident in his voice.

"Miss Evans, you have made me the happiest man in the world by agreeing to become my wife. Please, allow me to introduce you to my family: my father, Brendan . . . my mother, Mira . . . my brother, Kieran . . . and the man who is my uncle in all but blood, Liam Doherty."

Any hesitation and uncertainty left over from the events of that awkward night two weeks past were instantly banished as Connor's mother—petite and slim, with the same sea-green eyes her son possessed, an impudent nose, and little wrinkles that fanned out around it like a cat when she smiled, embraced the taller Rhiannon in arms that were surprisingly hard and strong.

"Connor may speak of his joy, but it ain't nothing compared to mine at the idea of gettin' another daughter!" she said happily. "And more grandchildren to spoil! You *will* go straight to work and give me grandchildren, won't ye? Oh, Brendan, I can't wait!"

Rhiannon, expecting New England puritanism or at least some semblance of gentility, nearly choked at the older woman's baldly-spoken words. Before she had a chance to mouth a response, Connor's father, who had been shaking Sir Graham's hand and blithely shrugging off the admiral's surprise about how he'd managed to creep into the well-guarded harbor right under the noses of the British fleet, came forward, smiling in a way that made any lingering awkwardness about the reasons for the upcoming wedding to instantly evaporate.

"Ah, so my son spoke the truth about your beauty," he said, his warm amber eyes reflecting a cheerful, irrepressible spirit that was impossible not to immediately like. "I couldn't be happier to welcome you to our family, crazy and unconventional as we are. Pay no mind to formalities, lass, because we certainly don't!"

"You're Irish!" Rhiannon said impulsively, then clapped a hand to her mouth in embarrassment at her lack of manners. But oh, his voice was pure music, lilting and almost poetic to listen to, and everything about the man made her feel welcomed and happy inside.

"Half Irish, half English, and all American, lass."

"I have heard much about you," she said somewhat shyly. "All of it good. Your son told me that you were a hero during the last war between our two countries—"

The older man waved the words away. "Eh, that Connor, 'tis full o' nonsense he is, pay him no mind a'tall. "

Nearby, Sir Graham, distinguished and handsome, was trying in vain to wipe spit-up off his shirt.

"Tisn't nonsense at all," said the big, blue-eyed man who had come in with the group and had been hugging Maeve and her children as greetings had been exchanged. He too was Irish, with a broad, barrel-like chest and merry blue eyes. "And I should know because I was there." He put out his hand. "I'm Liam Doherty, longtime friend o' the family and adopted uncle. I'd bow to ye, lass, but I'm a bit stiff this mornin', and if I go down I doubt I'll be able t' make it back up."

Rhiannon smiled. "I'm pleased to make your acquaintance, Mr. Doherty."

"Liam," he corrected. "Just Liam'll do."

"Liam." She turned back to the man who would soon be her father-in law. "And what shall I call you, Captain Merrick?"

"She could call you 'Da' after they're married," put in Connor's mother.

"She can call me 'Da' now, if she likes."

"But she may already have a father," said the young man who had arrived with them. His hair, carelessly tousled like Connor's, was the same dark brown shade as his mother's but he had his father's smile and the same warm, laughing eyes. Like the rest of his family he was strikingly good-looking, and knew how to execute a bow as gallant as any Rhiannon had ever seen. "I'm Kieran," he said. "The baby of the family. I'm sorry if we're a bit . . . overwhelming. We take some getting used to, I'm afraid."

And so followed a morning of laughter and chaos, of shared memories and giggling children and talk of ships and wars and the sad state of affairs between Britain and the fledgling United States. At one point Rhiannon happened to look over at Captain Merrick and saw that he was no longer engaged in the conversation, that he was growing fidgety and restless, and constantly getting up and looking out over the sparkling harbor, sitting back down, and getting back up again to go to the railing once more.

He happened to look up, and caught her eye. And then he gave a barely perceptible jerk of his head toward the door, and moved toward it. A moment later Rhiannon, making her excuses, got up to follow him.

"I shouldn't be alone with you," she murmured, looking back over her shoulder. "It's not proper."

"You heard my Da," he said, guiding her toward a window so the light illuminated her eyes and found the copper tints in her hair. "We don't stand on formalities. Besides, I've missed you."

"I missed you, too—"

She never finished the sentence. He already had her up against the wall, bracketing her there with his hands on either side of her face, his head bent and his lips claiming hers. She couldn't move, pinned as she was between his body, his arms, and the wall behind her. Didn't want to move. She felt the raw, desperate hunger in him as the kiss deepened and his tongue sought hers. Her arms twined around the back of his neck, his hand came up to cup and fondle her breast, and sudden, delicious sensation stirred between her legs as he pressed himself against her pelvis, allowing her to feel the stabbing hardness of his arousal.

A servant was approaching. He pushed back, leaving her dazed and wanting more, and her gaze flashed downwards. She saw the bulge in the front of his pantaloons, and her eyes widened.

"See what I mean?" he murmured, scowling at the hapless servant. "I vow to keep you at arm's length but no matter what my intentions, I can't help myself when I'm around you."

He reached for her once more.

Again, more footsteps coming down the hall as another servant, carrying a tray of punch and glasses, approached. Cursing under his breath, he stepped back once again.

"You're going to get us into trouble, Captain Merrick."

"My dear Miss Evans, we're already in enough trouble. But never mind that. This just proves that my decision to leave for a bit is a good one. I wanted to tell you that I won't be around tomorrow."

"Where are you headed?"

"I don't know. Anywhere. Sail handling, gun practice, information gathering, who knows. My men are restless and so am I. I'll be back in time for the wedding."

He must have seen the way her face fell.

"Have no fear, Miss Evans," he said, with a trace of his wicked, roguish smile. He reached up and tucked a loose strand of hair back behind her ear, letting his fingers linger along her jawline. "I made you a promise, and Merricks always honor their promises. You'll have your groom at the altar. If, of course, you still want him."

"But what about your family? They'll be hurt if you go off and leave when they only just arrived."

"My family knows me well. They're not going anywhere, and I'll be back soon enough."

He held out his arms in silent invitation and she moved willingly into his embrace, trying not to think about her dismay that he was leaving again, trying to tell herself that he'd only be gone for a little while this time, trying not to think about that swelling in his pantaloons that beckoned her curiosity in ways that were best saved until her wedding night. And then he pulled back, cradling her face in his hands and tilting it up to his own before capturing her lips in another long, searing kiss that left her breathless.

"I'll miss you, Captain."

"I'll only be gone for a day."

"I wish I could go with you."

He grinned and touched her cheek. "A warship is no place for a young lady."

"You're a privateer, not a naval officer. I'm sure it's perfectly safe." Her tone became mockingly stern. "And I'll tell you right now, Connor Merrick, if you think to store me here on this island or some other 'safe' port while you're off risking life and limb, you have another thing coming."

He raised a brow, and the humor in his eyes only intensified. "I hope, Miss Evans, that you are not going to be hard to handle."

"And I hope, Captain Merrick, that you aren't going to be, either."

By sunrise Connor was more than ready to leave, though his destination was one he hadn't pursued with any real thought.

He just knew that he needed to be on the move.

The idea of his upcoming nuptials made him feel trapped and jittery. And his habitual restlessness had had him pacing the decks all night long, unable to sleep, his thoughts a whirling turmoil that flitted through his head and refused to be reined in to something he could make sense of. By the time morning came, he craved some outlet for his energies.

Impatient to be off, he rowed ashore and strode boldly into Sir Graham's open-aired library where his father, Liam Doherty, and the admiral himself were enjoying an early morning pot of coffee and complaining about their various aches and pains.

"Old knees, they aren't what they used to be," his father was saying. "Faith, the way things are going, I'm going to need a cane."

"Eh, ye think that's bad, do ye?" Liam piped up. "I've got the rheumatism so bad I can hardly get meself out o' bed in the mornin'. And they say these are supposed t' be the golden years!"

"Golden my arse," said the admiral, reaching for more coffee.

"Beggin' yer pardon, Sir Graham, but ye're what, six years shy o' fifty?" Liam scoffed. "Wait 'til ye get our age."

"Aye, Liam's right," said Connor's father, ruefully. He reached over to top up his coffee. "Used to be I could run up the shrouds like the nimblest midshipman. Now, what isn't hurting is creaking, and what isn't creaking is falling apart."

"Well, at least yer hair isn't all grey like mine is," said Liam. "Ye might feel old, Brendan, but ye still look twenty years younger than the calendar says ye are."

"My knees would dispute that, Liam."

Connor had heard enough. "Honestly, Da, your knees probably only hurt because of the cold New England weather," he said impatiently. "Stay down here in the tropics for a while and I'm sure the pain will go away."

The admiral let out a snort of disdain. "I doubt it. I've been noticing a stiffness in my shoulder, myself, when I get up in the morning. Ever have that, Merrick?"

"Aye, but mine's from an old injury. Just gets worse with each passing year. I hear that if you take tincture of—"

"That's it, I'm leaving," Connor said in exasperation. "You three sound like a trio of old men with one foot in the grave and the other on a banana peel. You should hear yourselves!"

"Where are you going?" asked Sir Graham, frowning.

"What are you, my keeper? I have a wedding to prepare for, and that requires collecting our priest." He plucked a muffin from the plate near the coffee pot and took a bite. "Does Peter still live on the northwestern side of the island?

"Yes, and he and Orla are expecting their first child. I'm sure he's quite capable of getting here himself."

"I'm bored. I need to be doing something."

"Sit and have some coffee," his father said, indicating an empty chair.

"I don't want coffee, I need to be moving. I was going to take the crew out to do some gun practice but instead, I'm off to fetch Peter."

"'Twould be easier if you sail there rather than take the overland route."

"That is my intention, Admiral."

Connor turned to leave, but his father had set down his coffee mug. "Wait. I'll go with you, Con." He smiled. "It's been years since I stepped foot on my beloved schooner. I miss her, and it would do my soul a world of good to take her tiller again. You don't mind, do you?"

Connor smiled. "I'd love to have you along, Da."

CHAPTER 13

Hello, lassie, Brendan thought as, ignoring the pain in his left knee, he clambered over *Kestrel*'s rail and found himself standing on the deck of the ship that had brought him such fame during the Revolution.

So many memories. Of how he'd met Mira because he'd gone to Newburyport with the drafts to have a schooner built, one that would be unique, unprecedented, and ahead of her time. Of the emotion he'd felt when they'd launched her into the Merrimack that cold autumn day back in '78, and how all of Newburyport had turned out to see her and the crowds had come from as far away as Boston. Of her incredible speed, of battles fought and won, of his terrible fall from the rigging after his encounter with the sadistic Captain Crichton had weakened him such that his injuries had left him in a coma for over a week. The rail, gleaming with new varnish in the hot sun, blurred beneath the sudden mist in his eyes and he reached out and touched it as though he could turn back time. Memories, of this gallant little ship that had been the second love of his life, catalyst to his love for Mira, teacher to his three children, memory-maker, protector, and friend.

Connor, in his restlessness and drive to succeed, was not caring for her as he should. With some part of himself that sensed rather than saw, Brendan knew that the schooner was feeling every one of her thirty-five years, just as he was feeling every one of his sixty-five. Her decks were spotless and gleamed in the sun, her lines neatly coiled, her standing rigging taut and her sails in good order, but Brendan knew, intuitively, that beneath the tidy decks and well-maintained planking of her hull, this ship that he had designed, this ship with whom he had made so many memories, needed maintenance that the eye could not see.

Maintenance that his Irish heart and soul could only sense.

Her frames are rotting. She needs to go home to Newburyport. To the shipyard. For a complete rehaul and rebuild.

Yes.

Or retirement.

"What do you think, Da?" asked his son, and in Connor's tall, lanky form and easy grin, Brendan saw himself at that age—restless, eternally optimistic and daring, the world at his feet. But Connor had an edge that Brendan had never had, a hot-headedness that must have come down from Mira's father Ephraim and Mira herself, and he was quicker to anger than Brendan had ever been.

"When's the last time you inspected her frames, lad?"

"I haven't. Maeve took care of all that when she had her. Told me Sir Graham made sure she got plenty of attention, just like the other ships in his fleet. She's held up well, hasn't she, Da?"

Brendan frowned.

"I think you should have a closer look at her beneath the waterline, Connor."

"She's fine, Da. Since when did you become such a worry-wart?"

"Just a gut feeling." He grinned faintly but he was troubled, and he sensed an unspoken plea from the little ship, perhaps even gratitude that he was here, that he would take care of her.

Except that he couldn't. He might be her creator, had even been her master once, but she belonged to his children now. They knew that. He knew that, even if *Kestrel* herself did not. In her soul, if ships had them—and Brendan firmly believed that they did—she would always be loyal to him, and him alone.

"Nathan!" he heard Connor shout to his nephew. "We're heading out to fetch Peter Milford from the other side of the island. Good day for a sail, don't you think?"

"Sure is, Connor. Are you going to let Uncle Brendan take the helm?"

Brendan, his hand still resting on the schooner's rail, smiled. "She is no longer my command. But I would love to take a tour of her for old time's sake."

"Nathan, can you assume the deck? We've got a fine wind coming out of the northeast and I'd like to take advantage of it."

"Aye, Con."

Brendan followed his son as they headed for the hatch. He was aware of the reverent gazes of Connor's crew, and the way they were looking at him made him realize that they knew who he was, that they'd heard the stories about his Revolutionary war exploits, no doubt embellished more and more with each retelling.

It made him uncomfortable.

The schooner was little changed from her earlier days. There, her stubby nose poking out her open port, was *Freedom*, the gun once manned by Mira and inscribed with the biblical verse "it is better to give than to receive." There, the spot where they said he'd hit the deck following that awful fall from the rigging. There, a memory of Dalby clutching his stomach with some imaginary illness. There, where he'd stood sketching battle scenes as the guns had boomed and musket balls had whined around him. He glanced aft at the tiller. Saw again little Maeve and Connor, even younger, both of them fighting for their turn at the helm while baby Kieran looked on in wide-eyed curiosity.

Where had all the years gone?

"Da, are you all right?"

"Aye, Con. Just reminiscing, that's all." He nodded to his nephew Toby, who favored his father Matthew in looks. "Let's go below. I want to see my old cabin."

Down the hatch they went. Brendan's knee began to complain even louder, and he lamented the loss of his youth and the way that he, as did all young people, had taken those years for granted.

Funny how you expected youth to last forever. And how one day you woke up and it was gone, and the person who looked back at you from the mirror was someone you no longer quite recognized while around you, almost everyone you met seemed to be younger. . . .

"Da?"

"Right behind you, lad."

It was somewhat cooler belowdecks after the baking heat topside. Brendan felt a knot of emotion welling up in his throat as his son pushed open the cabin door and they stepped into the small space that had once been his domain as captain.

The same little wood stove was still there, but Abigail's old quilt was long gone from the bed and the cabin was not the neatly ordered place it had been all those years ago.

"Faith, lad, you're as much of a mess maker as your uncle Matt," Brendan teased, nodding toward the scattered papers on the desk and the open sea chest from which clothes spilled.

"Well Father, I wasn't quite expecting company, otherwise I'd have tided up."

Father, not Da. As usual, his son was reverting to formality when he felt the need to defend himself.

Brendan decided to let it go. He looked at the lantern swinging gently from the beam above, the sea reflected on the inner curve of the hull, and there, the sparkling patterns from the water making a mosaic of light and shadow on an old black tricorne that someone had nailed to the bulkhead.

"Well, well," he said fondly. "My old hat. May I?"

Connor just shrugged and watched him with an uncertain smile.

Brendan reached out and wrestled the old black tricorne down. For a moment he stood holding it in his hands, smiling. Remembering.

He put it on, adjusting the fit.

Connor looked at him dubiously, and with the long-suffering amused embarrassment that most offspring had for their parents.

"Uh, Da . . . that style went out of fashion years ago."

"So it did." Brendan went to the small looking glass hanging above the pitcher and wash basin and lifted his chin. He turned his head, gauging his reflection. "I seem to have changed a bit since I last saw this old hat. Where did you find it, lad?"

"Tucked up inside one of the drawers. Honestly, Da, you look ridiculous. And old. I'm sure I can find you a nice beaver or round hat, either of which is far more fashionable than that old thing!"

Brendan grinned. "Perhaps I should grow my hair out a bit so I can have my old queue back to go with it."

Connor groaned. "Nobody wears their hair long anymore."

Brendan grinned, enjoying this bit of banter with his son. "I could always resurrect the fashion."

"Don't embarrass me. What will Mother think if you return wearing that outdated old thing?"

"Perhaps she'll see the man she fell in love with and married all those years ago." Brendan adjusted the hat to a more rakish angle and smiled into the looking glass. "In fact, I can't wait to show her. Now, shall we? You have a priest to collect, and I yearn to feel the old lady's decks beneath my feet once more."

Connor shot him another dubious look, shook his head, and led the way topside.

Rhiannon couldn't sleep.

That night she lay there in the darkness, thinking about Captain Merrick's restlessness and roguish grin and feeling the slightest niggling of doubt beginning to creep into her mind about this wedding, now just a few days away.

There was no denying that the American privateer was the stuff from which any woman's dreams were made: he was handsome, dashing, charismatic, and a strong and natural leader. He had a good sense of humor and a kind, warm-hearted family. But the repeated comments of those who knew him well were beginning to chip away at Rhiannon's initial excitement over the upcoming nuptials, and as she lay there in her bed watching the shadows from the palm trees outside moving across her high ceiling, she couldn't help but wonder—and worry—just what she was getting into by marrying this man.

This man whom everyone said was too restless—and too reckless—for his own good.

True, he was never dull, whether he was diving from *Kestrel*'s rigging, boldly tweaking his brother-in-law's nose, or rescuing prisoners from the hulks back in Portsmouth as the elusive Black Wolf, always only a step away from the hangman's noose.

But what would it be like to be married to such a man?

Would the infatuation she had for him turn to something else? Constant worry about what he might do next? Impatience with his actions? Even resentment?

And what had Maeve meant when she'd said that her brother needed someone to anchor him?

Rhiannon turned over in bed, and lay looking out the open windows and into the night beyond.

Connor Merrick couldn't sit still. That much was obvious, perhaps even painfully so. He'd just been gone for two weeks doing God only knew what (though Rhiannon had a feeling she knew exactly what he'd been doing even if God didn't), and the tension of having him around was beginning to show in Sir Graham's increasing impatience with him. The arrival of Captain Merrick's parents must only complicate things for the admiral, who was already caught between a rock and a hard place when it came to his wife's brother; to take action against him would not only upset Maeve but his in-laws as well, people with whom Sir Graham obviously enjoyed a warm relationship and who were about the nicest people Rhiannon could ever remember meeting.

Oh, what a coil.

She got up and went to the open window, the warm trade winds blowing through her unbound hair and carrying the scent of the sea.

What would Captain Merrick do after they were married? Would he take her north to his home in Newburyport and finally settle down? Or would he haul anchor and take *Kestrel* back to sea, plying the Caribbean in direct defiance of Sir Graham's wishes while she was left here, high and dry on land, worried sick about him and all but forgotten?

Rhiannon wished, suddenly, that her sister was here to advise her.

For she had a feeling that she was about to step into a hole from which there was no getting out.

The wedding took place two days later and for Rhiannon, it was a blur of images that she would take out and treasure in the days and years to come. Hot sunshine and exotic flowers. Sweating in her gown as Captain Merrick's petite mother Mira, along with Maeve and the

Reverend Peter Milford's wife Orla, made minute adjustments to her hair, her gloves, the choker of pearls that circled her neck. Wondering if the eternally restless Connor Merrick would actually follow through with the nuptials, and thinking about what Mira had told her to expect when it came to her wedding night. . . .

Her future mother-in-law had sat her down on the bed as a maid was drawing Rhiannon's bath earlier that morning.

"Now Rhiannon, there are some things ye should probably know about what happens when a man and a woman come together for the first time. I can see ye're scared, and since it's my son who'll be takin' you to his bed tonight, it's my duty to make sure you know what to expect."

"Oh, Mira, you are very kind but truly, I already know what to expect," Rhiannon had said, hugging Connor's tiny mother. "Alannah gave me a book to read last night."

"A book?"

"Yes. It said that that the best thing to do is to just lie there and count the cracks in the ceiling when it happens, because while it's enjoyable for the man, it never is for the woman, and for the sake of getting a child as well as to please her husband, it's a necessary duty she must endure."

Mira, eyes sparkling with laughter, had raised one brow. "Endure, eh?"

"It also said that it hurts. Terribly."

"Pity the author of such a book. Obviously written by a virginal spinster or someone who didn't share love with her husband." Mira had sat down on the bed beside her. "I guess it's a good thing I'm here to enlighten ye."

"Well, what does happen?"

"First off, Rhiannon, none of that is true. Your husband will want to kiss you, to start. To touch you, and hold you, and explore those parts of your body that nobody else except yourself has ever seen. And if you love him, ye'll want him to." She smiled. "Just as ye'll want to explore *him*."

Rhiannon had nodded, wide-eyed and hanging on Mira's every word. After all, she wanted to please her husband. She wanted to make sure she did this right.

"When a man likes what he sees in a woman, yes, he'll respond in ways that can end up makin' a baby. Men are made differently than we are, Rhiannon. Their part is the fist. Our part is the mitten. When a man loves a woman and wants to be with her, that part that's the fist'll get big and hard and strong; it's the part that goes into the mitten."

"Does it hurt when it goes in?"

"Only the first time. After that, it's more wonderful than anything you'll have ever felt in your whole entire life."

Rhiannon had nodded, her mind already trying to envision the picture that Mira had sketchily painted.

"So the book is wrong, then. . . . "

Mira had laughed. "Trust me, Rhiannon, the last thing ye'll be looking at or thinkin' about are cracks on the ceiling. And now, I could tell ye more I suppose, but I think I'll leave that to my son. It wouldn't be right if I revealed all of the mysteries that it's up to the two of you to discover together. But I will say this. He'll treat ye with love and kindness, just like his father always treated me, and you won't find a better man on this earth to take as your husband. . . ."

That had been hours before. Now, Rhiannon felt her heartbeat quickening as the carriage in which she was riding finally pulled up at the church and came to a halt. Beside her sat Alannah, and across from her was Maeve and Sir Graham, who looked splendid in full naval uniform.

Rhiannon thought again about all that Mira had told her. About fists and mittens and this thing that would happen tonight that would be more wonderful than anything, Mira had promised, that she'd ever felt before. She thought about Captain Merrick, standing in there at the altar, and suddenly she couldn't wait to see him.

A footman opened the door and the admiral handed her down.

Trembling a bit, she took his arm and they went inside.

It took her eyes a moment to adjust to the cool gloom of the church after the bright tropical sun and there, up at the altar, she caught her first glance of the man who would soon be her husband.

Rhiannon was used to seeing him garbed casually, informally, in straw hat and sandals and clothes meant for comfort in the hot sun. She had never seen him in formal attire, and to do so now took her breath away.

Her first glimpse of him was from the back. His chestnut curls had been carefully brushed forward in the current fashion, and he wore a short, cutaway blue tailcoat with a high, stand-up collar that was the height of fashion. Cream-colored pantaloons emphasized the length of his legs, and the buckles on his leather shoes shone. He was standing with the Reverend Milford and his cousin Nathan Ashton, and at first, it was only his broad back that Rhiannon saw and his hands clasped behind it; then, hearing the hush that fell over the small gathered crowd as Rhiannon entered the church, he turned around.

The look in his eyes was one that Rhiannon would never forget. It was one of admiration, gratitude, and sudden, speechless joy, and for a moment he could only stare at her; then, a slow, rakish smile of appreciation curved his lips, and his eyes crinkled at the corners as the smile widened to light up his entire face.

Around her people had stood up, and out of the corner of her eye she saw Captain Merrick's crew, the rest of the Falconer and Merrick families, officers' wives. Rhiannon, her hand tucked into the crook of Sir Graham's elbow, felt their stares upon her, heard the twittering of the assembled guests:

"My goodness, what a beautiful bride!'

"Look at that gown, isn't it just splendid!"

"What a gorgeous couple they're going to make!"

She swallowed against the suddenly dry spot in her throat and willed her shaky legs to move her forward, grateful for Sir Graham's strength and solid presence beside her because really, what was she doing, marrying this man she barely knew, this man whom her sister Gwyneth didn't even know she was marrying, this man who would take her to his bed this evening in just a few hours' time and have his way with her, this man, this man—

Oh, this man.

She reached his side and there, was guided to his left. She caught the scent of him—soap, clean clothes, bay rum. Nerves fluttered in her stomach and she worried that she would suddenly run from the church. And then Reverend Milford smiled his cherubic, comforting smile, and Connor Merrick was leaning down to whisper conspiratorially in her ear:

"Live a little, Rhiannon."

Rhiannon blushed, and suddenly everything was all right.

"Are you ready?" the priest whispered.

Connor Merrick nodded once, Rhiannon took a deep and steadying breath, and the next phase of her life got underway. . . .

"Dearly beloved," the priest began, smiling, and Rhiannon concentrated on a shaft of light coming down through the stained glass window behind the altar and tried to ignore the way the clasp of the pearl choker was scratchy against the back of her neck. "We are gathered here in the sight of God, and in the face of this Congregation, to join together this Man and this Woman in holy Matrimony. . . ."

The reverend's words seemed to fade, and Rhiannon was only aware of the tall, handsome god beside her, and again, thoughts of their upcoming wedding night. *Oh, dear Lord, am I doing the right thing?*

Do I have a choice?

"Therefore if any man can shew just cause why they may not lawfully be joined together, let him now speak, or else hereafter forever hold his peace."

An expectant hush fell over the church, and Rhiannon heard her heartbeat in her ears. And then the moment was past, and Reverend Milford was looking soberly into Captain Merrick's green eyes. "Connor, Wilt thou have this Woman to thy wedded wife, to live together after God's ordinance in the holy estate of Matrimony? Wilt thou love her, comfort her, honour and keep her in sickness and in health; and forsaking all other, keep thee only unto her, so long as ye both shall live?"

"I will."

A similar vow was asked of Rhiannon, and somewhat breathlessly, she answered, "I will."

And then Sir Graham was formally handing her over to her husband, his hand was firmly clasping her own, and he was promising himself to her, to have and to hold from this day forward . . . .

She heard herself promising herself to him, for richer, for poorer, in sickness and in health. . . .

"To love, cherish, and to obey, til death do us part. . . ."

There, a band of gold resting upon the Bible, and then his strong, broad, calloused hand was taking her own and sliding the ring onto her fourth finger, and his deep voice was proudly ringing out for all to hear:

"With this ring I thee wed, with my body I thee worship, and with all my worldly goods I thee endow; In the Name of the Father, and of the Son, and of the Holy Ghost. Amen."

They both knelt, prayers were said, and the beautiful words of the liturgy bound them together in the eyes of God and before the assembled congregation. The metal clasp at the back of Rhiannon's neck dug into the sensitive skin there, and she resisted the urge to reach up and rub at it.

"I pronounce that they be Man and Wife together, in the Name of the Father, and of the Son, and of the Holy Ghost. Amen."

There was sudden applause throughout the church, and then Captain and Rhiannon Merrick were turned to face the cheering congregation.

It was done.

CHAPTER 14

The rest of the day was a blur . . . an elaborate reception at Sir Graham's home, dancing, food, music, lots of hugs from the Merricks, congratulations from well-wishers, Connor's crew toasting her and elbowing their grinning captain, champagne, the lengthening of shadows, the giving of advice for a happy marriage from those who apparently enjoyed such unions, aching feet, blisters, and finally, the gradual dispersion of the assembled guests as the night began to close in.

"Dearest wife," Connor said, taking her hand after she all but limped her way through one last dance, "I think it's time we take our leave."

They made their excuses amidst much cheering and many toasts. Rhiannon felt like she was in a daze, a dream, that she would wake up and find herself back at Morninghall Abbey with Gwyneth and Damon and her dog Mattie. Things had happened so fast . . . were still happening so fast . . . .

What will you be like, Connor Merrick, as a husband? As a lover? Will you be gentle with me tonight? Patient? Generous and loving?

She shuddered with nervousness.

Or will you rush this and make what should be beautiful, hurried and painful?

Painful.

Oh, dear heavens, Mira had admitted that it would hurt.

How could it not?

Her small hand clasped in his, he led her out of the house. Out into the balmy Caribbean night. There, off to the east over the hills, the moon was starting to come up.

"Where are we going, Captain Merrick?"

"Please, Rhiannon . . . we are man and wife now. Call me Connor."

"Connor."

The name sounded nice on her tongue. *Connor.*

As did her new name: Rhiannon Evans Merrick.

Mrs. Merrick. She was a Missus now.

Rhiannon pinched her arm, but this strange daze-dream did not go away.

The breeze whispered against her skirts, lifted them to swirl around her ankles as they walked through the warm night. The coconut palms sighed in the light winds, and stars shone brightly above them. Her heart was beating hard in her chest. Would their wedding night be spent on the beach? In an inn? Back, God forbid, at Sir Graham's home?

"Where are we going?"

"I have a surprise for you."

He led her down to the beach. A small boat had been pulled up onto the sand, well beyond the breaking waves.

Her new husband released her hand. Bending, he pushed the boat backwards and into the surf and then, turning, lifted Rhiannon up in his strong arms and gently set her down on the thwart.

Moments later he had taken up the oars and was rowing them across the nearly glass-smooth surface of the harbor.

"So," Rhiannon ventured nervously, "is our wedding night to be spent aboard a boat?"

"Aye, but not this one."

"Which one, then?"

"Why, *Kestrel*, of course. I've sent the crew ashore for the night. The ship is ours. All ours."

"We'll be . . . alone?"

He smiled at her in the darkness, putting his arms and shoulders into powerful strokes that made the small boat cut through the water.

"All alone."

Through the darkness they moved, the rhythmic sound of the oars in the oarlocks, the steady splash and gurgle of the water, the whisper of the bow wake all soothing in this night of nights. And there was the schooner lying low and dark upon the water, a single lantern hung in the shrouds of her mainmast piercing the night and throwing a beam of light rippling across the water.

"Ahoy, *Kestrel*!"

"That you, Captain?"

"Aye, Mr. Bobbs."

As Connor hooked the boat onto the schooner's main chains and prepared to scale her side, Rhiannon hissed, "I thought you said we'd be alone tonight!"

"And so we shall be, dearest. But no ship is ever left without a watch, and Bobbs is it. I'll relieve him as soon as we're aboard, and then he's free to go ashore to spend the night as he wishes."

"Oh."

"Shall I board first and rig a bosun's chair for you? Or since you're the captain's wife now, do you want to give it a go as an able seaman?"

"You mean, climb up the ship's side . . . by myself?"

"Might as well start sometime." His grin flashed in the darkness. "Live a little, Rhiannon."

"What if I fall backwards and into the sea?"

She could feel his warm, laughing gaze upon her. "My dear Mrs. Merrick. Do you honestly think I would let that happen?"

"No, Captain Merrick. I don't believe that you would."

"Right, then. Let's see you show Bobbs how it's done. Take off your shoes and hand them to me."

Frowning but intrigued, she did. He tossed them lightly up onto the deck, where they landed with two dull thuds.

"And your stockings."

"My stockings?"

"Aye, Rhiannon. Your stockings. Bare feet will give you more purchase than silk."

"I can't possibly take off my stockings!"

He leaned close to her and said, somewhat wickedly, "Before the night is out, you'll be taking off much more than your stockings, my dear."

She gasped, and he laughed, and a moment later Rhiannon was discreetly lifting her skirts, hooking her thumb around her garters and peeling the stockings down her legs while hoping that Bobbs, on the deck above, couldn't see.

"Do you know, my own mother used to be a crewmember aboard this very ship," Connor said fondly. "She spent her time here dressed in the clothes of a common seaman, and was the best gunner *Kestrel* ever had. Had my father fooled the whole time." He put out a hand, silently asking her to relinquish the stockings. "You won't be the first young lady to be running *Kestrel*'s decks barefoot, Rhiannon."

She was mortified as she handed the balled-up stockings, still warm from her body heat, to her new husband. And even more so when he brought them to his nose and then gently rubbed them on his cheek, smiling.

His eyes met hers in the darkness, and his grin became downright wicked.

Rhiannon's throat went dry.

"Bobbs, throw down a line, would you?"

"Aye, Captain."

A rope snaked down from above. Connor bade her to raise her arms and gently passed the rope beneath them, quickly tying a knot to secure it. He turned her to face the thin strips of wood set into the schooner's curved hull.

"In time, Rhiannon, you won't need the rope around you, but tonight, it's there for extra security. You are not going to fall, but if you do, Bobbs has the other end, and I'm right behind you. Now, hold the rope in your hands, set your toes into these little slats that are built into the tumble-home, and climb."

"I think the job of being captain's wife is going to prove to be more physically demanding than I'd anticipated."

His grin was positively wolfish. "Ah, dearest . . . if only you knew," he said, and she knew he wasn't talking about climbing the schooner's sides.

She did as he bade, and as her toes found purchase and she pulled herself slowly up the side of the ship, secure in the knowledge that her husband was right there behind her, she realized that he was correct about bare feet being an asset here. Soon enough she had reached the rail by her own power and there, Bobbs reached out a hand to help her over it and onto the deck.

He grinned, and saluted. Saluted! *Her?*

"Welcome aboard, Mrs. Merrick."

She had no idea what to say. "Thank you, Mr. Bobbs."

"All right, Bobbs, you can get the hell out of here now," Connor said, coming easily up behind her. "And make it fast. The rest of the crew are raising hell down in Bridgetown . . . you can probably find them at the Rusty Anchor."

"Much obliged, sir," the seaman said, and moments later he was gone—leaving Rhiannon alone, quite alone, on the gently rocking deck of the Yankee privateer schooner *Kestrel* with her new and impossibly handsome husband.

She looked at him.

He looked at her.

"Wait here," he said, and leaving her there next to the shrouds that pinnacled up into the night sky, padded across the deck and down the hatch.

Rhiannon hugged her arms to herself and looked out over the water to the lights of Bridgetown. Oh, what was she supposed to do? Say? Think?

From the time she'd first seen him she had been fantasizing over this man, trying to find ways to be with him, dreaming about what it would be like to be kissed by him. To be held in his strong arms. And here she was married to him—and about to find out.

And she was afraid.

Mira's reassurances came back to her. *It's more wonderful than anything you'll have ever felt in your whole entire life.*

"Beautiful night out there, isn't it?"

He was back, with several blankets, two pillows and a bottle of wine.

She eyed the pillows dubiously, swallowed hard, and looked up into the night sky, where a thousand pinpricks of light marked heavens that looked so different from what she was used to back in England.

"I don't remember seeing stars like this back home. Look how low that Cassiopeia and the Little Bear sit in the sky."

"That's because we're in much more southern latitudes."

He headed aft, looking back over his shoulder at her in invitation.

"Capt— I mean, Connor," she said, hesitantly. "I . . . I don't know quite how to say this, but . . . well, I'm . . . I'm a little afraid."

He stopped, gave one slow, understanding nod, and smiled. "There's no need to be afraid, Rhiannon. We don't have to do anything you don't want to do. I told you that before."

"And that . . . that applies to . . . *this*, too?"

"This?"

"Well . . . you know."

"Ah. That."

"Yes, *that*."

"Tell you what. We don't have to do this. Or that. Or whatever it is you want to call it. How about we just sit back here in the stern together, our backs up against the transom, and share some wine while we look at the stars?"

"That sounds very romantic, Connor."

"The moon is up. It's a beautiful night."

"Our wedding night."

She looped her hand through his bent elbow and he led her aft, past the silent guns sleeping in their trucks, an open hatch, and finally, to the tiller. *Kestrel* moved gently up and down beneath them, and Rhiannon adjusted her balance to the motion. She could hear the soft wash of the sea against the rudder and a warm, sultry breeze whispering through the shrouds.

Did she want to do this? Or that? Or whatever *it* was called? Oh, dear God. She trembled in nervous anticipation.

You know he won't force you. You know he's a good man, bold and reckless, yes, but kind-hearted and honorable.

She watched as he spread a blanket on the deck and sat down, his back against the gunwale, his long legs stretched before him toward the tiller. He motioned for Rhiannon to join him.

She did, keeping a few inches between them while carefully arranging her skirts over her bare legs. Her nerves were tight, her skin prickling with anticipation.

"Don't be afraid," he said softly. "I don't bite."

"I'm sorry. I don't mean to be so nervous."

"Do you have any idea what happens in the marriage bed, Rhiannon?"

"A little."

"Tell me what you know."

"The man puts his fist in the woman's mitten and a baby is made."

"*What?*"

She laughed. "Well, that's what your mother told me."

"My mother." He shook his head, amused. "Leave it to her to come up with something like that."

"Oh, I know they're just euphemisms, Connor. But I adore your mother, and she was trying her best to be reassuring."

"My family thinks the world of you," he said at length. "And I can't tell you how proud I was when you walked into that church this afternoon, Rhiannon. My heart was swelling so large that I thought it would burst the confines of my chest. You were beautiful. You *are* beautiful. You took my breath away."

"Is this how husbands seduce their new brides? By endless flattery and compliments?"

"What?"

"Oh, never mind. I was in jest."

"Were you? Because I was not." He gave her a sidelong glance, then uncorked the bottle of wine. He held it slightly aloft, and looked her in the eye. "To my beautiful wife. May God bless our marriage."

He drank from the bottle, wiped his lips with the back of one broad hand, and handed it to her.

She looked at it, smiled, and raised it to her own mouth. And then: "To my dashing husband. And, our marriage."

Madeira. She took a long swig of it and handed it back to him.

They sat there together, *Kestrel*'s gentle rocking going far to soothe Rhiannon's nerves. Connor took another drink, and handed her the bottle. She did the same.

Another.

"I feel as though we know so little about each other," she said, as the wine gently warmed her blood. "We've only known each other for three weeks, and for most of that time you were away."

"What would you like to know about me?"

"I don't even know where to begin."

"Well, since I know as little about you as you do me, how about I start?"

"All right."

He took another drink and set the bottle down between them, leaving his hand lingering on it, his knuckles just brushing her outer thighs through the thin muslin of her gown. "Where were you born?"

"Wales."

"I already know you have an older sister, of course. Gwyneth. And another sister, Morganna, yes? Tell me about your parents."

"They died a long time ago. I don't remember them well . . . Gwyneth raised Morganna and me."

"What's your favorite color?"

She thought of his eyes. "Green."

"What do you like to do for enjoyment?"

"Read. And imagine myself to be the heroine in the novels that I most enjoy."

"What's the one thing you want to do before you die?"

"That's an odd question."

"So it is. I'm sorry. I say whatever comes into my head, and half the time what comes into it surprises even me."

"Well . . . I guess I would like to finish learning how to swim."

"We can make that happen."

"And I hope I do you proud as the captain's lady."

His hand left the bottle and settled upon her kneecap. "You do me proud already, Rhiannon."

She could think of nothing but his hand, resting there on her knee. How warm it felt. How large it was. And how it was making the skin tingle all around it.

"I can learn to swim, but I don't think I'll ever dare to go aloft, Connor."

"We all have our limits."

"I doubt that the word *limits* is one that could ever be applied to you, sir!"

He laughed. "Lots of people are afraid of heights."

"I'm ashamed of my fear. Especially when I see how freely you live your life. You leap from the rigging and swim in the moonlight and laugh in the face of terrible storms. Your little nephew idolizes you. Your crew, I think, would follow you to the ends of the earth and back. I see you climbing aloft and going so high up that it makes my stomach feel funny just watching you. I would never, not in a million years, dare to do that, and yet there's a tiny part of me that wishes that I did. That I could."

He nodded slowly, and his thumb caressed the inside of her knee.

"You have lived a rather sheltered life, haven't you, Rhiannon?"

"Well, in comparison to you, I suppose I have. This is my first real adventure, you know."

"And here you got more than you bargained for."

Oh, his hand there on her thigh was making her feel very strange indeed.

Rhiannon shivered, suddenly.

"Are you cold?"

"No."

Suddenly shy. Nervous. Unsure. But not cold.

Even so, he shook out one of the blankets that he'd set on the deck and placed it over her legs, and then stuffed a pillow behind them, cushioning their backs against the curve of the gunwale. The pillow was small, too small for a back as broad as her new husband's, and he was gallantly giving most of the space to her. Growing bolder from the wine, Rhiannon shifted her weight, and leaned against his shoulder instead.

"Ahh," he said, and pulling his arm free from between their bodies, curved it around her shoulder to draw her close. The weight of his arm was delicious, and she fit against him as though she'd been made to. And he smelled good. Clean, fresh, untamed. Salt wind and shaving soap.

She snuggled a little closer.

This was nice. Very nice.

"I wish I knew the names of all those stars," she said, resting her cheekbone against his shoulder and turning her gaze skyward. Beyond his handsome profile, the tall spire of the mainmast and the cross-hatched shrouds that supported it made black silhouettes against the vastness of the night sky. "Do you know their names?"

"It's a mariner's duty to know them."

"Connor?"

"Yes, Rhiannon?"

"Will you kiss me?"

He gave a little laugh, pulled his hand free from behind her shoulders, and turning his body slightly so that he was looking down at her, put his fingers beneath her chin.

"I would love to kiss you."

How beautiful his eyes, crinkling at the corners with laughter, were in the starlight. How long his lashes were, how handsome the cut of his cheek, jaw and chin. He spread his fingers, gently pushed them along one side of her jawbone, and coaxed her to lift her chin.

His mouth was very close.

Rhiannon shut her eyes as he gently touched his lips to hers, his hand still alongside her jaw, his fingers now threading into her hair and holding her head steady. She twisted a bit and pushed herself closer to him, one hand coming up to palm his chest and explore the hard muscles beneath his waistcoat. Of their own accord, her fingers began to unbutton the garment and soon it lay open, only his fine lawn shirt separating her questing hand from the bareness of his chest. The pressure of his mouth against her own grew harder and more insistent, igniting a vortex of sensation between her legs that both thrilled and frightened her, and she felt her breath beginning to come hard as her body responded to him.

Slowly, they each pulled back, neither one ready to break the kiss, his hand still cradling her jaw and cupping the side of her head.

"Oh, my," Rhiannon said, a little breathlessly.

"That wasn't so scary, now, was it?"

"No. No, it was . . . quite nice."

He just smiled, and drew her close yet again.

Their lips met a second time, his growing more insistent, and she felt his breath coming hot against her cheek now as his tongue slipped out to circle her lips, to push inside her mouth and touch and taste her own. She pressed closer to him, feeling odd sensations moving through that private place between her thighs, through her breasts and along the nerve endings of her skin, and needing something she didn't understand.

And then, as though he could somehow know just what it was she wanted, his hand cupped her breast and his thumb roved gently over the nipple.

Rhiannon gasped into his mouth, suddenly unsure.

He pulled back just the merest fraction, brushing kisses against her cheek, down the sensitive side of her neck, his teeth gently nibbling at her ear lobe and his thumb, oh, his thumb, brushing over her nipple, over and over again until she thought that part of her was surely on fire.

"Frightened yet, dearest?"

"Only of these sensations I don't recognize."

"They are nothing to fear."

"What . . . what are they?"

"They are what your body does to prepare itself for love," he murmured, against the hollow of her collarbone. "I have them too."

"Do you?"

He pulled back then, and caressed her cheek with the rough pad of his thumb. It was impossible not to trust him, not to fall in love with him, when he smiled at her like that. "I would be less than honest if I were to say otherwise."

"But your body is . . . different than mine."

Hard where mine is soft. Hairy where mine is smooth. Strong where mine is delicate.

He gently took her hand and guided it to his crotch. "Touch me," he said quietly.

Fascinated, she stretched her fingers toward his pantaloons. Beneath the warm fabric his flesh was hard and bulging, like it had been that night after their swimming lesson. And after the kiss at Sir Graham's house.

"See?" he said, gently.

"But why. . . ."

"You really are an innocent, aren't you?"

She blushed. "I hope that's not a disappointment to you."

"It's a delight. You're a wonderful gift that has never been opened by anyone else, never been sullied by another, and all mine to enjoy."

"But, this part of you. . . . Why is it like this sometimes, but not others?"

"Well, when a man desires a woman, nature makes it such that his . . . his, um . . . oh, hell. That is to say, his—"

She smiled, enjoying his uncharacteristic discomfort and thinking about fists and mittens. "Really, Connor. You're a sailor. Just say it."

"His cock responds to her in a way that makes it possible for the man to impregnate the woman. It . . . changes."

"You're going to make me pregnant tonight?"

"Do you not want children?"

"Of course I do! Lots of them!"

"Just because we do this—"

"You mean *that*—"

"Doesn't mean it will result in a child."

"But you're saying it might."

"Yes, it might."

"I see. May I touch your . . . cock, Connor?" She took a deep breath. "Can I see it?"

He reached down and unbuttoned his pantaloons, and then lay back against the curve of the gunwale, watching her with a little smile.

Shyly, Rhiannon reached out, pulled down the flap front, and touched the warm flesh that was suddenly revealed to her gaze in the starlight shining down from above. She rather wished she'd asked Mira to tell her more, because how could men possess something of this size and keep it safely contained behind fabric, buckskin, leather or silk? Fascinated, she ran her forefinger over the length of this strange part of him, finding it both soft to the touch but hard as rock beneath the velvety skin, warm and rigid and strangely exciting. As she explored the soft, bulbous tip with her fingers, the whole organ seemed to grow even bigger.

Her new husband gave a soft groan, and she saw that he had tilted his head back against the gunwale, his eyes half closed.

"Do you mind that I'm touching you?"

"No, I quite enjoy it," he said, then sucked in his breath as her fingers circled and squeezed the tip, and then wandered down to explore his testicles in their bed of soft auburn hair.

"Does this hurt, when I do this?"

"No, Rhiannon. But for now, I think you should stop."

"Why?"

"Because I want to make this last. To make it special for you."

"What about making it special for *you*?"

"It will be."

"It's going to hurt me, isn't it?"

"Who told you that?"

"I read it in a book that Alannah gave me last night. That it's very unpleasant for the woman, and the best thing you can do if you're a woman is just close your eyes and look at cracks in the ceiling until the awful moment is past."

"Awful moment? Rhiannon, if this is the education you've received through reading books, I think you should pursue other hobbies. You've been woefully misled."

"I know . . . your mother set me straight. She said it's more wonderful than anything I'll ever feel in my whole entire life." She swallowed, hard. "But she also said it would hurt. The first time, at least."

Catching her wrist, he gently guided it away from himself. Then he leaned close, his handsome face blotting out the stars above. "Dearest, the first time it may indeed hurt for just a little bit. But it won't for long, and I give you my word—indeed, my promise—that you'll soon forget you ever felt any pain."

"You promise, Connor?" she said in a little voice.

"My promise." He reached up and traced her lower lip with his finger. "But you must trust me."

"I . . . trust you."

And then he began to kiss her once more, brushing gentle, feathery kisses along her jaw, nibbling at the corner of her mouth, licking at the seam of her lips until she finally opened to him with a little moan and began to boldly kiss him back.

He tasted of wine. She felt his hand in her hair, the thick tresses falling down around her shoulders as one by one, he loosened the pins and allowed her glorious mane to tumble down her back. One of his arms went around her, supporting her, and her world swam as he carefully eased her down upon the blanket. He turned onto his side, propped his head against his hand, and grinned down at her as he spread her hair out on the pillow, running his fingers out over each thick, lustrous hank.

"Comfortable?" he asked softly.

Her eyes very wide, her body throbbing in ways that were making her want to squirm, she nodded up at him.

He reached out and tenderly grazed her forehead with his knuckles, traced a path down the hollow beneath her cheekbone, and let his hand drift down her neck.

Over her collarbone.

And to the bodice of her gown, such thin, helpless protection against a hand that looked so broad and dark and masculine against the pale blue fabric. A hand that could expertly wield both sword and pistol, a hand that had probably killed, a hand that expertly steered this beautiful ship, a hand that knew how to make a woman ache and tingle in ways that were beyond her most fervent imaginings.

A hand that was now tracing the edge of her neckline, following the fabric where it lay against her skin and sending heat radiating out from every place he touched.

Please touch me again, there, Connor.

She only thought the words, but he must surely be connected to her in some mystical way because she only had to think them before those same fingers that were moving along the edge of fabric were dipping beneath it, sliding between gown and chemise and finding the upper curve of one breast. He knew what she wanted, what she craved, what she dared not ask for shame of being thought a strumpet, and she sucked her lower lip between her teeth as his warm, calloused fingers began moving over her nipple, this time with no muslin between them and the burgeoning peak.

"Ohhh," she said a little breathlessly, and clamped her legs shut against the building ache.

"Awful?" he teased.

"Not yet, Connor."

"Shall we continue?"

She made a noise that she couldn't recognize, something between a moan and a reply in the affirmative and closing her eyes, sank back into the pillow. She heard her own breathing growing more labored as he gently rolled her nipple between thumb and forefinger, felt sensations gathering between her clamped legs, felt an alarming wash of wetness down there that was unfamiliar and mortifying and oh, thank goodness that he could not know about *that*—

His lips brushed her nipple, and Rhiannon stopped worrying.

His mouth closed over it, and Rhiannon stopped thinking.

He began to suckle her, and Rhiannon nearly stopped breathing.

Sweet torture. She whimpered deep in the back of her throat and arched upward, unconsciously giving him access to her body, willing him to take more of her breast, now throbbing and tingling as though on fire, up into his mouth. He did, laving the nipple with his tongue, tracing circles around it and finally suckling it hard, pulling it deep, deep up into the hot cavern of his mouth and causing that sensation between her legs to become almost unbearable.

"Ohh, please stop," she said breathlessly, turning her face away. "I can't bear this!"

He pulled back, and cool air swept against her nipple where his mouth had left it wet. "Does it hurt?"

"No! Yes! It . . . it feels strange, and I'm afraid."

The deck moved gently beneath them as the tide began to turn.

"There is nothing to be afraid of, Rhiannon. Can you trust me on that?"

"What is this strange feeling, Connor?"

"It is called desire, my dear. It is perfectly natural."

She stared up at him.

"Just relax, and enjoy this . . . this adventure." He smiled down at her, and gently palmed the side of her cheek. "Isn't that what you've been telling me you wanted? An adventure?"

"Yes. . . ."

"So be brave, my sweet wife, and see where it leads you."

She took a deep and shaky breath and willed herself to relax, but a thin layer of perspiration had broken out the length of her spine and her body felt awash in heat and shivers and strange sensations that were not quite pain, but oddly pleasurable. He drew his shirt off over his head and moved back over her, his handsome form blotting out the panorama of stars so far above.

His hot mouth found her other breast now, kissing it, licking it, until Rhiannon's toes curled and her breath came raggedly through her lungs. And then, just when she thought she couldn't take it anymore, he reached down, found the hem of her gown and pushed beneath it.

Oh, it felt good, his hand warm against her shin, her knee, working its way upward toward that shamefully wet place between her legs and carrying the hem of her gown with it so as to expose her legs, and in horror, Rhiannon realized he was going to touch her *there*.

He was still suckling her breast. She gasped and shut her legs against him, embarrassed that she was . . . leaking something down there.

"Rhiannon, dearest . . . open to me."

"I'm ashamed!"

"There is nothing to be ashamed of."

But oh, dear God, she could feel the wetness between her legs and she didn't understand it, didn't know where it had come from or what caused it, and the idea that he, her new husband, handsome, virile and eager to please her, was going to find out that she was defective, that she— oh, God, she *leaked*—was mortifying beyond belief.

His fingers moved into the wetness, and Rhiannon wanted to die from humiliation.

And something else.

"You are beautiful," he breathed, lifting his mouth from her breast. "So sweet and wet."

"I'm sorry," she gasped as the same thumb and forefinger that had brought such pleasure and strange sensation to her breast, began to move gently into her hot, wet curls. "You have a defective wife, one who . . . one who— "

"Is beautiful and precious and making me hard with desire."

"*Leaks!*" she cried.

At this he just gave a little laugh and began working his fingers within her curls, stroking her gently down there until she began to whimper and moan. His thumb found a hidden part of her deep within the slick wetness and gently rolled it between it and his forefinger, causing her to cry out in delight.

Was it wrong that she was enjoying this? Oh, dear heavens, how could he like the fact that he had a wife who was all wet down there, who wasn't what he was surely bargaining for when he married her, who was hot and beginning to perspire and whose hair lay in thick, dampening tangles around her face?

His head moved lower and she felt him shift his weight, draw his hand away from that private, aching place between her legs—*oh, please put it back!*—felt his lips gently nibbling the inside of her knee, his teeth grazing her skin and now moving upward, his tongue licking against the inside of her thighs and moving higher . . . higher.

"Oh," she said, in something like a sob, "Oh Connor, no, I'm too embarrassed, I can't—"

"Yes, you can," he murmured against the warm skin of her thigh, and she felt his lips whispering higher and higher, getting ever closer to that hot, wet part of her that had become the very center of her existence.

"Open to me, dearest," he commanded, and when she took a deep and shaky breath and opened her legs just the slightest bit, he moved his weight yet again to kneel between her legs, put his hands on her bare thighs, and gently, carefully, opened her himself.

There he remained for a long moment just looking at her, and Rhiannon opened dazed, confused eyes, watching his face for any sign of disgust, disappointment, or horror.

And found none.

"You are a virgin," he said softly. "Of course you don't know that this is how it's supposed to be. That just as a man grows hard and large and stiff with desire for a woman, so a woman grows hot and wet, so as to ease his passage into the deepest recesses of herself. There is nothing to be ashamed of."

"You are not . . . horrified?"

"Let me show you how horrified I am," he said, and still holding her thighs open, he bent his head and resumed kissing the inside of her thighs.

Rhiannon relaxed into the pillow, feeling the sensation between her legs building, wishing desperately with some part of herself that dared not give voice to it that he would put his mouth there, that he would put his tongue there, that he would bring to that place the same searing, building, pleasure-pain that he had brought when he'd taken first one nipple and then the other into his mouth. Surely he must have been able to read this thought too, because in another moment she felt his mouth moving higher, into the warmest recesses between her legs, and daring to open her eyes she saw that his head was there, buried between her thighs, and he was— he was—

Kissing her.

There.

She gave a little cry at the first touch of his tongue to her inner flesh and instinctively tried to close herself to him, but he anticipated it and held her legs wide, pushing them even farther apart as his kisses there became gentle licks, then long strokes of his tongue against her slit, and she was gasping and arching against the blanket, bunched now beneath her, as he relentlessly licked and suckled her. She gasped, her hand anchoring in his hair, her breath coming in half sobs, and little whimpers escaping the back of her throat as she felt his tongue licking and tasting and stabbing. And then his thumbs moved on either side of that swollen, hardened bud down there, opened her even further to his ministrations, and she felt his mouth, hot and wet and warm, fasten upon her there.

And begin to suckle, hard.

Rhiannon bucked upward, caught in the first climax of her life, and as she cried out, her body convulsing, her husband caught her cries in his mouth and guided her hand to himself. She gripped him hard as the ache inside her peaked and pulsed, and then lay back, panting, her cheeks damp with perspiration.

"Put me inside of you," he said softly. "You are ready now."

Fist to mitten.

"Inside of me . . . "

He merely smiled, slid his hands up to either side of her face to cradle it lovingly between his palms, and looked down into her eyes.

"Trust me," he said.

And then he was kissing her once more. She did as he asked, her tiny hand gripping his huge and erect organ and guiding it to that hot, still-throbbing, and oh-so-wet place between her legs, instinctively knowing where it was meant to go. Sighing, her arms came up to wind around her husband's back as he found her entrance and slowly, agonizingly, began to push himself inside of her. The pleasure-pain swirled within her once more and her lower belly seemed to clench in on itself, building once more to that strange explosion of senses that had left her breathless and near tears just moments before. Rhiannon shut her eyes, tensing with fear and expectation, and felt him kissing her eyelids, her cheeks, his breath now hot and ragged against her temple as he reached down and adjusted himself and lay there, balanced on his elbows.

"Are you ready, dearest?" he asked, against her flushed skin.

"I . . . I think so."

"It will only hurt for a moment. Then, it will be nice again."

"You promise?"

"I promise."

She locked her arms around his back and then felt him surging forward, sliding deeply into her, and then a sharp, piercing pain that caused her to cry out in surprise. He lay still within her for a moment, gently kissing her face, reassuring her and holding himself in check; then, as she recovered from this surprise, he pushed forward once more, expanding her flesh and going deeper and deeper inside of her until she thought she might break.

She opened her eyes and saw just his bare shoulder, blotting out the stars above.

He pulled back and began to slide out of her, and instinctively Rhiannon pushed herself against him, not wanting him to leave her, not wanting this to end, and hoping that there was more to it than just this.

And apparently there was, for a moment later he was pushing back inside her, filling her and stretching her even more deeply this time, and the searing ache inside of her began to build once more; he pulled back again, and instinctively recognizing the ancient rhythm, Rhiannon began to move with him.

His breathing came hard and fast. The muscles in his great shoulders and arms stood out. She pushed upward to meet each long, driving thrust as he began to build speed and force, and just when she thought she could take it no longer he stiffened, gave a hoarse cry, and plunged into her a final time, igniting the explosion within her yet again until she, too, began to climax and, crying out with the beauty of the moment, clung to him with all the strength in her newly-awakened body.

For a long moment they lay together, he still deeply within her, his weight on his elbows, his head drooping so that his hair fell upon her shoulder. Her arms were still wound around his back. She felt warmth and moisture running between her legs, and wondered if it had come from him or from herself and found, in the aftermath of bliss, that she no longer cared.

"Was it so awful?" he finally asked, his breath warm against the curve of her neck.

"Terrible."

"Just goes to show you shouldn't believe everything you read, Rhiannon."

CHAPTER 15

Eventually he eased himself out of her. They pulled the pillows together, turned over onto their backs and lay gazing up at the heavens above, his arm comfortably under her head, her body snuggled close to his and her hand resting on his bare chest.

"You have made me the happiest woman on earth, Connor Merrick."

He smiled, turned her against himself, and kissed her hair.

If there was indeed a heaven, Connor figured he had found it.

His mind, usually so restless and unable to settle on anything for long, felt content and quiet, and for once he was happy to just lie here without the need to fidget. If making love to Rhiannon could do this to him she was a powerful drug indeed, and he looked forward to a lifetime of such therapy. He drew her close, inhaling the scent of her hair as it tickled his cheek. It smelled of lemons and innocence.

Beneath them *Kestrel* rolled gently, rhythmically, reminding him that he had places to go, things to do, a cruise to ready for on the morrow.

Instead he yawned and blinked hard, trying to keep his eyes open.

His bride was saying something. . . .

"What was that?" he murmured, his voice sounding distant and thick to his own ears.

"I was just saying that I hope you don't mind taking me back to England for the birth of Gwyneth's baby," she said. "I couldn't and wouldn't miss that for the world, Connor."

"All these babies," he murmured, watching Cassiopeia rolling back, rolling forth, with the gentle rocking of the ship. His eyes drifted shut.

"Yes, all these babies," Rhiannon said, turning in his arms and gazing down at him. "Connor, are you listening to me?"

"Hmm?"

"We were talking about babies."

"Aye, you said you wanted one."

Rhiannon reached down and smoothed a thick lock of curling hair back from his forehead, admiring the shape of his eyes and gently tracing the little crinkles at their corners. She was rewarded with a smile.

"I do want a baby. Gwyneth is having one, Maeve is soon to have a fourth, and you and I both know there's nothing that would please your mother and father more than to have another grandchild to spoil."

"Yes, they make no secret of that fact. But I think we shouldn't rush the idea of a family, Rhiannon," he said sleepily. "There's no hurry."

"Why not?"

"My profession isn't exactly a safe one. I'm a privateer. I could be killed in battle, lost at sea in a storm, captured and sent to a British prison. I can't set foot in England without considerable risk, no matter how much you'd like to go back there."

"Do you mean we won't be able to go back to England to be with Gwyn when her time comes?"

"I didn't say that," he said, closing his eyes as she played with another short curl, winding it around and around her finger. "You want to go to England, Rhiannon, I will take you."

"Oh," she said, frowning as she considered the risk at which he was willing to put himself for her sake, and her sake alone. "Then why don't you want to start a family, Connor?"

"I'm a privateer. It wouldn't be fair to a child, or to you for that matter, if something were to happen to me." He opened his eyes and looked at her intently before letting them close once more. "I had, and still have, the most wonderful father in the world. While I will never be the man that he is, I can't imagine growing up without a *Dadai*. I won't do that to any child of mine."

"If you're so certain that privateering is going to get you killed, then maybe it's time to give it up."

"I can't. Too much money to be made. And there's a convoy gathering in St. Vincent and ready to sail for England as we speak. I mean to pluck it like cherries from a tree."

Rhiannon frowned. A convoy. Fighting. Privateering. British ships. Cannons blazing. People shooting at each other. She felt a deep sense of unease.

"I don't like this, Connor. You've given me something to worry about."

"Nothing to worry about, my dear. I have the fastest ship on the Atlantic. Going to windward, there's nothing that can catch me."

"Nothing?"

"Nothing."

"Pride goeth before a fall, Connor."

He just smiled and said nothing as she played with a crisp lock of his hair that curled obstinately around the top of his ear.

"Connor?"

"Yes, love?"

Love. "Am I your love?"

"Hmm?"

"Connor!"

"I think I need to sleep, Rhiannon," he said, and a moment later, his breathing grew deep and rhythmic and the arm that curved around her shoulders became heavy. For a long time Rhiannon lay there gazing down at him, the errant curl above his ear still caught in her fingers, the gleam from the thousands of stars above silvering the bridge of his nose, the sculpted curve of his firm, sensual mouth. For if Connor Merrick was beautiful awake and in the glaring honesty of full daylight, here, asleep and under the stars, he was an enigmatic god.

She thought of the heights he had brought her to such a short time ago and lay her head down upon his chest, listening to his breathing and the steady beat of his heart beneath her ear. He mumbled something in his sleep, resettled his arm around her shoulders once more, and finally Rhiannon, too, closed her eyes.

Wrapped in the gentle embrace of his new bride, Connor Merrick lay dreaming.

As he drifted down through the tiers of sleep, his mind traveled back over the years and he was once again a boy, maybe Ned's age, maybe a year or two older, standing with fists clenched and chin mutinous while the other boys circled him and called him names.

"You're stupid!" taunted Jeremiah Lunt. "Stupid, stupid, stoo-pid!"

Connor took a swing at him.

"What's seven times five, Connor?" piped up Tom Johnson, as he threw a ball over his head to Jeremiah. "Go 'head, tell us what seven times five is!"

"He can't," jeered Jeremiah. "He's stoo-pid."

"You call me stupid once more and you're going to be spitting out teeth," Connor said, clenching his fists even harder.

"Oh? Then what year did Columbus discover America?"

"What's a pronoun?"

"I'm still waiting for him to tell you what seven times five is."

"He can't, because he's stoo-"

Connor's temper exploded and he threw himself at Jeremiah, his fists flying. He may be stupid, but damn it all, he knew how to fight, and he'd teach Lunt a thing or two about calling people names—

'Fight!" someone yelled, and then there was only his rage and Jeremiah trying to hit back, once, twice, before he panicked and tried to flee, but Connor ran him down and brought the other boy slamming to the ground, chin first, hitting him hard, harder—

"Connor Merrick!"

Someone was hauling him off Jeremiah, who lay crying in the dirt outside the little one-room schoolhouse. The red haze in front of his vision cleared and he found himself looking into the angry face of the teacher, Mr. Preble, whose hand had caught the fine linen of Connor's shirt and now had it bunched in a choke-hold at his throat.

"Fighting again, Mr. Merrick?"

Connor struggled in the man's grasp and around him the other boys started yelling.

"Connor started it!"

"Aye, Jem was just mindin' his own business when Connor started swinging!"

Jeremiah, wiping at his bleeding nose, glared at Connor from sullen eyes. "Aye, he started it. Just because his boglander father went and made himself famous back in a stupid war that nobody cares about anymore—"

Connor lunged for the other boy. "Don't you ever call my Da a boglander, he's a hundred times the man your father ever was and ever will be!"

Mr. Preble grabbed him by the ear so hard that Connor expected to reach up and find blood. He dragged him away from the other boys and back into the cold schoolroom, but they followed him, their taunts ringing in his ears.

"Stoo-pid!"

Mr. Preble shoved him down into a chair, and he felt blistering pain as the teacher cracked him across the knuckles, hard, with a cane.

"You'll never amount to anything, you worthless rapscallion," the old man snarled. "You're unteachable, you don't pay attention, you're as wild as your mother before you."

"They called me stupid," Connor said hotly. He massaged his knuckles, already turning red beneath the welts left by the cane.

Welts that joined those left from the last caning several days before.

"You *are* stupid, but it's because you don't pay attention! What is the matter with you? You spend your days looking out the window, starting trouble, failing tests, getting into fights. What do you think you have to prove, Mr. Merrick?"

Connor stood up.

"I'll show you," he said, meeting the teacher's eyes. "I'm going to become a privateer just like my father. I'm going to make Newburyport proud, I'm going to make my family proud, and I'm going to be more famous than anyone this town has ever bred. You can take your damned primer and hornbook and stuff 'em right up your arse!" And then, before the teacher could catch him he was off and running, not for home, because his own pride would never let him admit to his father and mother that Mr. Preble beat him on an almost daily basis, but toward the waterfront.

Where the seamen, the fishermen, the drunks, the troublemakers, and the old salts gathered.

Where nobody would ever call the son of Captain Brendan Jay Merrick *stoo-pid*.

Where he, Connor, felt right at home.

CHAPTER 16

Something was rubbing at her foot.

Rhiannon jerked it back and turned over. Light burned against her eyelids, and opening them, she saw that it was dawn.

The sun was on its way up, painting the eastern sky in bands of lemon, mango, and purple.

Again she felt something rubbing at her foot, and then, an impatient, "*Meee-ow!*"

Purring loudly, the cat padded up toward her face and began rubbing itself against Rhiannon's nose. It was obviously hungry.

And its master was nowhere to be found.

Rhiannon sat up, groaning. She must look a sight. Her back was stiff from lying all night on the open deck. She felt sore between her legs, and her lips were tender and bruised from kissing.

"*Meeeee-ow!*"

She pulled the blanket around herself. Oh, God, the crew was surely going to come back soon, and she couldn't think of a greater humiliation than to be seen in such a sorry state. She needed a bath, she needed a brush for her hair, she needed—

"Good morning, Rhiannon."

It was her husband, coming up from the aft hatch and carrying a tray in his hands. He looked fresh and rested, the formal clothes from the previous evening long discarded in favor of his usual casual attire: canvas pantaloons cut off at the knee, an open shirt and the straw hat, through which the first rays of sun were already beginning to leave tiny checkers of light across one of his cheeks.

Oh, he looked delicious.

"Good morning, Connor."

He came to sit beside her. The breeze, wafting over the water, picked at his open shirt and she longed to touch the tanned skin of his throat, to feel again the hard play of muscles underneath.

"I brought you some breakfast," he said, and gently shooing the cat aside, set the tray down on the deck. Delicious smells assailed her. Two mugs of strong black coffee, a pitcher of cream, cubes of sugar in a little pot, a spoon, and there, a chipped bowl of oatmeal. She picked up the bowl, its steam rising to fill her nose, its warmth delicious beneath her palms. It wasn't just oatmeal but something more, something made with skill and care, thick and golden and liberally stuffed with big, plump raisins and chunks of exotic fruit.

"You made this?"

"I did." He smiled disarmingly. "I'm not the smartest man to ever walk the earth, but I do know how to cook."

"That's a skill most sea captains probably don't have," she said, digging the spoon into the oatmeal. "Oh! This is good!"

"Aye, someone in the family had to learn how to cook," he said, grinning. "God knows my mother never mastered the art."

"Didn't you have servants? A cook?"

"Oh, we did, but my mother enjoyed trying. Nearly poisoned us all whenever she'd set her mind to baking a pie or a cake." He watched her tuck into the oatmeal, obviously delighted with her appetite. "I figured that if she couldn't cook, maybe I could. Might come in useful some day."

"It's coming in useful right now. This is delicious."

"I put mango in it, and papaya, too. And some spices we took off a recent prize bound for Europe."

"Did you already eat?"

"I did. I'm an early riser, I confess."

"Do you ever sit still, Connor Merrick?"

He leaned forward and kissed her cheek, and perhaps he might have done more if it weren't broad daylight with dozens of ships moored around them. "Not for long. Now finish up, because I have a surprise for you this morning."

"A surprise?"

"Aye. Your next swimming lesson."

What was she supposed to wear?

He had found her an old black shirt that wouldn't reveal too much when wet, a pair of cut-off canvas trousers that he said belonged to Toby and reached nearly to her ankles, and a straw hat, much like his own, to protect her fair face from the sun.

And then he began pacing the deck, back and forth, back and forth, as restless as ever as he waited for his crew to straggle back from a night of in-town carousing.

Nathan and Toby were the first to arrive. Toby blushed to the roots of his flaming red hair when he saw Rhiannon, and Nathan politely removed his hat to reveal his thick, sun-bleached locks. It didn't take long for the rest of the crew to return, most of them sporting dark circles under their eyes, expressions of exhaustion and overindulgence, and the unmistakable signs of hangovers.

"And how was your wedding night, *Capitaine*?" asked Jacques, with a knowing grin. "Quite an outfit the missus has on there, eh?" He looked tipsy and a bit of drool followed the cleft of his split-scarred lip and clung to his chin, and it was surely only that which saved him from his captain's ire as Connor turned irritably on him.

"My wedding night is none of your damned business, and have a care what you say around the new Mrs. Merrick or I'll scald your arse in pig's fat and feed you to the fishes."

"Sorry, *Capitaine*. It's the rum talking."

Connor shook his head and gave him a good-natured shove. "Go to your hammock and sleep it off, you wretch."

Jacques attempted to salute, turned green, and promptly vomited on the deck. Around him, laughter ensued.

Connor swore under his breath and relinquishing the deck to Nathan, took Rhiannon's arm and guided her to the rail.

"I'm sorry," he muttered, glancing over his shoulder at Jacques, who was being given a mop and a bucket of seawater by an unsympathetic Nathan. "My crew are a bunch of ill-behaved rascals. Not good company for a lady, I'm afraid."

"I'll get used to them," Rhiannon said cheerfully. "And really, Connor, I'm not so easily offended as all that."

"Shall we head ashore then, for our lesson? I can rig a bosun's chair if you like."

Rhiannon gazed down at the clear, turquoise water below. "No. If I'm going to be the captain's wife I need to learn how to be something of a sailor, and that means getting off a ship as well as getting on it."

"What a brave girl you are!"

She laughed. She didn't feel very brave. But she was determined, and that would have to do.

"I'll go first," he was saying. "Watch how I do it. Watch my hands, and where I put my feet. Watch how I hold this line in my hand."

Nimbly, he put a leg over the rail and still holding her gaze, moved quickly down the side of the ship and into the boat that one of the returning crew had left bobbing in the water below.

It wasn't that far down. Not really. *Kestrel* was a lean, trim vessel, and she sat low in the water. It wasn't that far.

I can do this.

In the boat below, her husband looked up and gestured for her to take the line. The boat, as *Kestrel* herself was doing, moved in the water. Up and down. Up and down. "You can do it, Rhiannon. Toby's right there. He'll keep an eye on you, and I'm down here. Trust yourself."

"Trust myself."

He grinned then, his eyes twinkling. "Live a little."

Rhiannon sensed someone near her shoulder and yes, there was Toby, ready to help if she needed it.

"Don't help me," she said. "I want to see if I can do this by myself."

"As you please, ma'm."

Keenly aware of the fact that she was wearing cut-off pantaloons—oh, how scandalous!—Rhiannon took the rope, put one leg over the side and with her toes, found the little wooden slats that served as footholds. She took a deep and steadying breath, aware of two dozen pair of eyes upon her and one very green, very handsome pair, below.

"Have faith in yourself," her husband called up from the boat.

She couldn't trust herself to speak. Taking a deep breath and clinging to the rope, she let herself down a little more. This wasn't so bad now, was it? She was no delicate, simpering creature; she had arms that were strong, balance that was good, nerves that were standing up to what was quite a test, given her fear of heights.

She lowered herself further down and stopped for a moment, resting. *Kestrel*'s rail was level with her eyes now; she could smell the hot sunlight and dried salt against the varnish. She descended some more, searching for toeholds, and then felt strong hands go around her waist. Her husband's hands.

"I've got you," he murmured. "Well done."

She let go of the rope, turned, and flung her arms around his neck.

Above her the crew let out a roaring cheer: "Hip hip, huzzah! Three times three for the captain's lady!"

Rhiannon found herself blushing, and it was all she could do not to let out three cheers herself.

Connor settled Rhiannon on the thwart, took up the oars, and as she turned to wave happily at his crew aboard the schooner, shot them a gesture that his wife wasn't meant to see and put his back to the rowing.

He was looking forward to their swim. One would have thought that the tender, intense lovemaking of the night before might have satisfied him for a time, might have cooled his ardor for this innocent but mischievous girl-woman he had married, but no; he'd had a taste of her, and now he wanted more.

Much more.

Thank God they weren't in England. He couldn't imagine trying to teach her to swim in one of those infernal bathing machines. No, here on Barbados he could clothe her in more functional attire, find some sheltered cove, and have all the privacy he could desire without fear that someone would spy on them and see his wife's long, lean legs and high, firm breasts revealed by wet clothes.

He looked at her sitting opposite him, a smile on her face, her beautiful hair caught in the loose thong of leather he'd found for her and hanging down her back. Maeve, he recalled, had worn her hair much the same way during her Pirate Queen days, and perhaps some might have found the clothes, the hair, and the bare ankles shocking and unacceptable.

Connor thought they were perfectly wonderful.

He thought again of last night. Of how hot and tight and wet she had been when he had so carefully eased himself into her. He had not known what to expect, making love to a virgin, and his rather dim expectations of the act had been surpassed by the delicious reality. Yes, he had introduced her to the art of lovemaking and she was likely sore and tender this morning, but she had not complained, and the fresh, rosy glow to her cheeks, the lush color in her lips, the sparkle in her eye were all testimony to the fact that she had enjoyed it, enjoyed that "awful moment," more than she had dreamed possible.

"What is so funny, dear husband?"

"Oh, I was just thinking about last night."

She blushed, but her eyes brightened and the corner of her mouth turned up in a shared grin. "Ah. That awful moment."

"Are you sore this morning, dearest?"

"I am, but it was worth it."

"You won't be sore, the next time."

"When can we do it again, Connor?"

"When you're feeling up to it."

"What a considerate man I've married."

Connor sincerely hoped she'd be "up to it" within the next hour, because he had some things in mind to top off their swimming lesson.

"I suppose I should write to my sister to let her know that I'm married now," she said, reaching out to trail her fingers in the water as Connor's powerful arms drove the boat at an ever-increasing speed toward the shore. "I wish I could see her face when she opens the letter!"

"I wish I could see Morninghall's," Connor returned wryly. "I'm sure he wanted more for his sister-in-law than a Yankee rogue with a price on his head."

"Who cares? He's not the one marrying you. I am." She reached out and laid her sweet little hand on his knee as the rowed. "And I am more than happy with my choice."

Connor just smiled. He was used to idol worship from Toby and his little nephew Ned, but they were both young and didn't know what a true cock-up he really was. They didn't know, as his parents knew, as Nathan knew, that math and numbers and chart-reading came hard to him and that if he tried to read a book he might get three paragraphs into it before he realized that he had little recollection of what he'd read, and he'd have to go back and read it all over again and sometimes the words made no sense or made him get a headache, which only added to his frustration; even so, his mind would be thinking of something else, and in the end its wanderings would win out over the book. Mr. Preble, of course, had been right: he was unteachable, probably stupid, but as long as nobody except his parents and Nathan—who could plot a course and read a chart when the numbers were all a'jumble in Connor's eyes—knew his shameful secret, he figured he could get by all right.

And if he couldn't be smart, well, he could still beat Nathan at chess. And he could be brave. He could be lucky. And he could be a good husband to this woman who seemed to think he could walk on water, when it was all he could do to read a chart.

He had observed the way his father had treated his mother all these years and he would treat his own wife with the same gentle respect, kindness, and reverence. He was his father's son, wasn't he? He would take good care of Rhiannon. He would help her to let go of the limitations imposed on her by what the world expected of gently-bred young women—limitations that his own mother had flaunted—and together, they would have a good life. And in the meantime he would be the best privateer he could be and take as many prizes as he could before the war ended—as some day it surely would.

His father was a naval architect, good with figures, brilliant even, for he could design a ship and make minute calculations that would result in increased speed, stability, and gun-carrying ability. His father was a brilliant man and a brave one, and if there was anyone in the world that Connor wanted to emulate, it was him.

He would never be good with figures.

But he already was a damned good privateer, and before the war was over, he'd be a famous one.

CHAPTER 17

He took her to the same little cove where they had spent the forbidden nocturnal rendezvous that had landed them in such trouble. Boating the oars, he let the forward momentum carry the little craft smoothly onto the beach, where its bow crunched against the sand and lurched to a halt.

In daylight, Rhiannon saw that a small headland extended out into the sea for a distance, shielding the cove from the gazes of anyone who might be watching from ships in the harbor; a thick tangle of exotic trees screened the cove from Sir Graham's house, and there was nobody here except a colorful parrot squawking from a nearby branch.

At night this had been a somewhat frightening place, the water deep and mysterious. Now, she could easily see the bottom, and the play of morning sunlight sparkling over the surface of the sea was soothing. Pretty.

Connor helped her out of the boat and pulled the little craft farther up onto the beach. She watched the play of strong, hard muscles in his arms as he worked, and the way his rich chestnut hair curled against the back of his neck beneath the brim of his straw hat. She wanted to touch him. To feel his arms around her, his lips against hers, and that delicious, intoxicating sensation of having him on, along-side, *inside* her, surrounding her with his strength and protection once again.

Yes, she wanted to touch him.

And, as he straightened up after beaching the boat, she did.

Just her fingers, reaching up to trace the hard bulge of his forearm, the crisp hairs there that lent roughness to the texture beneath her fingers.

He paused, and that slow, slightly lopsided, and alto-gether charming grin that did strange things to her insides curved one corner of his mouth.

"Well, now," he murmured softly.

She smiled.

He reached down and pulling off his shirt, balled and tossed it into the boat.

She pressed closer to him, shyly sliding her hand up past his elbow and to the rock-hard muscles of his upper arms. The base of his neck. The side of his jaw, slightly bris-tled beneath her palm, hard and scratchy and manly.

"You look like a pirate," she said.

"And you look delicious."

"Will you kiss me, Connor?"

"You have to tag me, first."

"What?"

He laughed, and moved backwards into the water until he was thigh-deep in the gently rolling surf.

"That's not fair."

"You want to learn how to swim, don't you?"

"Of course, but you have an advantage!"

She lunged forward, the water roiling around her knees and soaking Toby's cut-off pantaloons, but he just laughed and moved farther back.

"Connor!"

He stood there with arms crossed, waist-deep now, the gentle swells swirling around his navel. His smile grew.

"Ah, the water is nice," he mused. "You really should join me."

"Come back here!"

"No, you come and get me."

She waded farther out. He let himself fall backward until he was floating quite happily on his back, wiggling his toes at her as the waves moved past him and toward the beach.

Rhiannon waded farther. She could feel the water up around her rib cage now, her breasts. Her husband was tantalizingly out of reach, looking up, briefly, to check on her progress before folding his arms behind his head, gazing up at the cloudless blue sky and every so often, kicking a little to stay just out of reach.

Rhiannon was in up to her collarbone now; the waves were coming up to and lapping her throat, her chin, and suddenly a particularly large one lifted her straight up and off the bottom for a full second.

She stifled her cry of fear and surprise, her feet on the sea bottom once more. Connor eyed her from a few feet away, and turned agilely in the water until he was treading it.

"Feel the power of the sea?" he asked, knowing what had just happened.

"I feel it, and I'm frightened by it."

"There's no need to be frightened. It's a wonderful and magnificent thing, the sea, and you know I won't let anything happen to you."

Rhiannon stood there for another moment, rising up on her tiptoes to try to keep her chin above every swell that washed past on its way to shore.

Connor turned on his side and kicked a slow circle around her.

And behind him Rhiannon saw another wave coming, larger than the one that had stolen the bottom out from beneath her feet for that frightening moment, a wave that moved beneath him, lifted him up, and now came straight at her.

She felt its immense power, felt it shove her straight up with it. Her arms flashed out to retain her balance, the bottom dropped away from her feet and a moment later, Rhiannon was swimming.

Swimming.

"Keep your fingers together," Connor called, deliberately moving away but paralleling the beach. "Cup and push the water past you. Stiffen your legs. That's it. Yes! Yes, Rhiannon! You're doing it!"

And she was. She felt her fear suddenly become joy, and her joy become exhilaration, and then she was laughing as she paddled clumsily toward her husband.

"Trust the water, Rhiannon. Trust yourself. Feel it buoy you up, as salt water does, and stop stretching your neck up and out but just relax, let the water come up around your chin, your ears; you won't sink."

"Promise?" she gasped, breathlessly, as she paddled closer to him.

"I promise."

She swam to him. She swam with him. He taught her how to turn in the water, to flip over onto her back, her side, and back to her stomach again. She followed him out into the cove just a little farther, and as they swam slowly over a coral formation some four or five feet down, she tucked her chin and tried to see it.

"It's a beautiful world down there, Rhiannon."

"I wish I could see it."

"You can. Follow me."

"Underwater?"

"Yes."

"But how am I going to be able to see?"

"The same way you see on top of the water. By opening your eyes."

And then, before she could protest more, he took a breath and angling his body, dived beneath the surface.

Trust him.

Rhiannon took a deep breath, pinched her nose shut with two fingers, and ducked her head into the water; at first she was afraid to open her eyes but curiosity got the best of her, and when she did, she realized that she had entered a whole new world.

She let herself sink down, and holding her nose with one hand, letting her feet rest on the rounded surface of a huge chunk of coral that looked like a brain, realized that there was a beautiful yellow and blue fish swimming just inches from her nose.

It stared at her.

She stared at it.

And realizing she was getting short of breath, pushed herself to the surface.

Connor was standing only a few feet away, his grin about as broad as she had ever seen it.

"I am so proud of you," he said, and beyond his grin, beyond the way his eyes crinkled at the corners with a roguish merriment, she could see the heat building in his gaze and knew that he wanted her.

As she wanted him.

He moved closer to her, swam past her, and headed inshore.

She followed.

Well past the coral, he stood up in waist-deep surf, the water streaming down his chest and sparkling in the sun.

Rhiannon joined him.

He caught her as she moved close, pulling her wet body up against him, sliding his hands around the small of her back and pressing her hips against his own. Desire flared in her as she felt his arousal stabbing against her belly, and despite the lingering soreness between her thighs, she felt herself wanting him all over again.

His hips still against hers, his arms still around her lower back, he gazed down at her.

"I want you, dearest wife."

"Here?"

"Why not?"

"Because . . . someone might see?"

"They can't see what happens underwater," he said wickedly. He moved backward and as he did, his hands moved lower, curving over her bottom, squeezing her. She gasped and glanced nervously toward the beach, but he was right. They were alone. There was nobody there.

Considerate as always, he turned her so that the rising sun was behind her and not in her eyes; then, lowering his head, he kissed her.

His lips were wet and salty, hard, demanding, and hungry. Her breasts were crushed against his bare chest and her heartbeat began to bang out a frenzied beat as his tongue swept into her mouth and his hands drew her hips even closer, pressing them hard, hard into himself until she was grinding shamelessly against his thick and swollen member. She groaned deep in her throat as his hands moved lower, finding her cleft beneath the fabric of the old trousers, stroking it and causing her to catch her breath in surprise and wonder.

"You are a wicked man, Connor Merrick," she managed, pressing her forehead against his wet shoulder.

A gull winged past but he only laughed, found the buttons of her pantaloons, and in one quick move, had them unfastened and in the water around her knees.

"Connor, someone will see!" she squealed.

"Who?" He walked a step or two backward, allowing the rising water to shield them further, to shield what his fingers were doing beneath the surface to the soft, sensitive skin of her inner thighs now that he had full access to them, tracing up and down, coming a little closer to her slit with each upward pass.

"S-Sir Graham . . . someone in a boat . . . the—*oh!*—the fishes, oh, oh, please—"

He spread his fingers, forcing her to widen the stance of her legs, and there, deep underwater, he ran his hand back up her thigh. As she struggled to keep her feet, he played with her silken curls, teasing and touching her most sensitive parts until she was gasping, and then inserted a finger between the inner lips and pushed it deep inside her.

Rhiannon cried out and he quickly silenced her with his mouth, his fingers plunging further into her, beginning to stroke the innermost wall of her pelvis until she felt herself squirming, pleading, frenziedly biting at his mouth as he brought her closer and closer to release.

And then with his fingers still stroking deep inside her, he pressed his thumb against her swollen bud. Her knees buckled and with a cry she spasmed against his hand, and it was only the arm he had locked around her hips, and the hand that was bringing her to such sweet torment, that saved her from slipping beneath the surface and drowning right then and there.

She hung there, shaking and convulsing, and then he withdrew, waded farther out into the surf, turned her so that his own big body shielded her own from the beach and unbuttoning himself with one hand, allowed her to feel him.

He swelled against her, huge and hardened and completely filling her hand, and as he bent his head to kiss her once more, he put both hands beneath her, lifted her up with the help of each incoming wave, and planted her firmly atop himself.

"Oh . . . oh, Connor. . . ." She felt him sliding deep, deep, deep inside of her, touching areas inside of herself that she didn't know existed, and then he was lifting her up with strong hands and, to the rhythm of the incoming tide, he began to move inside of her.

Up and down, deeper and deeper until—

He suddenly clenched his teeth and tipped his head back, holding in his own hoarse cries as he spilt his seed deep within her and she climaxed once again, her body convulsing around his shaft. For a long moment they both stood there, he on shaky legs, she with hers wrapped around the back of his thighs, her cheek pressed against his chest and his heartbeat thundering like a racehorse beneath her ear.

CHAPTER 18

"Don't you two have a honeymoon to be off on?" asked Alannah, who looked up as Connor strode boldly onto Sir Graham's verandah, his new wife in tow.

"We're hungry."

"And soaked. Did you two fall off the boat or something?" She peered at Rhiannon in horror. "What on earth are you *wearing*, Rhiannon?"

"Connor gave me a swimming lesson," she chirped, and slid a coy, worshipful gaze toward her grinning husband. "It was fun."

Maeve was sitting in a nearby chair. "Honestly, Connor, why you didn't rent a room at one of the hotels in Bridgetown is beyond me." She eyed her brother with disapproval. "You took her to *Kestrel* for your wedding night, didn't you?"

"It was romantic," Rhiannon piped up, coming to Connor's defense. "The beauty of the night beneath the stars, the ship all to ourselves. . . ."

"Bah," Maeve spat. She got up, her hand going to her belly and rubbing it absently. "He'll be taking you privateering, next. Damn, how I wish this baby would come. He's kicking a hole through my blasted gut."

"Must've inherited the Merrick restlessness," Connor said. "Is there any food around here, Sis?"

"Go pillage the kitchen. But Mother's baking. Don't say I didn't warn you."

Connor visibly paled. "God help us."

"Aye, isn't that the truth."

"She's not expecting us to *eat* it, I hope."

Rhiannon glanced from one sibling to the other. "Why such trepidation?"

Maeve was shaking her head. "We don't eat Mother's cooking."

"Hazardous to one's health, it is."

"I should go change, first," Rhiannon said. "I don't want to face your mother wearing boy's clothing and looking like a drowned rat."

"You're fine just the way you are," Maeve said off-handedly.

"And I'm starving," Connor said. "Let's go see what's in the kitchen."

The smell of something burning grew stronger as they moved toward the back of the house, and by the time they entered the kitchen, a thick haze of smoke was wafting through the open door. Inside, they found Ned hastily fanning the smoke to try and chase it out the windows, and his grandmother at the hearth, struggling to close the great bake oven set into the bricks and cursing like a seasoned pirate while more smoke roiled out and around her.

"Mother, *what* are you doing?" Rushing forward, Connor gently pulled his petite mother out of harm's way and slammed the iron door shut with a poker. "Honestly, you're going to burn down the house."

Grinning happily, she straightened up and passed the back of one hand across her soot-stained forehead. "Ned and I are makin' molasses cookies."

"Making them, or burning them?"

"Oh, you mean the smoke? That ain't from the cookies. We tried to make a tart earlier, and I think I put too much fruit in it. It overflowed and got into the oven and now it's the spill that's burnin'."

"So where's the tart? I'm starving."

"On the work table there."

Connor glanced in the direction his mother indicated. Something unrecognizable sat smoking in a deep pan, with a blackened top that might once have been a pastry crust.

He sighed. "So where are the cookies?"

"Still in the oven."

"Mother, they're going to taste like smoke. You have to take them out."

"Now Connor, don't you be telling me how to cook. I've been doin' it all my life."

"Aye, and poisoning people the whole time through," he said. "Why don't you and Rhiannon go have a cup of tea and Ned and I will finish up here?"

"I'm trying to be a good grandmother, Connor. Grandmothers make cookies with their grandchildren!"

"You *are* a good grandmother. Isn't she, Ned?"

The boy, who'd been watching this exchange with uncertainty, nodded. "The *best*!"

"Well, I don't know about that," Mira said. "I burned my finger on that tray earlier and I'm afraid I taught Ned a new curse word."

"Oh, no, I already knew that one from my mother," Ned assured her. "But if you have any other curse words that a good sailor should know, Grandma, I would be in your debt if you would teach them to me. See, Uncle Connor? She's a wonderful grandmother!"

"And she's a wonderful mother, too," Connor added, gently guiding Mira toward the door. "But there's a time and place for everything and your place, Mother, is not the kitchen. In fact, why don't you practice being a good mother-*in-law* and go help Rhiannon find some dry clothes? I believe her trunk is still upstairs in her old room."

"Speaking of that trunk, we should probably have it brought to *Kestrel*," Rhiannon said.

"No, I think it should stay here."

"Why?"

"Because when I head off to work, you'll be staying here, that's why."

Rhiannon frowned. "Work?"

Ned piped up. "Uncle Con, are you going privateering?"

"This is a discussion best had at another time," Connor said, noting his wife's sudden frown. "Mother? *Please*?"

Rhiannon was still thinking about Connor's cryptic words when his mother turned to her and for the first time, noticed what she was wearing. But instead of shocked disapproval, the other woman only laughed. "Why, look at you! Are those Toby's clothes? Do you know, I spent months foolin' your father-in-law back in the Revolution, dressed as a boy and pretending to be a gunner on his ship. Time of my life, it was." She turned to her son as he wrapped a heavy cloth around his hand and, choking on smoke, pulled a tray of blackened discs out of the oven. "Connor, I'll leave you and Ned to finish up here, and Rhiannon and I will see you out on the verandah. Don't forget the cookies!"

Connor set the tray on the wooden worktable and gazed ruefully down at the ruined treats. "I think, Mother, that you already have."

Like all large houses belonging to people of means, the Falconer mansion had a sizeable staff. It was a good thing, too, because when Rhiannon, now dressed in a pale rose gown, reappeared on the verandah where Mira, Maeve, and Alannah were already gathered, she noticed that food had been put out—and it wasn't burned tart or blackened molasses cookies.

There was tea and raisin cakes and papaya laid out in a pretty dish. Banana muffins. And some sort of fruit punch in a large glass pitcher.

Connor, carrying a tray of blackened cookies with young Ned trailing in his wake, joined them a moment later. He set the tray down on a little table near the railing and looked out over the bay, his fingers restlessly tapping a rhythm against the wrought ironwork. "Where is Da? And Sir Graham?"

Maeve was eying the tray with a dubious eye. "Gone to look at the new statue in town of Lord Nelson. Then off to talk ships, I'd imagine."

"Come here, Ned. We have gulls to feed."

The boy joined his uncle at the railing while Maeve poured tea for everyone. Rhiannon had just gotten comfortable when there was a small commotion outside the door and the admiral, accompanied by his flag captain, Liam Doherty, and Connor's father—wearing a black, old-fashioned tricorne hat—came through the door.

"What's all that smoke?" Captain Lord asked, frowning and looking around in alarm.

Maeve grinned. "Mother's been baking."

"Burnin', more like," said Liam, pulling out a chair.

"Oh, stow it, would you, Liam? What kind of grandmother would I be if I didn't bake cookies with my grandchildren?"

"A merciful one."

"Grandmothers are *supposed* to bake cookies!"

"Aye, bake 'em, not burn 'em." Liam grinned as Mira's eyes began to flash. "God almighty, ye'd be better off takin' the lad out fishing. Or sailing. Or teaching him how t' fire a gun. Anything but the kitchen."

Mira pursed her lips and folded her arms across her chest, and Sir Graham, watching this exchange, wisely intervened by picking up a banana muffin from the blue-and-white plate that sat in the center of the table.

"Well, they look perfectly fine to me," he said, and took a bite.

"Your cook made the muffins and cakes," Mira said. "Ned and I made molasses cookies. But I'm afraid you missed them."

Rhiannon noted Brendan's swift expression of relief before he caught her eye and smiled. He knew, then, what they were all thinking. And he was silently laughing.

"Not all of them," Ned said from the railing, where he and his uncle Connor were busily tossing blackened pellets up into the sky; as they did so, there was a sudden melee of sound and several gulls came swooping down, screaming and trying to pluck the bits out of the air.

"He missed," Ned said, dejectedly, as the burnt bit of molasses cookie fell to the ground below.

"No he didn't," Connor whispered, with a sideways glance at his mother. "He just knows better."

The newcomers seated themselves. Connor came to stand behind Rhiannon's chair, his fingers resting atop her shoulder and gently stroking it through the thin muslin of her gown. She reached up and touched his hand, resisting the urge to lean her cheek into it.

Behind them, Ned pitched another blackened chunk of molasses cookie into the air.

The gulls screamed and flew away without touching it.

Across the table, Rhiannon saw that her father-in-law's lips were twitching uncontrollably.

"I see you haven't gotten rid of that silly hat, Da," Connor said, leaning over Rhiannon to pluck a piece of fruit from the plate.

Brendan made an expression of mock hurt. "I like my old hat!"

"*Old* being the definitive word."

"I think it makes him look quite young and handsome," Mira put in, with a fond look at her husband.

Brendan laughed, and his amber eyes were warm as his grandson came over and taking the tricorne, put it on his own head. "Is this really the hat you wore during the American War of Independence, Grandpa?"

"Aye, laddie, it sure is. But it looks better on you, I think, than it does on me."

Rhiannon watched the two, and the love that they had for each other, and felt her heart warm inside. It was good to be part of such a warm and loving family.

"And what do you think, Rhiannon?" Brendan asked. "Too old-fashioned? Or will Ned and I here set a new style?"

"I think we should find another one—" she glanced slyly at her husband, enjoying the good-natured banter— "just for Connor."

Her husband guffawed, and everyone laughed.

"So what's going on in town?" Connor asked, plucking a muffin from the dish on the table and biting into it. "Any news worth knowing about?"

Sir Graham leaned back in his chair and let Ned climb up into his lap. "Those pirates who'd set upon the merchantman that Alannah and Rhiannon were on have attacked a Dutch ship," he said tersely. "Killed the master and most of the crew, and have stolen the ship for themselves."

"They were a bloodthirsty lot," Connor said, taking another bite.

"Easier to deal with than the damned French, but they move from island to island and are hard to pin down. And now they've armed the damned thing. I suppose I'll have to send a frigate to subdue them."

"What sort of ship did they steal?"

"A large brigantine. Nothing a frigate can't handle but against anything smaller, she'll be formidable."

"It's the second ship they've taken this week," said Captain Lord, helping himself to a raisin cake. "I'd be happy to take *Orion* out and put an end to them, sir."

"Thank you, Delmore, but I'll send Captain Ponsonby in the *Athena*," the admiral said. "She's a frigate, with better maneuverability and inshore capabilities than a ship of the line."

"As you wish, Sir Graham."

Connor finished his muffin, went to the railing and looked out over the bay, his fingers restlessly tapping against the wrought ironwork. "Well, *Kestrel*'s more nimble and maneuverable than either of them, and I'm heading out tomorrow. I'm sure I can make short work of them in my . . . travels."

"Where are you going?" Sir Graham asked, frowning.

Connor grinned. "Off on my honeymoon cruise."

"Like hell you are." Sir Graham reached for a raisin cake. "Why don't you tell me what you're really planning?"

"Sorry, Admiral, but I don't report to you."

Brendan sighed. "Connor, lad, don't be rude."

"Rude? Who's being rude?" Connor said hotly, and Rhiannon saw the hard glitter that had come into his eyes. "I don't owe explanations to anyone. Where I'm going and what I'm doing is nobody's business but mine and my crew's."

"And *mine*, as long as you're sheltering in my harbor," the admiral snapped.

"I won't *be* sheltering in your harbor after tomorrow. I know enough to leave when my welcome's worn out."

"Connor, please—" Brendan said again.

"He knows damned well where I'm going. It's no secret there's a convoy gathering in St. Vincent and preparing to make sail for London. Do you want me to say it, Sir Graham? Oh, but wait. You don't want me privateering in *your* waters. Well, you have your job to do, and I have mine, and it's time for me to go back to work. Come, Rhiannon. I have no further business here."

Rhiannon, confused, embarrassed, and uncomfortable, sat unmoving.

"Rhiannon?"

She was aware of everyone's eyes upon her. "Actually, Connor . . . I would like to stay and have something to eat." She looked up at him, pleading with her eyes for him to quiet down. "And so, I think, would you."

In the sudden silence that followed her remark, one could have heard the waves slapping on the beach a half mile away.

Connor simply stared at her. A muscle twitched in the side of his jaw.

"You want to stay here."

She quietly met his angry green glare. "I would."

"Very well then," he said coldly, and turning on his heel, stalked toward the door.

"What an arse," Maeve muttered, watching her brother go. "Can't sit still for a damned minute."

But Rhiannon, torn between loyalty to her husband and trying to smooth things between him and their hosts, felt a sudden desperation. She pushed her chair back. "I must go to him."

"He'll cool off," Maeve said, offhandedly.

But her husband had his pride, and even though privately Rhiannon was inclined to agree with Brendan—that Connor was indeed being rude to their host—there was something to be said for the fact that Sir Graham, perhaps a little too accustomed to the position of authority he enjoyed, was patronizing her husband at best and treating him like a child at worst. It really *was* no business of Sir Graham's, what Connor did, or where he went.

Could she really blame her husband for his reaction?

She caught up to him at the bottom of the stairs. "Connor, wait."

He stopped, his back stiff with anger and his straw hat, still in his hand, crunched in his fist. "So now you know the truth about my family," he said, turning around. "We fight. A lot. I'm sorry you had to find that out so soon into our newly wedded bliss."

"Sir Graham was wrong to say what he did."

"Well, I'm glad you're on my side, after all. But I'm still leaving."

"And *you* were wrong to bait him."

He began to stalk toward the door.

"Connor, I'm your wife. You can't just walk out on me."

He paused again, and she saw his shoulders rise on a long, steadying breath before he turned around. She expected to see anger in his eyes, hardness in the set of his jaw, and she wasn't disappointed. He walked back to her, standing there with as much stubborn purpose as he himself was showing.

"I knew you were going to give me trouble," he said, but the heat had left his voice and the words were said with a certain fondness.

"And I knew you wouldn't be able to sit still for one moment."

"You're right. I can't. There's a convoy to catch."

"Don't go."

"I must."

"Then let me get my trunk."

"No." He caught her hand. "You'll stay here, Rhiannon."

"Where are you going?"

He set his jaw and began to turn away. "Now you sound like my brother-in-law."

"Connor, I know I angered you back there and I'm sorry for that, but—"

"You don't understand. I am going to work, Rhiannon, like all good husbands must do in order to support their families. And my work requires chasing, capturing, and burning British shipping as a private individual in service to and under the written permission of my country. That is my work. And where I conduct my work, on the gun deck of a well-armed warship, is no place for a gently-bred young woman."

"Your mother used to go aboard *Kestrel* when she was your father's ship!"

"My mother was a crack gunner, a fearless sailor, and as much a man as anyone in my father's crew. She could shoot and swear with the best of them." He reached out and tenderly smoothed a lock of hair from Rhiannon's forehead, the anger going out of him as swiftly as it had appeared. "But you, Rhiannon . . . you don't know how to shoot a cannon, you can't go aloft, there is no place for you on a warship. You'd be a distraction at best and in danger of being hurt at worst. No, you are far safer, here."

"You would just go off and leave me? Dump me here on your family like so much refuse?"

He turned and began to walk away. "It is for your own good."

"Connor!"

"And, mine."

He opened the door, walked out into the dazzling sunshine, and was gone.

CHAPTER 19

Mira found her sobbing in her room an hour later.

"Rhiannon! What the blazes are you wailin' about?" she asked half jokingly, but the very fact that she came into the room and sat down on the bed beside her daughter-in-law showed the depth of her compassion.

"Connor . . . he's angry with me. I was so embarrassed by the exchange at the table that I didn't know what to say or do, and both he and Sir Graham have been sniping at each other for the past three weeks. I only wanted them to stop."

"Sir Graham's short-tempered because he's worried about Maeve and the coming baby, Maeve's short-tempered because she doesn't feel well and is worried about Connor, and Connor's worried about proving to himself and to the rest of us that he's his father's equal. It's one hell of a mess, ain't it?"

"Proving that he's father's equal? But why? He has nothing to prove, he's wonderful just the way he is!"

Mira let out a heavy sigh. "Connor was raised on tales of Brendan's heroism and derring-do during the last war," she said. "When other children wanted to hear fairy tales at bedtime, Connor wanted to hear about his *Dadaí's* exploits as *Kestrel's* captain. If you hear enough stories about a person, I suppose that eventually that person becomes larger than life. People like Connor's father cast a tall shadow and are a tough act to follow."

"So Connor idolizes his father?"

"Aye, always has, and I suppose I should never have told him all those stories because now he'll do anything to prove that he's his Da's equal and Maeve's afraid he's gonna die trying."

"But why tell him such stories if they weren't true?"

"Who ever said they weren't?" Mira said, grinning. "They were true enough. Every single one of 'em. And I was there to vouch for that fact!"

Rhiannon just drew her feet up to her chest and wrapped a blanket around them, resting her chin on her knees and staring morosely out the window.

"Ye know," Mira said, crossing her arms over her chest, "if I were in your shoes I wouldn't just sit here and let him go."

"He already told me he doesn't want me aboard *Kestrel*."

"That's bullsh— I mean, that's ridiculous. Brendan didn't want me aboard her either, but that didn't stop me from going." Mira's eyes began to sparkle with mischief. "Come on. Let's go find Toby before the tide turns and that stubborn son of mine takes *Kestrel* to sea with it."

"Toby?"

"Aye. If he had one set of clothes that fit you, he'll have another. When that ship sails, you'll be on her."

"Connor will forbid it."

"Connor ain't gonna know."

Tarnal hell, Connor thought. The wind was out of the west, the tide was going in, and *Kestrel* wouldn't be going anywhere until one, the other, or both changed.

Jacques met him as he stalked moodily toward the hatch. "Where's *madam*?"

"On land. Where she belongs."

Jacques couldn't prevent a smirk. "Trouble in paradise already, eh, *Capitaine*?"

Connor bit back his reply and strode past Nathan, who was standing nearby coiling a line.

His cousin raised an eyebrow in silent question.

"We're weighing as soon as the wind changes," Connor snapped by way of explanation. "I'm fed up with Sir Graham's dictates. Does he think I'm one of his bloody captains? I'm an American for God's sake. He may be my brother-in-law, but we're on different sides of this war and I don't answer to him or anyone else in his Majesty's Royal bloody Navy!"

Nathan and Jacques exchanged glances.

"Can't sail without a full crew," Nathan said, spitting over the side.

"Aye, Captain," added Boggs, standing nearby. "Half the company's still ashore in Bridgetown."

"Then you can take one of the boats and go fetch everyone back," Connor snapped irritably. "There's a convoy leaving St. Vincent as we speak and as soon as that tide turns we're weighing anchor and going after it."

He stalked off toward the aft hatch.

"What about *Madame*?" Jacques asked. "Shouldn't we bring her back, too?"

"There's no place on a warship for a woman. I have trouble enough with distractions, I don't need another one."

"But *Capitaine*, you only just tied the knot—"

Connor turned around, his volatile temper close to blowing.

"Women need to feel treasured," Jacques said, making an expansive gesture with his hands. "How is *Madame* going to know how much you love her if you sail off and leave her?"

"Aye, Jacques has a point," Nathan grunted.

"You need to woo her, say the things that make her feel beautiful inside," Jacques continued, ignoring his captain's hardening gaze. "I know women, and I know what they like. Have you told *Madame* how lovely her lips are? How beautiful her mouth?"

Connor, his fists clenched, began to stalk back toward Jacques when suddenly Bobbs's voice cut through the buzzing sound in his head.

"Sir! Boat approaching from starboard. It's your mother."

Connor paused and looked over his shoulder. Sure enough, there was a boat heading toward them and in it were his mother, Toby, and several of *Kestrel*'s missing sailors.

"Well, how provident," he muttered, pasting a smile on his face for the benefit of his mother. "That's five, six, seven crewmembers you won't have to chase up when you head into town."

"Your mother's coming with us?" Jacques asked, stupidly.

"Hmph," Connor said. "I wish."

"You just said a warship's no place for a woman, *Capitaine*."

"Go to hell and rot, Jacques."

Moments later Mira Merrick, a basket in hand, was scrambling agilely up over the rail with Toby right behind her. In the boat were several other seamen who were already beginning to follow them up and aboard.

"Connor, dearest, I couldn't let you go sailing off without proper sustenance," his mother said, sliding her arm around his waist and steering him forward. "There was a second tray of molasses cookies that I'd forgotten to put into the oven. I brought them for you."

Inwardly, Connor groaned, wondering how many fishes would be poisoned when the cookies were pitched over the side—as they inevitably would be. "Thank you, Mother."

"Oh, don't thank me. It was Rhiannon's idea."

"Sweet revenge," he muttered.

"What was that?" she asked, glancing over her shoulder as she continued to walk forward with him.

"Nothing, Mother. Nothing a' t'all."

"I know I ain't much of a cook, but you're my darling son and the idea of you goin' off to fight the Brits without something good and solid in your stomach just fills my heart with dread."

"You are very kind, Mother. Perhaps you'd like to join us? I aim to go after that convoy, and Sir Graham can be damned."

"You know I can't, Connor."

"You're the best gunner *Kestrel* ever had."

"Your father wouldn't like it."

"Da is going soft."

"No he's not, he just wants to keep the peace." They had walked as far forward as they could get and there, Mira leaned out over the bow to peer down at the little hawk that was *Kestrel*'s figurehead. "Oh, good. I wanted to make sure it was just as I remembered it," she said.

"Why wouldn't it be?"

"Oh, you know. Time takes its toll on things. . . ."

Mother was behaving oddly, Connor thought. Very oddly. He turned and looked aft but there was nothing amiss, and the last of the sailors who had come with her was already climbing aboard.

"Well here you go, darling," Mira said, straightening up and handing him the basket. "You behave yourself and try not to make your brother-in-law too mad. And mind that you're not gone too long. I don't think Maeve's time is far off and you really oughtta be there for the baby's birth."

"Yes, Mother."

"Not to mention workin' on giving me another grandchild."

He actually blushed. "*Yes*, Mother."

She grinned, the endearing little wrinkles fanning out from either side of her tilted-up nose, and stretching on tiptoe, kissed him on the cheek.

Moments later she was gone, rowing the boat back to shore all by herself, the afternoon sunlight sparkling like amber diamonds in the craft's wake.

CHAPTER 20

"Follow me and be quick about it," Toby whispered, seizing Rhiannon's wrist and hustling her toward the hatch while his Aunt Mira kept Connor busy up in *Kestrel*'s bow. "We don't have much time."

"Take her to your cabin," One-Eye said quickly, moving to stand in front of Rhiannon in case his captain happened to turn around. "He won't think to look there."

"No, take her to Nathan's, it's got a better bunk," Jacques said.

"Christ," Nathan swore, and headed aft.

Well, so much for loyalty to their fearless leader, Rhiannon thought as Toby, Jacques and One-Eye, followed by several others, one of whom had her trunk, all of whom had breath that stank of rum, hustled her quickly down the hatch and forward. Above, she heard footsteps as Connor and his devious little mother, God bless her scheming heart, walked aft and Mira prepared to leave. "Stay outta sight until you're well out to sea," Mira had advised. "Once you've got Barbados well behind you, there's no more need to hide yourself. And don't. I want more grandchildren, and I ain't gonna get 'em if you're hidin' somewhere my son won't find you."

It was a good thing Rhiannon hadn't been eating something at that remark because surely she would have choked.

Now, led through the gloom by Toby and surrounded by grinning, laughing tars who seemed to think it quite funny to put something over on their captain, she was hustled into Nathan's cabin, offered a mug of rum, and then left to her own devices.

It was a tiny cabin with little place to stand, and only a bunk built into the curve of the hull. Sighing, Rhiannon sat down on it, put her feet on her trunk, and contemplated what she was going to say to Connor when she revealed herself.

Oh, he was going to be angry.

Too angry, probably, to continue work on making this grandchild that his mother so desperately wanted.

Beneath her the schooner rocked gently, and the small tin lantern that swung from the overhead beam cast a dim light over Nathan's cabin.

There was nothing to do but wait.

Wait for the hours to pass and the wind to change.

Wait for the sounds of the ship getting underway.

Wait for Toby to come and collect her.

Yawning, Rhiannon swung her feet up onto the bunk, put her head down on the pillow and closed her eyes. Moments later, she was fast asleep.

"Anchor's hove short, sir."

A crew stood at *Kestrel*'s windlass, bare-backed and sweating even though the sun was well on its way down.

"Get the jib and mainsail up," Connor said. "I want to be out of here before any of our Royal Navy friends know what we're about."

"Expecting trouble?" Nathan asked, heading toward the helm.

"I don't know what to expect, which is why I'd like to be ready for anything."

Moments later came the thunder of canvas as the trade winds caught the rising jib and *Kestrel* began to strain eagerly at her anchor.

"What's that convoy carrying?" Boggs asked. "Better be worth leaving that wench I found in Bridgetown."

"Damned if I know, but the pickings ought to be good," Connor said, watching as the great mainsail began to rise, the mast hoops crawling skyward up the mast with it. He was the picture of relaxed command, but inside his heart was churning as he remembered Rhiannon's face back there in Sir Graham's hall, her look of betrayal and abandonment.

Something twisted in his gut.

You should go back and get her, his conscience said. *Only married one day and you're already deserting her.*

"Oh, stow it," he snapped.

"What?"

"Nothing, Bobbs, just talking to myself. Where's that chart of the harbor?"

"Here, sir." It was One-Eye, handing him the map of Carlisle Bay and the surrounding coast.

Connor glanced at it, made sense of about half of it, and having gone through the motions, returned it to One-Eye.

"Give it to Nathan, he's got the helm," he said, and went to supervise the anchor's retrieval.

Some captain you make, his conscience continued. *But you have them all fooled, don't you? They all think you can walk on water, just because you're lucky. How confident do you think they'd be in you if they knew you can't even read that damned chart?*

"Haul! Haul! Haul!" came the cry, and the mainsail finally reached its full height and was sheeted home.

"Get the hook in," Connor ordered.

"Aye, sir."

The men at the windlass put their backs into it and moments later, the anchor came surging up from the bottom, swinging from the cathead and dripping a torrent of water back into the sea. The schooner began to drift, and her motion changed subtly beneath Connor's feet. The harbor was a deep mauve and purple shot through with orange from the sunset, and already, the riding lights of Sir Graham's flagship and several warships in the harbor were starting to glitter across the water.

Near the tiller Nathan had the chart open and was already plotting a course.

"Wind's backed to the northwest, Con," he said. "We ought to have a straight shot out of the bay and down around the southern coast of the island, and then it'll be clear sailing all the way into the shipping lanes."

"Happy hunting," Connor said, grinning.

"Happy hunting, indeed," Nathan agreed, and as the sun finally settled beneath the haze far off to the west, and the last of the color leached from the sky and the surface of the sea, the Yankee privateer showed her heels to Carlisle Bay, Bridgetown, and Barbados itself.

"Rhiannon! Open up. It's me, Toby."

It was some time before Rhiannon, curled up on Nathan's bunk and deeply asleep, realized that the knocking sound wasn't part of a dream, but reality.

She opened her eyes and saw the lantern swinging in the gloom.

"Rhiannon!" The knocking on the cabin door grew more persistent. "Are you all right in there?"

She got up, knuckled her eyes, and opened the door.

"I'm sorry," the boy said, blushing so hard that his freckles disappeared into the sudden profusion of color in his cheeks. "I didn't know you were sleeping."

"What time is it?"

"Near dawn. Barbados is twenty miles astern of us. Too late to turn back."

"Good."

"Are you ready to face the music?"

Rhiannon eyed the cabin. She wished there was a chamber pot, but that was something she'd probably have to find elsewhere. Heaven knew she couldn't do what the men did when it came to relieving herself.

Toby saw her predicament and his blush became downright crimson. "Do you, um . . . need an, um . . . "

"That would be nice," she said, blushing herself, and moments later he reappeared with what she needed. She disappeared back in the tiny cabin and wondered how on earth Mira Merrick had managed on a ship full of men, and determined to ask her when she next saw her.

She finished her ablutions, picked up the round hat that Mira had found for her and, cinching the rope belt around her waist a little tighter in order to hold up Toby's trousers, followed the youth topside.

Far beyond the long, plunging jib-boom, dawn was breaking and glowing gold against thin bands of cloud that sat poised on the horizon. Above, *Kestrel*'s pennants snapped crisply in the wind, and her great foresail and mainsail glowed with the colors of dawn. The sea hissed along her side as she met each long ocean swell with her starboard shoulder and Rhiannon, standing barefoot on a deck that felt damp and sticky with salt, inhaled deeply of the fresh sea air as the water around her turned a deep, vibrant azure.

From somewhere forward, the smells of cooking were already coming from the galley.

"Is he up yet?" she whispered, looking aft toward the tiller.

"Not yet, but that doesn't mean he's sleeping. If Connor gets four hours of rest a night, it's a rarity."

Rhiannon's eyes sparkled with sudden mischief. "He's going to be furious to find me aboard."

"Probably."

"Good morning, ma'm," said Nathan, with a short bow. "You'll have the devil to pay for this stunt."

"So I'm told."

"Here, have some breakfast," One-Eye said, thrusting a bowl of gray oatmeal into her hands.

Rhiannon looked up. The sunrise was strengthening against the pennant that flew from *Kestrel*'s foremast and was now glowing against the topgallant yard . . . that lofty sail, itself.

"What a beautiful sight," she said, spooning the gluey mixture into her mouth.

"The sunrise is even prettier up there," Nathan said, tipping back his tawny head to gaze aloft. "I'll take you up if you want to watch it."

Rhiannon felt the bottom drop out of her stomach and her palms were suddenly cold and sweaty. Her appetite gone, she handed the bowl back to One-Eye. "Thank you, Nathan, but I'm terrified of heights."

"Captain's coming," Bobbs announced, looking aft.

Rhiannon drew herself up and swallowed hard. Sure enough, her husband was coming up from below, the early sunlight glinting against his mahogany curls. He cut a dashing figure. He had foregone the straw hat and was dressed in the double-breasted blue pea coat that Rhiannon had first seen him in, a black kerchief knotted carelessly around his neck and his trousers, cut from a rough fabric that looked like sailcloth, hacked off just below the knee. As usual, he was barefoot.

"Top of the morning to you, lads," he said, glancing at the compass and then aloft.

"Same to you, Captain."

"Anything show up yet on the horizon?"

"Just a few clouds, sir."

Kestrel's captain took a spyglass from the rack, lifted it to his eye, and trained it on the eastern horizon. He was unaware that his wife stood a few feet away, admiring how handsome his shoulders were in the snug-fitting coat and wondering how long it would take for him to notice her. Around her, the men were snickering, elbowing each other, and whispering loudly.

"What is so funny?" Connor asked, without turning around.

"Nothing, sir."

"Aye, nothing a' t'all!"

Connor snapped the glass shut, replaced it in the rack, and swung to face them all. His sharp green gaze moved from Nathan standing stoically at the tiller, to One-Eye, to Bobbs, to Jacques, to Toby . . .

And to Rhiannon.

"What the *hell*?"

"Hello, Connor," she said, in a voice that was meant to be cheerful and confident but came out sounding like a squeak from a choking mouse.

"*Rhiannon?!*"

"Yes?"

Frowning, he came up to her, yanked off her round hat, and stood staring as her bright red-gold hair spilled down around her shoulders and tumbled down her back.

"How the devil did you get aboard?!"

"The same way as everyone else, I imagine. I took a boat, then came up the side."

"You know very well what I mean! Who is responsible for this?"

"I am."

"*Who brought you aboard?!*"

Rhiannon stood her ground. Beside her, Toby's brown eyes had widened behind his spectacles and he was starting to look nervous. At the tiller, Nathan peered up at the great mainsail and whistling, made a small adjustment to the schooner's course, and the crew began to look worried.

"A woman's place is with her husband," Rhiannon said, refusing to back down to Connor's glowering stare.

"*Your* place is safe in Bridgetown with my sister and my family!"

"No, it is with you."

Jacques raised his hand to the side of his mouth and as an aside to Bobbs, said, "*Madame* has spirit."

"Stow it!" Connor roared.

"Connor, I—"

"You didn't just row a boat out to *Kestrel* and come aboard all by yourself, Rhiannon. Who sneaked you aboard?"

She just smiled.

"*Who?!*"

"Your mother."

"My moth—" He paused in mid-sentence, unsurprised by this revelation but rendered temporarily speechless all the same.

"I know women," Jacques said importantly. "Once they get to plotting, we men just don't have a chance."

"I said stow it!"

"Aye, Captain. But if you ask me, the best way to a woman's heart is—"

Connor rounded on the Frenchman and at that moment, a cry drifted down from above.

"Sail ho, fine off the larboard bow!"

Connor threw one last, frustrated look at Rhiannon that promised full retribution later, stalked to the rack and grabbing a glass, went to the rail.

And just like that, Rhiannon found herself forgotten as the lookout shouted, "On deck! Another sail, far to the north'ard . . . and another!"

Rhiannon was forgotten, all right.

They had found the convoy.

CHAPTER 21

"Your orders, sir?"

Connor studied the sails of the distant convoy, so far off that he could barely pick out their royals and t'gallants from the haze and wispy clouds that lay heavily on the horizon.

His mind awhirl, he steadied himself against the rail and willed himself to take one thing at a time in order to try and reduce the confusion of thinking of too many things at once. Rhiannon. His mother's mischief. The convoy. *Damn.* He was keenly aware of Rhiannon standing somewhere nearby, and he still didn't know whether to be enraged or excited about her presence on the ship. She was one matter that must be dealt with. Then there was the convoy, beating to the north and presenting an opportunity that no self-respecting Yankee privateer could pass up—even if they *were* in Sir Graham's waters. Another matter that must be dealt with.

He took a deep breath. *First things first.*

"Run up British colors," he said. "They don't have to know who we are. *Yet.*"

Moments later the Union Jack streamed from *Kestrel's* gaff, and Connor hoped the ruse would fool not only the convoy so that he could get in close, but the Royal Navy warships that would surely be guarding the long line of ships itself. A thrum of excitement began to course through his blood and he felt suddenly unfettered, excited, and *alive*.

All but rubbing his hands together in anticipation, he strode confidently to the helm. There, Nathan had the tiller.

"If we keep on this course we'll close with them by nightfall," he said, shading his eyes against the late afternoon sun. "Easy pickings, after that."

Rhiannon was standing there too. "What are you planning on doing?"

Second things second. Time to deal with his errant wife.

"Rhiannon, go below and wait for me in my cabin."

"Why?"

"This is a warship. I don't want you on deck."

"You just said yourself that we won't close with that convoy until nightfall. So what is the hurry?"

Nathan cleared his throat and pretended to be engrossed in studying the binnacle.

The merriment faded from Connor's eyes. "Don't question me, Rhiannon. I told you to go below."

"Yes, but why?"

Because I can't concentrate on two things at once and you're a distraction, a huge distraction, that's why.

Nathan didn't look up. "Best not to question the captain's orders," he said matter-of-factly. "Always leads to trouble."

"He's not my captain, he's my husband."

"Then you have twice as much reason to obey me," Connor said impatiently, taking her hand and steering her toward the hatch. There, out of earshot of his men, she stopped and planted her feet.

"*Obey* you?"

"How quickly you forget your marriage vows, my dear."

"Marriage vows that were penned, no doubt, by a man. I'm staying here."

"You can't. I need to *think*, and I can't think if you're here distracting me."

"Distracting you from what? Recklessly attacking an entire convoy? You're insane!"

"And about to become very rich."

"I'm worried about you! This is madness!"

"For heaven's sake, Rhiannon, I'm under license from my country to attack, seize, harass, and make prizes of enemy shipping. That's what a privateer does. At the moment, we're at war with Britain and that's a British convoy. I'd be insane *not* to attack it."

"Flying the Union Jack is dishonest."

"It's the done thing. You want me to hoist the Stars and Stripes and go sashaying down on them like I've been invited to tea?"

"At least that would be honorable."

Connor, fighting a losing war with his temper, raked a hand through his tousled curls. At the tiller, Nathan was trying hard not to smirk. Connor could feel the familiar confused buzzing starting up in his head.

"Deck there!" came the cry from high above.

"Report!"

"Three more ships now, Captain. Maybe four. One looks to be a frigate."

First things first. Leaving Rhiannon standing there with stormy eyes, Connor hooked a hand in the shrouds, stepped up on the rail, and began to climb aloft.

He needed a clear head.

And she could never follow him there.

As *Kestrel* moved steadily toward the convoy that was now fully visible to the north, Connor came back down on deck, ordered the gun ports closed and the crew to lie low. For some time the frigate, capable of blasting them to kindling wood if her commander so chose, stayed close to the merchant ships like a shepherd guarding its sheep. Then, late in the afternoon, she wore ship and came storming down on them.

"Got our papers in order, Nathan?" Connor asked, grinning.

"Aye, sir. The British ones."

"Good. Toby, lad! Send most of the crew below. If that frigate yonder sees so many in our company, they'll know us for what we are. Especially with *Kestrel*'s design."

Nathan scratched absently at the light brown stubble on his jaw. "What about the missus, Con?"

"Yes, Captain? What about me?"

Connor turned and found his wife leaning against one of the schooner's guns, her arms crossed over her chest and her smile one of false sweetness. Oh, he couldn't wait to get his hands around his mother's neck for sneaking Rhiannon aboard. This was unacceptable. Totally, outrageously, unacceptable.

"Are you going to give me trouble, Rhiannon?"

"Already has, by the look of it," Nathan mused.

"You can stay on deck unless things get hot. But if I say go below you'll go, even if I have to bodily carry you myself."

The frigate, heeled over with the sea foaming at her lee bows, was growing closer.

Connor watched its approach and bit off a hangnail. "They'll be putting a shot across our bows right about—"

Boom!

"Now," he finished, straightening up. "Time to heave to. Everyone below except you Nathan, as well as Toby, Bobbs, and whichever one of you lot are capable of carrying off a passable English accent."

"What about me?" Rhiannon asked, watching the smoke drifting across the water from the frigate's challenge.

Connor eyed her dubiously. "Your accent wouldn't be false. But this is tricky business and I don't want you saying a word. In fact, stand over there with Toby so they don't notice you're a woman and wonder why you're aboard, and if I tell you to go below—"

"I know, I know. . . ."

"Good. I'm glad we understand each other," he said firmly, and throwing her a last, meaningful look, returned to the business at hand. Moments later, most of the crew had gone below and Nathan was putting the helm down. Like a well-bred horse obeying her master, *Kestrel* turned her nose into the wind and came drifting to a stop, her great sails luffing.

Rhiannon went to stand next to Toby, shifting her weight to keep her balance as *Kestrel* fretted beneath them, the long ocean swells passing beneath her, lifting her, settling her down in each trough before lifting her up yet again. She looked at the British frigate, its ports wide open and the ugly black snouts of its huge guns all aimed squarely at them, now hove to and lying to windward several hundred feet away.

"That frigate looks huge up close," she whispered to Toby. "I'm anxious for Connor."

"He's the best at what he does. Just like his father was."

"Why does he feel such a need to prove himself, Toby? He's so confident. Too confident. I worry so about him."

"A captain needs confidence to inspire his men. Have faith in him, Rhiannon. He's good at this."

A boat put out from the frigate and was now heading toward them, several tars at the oars and a smartly clad officer in the stern.

"Prepare to receive boarders," Connor muttered through a cheerful grin.

Rhiannon's blood was running cold. "I can't watch this. And yet I can't not watch it. I wish I'd stayed in Barbados."

Toby, who'd been watching his cousin and captain, turned to her in some alarm. "Want me to take you below?"

"No, I don't want to go below. But I don't want to see my husband shot down or hanged, either!"

Moments later the officer, accompanied by his coxswain, was standing on *Kestrel*'s deck and looking around with suspicious eyes. He was short, plump, and full of his own importance, with penetrating gray eyes, a stand-up collar that poked into the soft flesh around his jaw, and brown hair worn in fashionable spit curls.

"I am Lieutenant Treadwell of His Majesty's frigate *Diana*," he drawled. "Who are you and what is your business?"

Rhiannon could barely breathe. She watched in silence as her husband bowed deeply. "Mr. Merrick, sir, o' the English schooner *Kestrel.*"

"English? Looks like one of those damned Baltimore privateers to me."

"Indeed sir, she was that until me captain, an English privateer 'imself, took her as a prize. I'm her prizemaster, that I am, tasked with sailing her back t' London."

"You Irish?"

"Aye."

"Why sail her all the way back to England? Vice Admiral Sir Graham Falconer is in Bridgetown, surely you can have her condemned and sold at auction there."

"Ah, but sir, ye know that th' Royal Navy has nothing like these sharp-sailing, over-sparred American ships that can run circles around its fastest frigates. Admiralty in London is eager t' get its hands on one o' them so they can study and duplicate them." Connor turned and gestured expansively to the schooner's raked and towering masts. "Can ye blame 'em? Look at her. Is she not a beauty?"

"Simmons, go below and fetch her papers," the lieutenant snapped, but his mariner's eyes had warmed in appreciation as he studied the schooner's lean and predatory lines, her neat rows of guns, the sharp, backswept rake of her two masts and the jib-boom at her nose that seemed to angle out into forever.

"She is indeed," he said, watching his coxswain head below. "What kind of sailor is she?"

"Fast. Wet." Connor grinned. "Hard t' handle, just like a woman."

A faint smile curved the lieutenant's stern mouth. Moments later his coxswain had reappeared, a leather packet in his hand. With a lingering look at *Kestrel*'s square topsail so high above, the officer took the packet, opened it, and studied the papers that granted *Kestrel* permission to harbor in Barbados.

"These are signed by Sir Graham himself!" the man said, a crease appearing between his heavy brows.

"Aye, sir. That they are."

"Well then, since you are headed back to England all alone, and I'm sure those damned Yankees will lose no chance to reclaim such a singular ship as a prize, you will travel in convoy with us under the protection of His Majesty's frigate *Diana* and the sloop-of-war *Whippet*."

"Thank ye, sir. Much obliged." Connor bowed deeply and shot Nathan a wicked, conspiring grin as the British lieutenant looked up at *Kestrel*'s sails in admiration. His eyes were twinkling with mischief. "Indeed, we would be most grateful, sir, to sail in convoy with ye. Most grateful, indeed."

"Fools," Connor said under his breath, touching his hat and grinning as the Englishman and his crew went over *Kestrel*'s side and back down into the boat below. "That was easier than I thought."

"Gotta hand it to you, Con. That was a clever way to get us right in the middle of the convoy without 'em suspecting a thing. You're as cunning as your Da. Loved the Irish accent."

"All in a day's work. Keep your friends close and your enemies closer. Good hunting tonight, I say."

"Good hunting," Nathan agreed.

Connor picked up one of the cats which had wandered up on deck and was now twining itself around his feet. "We'll keep the crew lying low until dark. I don't want that supercilious prig out there thinking we're anything but short-handed and vulnerable." He stroked the tabby's sleek, shining fur. "Rhiannon, lass. What's the matter?"

"You can drop the Irish accent now, *Captain*."

"Sounded just like his father, didn't he?" One-Eye said.

"I doubt his father would ever stoop to such deceit."

Connor shrugged. "My father knew every ruse in the book and the ones he didn't know, he invented. Just ask Bobbs, here. His Da sailed with mine back in the last war."

"Tell her about the time Uncle Brendan snuck up on that British frigate in the dark and stole some of its crew for his own right out from under its captain's nose!" Toby said eagerly.

"Or the time he fooled another British warship into thinking he'd gone aground when he was in seas that were unmeasurably deep!"

"How 'bout the time he cleverly escaped the British admiral during the Battle of Penobscot?"

"I'm going below," Rhiannon said, the fear and tension of watching the exchange between her husband and Lieutenant Treadwell leaving her suddenly exhausted.

"Oh, do stay," Connor urged. He was in high spirits and eager, she could see, for the coming night's work. "We're about to have some fun."

"Fun?"

"Aye." Handing the cat to Rhiannon, he watched the English lieutenant scrambling up the frigate's tumblehome and the British tars preparing to hoist the boat back aboard. "Time to carry out our ruse. Bobbs! Douse that mainsail, would you? We'll pretend to limp along with just the jib and fore. Make sure her trim is sloppy. Let them think we don't know how to sail this lovely lady, eh?"

"That will slow her down considerably, sir."

"And that's my intent. I don't want to show our hand until it's time to run, and there's no sense letting our friends over there know how fast this thoroughbred really is."

Rhiannon put the cat down and headed toward the hatch, assailed by confusion, despair, a grudging admiration for her husband's cleverness, and worry. Deep worry. What would happen if the men on that frigate over there discovered who he really was and what he was up to? And what would Sir Graham do when he learned of such audacity?

"Rhiannon. A moment, please."

She turned and saw that her husband had replaced Nathan at the helm. He stood with a hand on the tiller as Toby, Nathan and One-Eye went forward to back the jib and get the schooner out of irons.

"Come and join me," he said, his smile spreading. "I don't want you to be angry with me."

She walked back to him, and allowed him to slide his arm around her waist. "I'm not angry with you, Connor. Just afraid of what will happen if they figure out your ruse."

"You knew what I was when you agreed to marry me," he said softly.

"I know. But seeing you in action, seeing how dangerous your work really is . . . I guess I was unprepared for how it would make me feel."

The frigate *Diana* was moving off, heading back toward the convoy it had been tasked to protect. Beneath them, *Kestrel* leaned over on the larboard tack as wind filled her jib and foresail and water began to hiss along her sides.

"I've done this before, Rhiannon. Many times. Everything will be all right."

"Only if Treadwell and his captain out there don't hang you once they discover your deceit."

"Rhiannon, I'm a privateer. The United States Navy is dangerously short on ships and cannot fight, let alone hope to win this war without the help of privately armed and financed vessels such as this one. Please, have faith in me."

"Faith," she murmured, unconvinced.

"Faith."

She nodded, and suddenly too tired to think, headed below.

CHAPTER 22

T he moon was already rising, the deep cobalt blue of the sea fading to grey as the sun sank into the west and night began to close in.

Sailing in loose formation with the rest of the convoy under jibs and foresail, *Kestrel* struggled to keep pace with the heavy, wallowing merchantmen as the ships, some thirty all told and helplessly strung out over several miles, beat to windward on a northerly course. Every man in her crew knew that the swift American schooner could sail circles around the convoy, and there was much sniggering and joking amongst her company as they deliberately held her back; in fact, even *Kestrel* herself seemed to be laughing, perhaps remembering distant times when her captain's own father had also practiced a wily cunning and brought glory to her name so long ago. Slowly, she dropped back, falling farther and farther astern as the merchant ships began to hang lights in their rigging and the two guard ships, *Diana* and the sloop-of-war *Whippet*, tried in vain to round up stragglers before nightfall settled in.

Connor had since relinquished the helm to Bobbs, and now he began to restlessly pace the deck as the last of the light began to fade.

He was trying not to think about Rhiannon. Trying to keep his mind on one task only, which was the one at hand.

First things first.

"Which one will we start with, Captain?" Bobbs asked as Connor took a night glass from the rack and put it to his eye.

It was a moment before Connor answered, and only he knew that it was because the night glass, which provided him with an inverted image in its circular field, presented challenges all its own for his poor brain which, at times like this, led him to believe it really was *stoo-pid*, and was having trouble making sense of what he was looking at.

"That one," he said, quickly shutting the glass and pointing out through the thickening gloom at a heavy merchantman that was laboring to keep up with the rest. She was a mile ahead of them, maybe more, but Connor had been studying her all day through a telescope that gave him far less trouble than the night glass. He had already discerned how many were in her crew, who commanded her, and the number of men who'd be needed to board her under cover of darkness, overpower her people, and sail her back to the closest port at which to condemn and sell her—probably Mobile, especially if they continued on this convenient northwesterly course.

"Who'll you send over in the boarding party, Captain?"

"I'll go myself with you and a dozen others and leave Nathan here in command. Let's get the mainsail up and start making some progress now that it's dark, *Diana* is back up in the vanguard and her consort is killing herself trying to keep the stragglers together."

"Seems rather audacious, Connor," said Nathan, from nearby.

"Just the way I like it."

Quietly, the crew raised *Kestrel*'s giant mainsail. It was trimmed to perfection, and the schooner's two huge wings glowed silver in the very last of the light as she eagerly began to gain speed.

"Douse the lanterns," Connor said. "And get that damned Union Jack off of her and run up her proper colors."

"Aye, aye, sir. Stars and Stripes."

Kestrel found more speed and water began to hiss against her leeward shoulder, the long ocean swells breaking over the bowsprit now and running the length of her deck before pouring back into the sea.

"Toby, lad. Where is my wife?"

"Below, Con. Told me she was tired so I set her up with some supper . . . figured it would be best to keep her out of trouble for the time being."

"Trouble," Jacques said, his ugly face looming in the nearby darkness, "Aren't they all? You know, *Capitaine*, the best way to win a lady's heart is to pay her a complement or two, even if you don't really mean them."

"I mean every complement I pay my wife, Jacques."

"Have you told her, lately, how beautiful her hair is?"

Connor walked to the weapons chest and pulled out a cutlass.

"Have you told her how luscious her lips are, how soft and smooth her skin, how all the green of the forests can't match the color of her eyes?"

Connor belted the cutlass and found a boarding pike.

"Jacques is right," One-Eye said importantly from several feet away. "Women like to be flattered. Maybe we can find something nice for you to present her with from that ship we're about to take. Some fine linens or silks, if we're lucky."

"Or maybe some exotic spices."

"Aye, spices! Maybe we can get her to cook us something worth eating, rather than this swill that Lunt keeps poisoning us with."

"Aye, good thinking, Bobbs. A woman's place is in the kitchen. Or in this case, the galley."

"I've got a tear in my shirt; if I'm real nice to her, think she might mend it for me?"

"I know women," Jacques said importantly. "The best place for them is between the sheets—"

A second later, he found himself staring up at his captain's broad shoulders from where he lay, flat on his back, on the schooner's deck. He raised himself on one elbow, rubbing at his throbbing jaw and feeling the warm trickle of blood running from a new split in his lower lip.

"*Capitaine*, sir, no disrespect to *Madame*! Just trying to help!"

But Connor, armed with a cutlass and two pistols, was already stalking off into the darkness.

"Really, Jacques," said young Toby from nearby. With a long-suffering sigh, he reached a hand down to help the Frenchman up. "I don't think my cousin, of all people, needs any advice when it comes to women."

They took the merchantman without a single shot being fired.

One moment the huge vessel, three-masted and thrice the tonnage of the swift raptor who slid silently up beside her in the darkness, was sailing along without a care in the world, her master safe in the knowledge that the two Royal Navy warships sent to protect them were on guard and keeping all threats at bay. In the next the crew, sitting around on deck smoking, drinking, chewing tobacco and swapping stories, found themselves surprised by grappling irons that came flying over the side; before they could even leap to their feet, their ship was secured to the black ghost-vessel that had appeared from out of nowhere and a barrage of men wielding pistols, cutlasses, knives, blunderbusses, and boarding pikes came pouring onto her decks.

The crew was terrified.

"Don't shoot! *Don't shoot!*"

"Give me what I want, and there'll be no bloodshed," said the tall, imposing one with the pistol aimed at Captain Roth's heart.

What he wanted, it seemed, was his ship.

"Round up the crew, Bobbs, and fetch me this tub's papers. And be quick about it." The man, garbed in a double-breasted pea coat and shorn canvas trousers, bare-footed and looking as if he would not hesitate to put a ball through Roth's heart, turned to the quaking master, bowed, and came up with a roguish grin. "I do apologize for the inconvenience. I'm Captain Connor Merrick of the armed American privateer *Kestrel*, and your ship is now my prize. The sooner we get this business over with, the better off we'll all be."

"Merrick? *Kestrel*?" Roth was staring at the privateer captain through the gloom. "Wasn't there some famous ship by that name captained by a Merrick during the last war?"

"My father," the American said, with no small degree of pride. "Just continuing on the family tradition."

Bobbs reappeared with the ship's papers. He handed them to his captain along with a lantern so that he could read them, and suddenly Connor wasn't laughing anymore, because Bobbs didn't know that he *couldn't* read them, at least, not with any haste and certainly not without a significant degree of difficulty, and for a brief, frightening moment, Connor felt his mouth go dry and wished, desperately, that he had brought Nathan along. Nathan knew his secret. Nathan would read the papers.

Dismissively, he handed them back to Bobbs. "I don't have time to go through something the size of a damned book," he snapped. "You read them while I go have a look around this tub and see just what it is we're dealing with."

There. He'd gotten out of that bind easily enough, and when he returned to Bobbs ten minutes later, he was told that the merchantman was loaded with rum, sugar, molasses, and indigo. The cargo, let alone the ship itself, would fetch a fine amount at auction at the nearest American port.

"Shall we send her into New Orleans, sir?" Bobbs asked.

"No, those greedy bastards'll take ten percent right off the top," Connor said. "We'll fetch more for her in Mobile."

"Too bad our own coast is blockaded. Sure would be nice to send her back to New England," said Amos Lunt, sharing a plug of tobacco with one of the English sailors.

"There's a big enough chance she'll be recaptured by a British cruiser as it is," Connor said tersely. "I'm not going to risk sending her all the way home. No, she's best sent to Mobile, and you, Bobbs, will command her. Take Lunt and your pick of the men here; that should be enough to see you safely into port as long as you show a clean pair of heels to any Britons who see fit to give you chase."

"Aye, sir."

Shortly thereafter, the merchantman's crew were locked below to be released in Mobile, the prize crew under Bobbs was silently setting a course toward the Gulf of Mexico, and Connor was on his way back to *Kestrel*.

He returned to rousing cheers and lots of happy back-slapping from his men, and the rum flowed like water that night.

At dawn, when the sharp-eyed officers aboard HMS *Diana* scanned the horizon and set about rounding up the stragglers who had fallen astern during the night, they found the merchantman *Peggy Lee* missing. Assuming she'd wandered off course in the darkness, *Diana* went off in search of her, leaving *Whippet* to guard, as best she could, the rest of the merchant fleet as it continued to sail north toward England—including the sleek black American privateer snugged safely in their midst.

A wolf amongst sheep.

And not a one of them suspected.

CHAPTER 23

Connor waited until the sun was up and *Kestrel* was once again laboring along under the pretense of unskilled seamanship. Then, satisfied that their deception held, he relinquished the deck to Nathan and finally went below.

He found Rhiannon in his cabin, sitting in bed with her hair loose around her shoulders and a book in her hand.

He was tired. Spent. But not so tired that the sight of his beautiful wife didn't immediately cause him to harden with desire as he shut the door behind him.

Rhiannon looked up at him. "Good morning, husband."

"Good morning, wife."

"You're tired."

"Aye."

She could see him eyeing the rise of her breasts above the light blanket that covered her.

"Come to bed, Connor." She put the book down and moved over, making room for him. Her eyes were full of promise. "I was just going to get up, but now that you're here. . . ."

"I don't want you to get up."

He pulled his shirt off from over his head, unbuttoned his cut-off trousers, and stepping out of them, tossed them over the back of his chair. His wife's eyes darkened as he stood there naked before her and suddenly Connor wasn't tired at all, despite the fact he'd been up all night.

He slid in beside her and they lay together, skin to skin beneath the blanket. Beyond the open stern windows he could see the unsuspecting ships of the convoy, and wondered which one he might pluck for tonight's prize.

And then his wife's hand was touching, stroking, fondling his growing arousal, and Connor, happily distracted, stopped thinking about ships.

For the next five nights, it was a repeat of what had happened aboard *Peggy Lee*, one prize after another boarded under cover of darkness right under the Lion's nose, *Kestrel* sailing innocently along in convoy during the day while her crew slept belowdecks, and another prize boarded and taken the following night, until nine merchantmen in all had inexplicably disappeared from the convoy.

"Think it's time to call it a day?" Nathan asked as he and Connor watched the brigantine *Betsy*, her lights doused and only her sails against the starlight marking her progress, sail off toward Mobile under the command of the small prize crew that Connor had just put aboard her. "We'll be pushing our luck if we keep at it much longer."

"It's not the luck I'm worried about pushing, it's the fact we're down to a skeleton crew. We've only enough men to sail back to Barbados, and no more to man out yet another prize. Aye, Cousin. Time to end what's been a very lucrative venture."

Dawn was breaking, and they were some three hundred miles south of Florida with a good stiff wind coming hard over *Kestrel*'s starboard quarter. Had they a full crew and no ruse of incompetence to pull off, Connor might have ordered the studding sails set on either side of the fore topsail. It was the perfect wind in which to fly them, but as he leaned idly against the rail watching *Diana* hauling her wind and heading their way, his gut instincts told him that it was, indeed, high time to make a move.

Fast.

"Think they've figured us out?" Nathan asked, following his cousin's gaze.

"I'm not about to stick around to find out. Call up what remains of the crew and tell them to stand by to make sail."

"Aye, Captain."

Rhiannon came up on deck then and saw her husband at the tiller, arms crossed over his chest, his handsome, angular jaw covered with morning bristle that he hadn't yet bothered to shave. She had been anticipating his arrival in bed, as she had done every one of these past several mornings, and had been looking forward to an hour of lovemaking before finally letting him grab a few hours of sleep. But not this morning. This morning, her husband was gazing intently past *Kestrel*'s masts and long, upthrust jib-boom, watching the British frigate far ahead of them coming back down along the line of ships that made up what remained of the convoy.

"Good morning, dear," he said, smiling.

"Good morning, Connor."

He leaned close, kissed her in full view of anyone who might be watching and murmured, "I think this morning's bed play is going to have to wait a bit. You'll forgive me, I hope?"

"Tired of me already, Captain?"

He laughed. "No, but I think that frigate yonder is tired of us. We're done here."

She noted the direction of his gaze and how fast that British frigate was coming on.

"It's best if you go below, Rhiannon. I think we'll see some action today."

"Action?"

"Aye. Our British friends have, I think, finally grown suspicious as to why—and how—ships are disappearing from the convoy every night. The game is up."

"You don't mean to actually *fight* them, now, do you?"

"I will if I have to, though I'd rather not."

"Your mother told me that *Kestrel* is aged. That she won't withstand heavy punishment from a Royal Navy warship."

"My mother was right."

He turned and caught Toby's arm as the lad hurried past. "Toby, get the guns loaded. Double-shotted, please."

"Aye, Captain."

"And get ready to hoist our *proper* flag."

The frigate was coming closer. Her gun ports were opening and she meant business.

"Time to show them our heels, lads," Connor said, straightening up. "Ready about."

"Ready about!"

Kestrel's great main and foresail were sheeted in and Connor, taking the helm himself, pushed the tiller hard over. The schooner responded instantly, swinging her long, lofty nose around toward the wind, closer and closer, until her great mainsail boom had swung over their heads and she was stern-on to the oncoming frigate which, seeing her make a decisive turn, was now coughing a plume of smoke from the chaser guns mounted in her bow; a split second later, the echoing boom came thundering over the water as her captain demanded that they heave to.

"Run up the flag," Connor said, grinning.

Moments later, the great red, white and blue flag with its fifteen stars and stripes unfurled itself to the wind, an audacious taunt to the frigate behind them.

Diana fired again and a half-mile astern, a plume of water shot skyward as the cannonball plunged into the sea.

"Are they going to catch us?" Rhiannon asked worriedly.

"Not headed to windward as we are. On this tack we're the superior with our fore-and-aft rig, and we'll leave them chewing their bow wake. 'Twould be another story, though, with the wind dead astern."

"Aye, that frigate would be deadly," Nathan added, looking up from where he was casting off the lashing on a nearby gun.

Rhiannon instinctively moved closer to her husband. He had made his work look so easy these past five nights, and observing his behavior, it had been easy to think it had all been child's play. Now she realized the danger he was in, the danger he'd been in all along, and her blood went cold at the idea of what might happen to him if *Kestrel* could not outsail that mighty warship back there. She doubted very much that Sir Graham would lift a finger to save him.

In the end though, her worries were for naught. The distance between *Kestrel*'s rudder and the sea boiling at *Diana*'s bows grew steadily throughout the afternoon, and though the frigate fired a few more shots in hopeless rage, she never came close to the Yankee privateer.

By the time night fell, the convoy—or rather, what remained of it— was hull down on the horizon, its lights winking like tiny stars in the darkness and *Kestrel*, her bow smashing up and down in timeless rhythm against the swells that paraded toward them from out of the night, was all alone on the vast Atlantic.

It took them two days to reach Carlisle Bay, and as they dropped anchor, a tight-mouthed Captain Delmore Lord was rowed out to meet them himself.

"How was your *honeymoon cruise*?"

"Fruitful," Connor replied innocently and without batting an eyelash.

Misunderstanding the deliberate *double entendre*, the Englishman cleared his throat and looked away. "I never thought I'd say this, but I'm glad you're back. Sir Graham is beside himself, and even your parents can't get him to relax. Lady Falconer is in labor."

Connor, privately thinking he was the last person on earth who might get Sir Graham to relax, especially if the admiral had gotten wind of his recent exploits, smiled happily. "Oh, good, I get to be an uncle again."

From out of the corner of his mouth Nathan, passing nearby, muttered, "Obviously, he doesn't know what you've been up to."

Guess not. Connor grinned. "Is my sister all right?"

"I don't know. She started having pains early this morning. Your mother and Mrs. Cox are with her now."

"No imminent danger, then?"

"How the hell would I know? I know nothing about childbirth!"

"Aye, well, neither do I. But what I do know is that I stink, and this harbor looks pretty damned inviting. It's tarnal hot here, don't know how you can stand it, Delmore, all rigged out in uniform like that. The admiral's not here. Why don't you join me and the lads for a swim?"

Captain Lord's aristocratic nostrils flared. "I could *never—*"

"Yes you could, and I won't tell if you won't."

"Impossible," Captain Lord said, with an abrupt and dismissive shake of his head. He drew himself up in lofty splendor. "I am a captain in His Majesty's Royal Navy, I can't go jumping off ships half-naked!"

"You do know how to swim, don't you?"

"Well of course I do, that's not the point—"

"Well then, never mind, Del. Far be it from me to force you to do something you don't want to do. Me?" Connor was already stripping off his shirt. "I'm not going to show up stinking like a pig after several days at sea, so I'm having a swim first. I'll join you up at the house, shortly."

And with that, he stepped up onto *Kestrel's* varnished rail, tossed a wicked grin from over his shoulder at the tight-mouthed Captain Lord, and threw himself into the sparkling blue waters of Carlisle Bay without a care in the world.

Rhiannon came up on deck just as Captain Lord, the morning sun glinting off the gold lace of his blue and white uniform, was rowed away in his boat. She stood at the rail watching her husband move through the clear blue water as though he'd been born to it.

Water streamed over his back, the well-defined muscles in his shoulders and upper arms, and he was thoroughly enjoying himself. Dear God, he was beautiful. And hers. All hers. She couldn't help but admire him. How could he be so blithe and cheerful in the face of danger, and so reckless that he'd sailed straight into Carlisle Bay with not a worry in the world about Sir Graham's possible reaction?

Surely, the admiral would guess what Connor had been up to, especially if news about ships missing from a certain convoy had made its way back to Bridgetown.

A little flutter gripped her stomach.

"Guess what, Rhiannon!" He swam near until his face, tanned and handsome and dominated by that wicked, perfect smile, was only several feet below her. "I'm going to be an uncle again. Maeve's having her baby."

"And you're taking a swim?"

"Need one," he said simply, and his green eyes crinkled at the corners. "Want to join me?"

"No, I'm not going to join you. I can't believe you're down there frolicking in the water while your sister needs you!"

"Needs me? Staying away from her while she's in the whelping box is my way of self-preservation."

"Connor! What an outrageous thing to say!"

He laughed, and their gazes met. Something warm and wanting fluttered deep in the pit of Rhiannon's belly and she realized that the more she had of this man, the more she wanted.

"Sir Graham's going to be very angry with you, you know."

"I can handle Sir Graham. Why don't you throw me that line there, dearest? I fancy I'm clean enough."

"The one wrapped around this cannon?"

"Aye, that very one."

Rhiannon knelt, picked up the end of the rope, and flung it down to him. Moments later her husband, dripping wet and looking delectable, was hauling himself up over the side, droplets of salt water clinging to his shoulders, his cheeks, and running from his tousled curls.

"You're shameless," she said with a helpless little smile.

"I know. I try to be." He stepped closer and pulled her into his arms. "Kiss me, Rhiannon."

"You're soaking wet! You'll ruin my gown!"

"The hell with your gown," he said, and a moment later she was wrapped fiercely in his strong, hard arms, his mouth crushing hers and the heat in the pit of her belly spreading to parts of her that knew only one way to relief.

Nathan, coiling a line some thirty feet away, just shook his head and turned away.

The baby was coming.

Connor and his father had taken poor Sir Graham to the library after the admiral had tried to enter his wife's bedroom during the hardest part of her labor, only to be rewarded with shouted epithets and hot accusations that he'd been the one to put the babe in her belly and damn him, this was the last, the very *last* one they were ever going to have. Of course, Connor and Brendan had no way of knowing that Maeve had screamed the very same words at her hapless husband during the birth of each of their previous three children, but Sir Graham had gone white with horror and fear at sight of his wife's distress and was all but inconsolable. Now, as the admiral paced the floor of the library, Connor and Brendan were both trying their best to calm him down.

"Faith, if this is the way the British admiralty behaves in a crisis, you're all doomed," Brendan joked, topping up his son-in-law's glass with fine Bajan rum.

"I'm worried sick about her, this is the last time I'm getting her pregnant, never again, I can't stand this, by God, I have to go to her—"

"Sit down, Gray, and drink some rum," Connor said impatiently.

"Aye, you'll be no good to Maeve if you wear yourself out pacing a hole in the rug," his father added. "What are you going to name the babe?"

Sir Graham gulped from the glass. "Damned if I know. Plenty of boy's names to be had, but we've run out of names for a girl."

"Run out of names?"

"Don't forget, Da, they name their children after famous pirates," Connor reminded his father.

"Why, there've been plenty of lady pirates," Brendan said, foregoing the rum and pouring himself a glass of punch. "But you've got to look beyond the Caribbean. We've an ancestor from Ireland who was a lady pirate. Grace O' Malley, her name was."

Danelle Harmon

"Grace! That's a fine name," Sir Graham said, draining and putting down his glass. He turned suddenly and nearly toppled over, only to be caught by Connor on one side and Brendan on the other.

It was to this scene, of the admiral flushed with drink and unable to stand, that Mira arrived a few moments later.

"Is she all right?" Sir Graham demanded, reeling.

Mira just looked at him, grinning. "Congratulations, Gray," she said. "You have a baby girl."

"And you and I," said Brendan with delight, "have another grandchild to spoil."

CHAPTER 24

They all took turns quietly filing in to see the baby and her exhausted mother, who hooked an arm around Sir Graham's neck, pulled him down to kiss him and begged his forgiveness for anything she might have said to him during the agony of birth.

"It's all right, Maeve. It's forgotten."

"Why Gray, you positively reek of rum," she said, frowning.

"Your brother and father got me soused."

"My father? Honestly, Da, for someone who doesn't drink, himself, you're shameless. . . . "

Brendan just laughed, his infectious smile lighting up his whole face.

"Needed doing, Sis," said Kieran who, having heard the news, had hurriedly left *Sandpiper* and come as fast as he could. "She's a pretty little girl. Got the family hair."

As indeed, young Grace did —a thick, soft, reddish cap of curling peach fuzz. She lay wide-eyed and comfortable in her mother's arms as her big brother Ned and two sisters Mary and Anne were brought to meet her for the first time.

Rhiannon noticed Connor's fingers drumming against a night table and knew he had reached the end of his patience for staying in one place. Moments later, her suspicions were confirmed.

"My mother and Da will be looking to us, next," he murmured, leaning close to her ear.

"For what?"

"Another grandchild. What do you say we go and work on making one of our own?"

"You're as shameless as your father!"

"More so. Come, let's go take a walk."

Captain Delmore Lord was working on some correspondence from the comfort and privacy of his great cabin aboard *Orion* when a midshipman brought him the news that the latest little Falconer had been born.

"Mother and child safe and well?" the captain asked, dabbing his sweating brow with a crisp white handkerchief and inwardly cursing the tropical heat.

"Well enough. But I heard some news down at the local tavern, sir. Seems an American privateer was found to be in company with that convoy heading for London. Plucked a sizeable number of ships right out from under their noses before showing a fleet pair of heels."

"What kind of ship was this privateer, Mr. Pettingill?"

"A black schooner, sir. Or so it's said."

Delmore took a deep and weary sigh and kneaded his forehead with his hands.

"Just thought you'd like to know, sir."

"Thank you, Mr. Pettingill."

"Are you going to tell the admiral?"

Delmore pushed his fingers through his thick black curls. Telling the admiral was, of course, the right thing to do. And the flag captain harbored no doubts about just who the American privateer was, especially given Connor Merrick's absence over the past few days. But did he really want to spoil Sir Graham's joy over the birth of his newest child by telling him of the raid on the convoy, and the likelihood that it was his American cousin who was responsible?

It is your duty to tell him.

"All in good time," he said, his gray eyes showing more purple than usual as he picked up his quill, plunged it into the ink pot and continued his letter. "For now, let him enjoy the blessings this day has brought him."

While Sir Graham was enjoying the blessings of his newest daughter, his errant brother-in-law was looking forward to enjoying the blessings of being a happily married man.

He and Rhiannon had gone back aboard *Kestrel*, deserted now with all but the scant watch—which consisted of a slumbering-in-the-sun Jacques—having gone ashore hours before. The heat seemed to bake the tar of the deck seams and even the guns, lashed tightly behind their closed ports, were hot to the touch when Rhiannon absently brushed her hand across the breech of one as they headed to Connor's cabin.

"I don't think I could live here in this climate," she mused, all but panting in the heat. "I feel like I'm going to wilt."

"Aye, these southern latitudes are too hot for me too, but at least one can cool off by jumping in the sea."

"Where will we live, Connor?"

"Where do you want to live, Rhiannon?"

"I don't know. It would be nice to be near my sister in England, but you're a man of the sea, and Morninghall Abbey is rather far inland." She smiled up at him. "To be honest, I really can't see you settling down and living in England. I don't think you'd be happy there."

"Happiness is the home you make, not where you make it."

"I know. And it's whom you make it with." She followed him down the hatch and below decks where it was noticeably cooler without the brutal tropical sun. "Where would *you* like to live?"

"I own a home in Newburyport. But I'd understand, Rhiannon, if that's too far away from your loved ones."

"You're my loved one now, Connor."

There, she'd said it. *Love.*

For a long moment he said nothing. He looked briefly uncomfortable, as though he didn't quite know how to respond to her words.

"Connor? What is it?"

With a pained smile, he took her hand and led her into the cabin. "You don't want to fall in love with me, Rhiannon. I'll just break your heart."

"You're my husband! Of course I'm going to fall in love with you. What a perfectly absurd thing to say."

"I'm reckless and take risks. Too many of them, most people say, and I doubt my life is destined to be a long one."

They were in his cabin now, and she took his hand and coaxed him to sit down on his bunk. He looked distressed, and gently, she reached out and pushed a tousled lock of hair from his forehead. "Why *do* you take so many risks, Connor?"

He shrugged. How could he explain the feeling of bees buzzing through his veins and making him unable to sit still? How could he explain how doing daring things made him feel invincible and gloriously alive? How could he explain that while some men might be addicted to the bottle or to opium or to cards, he was addicted to that wild, thrumming rush that only came when throwing himself at a dangerous situation and emerging the victor?

"I don't know," he said honestly. "I've just always been like this."

He went to the stern windows, open to catch what breeze managed to skate over the bay, and stood there looking out over the harbor, drumming his fingers against the sill.

She came quietly up behind him and laid her hand on his arm. "You have nothing to prove, you know."

"I have everything to prove." His fingers beat a quickening tattoo on the sill. "My father was a legend during the last war. He had the love and admiration of his crew, the entire town of Newburyport, was commended by Washington himself, whereas I—"

He broke off.

Whereas I can barely read. And certainly not a chart.

"And you think you need to be your father in order to be appreciated and admired, yourself?"

"He's a tough act to follow."

"What's wrong with being the man that you actually are, instead of the one who fathered you?"

"There are some things, Rhiannon, that you cannot understand."

"Maybe not, but there are some things that I can certainly see, and it is this. Your crew adores you. You're a natural, charismatic leader and your courage is infectious, so much so that I believe those men would follow you anywhere, do anything you ask of them. I don't understand where this drive to prove yourself comes from."

Connor turned abruptly from the window and began to pace once more. "I can't have this conversation. We didn't come here to have this conversation. We came here to make a baby, damn it, and I'm through talking."

"But—"

He took her into his arms and kissed her before she could finish the thought, intending only to silence her and distract her from pursuing this subject that he found vastly uncomfortable. For a moment she resisted, stiff beneath the forceful pressure of his lips, his mouth against her own, and then, with a little groan of defeat, her arms came up to wend around his neck and her breasts were pressing against his chest.

He forced her backward to his bunk, his hands already going around the small of her back, cupping her buttocks through her thin muslin gown and pulling her close up against himself. Her pelvis pressed against his arousal and he drove his mouth relentlessly down against her own, feeling a need to possess her, to silence her, oh, yes, especially to silence her.

Her mouth opened to him, and he plunged his tongue inside the honeyed sweetness of it, his breath coming hard.

She had asked him what he had to prove. She had told him he had nothing to prove. And she had told him that she loved him.

Loved him.

He sucked her bottom lip into his mouth, biting it gently as his hands rucked up the hem of her gown, her shift, found the bare, satiny skin of her bottom and squeezed.

She tried to fall backward onto the bunk but he held her tight, opening her cleft from behind with his fingers, plunging them within her and beginning to stroke until she caught her breath and tensed and reached for his arousal. Then, and only then, did he allow them both to sink to the bunk, her hands already freeing him from the containment of his pantaloons and guiding him to that sweet, hot, delicious part of herself that was able to focus and contain his thoughts, to make them its own, in a way that nothing in Connor's life had ever been able to do.

Their coupling was hard and fast and desperate. With a cry, she convulsed around him, sending him over the edge as well, and it was a long time before either of them talked.

That suited Connor very well indeed.

CHAPTER 25

By the time the afternoon sun was low in the sky, Captain Delmore Lord's conscience had finally caught up with him.

He had long since finished his paperwork and now sat sweltering in his great cabin, his feet sweating in their buckled shoes, his white breeches all but glued onto his legs, a trickle of perspiration running down his back beneath shirt, waistcoat and coat, and the points of his stand-up collar stabbing into his cheeks.

He stood up, faint with heat, and decided he had no choice but to tell his admiral the news that had been brought to him earlier.

It pained him to do so. He respected his admiral, found him to be a fair commander and a good mentor. He appreciated the fact that Sir Graham was in a tough spot, being highly placed in the Royal Navy and yet married to an American whose brother was currently wreaking havoc on British shipping.

Delmore took out his handkerchief and mopped his brow.

He didn't dislike Connor. What he did dislike was his own private envy of his American cousin's sense of unfettered freedom, and his boldness in pursuing it.

He stalked moodily to the great stern windows of the man o' war and looked out over the waters of Carlisle Bay. The dying sunlight painted the harbor in glittering white-orange diamonds where a puff of wind happened to move, and Delmore stood there for a moment, sweating, conflicted, and irritated.

They were at it again.

His irritation grew.

For there, several hundred feet away, that same American privateer schooner that had been the bane of his conscience all afternoon lay anchored, with the fools and idiots that made up his cousin's crew once more playing at their ridiculous game of seeing who dared to jump the highest from the rigging.

The answer to his dilemma came then to Delmore. He would go over to the schooner, confront his cousin directly, and ask him point-blank if his was the schooner that had wreaked so much havoc on the convoy.

Connor Merrick was a daredevil, a show-off, and a swaggering fool.

If he was indeed the privateer who'd inflicted such damage, Delmore knew he wouldn't waste the opportunity to confirm it.

"I'm scared!" Rhiannon said, laughing, as on wobbly knees, she climbed up onto *Kestrel*'s rail and crouched there,

Danelle Harmon

clutching desperately to her husband's hand and afraid to move. Below her, the water looked awfully far down; farther than she knew it actually was.

"What are you scared of?"

"I only just learned how to swim, and now you have me jumping off the ship?"

"You'll love it. It's fun."

"Yes, fun!" cried Toby, from nearby. He was minus his shirt and like Connor, clad in nothing but frayed canvas trousers. So was Rhiannon and the trousers she wore were Toby's, but a shirt and a sleeveless waistcoat to protect her modesty had been procured for her as well and now she stood, watching the late sun sparkle on the water below her and her heart beating like a woodpecker in her chest as she crouched, poised, on the schooner's rail.

Around her, the ship herself seemed to whisper, *I know you can do it. They're quite right. It's fun.*

"Live a little," Connor said, eyes twinkling.

"I'm afraid!"

He just smiled, and a second later joined her on the rail, his bare feet next to hers, her small hand gripped tightly in his own big, powerful one.

"What are you doing?" she squeaked. "You'll lose your balance and we'll both fall in!"

"Stand up," he said cheerfully, and doing so himself, pulled her erect.

Rhiannon, standing there wobbling in terror, had no time to realize the fact that, standing up, the water was that much farther below her because suddenly her husband cried, "Jump!" and, still gripping her hand, they were plunging through space and down toward the harbor below.

She had no time to even scream. It was only a short drop from *Kestrel*'s rail to the water and they hit it together, her hand still tightly held in his as they plunged beneath the surface and the water closed over her head. Their descent stopped in a hiss of bubbles. Rhiannon opened her eyes and saw him right beside her, lips curved in appreciation of her courage, and then he let go of her hand and helped guide her back to the surface above with a hand against her ribs.

She broke the surface to a thunderous roar of applause from the schooner's decks above.

"Three cheers for the captain's lady!"

"Hip hip, huzzah! Hip hip, huzzah! Hip hip, huzzah!"

"Next thing ye know, Captain, she'll be jumping from the gaff like the rest of us!"

Connor laughed, delighted, and looked across the several inches of water that separated him from his wife. Her hair was slicked back, showing the elegant shape of her head, making her large green eyes seem all the wider, her mouth all the fuller, and never had she looked more beautiful to him. Treading water, he moved close, and put his lips against her wet forehead.

"I'm proud of you," he said. "That took a lot of courage."

She wrapped her arms around his neck, nearly pushing him under. "I'm proud of me too, Connor. And you were right. It was fun!"

He kissed her then, hard, passionately, and in full sight of his entire crew; or rather, what remained of it after putting so many men aboard the captured prizes, and there was more cheering and a few ribald comments.

They clambered back aboard the schooner with some help from a rope and Toby, Jacques and Nathan.

"Don't just stand there, you wretches," Connor said good-naturedly, with a glance at his dripping wife. "Fetch the lady a towel."

Toby ran below to get one and One-Eye looked up at his captain, who was in higher spirits than usual.

"Hot evening, sir." Gazing up at the rigging, he pulled at the corner of his mouth. "I'll bet you ten dollars I can jump from a greater height than you."

"Done." Connor headed for the shrouds.

"Trouble coming from fine off the starboard bow," Nathan said wryly.

One could almost hear the collective groan as the few men who remained aboard the schooner looked up and saw the Royal Navy boat, with the impeccably uniformed Captain Lord sitting stiffly in the sternsheets, heading toward them.

"Just when we were about to have some fun," Jacques muttered.

One-Eye rolled his blue and brown eyes. "And he had to come along and spoil it."

"He hasn't spoiled anything, and the fun's just beginning," Connor said cheerfully, and headed aloft.

From the boat, a tight-lipped Delmore Lord watched his cousin deftly climbing the shrouds and wondered if he was going to make this interview even harder than he already expected it would be. On the schooner's low, lean deck, he could see a few men watching him with derision, perhaps even hostility. He drew himself up a little straighter and held himself still as his smartly dressed crew hooked onto the schooner's chains.

"Permission, Captain Merrick, to come aboard!" he demanded formally.

"As you please, Cuz," called down the man who was now standing at the cross-trees high, high above.

Delmore's lips thinned. He reached for a rope and climbed aboard the ship. There was young Toby Ashton, thin, gangly, and looking at him with some apprehension. Nathan, the dying sunlight gilding his tawny hair. Two crewmen he didn't know and of course, the beautiful Rhiannon.

He bit down the pain he felt at sight of her.

She was never yours to have. Somewhere, there is a woman out there for you. But it's not her.

"Del, my man!"

The British captain looked up. There was his foolish cousin still standing at the crosstrees, one arm hooked around a stay and looking down at him.

"Please come down so that I might speak to you privately, Connor."

"If you want to speak privately, why don't you come up here?"

Delmore groaned, inwardly.

"One-Eye and I have another contest going. Ten American dollars to the man who dares to jump the highest. I'll raise it to fifty if you care to join in."

"You're out of your bloody mind."

"Always am. So what do you say, Del? The view up here's fine, and the water's even nicer."

Around him Delmore could hear the snickers of the American crew, and he felt Rhiannon's expectant gaze upon him. His face reddened, and a muscle ticked in his cheek. He stood there for a moment, then walked to the rail and looked down at his men waiting in the boat below.

"You may return to *Orion*," he snapped. "I'll be along after I conduct my business with Captain Merrick."

"Aye, aye, sir."

He watched the boat move off, oars rising and falling, rising and falling, and turned back to the schooner. Nobody had moved. They were all watching him. Waiting.

"Well?" Connor Merrick called down from high above. "Are you going to join me, Del? You representing Britain, me representing the United States, and not a shot needs to be fired."

"I'm coming up there to talk with you, not to engage in your childish games."

"Come on up then. How about sixty dollars?"

"You're mad."

"Seventy!"

"Bloody insane."

But Delmore strode to the shrouds and removing his hat, tilted his head back. The sun was going down such that his cousin, so far above, was now nearly in silhouette.

Waiting.

Tight-lipped, Delmore placed his fancy over-large hat on the breech of a nearby gun and began to unbutton his coat.

The silence around him grew deafening.

The high, stand-up collar pressing into his jaw fell away and he felt a sense of relief and freedom. He shrugged out of the coat, and felt the sweat beginning to pour off him as though the heavy garment had kept it all contained. Carefully folding it, he laid it next to his hat.

Out of the corner of his eye, he saw a man with a split, scarred lip elbowing Nathan and grinning madly. Ignoring them, his mouth a tight, hard line, Delmore bent down and removed his shoes and stockings.

I'm doing this just to make it easier to climb, he told himself. But some wild, distant, previously unheeded part of himself knew differently.

He reached for the shrouds and began the ascent.

Below him, the scanty American crew began to clap in appreciation, and someone let out a cheer. His cheeks reddening, Delmore kept climbing.

And climbing.

He found his cousin sitting on the topsail yard, eyes crinkling with good humor, the water still trickling from his loose auburn curls and dripping down his neck and shoulders.

"A hundred dollars," Connor said, grinning.

The tic in Delmore's jaw twitched one last time before a faint, reluctant smile touched his hard mouth.

"Done."

"Damned fools," Sir Graham said irritably, watching the hi-jinks aboard the American schooner with a telescope pressed to his eye. He snapped it shut in irritation, for his head ached from the overindulgence of rum and it was hot enough to bake the burn right out of one of his mother-in-law's ghastly, inedible cookies. "That son of yours is going to get himself killed."

Behind him, Brendan Merrick was sitting in a chair reading a newspaper and trying, like Sir Graham, to find any whisper of breeze out here on the verandah. His knee was hurting tonight, and he wondered if it was going to rain.

"What are they doing now?"

"Jumping from that damned schooner's rigging."

"Good night for it," Brendan said, and went back to reading the paper.

"He's going to break his fool neck." Sir Graham wiped his sweating, pounding brow. "I say, if I *ever* caught one of my men engaging in behavior like that, I'd have him bloody keelhauled."

With a little sigh, Brendan put the paper down and joined his son-in-law at the railing. Together they watched two figures, tiny with distance, moving out along *Kestrel's* fore topsail yard.

"Come now, Gray," said Brendan. "Weren't you young once?"

"A long time ago. Before I had children."

"They age you, don't they? You worry about them, you fear for their futures, you do the best you can by them and no matter how old they get to be, they'll still be your children. But there comes a time when you have to just let go, and let them be the person the good Lord made them to be."

Brendan picked up the telescope and put it to his eye. Into the circular field came masts, spars, water, and there, yes, his beloved schooner. He found the mainmast and brought the glass up, studying the two men so clearly revealed by the magnification.

It was Connor, all right.

And the other one, just peeling off his shirt and tossing it down, down, down to the deck, was—

"Well, I'll be damned," he said.

He snapped the glass shut as his son threw himself off the yard and executed a perfect dive into the sea so far below.

"What is it?" Gray asked, reaching for the glass.

"Why don't we go and check on Maeve and the baby. Maybe get something to eat."

But Sir Graham had grabbed the glass and, as Brendan watched helplessly, was putting it to eye.

The admiral's roar nearly shook the paint off the railing. "Holy Christ above, is that my *FLAG CAPTAIN?!*"

From somewhere on the other side of the mansion, the sudden wails of a infant permeated the air.

"You've gone and woken your baby daughter," Brendan said, taking the glass from his son-in-law's hand. "Maeve will have your head."

"I'll have *Delmore*'s head for this, by God! I thought he of all people was beyond the reach of Connor's corruptive influence!"

"Faith, lad, the night is hot enough to melt the shadows off the sun. So they're cooling off out there? 'Tis about time he relaxed a little and learned to have fun."

"Fun? He's a damned captain in His Majesty's Royal Navy, he can't be jumping off yardarms like a damned fool!"

Sir Graham stormed toward the door, but was quickly caught by his father-in-law's hand. "Gray," he said, and his smile was wise, patient, and full of understanding. "Life is short, and just as we welcomed a little baby into the world today, none of us ever know when the good Lord is going to come and take one of us away. Let the lad enjoy himself while he can." He clapped the admiral on the shoulder. "It's good for him."

Sir Graham just raked a hand through his hair and pouring himself a glass of lemonade, went back to the railing, watching the distant contest.

Brendan joined him, a glass of the cool beverage in his own hand.

The shadows grew longer as they sipped their drinks and watched the distant competitors climb higher for each dive.

"Kind of makes a man wish he were young again," Sir Graham finally admitted, grudgingly.

Brendan took a last swallow of his lemonade. "You're only as old as you feel."

"Or so they say."

"Whomever *they* are."

Silence.

"Rather does look like fun. . . ."

"Aye, now. It sure does."

Night was coming on now. Blessed, concealing, conspiring darkness.

Sir Graham straightened up. He looked over at his father-in-law, and a slow, reluctant grin curved his lips as the two of them met each other's gazes.

Brendan smiled.

Sir Graham smirked and rubbed his jaw.

An hour later, when Mira went looking for them, she found an empty verandah, abandoned lemonade glasses and heard, coming from across the harbor in the direction of Kieran's sloop *Sandpiper*, loud splashes, her son-in-law's whoops and guffaws, and beloved Irish laughter that she recognized as Brendan's own.

She slapped at the mosquito sucking a hole in her arm and smiling, went to check on Maeve.

All was right in her world.

CHAPTER 26

In the end, Captain Delmore Lord ended up sharing a drink, laughter, and stories of their respective childhoods with his recklessly wild American cousin in the latter's cabin, and the subject that the Englishman had come prepared to discuss, was never raised.

Captain Lord went back to his ship that night feeling strangely liberated, and happier than he could remember being since he was a little lad in long ago Hampshire.

Connor Merrick went to bed that night beneath the stars, cradling Rhiannon in his arms and thinking about what she'd said about having to prove himself.

Vice Admiral Sir Graham Falconer and Captain Brendan Jay Merrick went to bed that night aching in places they didn't know existed, and the following morning could barely walk.

Connor came upon them both in the library, where his father and the admiral were enjoying a morning cup of coffee.

"Faith, that last jump really took a toll on my knee."

"You think your knee is bad? My shoulder feels like someone stuck a knife in it and twisted."

"I was stiffer than the wind out of the nor'east when I got up this morning."

"Well, it was your bloody idea, not mine."

"Nobody forced you to go, lad."

"You think I'm going to let my father-in-law show me up?"

Connor walked in, frowning. "What are you two talking about?"

"Ah, lad, just getting old. Getting old."

"I don't want to hear it. It's depressing."

Connor plucked a book from the shelves, flipped through it without looking at it, put it back, and sat down. Stood up. Went to the window. Came back.

"You make a body tired just looking at you," the admiral said. "Don't you ever sit still?"

"Not for long."

"How's my new daughter?" his father asked, rubbing his knee. "Did she get her sea legs yet?"

"Working on it."

Connor went to another shelf. Picked up another book. Put it back.

Brendan glanced at Sir Graham, and shifted painfully in his chair. "What ails you, lad?"

Connor turned, took a deep and heavy breath, and let it out. "Rhiannon's wondering where we might live. I haven't even given any thought to that. I'm not ready to settle down."

Sir Graham just looked at him and shook his head. "You should have thought about that before you tied the knot."

"You should have thought about that before you forced me to."

"Forced you to? It was your own reckless behavior—"

"Stop it, both of you," Brendan said wearily.

"She also said she loves me," Connor said, beginning to pace. "Imagine. *Love*! Why is it that that's all females think about? All they want? That's why we give them babies, so they *have* something to love!"

Sir Graham leaned his forehead on thumb and finger and slid his father-in-law a quiet, sideways smirk.

"Yes, speaking of babies," Brendan said innocently, "I do hope you don't waste any time on giving your mother and I another grandchild. We're not getting any younger, you know."

"*What?!*"

"Babies."

"For God's sake, Da! Have you no shame?"

"None."

"Right, I've heard enough. I was always told that it was the children who embarrass the parents, but you've managed to turn that belief on its ear. And honestly, Da, when are you ever going to get rid of that ridiculous old hat?"

"I like my hat. Brings back memories."

Connor shook his head, made a noise of impatience, and strode out.

"That's one hell of a mosquito bite you have on your arm, Mother," Maeve said, watching Mira absently scratch at a reddened welt on the inside of her elbow. "Stop digging at it and it won't itch so bad."

"Itch? It's driving me bleedin' mad. Our winters back home might not be as nice as yours are down here, but I wouldn't trade them for your bugs. These damned— why hello, Rhiannon my dear. Why don't you join us for a cup of coffee?"

Rhiannon, who had come over with Connor to see the new baby, shook her head and took a seat.

Mira eyed her in concern. "Everything all right? Fists and mittens and all that?"

Rhiannon's mouth dropped open and she blushed wildly.

"Honestly, Mother, some things are best not talked about." Maeve had been tense, irritable and of unpredictable temper for most of the time that Rhiannon had been here on Barbados, but finally looked serene and at peace as she reclined in a chair, little Grace at her breast, her thick, glossy chestnut hair pulled over one shoulder and spilling over the baby's tiny back.

"Well, I can tell when something's bothering a person, and my new daughter looks troubled. What ails ye, dear? That son of mine treatin' you all right?"

Rhiannon was not used to such plain-spokenness. She sat down, took a deep breath, and looked at the spritely woman who was her mother-in-law in some despair.

"I'm worried about Connor," she said, at last. "The longer I'm with him, the less I feel like I know him. It's as if he's hiding something."

"It's not like Con to be secretive," Maeve said. "Though it would take a fool not to figure out what he's been up to these past few days."

"Once a privateer, always a privateer," Mira said.

"It's not that," Rhiannon said. "Well, maybe it is. It's just that he's so—so *driven*. He puts all caution aside and does things that are reckless, if not dangerous. It's as though he thinks he has something to prove. If not to the world, then to himself."

"Ahh, and you're worried about him."

"I can't help but be worried about him. I'm afraid he's going to take one too many chances and end up getting himself killed."

Maeve's face had gone still and she looked down at her baby, her eyes troubled. Mira noted it and rising, touched Rhiannon's arm, indicating that she follow her out of the room.

Outside in the corridor, Rhiannon paused. "Did I say something wrong?"

"No, no, not at all," Mira said. "But you know, my daughter has the Irish gift of the Sight. She has visions, sometimes, of things that are about to happen, and she had a dream last night about death. I don't want to upset her."

"Death? Whose?" Rhiannon asked, alarmed.

"I don't know, and neither does she. But Maeve's not often wrong about such things."

"Now you have me really worried."

"I don't mean to upset you, my dear. Not much we can do about it, anyhow."

The two of them walked slowly down the hall. "Was Connor always like this? Even as a little boy?"

"Yes, I'm afraid he's always been a daredevil. Some would say, a troublemaker. Even back when he was in school we had our hands full with him."

"What happened?" Rhiannon asked, eager for this glimpse into her husband's formative years.

"Well, Connor never could sit still, and he wasn't much of a student. Had a hard time with school work, and was always gettin' punished for fighting with the other boys." Mira gave a sheepish smile. "Probably gets that from my side of the family."

Rhiannon nodded thoughtfully.

"He was constantly bloodying someone's nose, or gettin' himself into one kind of trouble or another. Connor's not stupid, but book learning came hard to him and still does . . . so he tries hard to find other ways to prove himself. "

"He has nothing to prove to me. I think I was already half in love with him back in England when he was rescuing all those prisoners from the hulks and endangering his own life in the process. He's perfect just the way he is. Why doesn't he see that?"

"Because he will never think he's perfect, until and unless he is his father."

Rhiannon grinned. "Surely, even he's not perfect."

"Maybe not," Mira said, smiling wistfully. "But he comes pretty damned close."

Sir Graham's staff put on a delicious afternoon meal of roast pig accompanied by great pitchers of planters' punch, lemonade, and Bajan rum. Liam Doherty, who was staying aboard Kieran's sloop *Sandpiper*, entertained them all with stories of his best friend's daring and clever exploits during the American War of Independence, much to the delight of everyone in his small audience except Brendan himself, who raised a hand, shook his head, and tried to change the subject.

"Faith, Liam, you exaggerate the details of that particular tale every time you tell it," he said, reaching for a second helping of pork. "Your memory's going, old man. It was only a few men we stole off that British frigate, not two dozen."

"Twenty-five, and there isn't a thing wrong with me memory."

"You stole twenty-five men off one of our frigates?" Alannah asked, amazed.

"Liam's telling tales, Mrs. Cox. It was all a long time ago. My complements to your chef, Gray. These papaya tarts are delicious—"

"Liam's right," Connor said, sitting beside Rhiannon. He had slipped off one sandal and, hidden beneath the tablecloth, was absently rubbing her ankle with his bare toe. "It *was* twenty-five."

"Now Connor, lad, you weren't even there."

"No, Da, but I've heard the story enough times from Mother, and she *was* there."

"It was twenty-five," she said, with an infectious, impish grin. "Under cover of night, your father sailed *Kestrel* right up to the British frigate that had been chasing us all day, sent a note across via two of his young crewmembers who were pretending to be local fishermen, and coerced twenty-five of His Majesty's tars to join our crew."

"You both exaggerate," Brendan said with a dismissive shake of his head, and looking up, caught Rhiannon's admiring gaze. He grinned, his honey-colored eyes twinkling. "Don't believe a word they say," he told her, and talk moved on to little Grace, ships, appreciation for the meal, and how hot the day had been. Eventually, Maeve excused herself to go feed her baby. Liam nodded off in his chair and began to snore. The plates were cleared, Ned clambered up on his grandfather's lap and asked him to tell him more stories of the American Revolution, and even Connor, usually unable to sit still, stifled a yawn.

"Let us go take a walk, Rhiannon," he said, poking around with his bare foot beneath the table until he found his other sandal. "I've been sitting too long."

He got up, tall and handsome, his curls haphazardly tousled and his long, well-muscled calves and bare feet tanned beneath the ragged fringe of his canvas trousers. He helped Rhiannon up from her chair and, making their excuses, they headed downstairs and outside.

It was early evening and the heat of the day was subsiding, the ever-moving trade winds rustling through the coconut palms. The shadows were long as they walked down the path toward what Rhiannon had come to think of as their own little cove.

"Oh, look," she said. "Someone's hung a hammock between those two trees."

Letting go of his hand, she walked over to the net crescent, tried to sit in it, and was promptly dumped into the warm sand as it flipped over. In a tangle of skirts, she came up laughing as immediately her husband was there, reaching down to help her up.

"Silly girl," he said fondly, "hasn't anyone ever shown you the right way to get into a hammock?"

"I'm afraid not." She brushed sand off her arm. "Perhaps you can instruct me!"

With his back to the hammock, he sat down and in one quick movement, brought his legs up. The contraption swung gently as he stretched comfortably out in it. He looked over at her, his mouth curved in that playful grin that she so loved.

"See? It's not so hard."

"You're a show off, Connor Merrick."

"I'm lonely. Come join me."

She eyed the swinging hammock dubiously, but he reached a hand up and as she took it, he yanked her down on top of himself; the hammock swung dangerously and Rhiannon let out a little shriek, but he hooked an arm around behind her to steady her and a moment later, she found herself stretched out alongside and partly atop him, her head comfortably pillowed in the cup of his shoulder, his heart beating beneath her ear and the trees, the sky, moving gently back and forth, up and down, as the hammock swung gently with the last of the momentum.

"Mmmm," he murmured, his arm cradling her close. "This is nice."

They lay there together, listening to the surf down on the beach moving rhythmically against the shore, the chattering of monkeys in a distant tree, and feeling the trade winds playing with their hair.

Rhiannon's hand slipped beneath Connor's shirt.

"I could touch you all day," she murmured, her fingers circling the small, pebbly nipples before moving out over his chest.

He just smiled, looking at her with a lazy, assessing gaze that reminded her of a predator at rest, watching her and waiting to see what she would do.

"Do you think anyone can see us?"

"I don't know. Do you care?"

"Well, of course I care."

"You are my wife now, Rhiannon. Mine. We don't need to hide our feelings for each other from anyone."

And with that, he took her hand and guided it down to his pantaloons, where she felt the strength and power of his arousal pushing up, hard, against the fabric.

Rhiannon's head jerked up, and she looked toward the house. "What if someone comes and finds us?"

"Live a little, my dear." His grin was wicked.

And with that, he shifted slightly in the hammock and, still holding her hand against himself, hooked his other arm around her neck and pulled her down to kiss her.

Rhiannon melted beneath the delicious onslaught. He tasted of papaya tart and the rum with which he'd washed it down, and his mouth was firm and insistent against her own. Beneath her hand he swelled full and hard, and as her lips parted to receive his tongue, as her senses began to swim with delight and anticipation, she rubbed him through the rough canvas trousers.

"Maybe we'd better . . . go aboard *Kestrel*," he managed, between groans.

"Live a little," she parroted, rubbing him harder.

"Live a little? Hmph! I think I'm dying."

She laughed, running her fingers up and down his bulging length until he reached down, found the hem of her gown and tossed it over himself, covering their actions from anyone who might come upon them.

"You're shameless, Rhiannon Evans Merrick."

"I just have a good teacher."

Her hand now hidden beneath her own skirts, she traced her fingernail along his arousal, swelling thick and hard beneath the rough canvas of his pantaloons. It was a wicked, sinful feeling with a sense of urgency about it to be doing these things out here in broad, albeit fading, daylight where anyone might come along and see. She heard his breathing change in pitch as she explored him through the fabric, and delighted in watching the effects of her newfound power over him, delighted in the fact that she could make him helpless, because even if she could not make him love her, well, she could make him want her and maybe, for now, that had to be good enough.

For now.

Maybe some day he will come to love me. Some day, when he realizes he doesn't have to be his father, that he doesn't have to try so hard, that he has nothing to prove to anyone, when—

He was kissing her again, his breath coming hot against her cheek, one hand lifted to massage her breast through the light muslin of her gown until she, too, was breathing as harshly as he.

She felt the familiar heat building in her blood as his kiss became more urgent, a delicious onslaught against not only her mouth and tongue, but her senses themselves. Growing desperate now herself, Rhiannon unbuttoned him and suddenly his hard, hot length was in her hand. He groaned. The kiss deepened. She stroked him, squeezed him, and then rubbed her thumb once, twice, over the head, delighting in the increased tempo of his breathing, the sound of her own pulse growing quicker in her ears. At last he reached down and caught her hand, his pale, sea-colored gaze locked intently on her dark green one as he broke the kiss.

"You're a wicked woman, Rhiannon, and I wouldn't have you any other way."

"Come inside me, Connor. If you can."

His eyes smiled, and little crinkle lines fanned out from their corners. "If I *can*?"

"We're squashed together on a narrow hammock that is bowed beneath our weight. It's not like there's a bed beneath us."

"My oh my, do you have a lot to learn."

And with that, he stroked her own inner flesh until she was panting and gasping. Then, shifting position, he hooked a thumb in her drawers, pulled them down as she willingly lifted her hips to accommodate him, and maneuvered her atop himself. Beneath them, the hammock moved wildly for a moment and then settled, swinging gently back and forth.

"Aren't you supposed to be on the top?" she asked, puzzled.

He just grinned and, his hands bracketing her hips, lifted her up and off him. "Put me inside of yourself, Rhiannon."

Squeezed within the tight confines, she found him once more. She adjusted her own position until he was poised at her entrance, now damp and slick with her own readiness for him.

"I want you, Rhiannon," he murmured, his eyes darkening as she slowly rubbed him back and forth along her cleft, teasing them both. "Our marriage might have been forced, but by God, you're the best thing that ever happened to me."

And with that, he lowered her down atop himself and entered her, the huge, hot length of him beginning to fill her, to stretch her, deeper and deeper, inch by delicious inch, until they lay locked together, both of them now trembling with need.

"Take me, Connor," she breathed as his hands, hard with callous but sensitive enough to know just how to pleasure her, began to lift her up on top of himself and then to lower her back down, building a rhythm that would take them all the way to where they both wanted to go. "Make me yours all over again."

She tried to reach down to kiss him, but with the bow of the hammock it was impossible and all she could do was lay there, speared on his shaft, lifted up and down by his powerful hands until she felt a searing climax beginning to build within her, until she bent her head and bit her lip and began to whimper deep in her throat, until with a sudden groan, he stiffened and spilled his seed deep within her A moment later her own senses shattered; she cried out and convulsed all around his still-quivering shaft, and then, as she all but collapsed on top of him, his fingers found her hidden, swollen bud and stroked her hard until she came a second time . . . a third.

They lay there together, both damp and panting, the hammock swinging like a cradle beneath them. The shadows lengthened. Eventually they separated, and she settled down to lie beside him, tucked up against him with his arm holding her close, her head pillowed in the cup of his shoulder.

"I wish we could stay here all afternoon," Rhiannon murmured, idly tracing the groove of his breastbone with her fingers.

He stretched, put a foot out and down, and rested it on the ground below so that he could idly rock them back and forth in a gentle, peaceful motion. "Well, we can stay here until the mosquitoes come out, at least."

"I can hear your heart beating beneath my ear."

"Good. Nice to know I'm still alive after that."

She laughed and inched a little further up so that she could look over at him. A dark shadow cloaked his jawline, and in the late afternoon light his lips looked sculpted, firm, and noble. She reached up and put her forefinger into one of the loose curls that hung down over his forehead, stretching it out and watching it spring back, admiring the thick, glossy waves of his hair and thinking he was quite possibly—no, quite probably—the most handsome man on earth.

A god, she had thought, when she'd first met him.

He glanced over at her, smiling. "Have you given any more thought about where you'd like to make our home once we leave here, dearest?"

"I'd be happy to live in Newburyport with you, Connor. I adore your family . . . your father, your mother, even Liam Doherty. And if Toby and Nathan are also there, well, it makes it all the better."

"How so?"

"I lost my mother and father when I was young, and had only Gwyneth and Morganna. I didn't have a big family, and even though I love my sisters, my place is with you. Your family is now mine. If you promise that we can go to England once a year to visit with my sisters, I would love to make my home in Newburyport with you."

"You're a treasure, dearest heart. And I would be happy to bring you to England as often as you like." He grinned, and she saw the tiredness coming into his smile, into his eyes. "Or rather, as often as I can slip past the blockade."

"I'm sure, Connor, that if your father can do it, then so can you."

He smiled, his eyes slipping shut. "How nice that you have such faith in me."

"I've seen you in action, remember."

"Mmm, well, you are about to see me out of action, because I'm getting quite sleepy... nap with me, Rhiannon?"

He lay on his back. She, on her side facing him, was already snuggled as close as she could get to him, his powerful arm curving around behind her neck and shoulders, her body lying alongside his, dwarfed by it, warmed by it, sheltered by it.

This is heaven, she thought.

She wondered what life would be like in Newburyport, an American town, foreign and far away and with a climate that was surely colder than Britain's could ever be. But Connor would be there. His family, tight-knit, quirky, warm, delightful, and already embracing her as one of their own, would be there. She didn't care where they lived as long as she could be with this man for the rest of her days, and to have her new family there made it all the sweeter. She put her palm over her husband's heart, watching the steady rise and fall of his chest, listening to his breathing slow and grow rhythmic as he relaxed beneath her and the hammock stopped its slow swinging as his foot, eternally restless, finally fell still.

She knew, with the intuition of the intimately connected, the exact moment he fell asleep and left her. She moved her head to look up at him, at his angular jaw, his slightly parted lips, his dark lashes lying fanlike against his cheeks.

"You are beautiful," she whispered, her heart swelling with emotion as she gazed upon him. "And I love you."

His other arm lay over his chest, the fingers lax, and as she settled back down against the cup of his shoulder and looked at that hand ... the small scar between thumb and forefinger, the short, well groomed nails, the length of the fingers, the breadth and strength across the back of the palm, she saw something she had not noticed before.

His little pinkie was crooked and bent, not coming straight off the knuckle like the rest of his fingers, but at a slight angle to it. Idly, she wondered if he'd gotten it caught in rigging, or injured it in some way aboard ship. Heaven knew there were a thousand ways for a mariner to get hurt. She yawned, and blinked, and looked again at that slightly crooked finger, and eventually fell asleep to the sound of his heart beating steadily beneath her ear.

CHAPTER 27

Several days later Brendan, accompanied by an exuberant Ned, rowed himself out to *Kestrel* and asked permission to come aboard.

"For heaven's sake, Da, she's your ship. You don't need to ask permission," Connor said, reaching a hand down to help his father over the rail. "You and your formalities!"

"She may be my ship, but you're her captain."

"Yes, but you were her first. And, her best." He grinned as the elder Merrick respectfully removed his tricorne as his feet touched the deck. "And when are you going to get rid of that dreadful hat?"

His father gave a distracted smile but didn't rise to the old joke. "Do you have a moment, Con?"

Connor saw the tension in his father's face and his teasing grin immediately faded. "Of course." He beckoned to his cousins and One-Eye, lounging near the stern. "Toby! Go find a drop-line and see if you can show Ned here how to catch a fish."

"Aye, Con. I'd be happy to."

Brendan mustered a smile as the youth approached. "Faith, Toby, you grow another inch every time I see you. Your parents aren't going to recognize you when we get you back to Newburyport."

"I wish *I* could go to Newburyport!" Ned cried. "Can you take me?"

"Your mother would skin me alive," Connor said.

"Yes, when *are* we going back to Newburyport?" asked Nathan, coming up to shake his uncle's hand. "I'm sick of this heat and we're about as low on crew as it's possible to get and still sail the old lady home."

"That's what I came to talk to you about." Brendan waited until Toby had led Ned off to the stern, then went to one of the starboard guns and leaned wearily against its truck. "Your mother isn't feeling well. She wants to go home."

"Mother? Not feeling well? What's the matter?"

"I think the heat is getting to her. She's a New Englander and not made for this climate. Neither am I, for that matter. But she's not herself, and that worries me." Brendan cast a glance toward Ned, who was busily lowering a drop line off the schooner's stern while Toby looked on. "Kieran wants to stay here and visit with his sister. I was hoping you'd take us home in *Kestrel*."

"Sure, Da. We can leave any time you wish."

"How long will it take you to provision?"

"We could be out of here on tomorrow's tide."

"Good. I'll tell Maeve, then. She'll be disappointed, but I think it's best we leave sooner rather than later." He took off the old black tricorne, ran a hand through hair that was still as thick and tousled as his son's, and replaced the hat.

"Probably just as well, anyhow. The old lady here needs to spend some time in the yard. Her frames beneath the planking are rotting, you know."

"She's as seaworthy as the day she was launched."

"No, she is not. She needs work in places that a body can't see, Connor. Trust me on that."

"She's *fine*, Father. You worry too much."

A shadow came over Brendan's face at his son's use of the formal word. *Father*. But he said nothing, and reached out to touch *Kestrel*'s smooth, varnished rail.

"Besides," Connor said, noting his father's uncharacteristic demeanor, "how would you know such a thing?"

"Don't ask me how I know, I just do. And furthermore, I know something else and so does Sir Graham." He shot a sideways glance to his son. "Something about a certain convoy being plucked clean by a mysterious, sharp-sailing Yankee topsail schooner?"

Connor grinned and rubbing his jaw, caught Nathan's eye.

"You've worn out your welcome here, lad. All the more reason to go home before you force your brother-in-law to throw you in jail."

"He wouldn't dare."

"Don't underestimate him. You've put him in a ticklish spot, with his duty and his men's expectations on one side and his wife's family on the other. I don't envy the man."

"When did he learn of this . . . Yankee schooner?"

"He got a dispatch this morning—and a formal request for his help in finding and apprehending certain *said schooner*. You try his patience, Connor, and this time you've gone too far."

"Nothing like an angry British admiral."

"Your father here isn't too happy about it, either."

"Yes, right, I'd forgotten. You sided with the Federalists. You were against this war from the beginning, you who made your fortune during the last one and would deny me the chance to do the same. You'd probably be just as happy to see New England secede and join the British, wouldn't you?"

"Easy, Con," Nathan said, putting a hand on his cousin's arm.

But Brendan did not rise to Connor's tightly-voiced taunt. Instead, he turned and smiled as Rhiannon, garbed in a mint green muslin gown and wearing a bonnet to protect her face from the sun, came up from below.

"Good morning, lass!"

"Hello, Brendan," she said, and instead of offering her hand, happily allowed herself to be swept up in his strong, wiry arms. But something wasn't right here; she could see it in Connor's tense stance and tight mouth, and in her father-in-law's troubled eyes, normally so carefree and laughing.

"Is everything all right?"

"We'll be weighing anchor tomorrow and heading home to New England," Connor snapped. "Mother is not feeling well, and Sir Graham would like my head on a pike to parade through the streets. I'll send you back with my father and Ned so you can collect your things from the house and make your farewells."

"But this is so sudden. . . ."

At that moment there was an excited squeal as Ned pulled a fish up over the transom with Toby's help. Holding the wriggling creature in his bare hands, the boy came running toward them, his face glowing. "Grandpa! Uncle Connor and Aunt Rhiannon! Look what we caught!"

As Rhiannon exclaimed over the boy's catch and Connor proclaimed it bigger than any fish he'd ever seen, Brendan knelt down and examined the animal. Its gills were desperately opening and closing. "That's a fine fish you have there, Ned. And now, unless you intend to eat him for supper tonight, I think you should let him go before he dies."

"Of course, Grandpa. I don't want him to die." Carefully carrying the fish, the boy hurried back to the side, leaning far out over the rail so as to lessen the drop to the water as he released it.

"Little lad's got a good heart," said Brendan, his eyes fond as he watched his grandson.

"Aye, he sure does."

"Well, I'm off now to go check on your mother. Will we see you at dinner tonight?"

"Nay, I've work to do here. Give everyone my farewells."

"You'll be missed, Son."

Connor just shrugged.

"I know that you and Maeve don't always see eye-to-eye, and Sir Graham is in a tough spot with wondering how to deal with you, but think of how it'll affect the twins if you don't come to say goodbye." He glanced at his grandson, waiting eagerly by the rail. "And little Ned."

Connor's gaze slid helplessly to his nephew, and he sighed in despair.

"Aye, Da. I'll be there."

Their last meal on Barbados was one of stuffed fowl, shellfish, hot bread with guava jelly, rum, and a sugar cake that was much the better for the fact that Mira Merrick, who had skipped the meal and kept to her room with a headache, had had nothing to do with its creation.

Tension hung in the air. Sir Graham purposely avoided making conversation or eye contact with Connor. Connor's smile was tight, his manner flippant, his foot beating a relentless tap-tap-tap beneath the table until Rhiannon finally squeezed his hand and managed to quiet him. Alannah Cox made an excuse to leave the uncomfortable atmosphere as soon as dessert was served and Delmore Lord followed suit a few moments later. Someone commented about the weather, which was unremarkable. Finally Brendan, his eyes dark with worry, excused himself to go be with his wife, and Ned, who had been uncharacteristically subdued all night, climbed up onto his uncle's lap with a book in his hand.

"Do you all really have to leave tomorrow, Uncle Connor?"

"Aye, lad. We really have to leave. But perhaps Rhiannon and I will come back in the springtime. Or your mother and da will bring you north so you can spend the summer with us in Newburyport. Wouldn't that be fun?"

"I'm going to miss you," the little boy said, his bottom lip quivering before he quickly looked down at his book to hide his unmanly display.

"I'm going to miss you too, Ned." And then, to distract his nephew from his coming tears, "What've you got there, eh?"

"My favorite book, *Robinson Crusoe*. I was hoping you'd read to me before Mama sends me to bed."

For a moment, there was silence.

"Well, this ought to be interesting," Maeve said cryptically.

Connor shot her a glare. "Stow it, Maeve."

The boy was oblivious to the tension between the two. "Will you read to me, Uncle Connor?"

"It's getting rather late, lad," Connor said, a little too quickly. "We've got to be up early. Perhaps Auntie Rhiannon can read to you . . . I'm not very smart, you know. She's got a better voice for storytelling than I do, anyhow."

The boy's face fell.

"How about I tell you a story, instead? Once, there was this huge ship called—"

"I don't really want a story, Uncle Connor. I just wanted to have a last memory with you and my favorite book so that after you leave tomorrow, I wouldn't be so sad. But never mind. I understand."

The boy slid down from his uncle's lap.

Connor began to fidget.

And Rhiannon, frowning, exchanged a glance with the equally confused Sir Graham.

What's going on, here?

Damned if I know.

Rhiannon saw the stricken look on her husband's face as Ned headed quietly for the door.

"The least you could do, Connor, is read him his favorite story," Sir Graham said reprovingly. "It's not that much to ask, is it?"

Rhiannon had never seen fear in her husband's eyes. But in that brief instant, she saw a sudden flash of panic before he suddenly seemed to collect himself.

"Ned, lad."

The child paused at the door and turned, the book still clutched in his hand.

"I'm sorry. I guess I can read to you."

The boy ran back to his uncle and clambered up into his lap. Connor mustered a fleeting grin, cleared his throat and, taking a long time to open the faded, well-worn cover, finally put it on the table before him.

"Thank you, Uncle Connor. I know the story by heart . . . but I just wanted to hear it told in *your* voice."

Rhiannon saw her husband take a deep breath and turn a page, then turn it back again and draw his brows close as he stared down at the print, little Ned snuggling comfortably against his shoulder.

Rhiannon smiled, anticipating the familiar words and wanting, like the child, to hear the beloved old tale in her husband's deep, comforting voice:

I was born in the year 1632, in the City of York, of a good family, though not of that country, my father being a foreigner of Bremen. . . .

But Connor had not started reading. Instead he was biting his lip, peering down at the page in what appeared to be deep concentration, and doing everything he could to buy time.

"Uncle Connor?"

Connor Merrick began to read.

"I was . . . dorn in the year 1326, in the York of C-City, of— of a doog f-family—" he flushed, his face going crimson with humiliation—"th-though ton of th-that tunkrey. . . ."

A deep, awful, embarrassed hush fell over the room as the sudden realization sank in.

Connor slammed the book shut and glared up at the open-mouthed faces, the looks of astonishment and dawning pity all directed at him.

"So I never learned to read," he said flippantly, but in his eyes Rhiannon saw his deep and abiding shame. "Is that such a crime?"

Sir Graham cleared his throat and looked away. Maeve stared morosely down at the floor and little Ned, still lying against Connor's chest and shoulder, reached out and found his uncle's hand.

"I don't care if you can't read, Uncle Connor. I love you just the same."

Rhiannon wanted only to save her husband from further humiliation. "I think we should take our leave, Connor," she said quietly. "We need to catch the tide first thing."

But Sir Graham was staring at his brother-in-law. "If you can't read, how the hell can you look at a chart and plot a ship's course? Read manifests? A compass? What the devil kind of captain *are* you?"

"One who's lucky enough to have a cousin named Nathan who does those things for me," Connor shot back. "Never did guess, did you? None of you did. And now you know my shame. Now you know why I am the way I am, why I've spent my life trying to prove myself to be something I'm not, and what I'm not is smart. But I *am* smart enough not to stay here and have you all look at me with pity, and if you have nothing more to say about it, then neither do I." He hugged the boy and gently set him down as he got to his feet. "Good evening. I'll see you all in the morning."

Back stiff with pride, he stalked to the door.

Rhiannon ran after him and caught up with him out in the hall.

"Connor, wait."

He turned then, his eyes hard with humiliation and anger. "You married an idiot, Rhiannon. I'm sorry."

Never slowing his pace, he continued toward the door and outside, wanting only to put as much distance as he could between himself and everyone back in that room who'd witnessed his ultimate humiliation. Ned, who idolized him. Sir Graham and Maeve. And his wife, who would never look at him with the same infatuated awe ever again, and in whose eyes and estimation he'd surely just plummeted. His wife, who now knew him to be less than a man. She, who liked to read books. She who *wasn't* stupid, she who was all the things that he was not and could never be.

Oh, the mortification.

"Connor."

He was nearly to the beach where the little boat, drawn up on the sand away from the tide, waited. Hands fisted, he turned, thankful for the darkness that hid the shame in his eyes.

"Don't pity me, Rhiannon."

"I don't pity you." She took a step closer to him and slid her hand up his chest, gently stroking it through the shirt, trying to calm him. "How could I ever pity a man whose courage causes him to leap with joyful abandon into the unknown? Who is a master at chess, so much so that not a man of his acquaintance can best him? A man whose wiliness netted him two thirds of a rich convoy with none of them the wiser?"

He just looked away, his mouth a hard slash of pain in his face.

"Your shame is not my own, Connor," she said. "I am proud of you. In awe of you." She faced him squarely. "In *love* with you."

"You're only in *love* with me because you're young and impressionable and I do reckless, daring things."

"That's bollocks, Connor."

He gaped at her. "Where did you learn such a word?"

"From your crew, and I hope to learn a good deal more such words if I'm going to be a proper sea captain's wife. Furthermore, it makes me angry that you think I love you because I'm a silly eighteen-year-old girl who's only interested in daring deeds and displays of manly courage. Well, I'll tell you something, Connor Merrick. I'm in love with the man who cares enough about others to continuously risk his own life to save theirs. The man who is good and gentle and kind and caring. The man who got his own stuffy cousin to learn how to have fun, the man whose crew adores him and would follow him to the ends of the earth, the man who, at great risk and sacrifice to himself, took the time to give a little boy he loves a parting gift so that that little boy won't be so sad after he's gone. That's the man who's stolen my heart, Connor. Not the daredevil, the show-off, or the cocky privateer captain."

He just looked at her, confused, and Rhiannon saw the exact moment when he began to dare to believe her words. A softening in his stiffened stance. A relaxing of the hard, poised muscles beneath her fingers.

"It doesn't matter if you can't read," she continued. "You have Nathan to help you with what you need aboard ship, and you have me to help you everywhere else. The only person ashamed by this is you, because I couldn't care less. We're husband and wife now. Two who have become one, and your strengths are now mine, just as mine are now yours. Together, there's nothing we can't do."

He looked away. "I can't see the letters right," he muttered. "They face all different directions. Sometimes they're upside down. And when I try too hard to make sense of them, my head hurts and I feel like I'm going to vomit. Honestly, I don't know how any of you can put up with such torment just for the sake of being able to read."

Most of us don't, she almost said. But he didn't need to be told he was different. He already knew that he was. The sadness came from the fact that his idea of "different" was, in his own eyes, "inferior."

"My teacher tried to beat it into me," he said, turning and untying the boat from the large chunk of driftwood to which he'd secured it. "He said I was unteachable and maybe I was, because I was more interested in looking out the window than at my hornbook or worse, that damnable New England Primer. Never could make much sense of either of them and never cared to, either."

She nodded toward his hand with its little crooked finger. "Was it that same teacher who broke your pinkie?"

"Aye. I was daydreaming, and he wanted to get my attention. I daresay he did . . . though he was never able to get my mind to stop wandering. Nobody has. I can't read. I can't rein in my thoughts. I can't think of more than one thing at a time without getting confused and frustrated and ultimately, angry."

She caught his arm as he began to push the boat out into the water. "Think of the things you are, Connor, and the things you *can* do. The gifts you've given to others. You're a man who knows how to live life to the fullest and whose enthusiasm for it is infectious. And I'm just one of many whose life is much the richer for your presence in it. You've opened my heart and soul to a whole new world. You taught me how to swim. You taught me how to jump out into the unknown with faith and joy. Maybe someday, you'll even teach me how to take a few steps aloft." She smiled. "But just a few. Because we all have our shame, Connor, and mine is my fear of heights."

He finally paused, took a deep, bracing breath and looked down at her, overwhelmed at what she had just said.

"You're an amazing woman, Rhiannon Evans Merrick."

"And you, Connor Merrick, are an amazing man."

He reached down and drew her up against him, folding her against his chest, his strong, hard arms going around her and all but crushing her to himself. She felt him lay his cheek against the top of her head; then he gently pulled back, raised her face to his own and, looking deeply into her eyes, said the words she'd longed, with all her heart, to hear.

"I love you."

Tears filled her eyes as he bent his head to kiss her, and as his lips claimed hers with hunger and gratitude she thought of Connor as a little boy, abused and mistreated so terribly by those who did not understand him, who didn't try to understand him, who tried to make him be exactly like everyone else. Now she knew why he was so driven to prove himself. Why he took the risks that he did, why he had made his father's long ago exploits a benchmark by which to measure and define his own successes.

Connor Merrick might be able to outsmart the British and play a superior game of chess, but underneath the recklessness and the swagger was a little boy who still believed that he was stupid, worthless, and was desperate to prove himself.

And for Rhiannon, it all suddenly made sense.

"Honestly, Brendan, I'm quite capable of boarding our old friend *Kestrel* here, myself," Mira said as she ignored his offered hand and came aboard the schooner the following morning. "I'm gonna be fine. Stop yer worryin."

Her, Brendan's, and Liam's trunks and belongings had all been brought aboard earlier, the schooner hastily provisioned, and goodbyes already said to the Falconers and Kieran, who was staying behind for a longer visit with his sister and her family. The youngest Merrick stood now aboard the deck of his sloop *Sandpiper*, watching them as they prepared to get underway. Gulls wheeled over Carlisle Bay and Connor's fingers were drumming in agitation as he eyed his mother and sent his scanty crew forward.

"Let's haul in the hook and get the hell out of here," he said to Nathan. "I want to clear Barbados well before any of Sir Graham's frigate captains decide to take matters into their own hands where *certain Yankee schooners* are concerned." He shot a glance at his father, but Brendan had paused to help Mira, who looked pale and waxen as she went to lean against the old cannon that someone, long ago, had dubbed *Freedom*. "Mother, you are ill. Let *Dadaí* take you below."

"I don't want to go below. I want fresh air."

Liam reached his great bear paw of a hand down to her. "Come, Mira. Con said ye can have your old cabin, just like old times."

"I said, I'm quite happy to stay here on deck, damn it!"

"Damnation," Connor swore, and stalked off across the deck. "Can't reason with a female no matter what. Get the jib and mainsail on her, Nathan." And then, lowering his voice for his cousin's ears alone, "Did you get a chance to study the charts? I'd hate like hell to hit a reef or some other godforsaken obstruction as we round the island."

"Aye, Con. No worries."

Connor nodded. His secret was safe with his cousin but nevertheless he went to the helm, pretended to engross himself in studying the charts laid out there—charts whose numbers were back and forth and upside-down—and saw Rhiannon, garbed in a lemon-yellow muslin gown with tiny white flowers dancing around the hem, bringing a glass of cold lemonade to his mother.

His heart warmed at his wife's simple gesture of kindness. He'd bet his eyeteeth that Rhiannon would find a way to get his mother to go below and rest, even if he and his father could not.

Sure enough, his mother, wiping her brow with the back of one hand, nodded at something Rhiannon said and a moment later, was following her below.

"She's a good lass, that one," Brendan said, joining Connor at the helm. "It does my old heart good that you married such a kind and caring woman."

"What, no jokes about working on grandchildren?"

"Not today, lad. Not today."

"Is Mother all right?"

Brendan looked away. "She'll be better once she's home."

Forward, several men were at the windlass, working to bring the anchor in while Toby leaned out over the bows, watching its progress.

"Anchor's hove short, Con!"

"Bring it in and let's go home."

A rousing chorus swept through the ship. "Three cheers for home!"

"Three cheers for our captain!"

"Three cheers for the captain's father, who brought this ship to glory in times of old!"

"Hip hip, huzzah!"

Brendan touched his old black tricorne to them, his smile pained and fleeting.

"See, Dad? You're a legend."

"'Twas a long time ago, Con. And legends, like snowballs, have a way of getting bigger and bigger the longer they roll and the farther they travel. Unless you have anything you'd like me to do up here on deck, I'm going below to be with your mother."

"I've got it all under control."

Brendan watched the men haul in the dripping anchor and secure it to the cathead, and beneath their feet the schooner began to move, her long, stately jib-boom swinging slowly around as the trade winds filled her jib and his son's hand confidently guided the old ship out of Carlisle Bay. He waved a final time to Kieran and his youngest son waved back, and something tugged at Brendan's Irish heart. A premonition, perhaps, not unlike something his daughter might have felt. A lament for days gone by, a deep, intuitive concern that Connor, in his never-ending quest to prove himself, was going to push *Kestrel* beyond her limits.

A sense of impending disaster.

For Brendan knew that his beloved schooner, like himself, was feeling her age.

And he knew that he wasn't wrong about the rot beneath her planking, and within her very bones themselves.

But he had other matters that worried him far more, and leaving the schooner in the care of his son, headed below.

CHAPTER 28

The wind filled in from the east and cooled the baking deck, and with all her canvas set hard against it, *Kestrel* was soon charging along on a beam reach with the log registering nine knots. Flying fish leaped up and over the driving jib-boom, and the two cats came running as one occasionally landed, flapping, on the deck. The bright green dome that was Barbados fell steadily astern, and Nathan charted a course that would take them past the tiny island of Bequia, then St. Thomas and through the beautiful blue-green waters of the Sir Francis Drake Channel. They made good time.

A day after they left Barbados, Rhiannon found Connor at the tiller and studying the distant horizon. Clouds were thick in the sky but to the north, far beyond the plunging jib-boom, the horizon showed bright blue and the wind remained steady out of the east.

"Glad to be headed home?" she asked, curving her arm around his waist. He was barefoot and garbed in his usual cut-off pantaloons, but the wind was brisk this morning and the snug, double-breasted pea coat showed off his powerful shoulders and lean physique.

"Always glad to be headed home. I just wish we'd been able to find more men to sign aboard back in Barbados. I hate being so short-handed."

"Seems to me you have enough to work the sails and stand the watches."

"Aye, but not to fight the ship if need be."

"Why would we need to fight? Didn't you have enough of adventure and riches with that convoy?"

"I have no way of knowing how many of those ships actually made it to Mobile without being recaptured or lost. And I'm a privateer, Rhiannon. If I see something that looks like a worthy prize, I'm not going to just steer clear of it."

Rhiannon sighed in despair. Her husband seemed even more restless and tense since they'd left Barbados; was it because of worries about being short-handed when it came to crew? Or was it the fact that his father was aboard that had him desperate to prove himself?

It would not do, Rhiannon knew, to ask.

"How is my mother this morning?"

"I just visited with her. I brought her some refreshment, but she declined it and said she just wanted to stay in bed. I'm worried about her, Connor. She's cold one minute, and hot and sweating the next."

"Where's my Da?"

"With her, of course."

Connor nodded. He felt a faint stirring of unease which he quickly tamped down. His mother would be fine. She was his mother, for God's sake. One of his parents. Parents were infallible. They were there for you from the moment you came bawling out of the womb, there to soothe childhood hurts and youthful broken hearts, there to advise and listen and love; they were there for you every moment of your conscious life, as constant as the stars in the sky or the tides in the sea.

Nothing to worry about.

He dismissed his unease and turned his bright smile on his wife, who looked particularly fetching this morning in a pale yellow gown with little blue ribbons decorating the open sleeves. She had borrowed one of his straw hats and her hair, not quite red, not quite gold, was caught in a strip of leather and tumbled down her back.

Desire stirred in his loins. Though his parents occupied *Kestrel*'s main cabin, there were other places on the ship that he wouldn't mind taking his wife. Leaning his thigh against the big tiller to keep the schooner steady on her course, he bent down and brushed his lips over Rhiannon's temple; then, enjoying her fresh, lemony scent, he recklessly licked the skin behind her ear.

"Really, Connor, not here!"

"Why not? You're gorgeous and I can't help myself. Besides, it's just a kiss, Rhiannon." He grinned, his eyes warming with a teasing light. "Live a little."

And then, before she could say anything more, he pulled her close, pushed a hand beneath her hair and loosened it to fly free in the wind. There. that was better. Rhiannon, just the way he liked her, unfettered, happy, enjoying the elements. His put a finger beneath her chin, tilted her face up to his, and claimed her lips in a long, searing kiss that left her heavy-lidded with desire and he with an erection that pressed painfully against his drop front.

"This is going to be a long passage," he muttered, as a head came up above the hatch and he saw Toby's bright red curls. "I want you, Rhiannon. Badly."

"There's always tonight underneath the stars if we're quiet."

"Jacques has the watch. And he's a nosy old woman who doesn't miss a trick."

She sighed and moved into the protective circle of his arm, leaning her head against his collarbone and inhaling deeply of his salty, wind-cleansed scent. "You're right. This *is* going to be a long passage."

"How long will it take us to get to Newburyport?"

"Depending on the wind, about a week and a half."

Rhiannon groaned. "Perhaps you should have someone other than Jacques stand the watch tonight."

Her husband laughed and tipped his head back to check the pennants so high above, now streaming out to larboard in the wind coming over the beam.

"Ever sail a ship before, Rhiannon?"

"Oh no, surely, I couldn't!"

"Of course you could. Here. Take the tiller."

"I'm afraid! What if something happens?"

"What's going to happen? I'm right here. It's not hard. The sails are set and well trimmed, the wind is steady, our course hasn't changed and all you have to do is hold the tiller and keep her on course."

"How do I do that?"

"See the compass there, in its box? Look at where the needle points. See how the letters on the compass are there, with the N at the top, the S at the bottom, and our heading is right there between the N and the W?"

"Yes . . . ."

"Just keep it there. And you'll do fine."

"All right. I'll give it a try. But don't leave me here by myself!"

He laughed and passed her the thick, salt-encrusted rope that was attached to the tiller, put there to take some of the strain off the helmsman in rough seas and weather.

Her heart pounding with something that was more excitement than fear, Rhiannon stepped into her husband's place, wrapped her hand around the tackle and put her other one on the smooth, varnished wood of the tiller.

And then he let go and stood back.

"Oh, my!" Rhiannon cried excitedly, as she felt the schooner come alive in her hands, felt the ship's very soul entrusted so lovingly into her care. She thrilled at the feel of the rudder's bite so far beneath and below her, thrilled to the feel of the beautiful ship cutting through each long, frothy swell, thrilled to the feel of all that power of the wind, from deck level to some ninety feet above, where the strong easterly made hard drums against the sails; all of it, that power, held in her hand; she had ridden horses, felt the strength of the animal through the reins, and this was no different. Suddenly she understood what sailors through the ages had always known. That ships had souls. And that *Kestrel* was not just a machine, an inanimate object of wind, wood, and canvas; in Rhiannon's hand, she was a living, breathing being, alive, responsive and spirited.

She threw back her head and laughed. "Oh, Connor, this is wonderful!"

He grinned, and his eyes looked all the more green in the bright sunlight reflecting off the deep, foaming sea around them. "Well, what kind of captain's lady would you be if you didn't know how to steer a ship?"

"Teach me more! What happens if I push the tiller to larboard?"

"She'll round up. Her nose will come into the wind and we'll have to sheet in the sails."

"What happens if I push the tiller to starboard?"

"She'll fall off, and we'll have to ease out."

"How do you know where we're going?"

"The compass and the charts."

"Charts? Which one?" She saw a thick, yellowed paper, curled and water-stained at the edges laid out on the binnacle, its corners weighed down by bar shot. "That one?"

"Mind your ship, dearest. The foresail's starting to luff. You've brought her a little too close to the wind, so let her fall off a bit."

"Oh! Oh, I'm sorry. . . ."

He leaned down to kiss her. "No worries, my dear. It's all part of learning."

Nathan was coming up on deck now, his tawny hair blowing in the breeze. He looked aft, saw Rhiannon's excited face as she steered the ship while her husband, standing protectively beside her with his arms crossed over his chest and his bare feet planted against the schooner's roll, looked on. He grinned and, with the two cats following him, headed forward.

Connor saw Liam come topside. And there, that ridiculous old black tricorne also coming up through the hatch as his father appeared on deck.

Connor grinned. "Good morning, Da."

Out of long habit his father glanced aloft, checking the direction of the wind and the set of the sails. "Good morning, you two. Is he trying to make a helmswoman out of you, Rhiannon?"

"Oh, Brendan, this is so much fun! I can *feel* her. She's alive, isn't she?"

Something changed in her father-in-law's face; a recognition of a kindred spirit, a shared understanding, a new respect for her as she excitedly told him of her new-found joy. He smiled then, a warm, dazzling gesture that made her feel as though he knew what nobody else in the entire world could possibly describe and understand about what she was feeling as she stood there at the tiller and felt *Kestrel*'s very soul. He understood. Of course he did.

"Aye, lass. She is."

Connor shook his head. "You two and your sentimental, romantic nonsense. She's just a ship. How is mother this morning?"

His father wouldn't meet his eye. "She'll be all right."

"Good. Because when you came up on deck just now you looked awfully worried, Da."

Connor shouted an order to the men who had come topside, Rhiannon caught her errant hair and secured it once more with the strip of leather, and Brendan turned to go below. He was just about to descend the hatch when a cry from high above broke the early morning symphony of wind and sea and spray.

"On deck! Sail up ahead! Fine on the larboard bows, hull up!"

"Keep her on course," Connor said to Rhiannon who stared at him, wide-eyed and suddenly nervous, as he stalked to the lee rail and, plucking a telescope from the rack, put it to his eye.

"Hmph," he murmured, and grinning, handed the glass to his father.

Brendan looked at the distant ship, almost indiscernible from the horizon, for a long time before handing the glass back.

"Leave her be, Connor."

"Leave her be? She's big, wallowing, and probably unarmed. I bet we could take her with nothing more than a shot across the bows."

"It's your decision. But I would advise against it."

"What are you, mad?"

"No, but I don't think that ship is what she appears."

"Your eyesight's failing you as much as your knee if you think that's anything but a fat British merchantman with probably less crew to sail her than we ourselves have."

"And if she is that, and you do take her, how can you spare the crew to sail her?"

"Oh, for God's sake, Father. Your prudence is wearisome. Easy pickings, if she is indeed British."

Two captains and only one ship between them. Not even a day out of Barbados and already he felt manacled, his ambitions neatly stifled, and he suddenly resented his Da for his caution when it went against everything he'd ever been told about him. Frustrated, he shot a glance at Rhiannon, still at the tiller and dutifully holding the schooner on course, then stalked away from his father. What the hell did his old man know, anyhow? Had he gone blind as well as soft in his dotage?

"Your orders, Captain?"

It was One-Eye, addressing his question to Connor but looking, as though for guidance, to Brendan who still stood at the rail.

The hero.

The legend.

And Connor was suddenly angry.

"Get the t'gallant on her and let's keep to windward of our fat friend up there as we close in on her. She's poorly handled. Isn't even flying her topsails. And run the British flag up our gaff so she doesn't know who we really are. We won't attack, but if she's going to be sailing the same course we are, I damn well want to hail her and find out who she is. I hate surprises."

Connor glanced once more toward his father as he headed aft to take the tiller from Rhiannon but Brendan, still standing all alone at the rail, never saw. He remained there for a long time, then, his eyes troubled, went back below.

CHAPTER 29

B rendan, favoring his bad knee, made his way back to the schooner's main cabin.

It was little changed from the days when he and Mira had shared this small space. The little woodstove was still there, the old bunk, the same beams and sweet curve of the hull.

He put his hand against the wood. It was cool to the touch, firm and hard and familiar.

But what lay beyond it? What weakness deep in *Kestrel's* old frames?

He was worried, though he would do his best to hide it from the others. He was worried about Connor's reckless determination to prove himself equal to a legend that Brendan didn't feel he deserved. He was worried that *Kestrel*, despite all outward appearances, no longer had the strength of hull to stand up to the onslaught of cannonfire, or even a particularly strong storm.

And he was worried about his beloved wife.

Worried sick.

"*Moyrrra*," he said quietly, going to the bunk where she lay. "Can I get you anything?"

"Another blanket," she mumbled. "And a linstock . . . gotta make sure the gun is pointed low . . . fire on the uproll."

"What?"

"And where's Matt? Is he sneaking off without me again?"

Brendan knelt gently beside the bunk and took his wife's tiny hand. It was hot and dry, and fear suddenly gripped his heart.

"*Moyrrra*, my love. *Stóirín.* You're here, with me. On our old friend, *Kestrel.*"

She turned her head on the pillow then, and her pale green eyes were distant and unfocused. She looked at him. Through him. A trickle of sweat ran down from her temple and she closed her eyes once more.

"Brendan."

"I'm here, *mo bhourneen.*"

She looked over at him, her gaze lucid once more. "I love you . . . have always loved you, more than I ever loved anything else in my entire life. If I could do it all over again, I wouldn't change a thing."

He swallowed hard against the rising tide of emotion. "I wish we'd never come south. We should have stayed in Newburyport, long, cold winter or not."

"No, Brendan. I needed to see our grandchildren . . . one last time."

Tears suddenly burned behind Brendan's eyes and choking back the lump in his throat, and the sudden, desperate pounding of his heart, he gripped his wife's hand all the harder. He didn't trust himself to speak.

"I'm so sick, Brendan. I'm not going to get better. You . . . you know that, as well as I do."

"It's the fever talking, my love. You need to rest. Please, please rest. I will stay right here."

"I know you will."

"I'll never leave you. Not in this life, or the next. *Never*."

"I know you won't." She shut her eyes once more. "Oh, God . . . I'm so cold."

She didn't see the tears slipping from his beloved eyes and slowly tracking down his cheeks, didn't feel his trembling hands or hear the strange, guttural sounds coming from the back of his throat as he tried to choke back sudden, towering sobs that threatened to overwhelm him. But she felt the hard warmth of his body as he carefully climbed up into bed beside her, took her in his arms, and cradled her tenderly to his chest.

There, his tears melded with the trail of perspiration that trickled down her brow.

And above, his son, oblivious to just how critical his mother's illness was, continued to send the willing little *Kestrel* closer and closer to her date with destiny.

A date that would be her final one.

"What do you make of her, Con?"

Toby had joined him, and now the two of them stood well forward at the larboard rail, watching the distant ship.

Connor was aware of the way his young cousin was watching him, hanging on his every word. It was hard not to feel a bit swelled up by such open admiration, hard not to derive confidence from it when that same confidence had been dented by his father's admonitions only an hour before.

Confidence that made him reckless.

Connor's fingers were drumming against the hot breech of a nearby gun.

"She's riding low in the water. Looks like they're hoisting topsails now, maybe her royals, too."

"Think they've gotten spooked by our presence?"

Connor grinned. "Looks that way, doesn't it?" He turned to One-Eye, coiling a line nearby. "The wind's veered a point. Let's get the stuns'ls on so we can run down on her before she can take advantage of it. She'll be faster than we are with it abaft the beam, but given how sloppily she's being handled, I think we'll have the advantage if we fly the kites."

"Aye, Captain."

There was movement behind him. It was Nathan and Rhiannon, who had given the tiller over to Jacques.

"I thought you said we wouldn't attack," Nathan said, frowning.

"I'm not attacking. But only a fool would blindly share sea space with a ship whose colors and intent are unknown."

Rhiannon reached out and touched his arm. "Are you sure we should be doing this?" she asked gently.

Sudden anger lanced through him. "For God's sake, I'm the damned captain here. Why is everyone questioning my judgment? First my father, and now you two."

She didn't back down. "I'm not questioning your judgment, just your actions. Your mother is ill, Connor. Sicker, I think, than your father is either letting on or willing to admit. I'm sure he'd like to just get her home without incident or delay."

"Hailing that ship and discerning her identity will take all of fifteen minutes, and we'll *all* sleep better tonight for my having done it!"

She had found a chink in his armor, but to acknowledge it would be to admit weakness or error, and that was something he could not do. Not with everyone looking at him for guidance and orders.

And not when his father was aboard, the first time they had ever sailed together in wartime, the first chance that he, Connor, would have to show him that he was his son and equal in every way.

One-Eye and several others were climbing the shrouds now, going aloft to set the studding sails that would extend the surface area of *Kestrel*'s square topsail and make her all the faster with the wind coming off their starboard quarter.

The distant ship, rolling heavily in the seas, was now directly off their larboard bows, the distance between them rapidly decreasing.

"Ease out the main a little more," Connor snapped, willing more speed from the schooner. "We'll fire a shot across her bows and get this business concluded before anyone even knows what we're about."

Time went by too slow for his liking, and his fingers drummed a faster tattoo on the rail. Finally, high above their heads, the studding sails were on and sheeted home at a speed that had Connor frowning.

"We need more crew, Con," Nathan said quietly.

"Stow it."

Connor gave the order to let the schooner fall off a point. Around them, the sound of the hull cutting through the sea changed in pitch as *Kestrel* began to run hard and fast, chased now, by the long ocean swells and the wind itself.

Ahead, the ship was growing larger as *Kestrel* eagerly closed the distance on her.

A sudden hush fell over the deck, and feeling it, Connor turned.

There was his father standing a short distance away, his face pale beneath that absurd old hat. He looked confused. Lost.

"Da, what is it? You're not sick, too, are you?"

"No, lad. I'm not sick. I need to talk to you. It's about your—"

"Captain!" It was Jacques at the helm. "She's tacking! Your orders, sir?"

"Look, Da, I can't talk right now. Can it wait?"

His father looked up and across the rapidly decreasing stretch of water to the merchant ship. She had come about and was now on a beam reach, running almost perpendicular to them, and it occurred to Connor, in that moment, that it was a bit odd that she would be doing that instead of taking advantage of the easterly wind in an attempt to get away.

One-Eye hollered down from above. "Captain, she's not flying any colors!"

"Two points to sta'b'd," Connor called tersely to Jacques at the tiller.

"What was that, sir?"

"Two points to sta'b'd! Stay to windward of her, damn you!"

"Shear off, lad," said Brendan, quietly.

Connor stabbed his fingertips into his temples and shut his eyes as he tried to focus his thoughts and control his temper.

Danelle Harmon

"Don't worry, Da, I know what I'm doing, I've got it all under control."

Kestrel was all but flying now as the wind sent her closer and closer to the merchantman, a ship thrice her tonnage and still continuing on that strange and intersecting course.

"Connor, I—"

His temper blew. 'You know what your problem is, Father? You've lost the fire in your belly, that's what! Or maybe you never had it to begin with and all those stories about you were one big, fat lie. There's a war going on! You built this ship for war, and now you want us to run away and hide! I wish you would just get the hell off my deck and go away, you're distracting me, I can't think, damn it, *I can't think*!'

"Connor!" Rhiannon gasped, trying to pull him away from his father.

"Well it's true! Lies, all of them. Lies!"

Brendan just looked at him, his eyes tragic.

Connor, feeling as though his head was going to blow apart, stalked away, hurt, humiliated by his father's actions, and betrayed by the dawning truth—a truth that he had spent a lifetime believing, a truth that was now coming apart before his very eyes. To think that he'd been raised on stories of his father the legend. To think that all these years, he'd been deceived into thinking his father was someone, something he was not, and he suddenly felt like a fool for having been duped for so long. "It's true! It was all a lie, wasn't it? All those stories that Mother and Liam told me, they were nothing but nursery tales, embellished each time in order to make you look like the hero you never were, to make me see you as bigger than you really are, *to make a little boy worship you*! You're a sham, Father! You're an old man, a fake, and worst of all, *you're a damned coward*!"

A terrible silence fell over the ship, and even the seas beneath *Kestrel* herself suddenly seemed to hush.

Clenching his fists, Connor turned to Nathan, hating him for his silently condemning eyes. Hating all of them for the way they were looking at him as though *he* was the one who had done something terribly, unspeakably wrong here. "Fire a shot across that pig's bow. I'm done wasting time."

"Aye . . . sir."

Quietly, Nathan turned to give the order, and a moment later *Kestrel*'s most forward gun banged out an impudent demand that the other ship heave to. The ball skipped across the water, slicing harmlessly through the crests of blue, blue waves before finally sinking.

The other ship did not heave to.

And in that moment Connor, leaping barefoot up atop the old gun his mother had dubbed *Freedom* so long ago, saw movement along her steep sides, and to his horror, gun ports, previously closed and their seams blending in against the paintwork, yawning open. One by one by one.

They had found the armed pirate ship.

"Oh, *Christ*," he swore, and turned to shout an order for *Kestrel* to head up and to run like she had never run before.

It was too late.

With an unholy, ear-splitting roar, the other ship's great broadside flashed orange and a hail of iron came slamming into the little schooner.

Kestrel never had a chance.

As she obeyed her captain's frantic command to turn away from the danger, her sails in confusion and her sleek black side coming straight on to the bigger ship as she came about, the hail of iron found her. An eighteen-pound cannonball smashed into one of her two boats, sending an explosion of deadly splinters in all directions and reducing it to kindling wood in its cradle. Others tore into her rigging, sliced through sails and severed her standing rigging, bringing spars, cordage, and the topsail's yard crashing and bouncing off her deck in a deadly rain of debris. The proud studding sails that had sent her so swiftly down upon her quarry were cut to ribbons. Several of her guns were upended, her captain was hurled twenty feet into one of them, and everywhere there was screams of pain and confusion and the smell of smoke.

"Connor!" Rhiannon screamed, picking herself up from the deck where she had fallen and peering desperately through the smoke. "*Connor, where are you?*"

She never felt the gash on the back of her hand that spilled blood down her arm and onto her pretty yellow gown. Her ears ringing, her senses dazed, she stumbled across the wreckage on deck. She saw Jacques, groaning and crawling on hands and knees near the untended tiller. One-Eye, desperately trying to get old Liam Doherty out from beneath the jagged, broken spar that had been the topsail yard, now lying in pieces across the deck. Nathan, grabbing an axe and hacking desperately at rigging in a frantic attempt to free the schooner from the tangle of sail, rigging, and spars that hung, swinging, from a few last lines so far above, Toby running to take the tiller as *Kestrel* lay helpless and vulnerable under the other ship's guns, and

Brendan, bending down beside a man lying draped and face-down across one of the overturned cannon, arms and head hanging, apparently dead.

A man with canvas pantaloons cut off at the knee, bare feet and calves, and a straw hat, spattered with blood, lying upside down on the deck beneath his head.

"Connor!"

Rhiannon was running now, sobbing as she leaped over debris on deck, slipped in blood, and plunged to her knees beside her father-in-law. She grabbed one of her husband's hands, her thumb feeling for a pulse at the wrist.

"Uncle Brendan!" It was Toby calling from the tiller, his voice rising in fear. "They're running out their guns again!"

Brendan, blinking and dazed, looked up.

Toby's voice rose in a scream of terror. "What shall I do?"

Numb with loss, Brendan blinked again, trying to clear the fog in his head. *Do?* His precious Mira, dying below. *Kestrel* hit hard, probably fatally. And Connor. Connor, his beloved son—

And then someone touched his arm, and feeling as though he was looking at her from far, far away, as though from the body of another person, he gazed down into the face of his new daughter whose huge green eyes were staring pleadingly up into his own. "I know what you think, but Connor's not dead," she said vehemently. "He has a pulse, Brendan. *He's not dead.*"

"Not dead?"

Her grip on his arm became desperate, and the pain of awareness began to bite through the blessed numbness, clearing it away, laying the path ahead of him bare. "Don't give up on us, Brendan! The fate of everyone on this ship is in your hands, and yours alone. They're all looking to you to save us. Please. Please don't give up."

Toby's shrill voice cut into his thoughts. "*Uncle Brendan!*"

Brendan saw Liam, limping, making his way toward him, and their gazes met.

And in that moment, Brendan knew what he had to do.

They had too much damage to turn and make a run upwind, as Connor had tried to do in that horrible moment before they'd been hit. And there was no way—no way—the little ship, outgunned, outmanned, and mortally wounded, could win against her towering rival in a sea fight.

But she would have to.

He stood up and seized a speaking trumpet lying nearby. "Put her back on her original course," he shouted to his young nephew. "Quickly."

Relief mixed with terror in young Toby's face, and Brendan felt his beloved schooner loyally answering the rudder as the youth let her fall back off the wind on a course that would now, with the big ship forging ahead of them, take them directly across its wake.

That one decisive move immediately rendered the other ship's broadside useless—for the time being.

"God almighty, it's about time ye took control of this situation," Liam muttered. "What next, Captain, old friend?"

"Run out the starboard broadside. Double-shotted. In less than a minute, we're going to cross her wake, and it will probably be our one and only chance to rake the hell out of her."

Liam turned, cupped his hands to his mouth and bawled, "Sta'b'd guns! Load up with grape, double-shotted!"

Kestrel's small crew immediately ran to carry out Brendan's order, and it was only then that he finally knelt and, sliding his hands beneath Connor's arms, gently lifted his unconscious son off the gun and dragged him up into the comparative shelter of the gunwale.

"You should go below, Rhiannon."

"I can't leave him."

Her father-in-law smiled, and she saw respect in his kind, honey-colored eyes. "No, I don't think you can. Nor would I want you to. But since you insist on staying up here on deck, at least sit down, keep your head down, and say a prayer or two for us all."

She lowered herself to the deck and put her back up against the gunwale, holding out her arms as Brendan dragged his son up against her and tenderly laid him in her open embrace. Blood ran from a cut in his scalp and trickled down the stubbled line of his jaw, and seeing it, Brendan turned away.

Her voice brought him back to the present.

"Are we going to survive this?

He just looked at her, and she saw something deep and unspoken in his gaze. "Some of us will, lass. But not all."

"Sta'b'd guns loaded and run out, sir!"

He looked down at Connor, his eyes dark beneath the shadow of the old tricorne that his son had taken such delight in teasing him about. "I must leave you now. Be strong."

Kestrel, wounded, bravely surged forward, her long bowsprit and jib-boom now sliding past the ornate stern quarter of the other ship as Brendan went to the rail where all could see him.

"Fire!" he shouted, and one by one *Kestrel*'s guns spoke as they passed astern of the other ship, each one leaping back on its tackles, coughing a plume of smoke and flame and making the deck thunder beneath their feet. In a crashing shower of glass, the big stern windows imploded and screams issued from deep within the enemy ship as *Kestrel*'s broadside ripped through the big vessel from stern to stem, cutting down everything in its path.

"Just like old times, Brendan," said Liam beside him.

"Just like old times."

Except Mira was not here. Mira, who—

He was desperate to go below, to return to her, but again he saw the pleading eyes of his new daughter, felt the heavy responsibility that had been thrust upon him, saw the relief and trust in the eyes of everyone around him and knew that he had a duty here, first.

"Nathan."

His nephew was there, touching his temple in a salute. "Sir?"

"Send someone below to check for damage." And then: "Who is your best gunner?"

"One-Eye is, sir."

"Our foe is preparing to wear ship, and we must prevent that from happening at all costs if we want to avoid another broadside. Is your man good enough that he can take out her steering, Nathan?"

"I reckon he is, Uncle Brendan."

"Put him to work, then. Larboard guns this time. Quickly."

Off to starboard the enemy ship was beginning to make her slow turn, preparing to bring her full broadside to bear on them once again, preparing to finish what she had started, and Brendan knew he could not let that happen.

Someone was at his elbow. "We took a bad hit below the waterline, sir. Larboard side, just abaft the cathead. She's taking on water."

"Get the pumps going."

"Aye, sir."

He studied the other ship. She would run them down in no time. There was nothing to do but make a big, sweeping turn to larboard in an elaborate dance to avoid that deadly broadside, to head back up and try for another shot at the stern . . . and the ship's Achilles heel, her steering.

He laid a hand on the rail. *One last dance, lassie,* he murmured to the little schooner. *I know your wings are broken, that you* can *no longer dance, but please, love . . . try your best.*

"Ready about!" he called.

"Ready about!"

"Load up the larboard guns!"

Kestrel's long, jaunty jib-boom began to make her sweep around the horizon . . . northwest . . . west . . . southwest . . . south . . . across the wind, more debris falling from above as her great booms went over . . . .

Come on, lassie. Dance. . . .

East. . . .

"Larboard guns all loaded and ready, Captain!"

Kestrel completed her turn, and once more her proud jib-boom took aim on the other ship's wake.

Musket fire began to rain down from above, pinging off the guns' iron breeches.

"Get ready, lads," Brendan said, striding to where the man named One-Eye waited at the most forward gun.

Another moment . . . another. . . .

Now.

"Cripple her."

One-Eye bent, sighted along the gun's breech, and as the schooner began to rise beneath the next swell, lowered his linstock to its touchhole. The cannon flung itself backward against the breeching with an angry roar, and the ball spit harmlessly into the water several feet below the rudder post.

"Try again," Brendan said, steadying the man with a hand on his shoulder. "Wait until she's poised at the very top of the wave crest, just before she slides into the trough. It'll give you a more stable platform."

"Aye, sir!"

One-Eye went to the next gun down the larboard line. A second later it belched out its fury in a cloud of fire and smoke, and a great cheer went up from *Kestrel*'s men gathered at the rail as this time the ball found its mark, slamming into the rudder post and severing the tackle that led to the great wheel above.

"Got her!" Liam crowed, smashing his fist into his big, meaty palm. "Damn her to hell!"

"Three cheers for Captain Brendan!"

"Hip hip, huzzah! Hip hip, huzzah! Hip hip, huzzah!"

From the great ship that towered over them, they heard men screaming in a strange dialect of Spanish, Dutch and God only knew what else, people wildly trying to get the now useless rudder to answer the wheel, and the sounds of fear and chaos as the vessel drifted helplessly out of control.

"I think we're done here," Brendan said. And with that, he gave a tight smile that never reached his eyes, and headed for the hatch to go below.

Liam stood where his friend had left him.

"What did we just see?" One-Eye asked, staring in awe after the lean, lanky figure.

It was Toby, also gazing reverently at that same retreating figure, who answered. "What you just saw," he said, "Was the legend."

CHAPTER 30

Whither shall I go from thy spirit? or whither shall I flee from thy presence? If I ascend up into heaven, thou art there; if I make my bed in hell, behold, thou art there. If I take the wings of the morning, and dwell in the uttermost parts of the sea; Even there shall thy hand lead me, and thy right hand shall hold me.

— Psalms 139: 7-10

Brendan was all but running once he had disappeared down the hatch, desperate to reach the stern cabin and his beloved Mira.

She lay where he had left her, her chest steadily rising and falling, her hair damp with sweat.

Swallowing hard, he poured water into the pitcher, dipped a cloth in it, and tenderly bathed his wife's forehead. Her cheeks. Her arms.

Her eyes drifted open.

"Did you save the day, love?"

He reached out and took her hand, gently touching the cooling water to her knuckles, her fingers, her palm. "It was a combined effort."

"Connor . . . I wonder if he'll ever learn."

"Ah, dearest. He's not so different from me at the same age."

"Except he has a temper . . . you never did."

"Gets it from you, I imagine."

She smiled weakly, and closed her eyes once more. "I imagine you're right."

They sat together in silence. Beneath his feet, Brendan felt the deck listing slightly forward, and to larboard.

Mira, he knew, felt it too. "How bad is it?" she murmured, her eyes still closed.

"Bad enough."

"I heard it hit. Felt her shudder . . . heard her cry."

"I know, *Moyrrra*. I heard her, too."

"She's been a good ship."

"None better."

"You're weeping, Brendan. I can hear it in your voice."

"Aye, lass." He choked back the tears. "I am."

"No reason to cry . . . three wonderful children . . . beautiful grandchildren . . . a lifetime of love and memories and happiness."

"A lifetime."

Strange creaks and groans echoed through the stillness.

"Might still be able to save her if ye rig a canvas patch over the hole."

"It's no use, dearest. Too much rot in her frames."

Mira was silent for a long moment, and then she smiled. "Kind of fitting, ain't it. Just you and me and her. The three of us. Just as it used to be."

"Just as it should be."

"Will you make the effort to get off before she goes?"

"I told you I won't leave you, and I won't."

"I ain't goin' nowhere. Came into this world on a ship, and I'll go out on one, too."

The tears were running down his face, openly now. "I'm sorry I couldn't get you back to Newburyport, *Moyrrra*."

"Ehhh, what's Newburyport . . . home is here with you. With *her*. And it always will be."

"Yes," he murmured, his gaze distant through his tears. "It always will be."

"C'mon, Connor, wake up," Nathan said, kneeling down beside his cousin. He put a thumb against his captain's eyelid, pushed it up, and frowned as he saw the green eyes rolled back in his head and unresponsive. He took his hand, limp and heavy in his own, and slapped the wrist hard, once, twice, three times. "Ain't no time for taking a nap. You're needed."

"I can't wake him," Rhiannon said worriedly, and shifted beneath his dead weight, trying to relieve the numbness where her tailbone had been pressing into the deck. "I'm scared, Nathan."

Nathan shot a look over the rail. Far off now, tiny with distance and her sails a black silhouette in the setting sun was the pirate ship, no longer a threat. But Nathan knew there were other, more insidious threats and now, with Connor out of action, his uncle Brendan below, and everyone looking to him for guidance, he found himself in command.

A shadow fell over them. Liam Doherty was there, his blue eyes grim.

"How's the patch holding?" Nathan asked. Together, he and Toby had dived down after heaving to and, swimming deep underwater, had managed to place a large patch of sailcloth over the ragged hole below *Kestrel*'s waterline, passing ropes down under her keel and back up her other side and snugging the repair tight.

But the pumps had been going all afternoon. Constantly.

"It's not," Liam said soberly. "There's a foot and a half of water in the cable tier. And rising."

Rhiannon, gently stroking Connor's hair, looked up in alarm. "I thought the patch was supposed to keep the water out."

"She's an old ship, lass. A patch can only do so much before the sea claims her own."

"Is the sea going to . . . "

She could not finish the question, and Liam looked away.

Silence. The sun sank a little lower, and a deep, red-orange glow began to fire the sky to the west.

"Probably ought to think about getting everyone off soon," Nathan said quietly to Liam.

"Aye, lad. I wouldn't leave it too long."

"How many people do we have left on board?"

"Twelve."

"And only one boat," Toby said, approaching. "The other's no good. Smashed to bits."

The wind had steadily died throughout the afternoon and now, only a slight breeze moved sluggishly through what was left of *Kestrel*'s sails. Her long, proud jib-boom still pointed toward the north, but her topmasts were gone and Nathan knew that only a few strained, weary stays kept that jib-boom supported and the whole rig from collapsing in a heap on deck.

Kestrel rolled heavily on the long swells, and not with her usual grace.

Nathan, noting it, cast a glance toward the stern where the single remaining boat waited on its davits. "Boat won't hold more than eight," he said.

"I think we might get nine, maybe ten into it. Should be all right, as long as the seas stay calm and the wind continues to go flat."

"That's pushing it, Liam."

"We don't have a choice, lad."

"Where are we?" Rhiannon asked, growing increasingly worried.

"Two hundred fifty miles northwest of Puerto Rico. Deep ocean."

Silence.

"We'd better gather water and some supplies and get them into the boat," Nathan said. "This far from anything, we might be at sea for days before anyone finds us."

Liam stood where he was, looking around, his eyes strangely moist.

"Never thought it would end here," he said softly. "Not like this."

A cannonball that had been dropped to the deck in the haste to load the guns suddenly began to roll forward, gathering speed as it went, before finally angling off toward the larboard bow and lodging against the gunwale.

"Come on," Nathan said, taking the old man's arm. "We don't have much time."

The color of the sea went from a deep, deep blue and then to purple as the sun sank lower in the sky, and supervised by Nathan, the schooner's crew hurriedly gathered supplies. A keg of water. Dried fruits and salted meat. By the time they were hurriedly loaded and secured into *Kestrel*'s remaining boat, swung out on its davits over her stern, the deck had a noticeable pitch in it.

Brendan, a cat under each arm, came up from below and stood there quietly watching the proceedings. His face was in shadow beneath the black tricorne. Unreadable.

He had left Mira asleep in her bed, sweating-hot, restless, and slipping away from her brief moments of lucidity once more. Here, topside, Liam and Nathan seemed to have the situation well under control without his help. But he had done what they had asked of him.

There was nothing left for him to do.

He walked over to the boat, which Nathan and Liam were preparing to lower down into the sea below. Wedged amidships, the big keg of water took up a lot of room, but it was necessary. So, too, were the canvas bags of food.

He was not needed here.

He left them lowering the boat down toward the water and looked up and around the horizon. The enemy ship was gone, and the sea was empty for as far as the eye could see in all directions. A majestic sunset was starting to turn the sky purple and orange, the colors reflected on the water, water that, as dark and mysterious a blue as it had been an hour earlier, he knew was probably amongst the deepest in the Atlantic ocean.

A fitting grave.

He was largely ignored as Connor's small crew hustled to round everyone up and get them into the small boat. He saw the fear in his young nephew Toby's eyes, the anguish in Liam's, the stoic determination in Nathan's as he cast a glance forward and noted, as Brendan had done when he'd come topside, that *Kestrel* was now low in the water at her bow. Waves were beginning to slosh against her dolphin striker. Soon, perhaps in another hour, her proud and lofty jib-boom would be awash.

And there was Rhiannon, still sitting with her back against the gunwale, his beloved son wrapped securely in her arms. She was quietly sobbing.

He walked over to her and, his knee paining him, knelt down.

"You'll take good care of him for me, won't you, lass?"

She looked up then, her lovely green eyes awash in tears. "You're not going with us?"

He quietly shook his head. "No. I'm not."

"But you have to, you can't stay here, you'll— " she gulped back the tears. "You'll—"

"Hush, lassie. Tears won't change things."

He could not tell her that there wasn't enough room in the boat, already starting to fill up as one by one, the schooner's crew climbed down her side and found a space in the little craft. He could not tell her that it wasn't where he wanted to be anyhow, that his place was here, with his beloved wife and the ship that had brought them both together all those years ago, the ship that had been a living, breathing part of their history together, the ship that had been, if truth be told, the only other woman he had ever loved with every bit of his Irish heart. He didn't want to get down into the boat, but he couldn't tell her that, because she would never understand. And she, like the others, might feel guilty for taking a spot that could have gone to himself, and refuse it.

It was an argument that he would not enter.

"I'm going to help you get him down into the boat now, dearest," he said gently, as she quietly knuckled the tears slipping down her cheeks. "The others are all waiting for you. Promise me you'll care for him. It's all I ask."

He saw her chin quivering, the sobs choking the back of her throat, one of them escaping in a cry of pure anguish. She nodded jerkily, and unwrapped her arms from around his son. Arms that had held him so tightly against herself, safe within her embrace while her tears fell steadily into his hair.

Brendan bent down, slid his hands beneath Connor's shoulders and the back of his knees, and quietly stood up, holding his grown son in his arms. Nearly thirty years ago, he had held this same beloved soul as a tiny infant, restless and squalling even then, and all the years that had elapsed since didn't change a blessed thing. Connor was his son. And he would love him until his last, dying breath.

His daughter-in-law drew herself up and walked to the rail where below, the boat, already overloaded with people and supplies, rode low in the water. Liam stood there at the rail waiting to help her down, trying to hide the tears in his eyes by quickly knuckling them away.

There, the girl turned.

"Good-bye . . . *Dadaí*."

"Good-bye, dear Rhiannon. Remember your promise to me."

"I will remember."

He nodded. She was ready to break down, and he would spare her that. He stood there cradling his son in his arms, wanting the moment to go on forever, to never let him go, while Liam helped her over the rail and hands below stretched up to help guide her safely into the boat.

And then he bent his head and kissed his son's forehead. "I love you," he murmured, seeing the tousled auburn hair, so much like his own had been in his youth, behind a blur of tears. "I love you, Connor. And I'm proud of you."

Connor was his equal in height and weight, but Brendan's strong arms did not falter as he handed his precious burden to Liam, who wrapped a rope beneath his arms and, with Brendan's help, slowly lowered his unconscious body down toward the upraised hands and arms below. They both watched, the last two men on the ship, as Toby and One-Eye helped settle him across Rhiannon's lap, and someone laid a light blanket over him.

"Just as well he's unconscious," Liam said quietly. "He'd never let you do this."

Brendan nodded, and put out his hand.

"Good-bye, Liam," he said hoarsely. "You have been the best friend a man could ever ask for. Take care of him for me. All of them."

Liam's blue eyes flooded with tears and he shook his head. "I'm staying here with you and Mira and *her*. I'm not leaving."

"You have to, old friend." He smiled, not letting go of the firm clasp he had on his best friend's hand. "We've been through a lot together, Liam. Trust me, just this last time."

"Don't tell me you have a plan?"

Brendan smiled. "Don't I always?"

Liam, torn, looked at him uncertainly. Tears ran freely down his cheeks.

Beneath their feet, *Kestrel* leaned a little farther into the water.

"Now go," Brendan said. "I'll catch up with you later."

Unable to speak, Liam nodded jerkily and the two men embraced, Liam now blubbering like a baby, his tears wetting Brendan's shirt as Brendan quietly slipped a folded letter, one that he'd penned after Mira had slipped back into her delirium just an hour before, into his friend's pocket. He stood back, suddenly remembering two more who could not stay, and there, saw the two cats nearby, staring toward the schooner's bows. He reached down, picked each one up under his arm, and handed them gently down to the people below. Liam made an odd sound of anguish in his throat. And then, without another word, he turned, went over the rail, and joined the others in the boat.

"Oars out," he choked out, swiping at his eyes. "Shove off."

Brendan stood there, the burning colors of the sunset gilding his hair beneath the old tricorne, turning it the color it had been all those years ago as he watched the little boat, cramped to overflowing and so low in the water that he dared not to think of how it would handle any sort of a sea, move steadily away. He did not, of course, have a plan. Not this time. It was a lie, and Liam probably knew it. But maybe he did not. It didn't matter. He would be safe.

He would look after his and Mira's children until his dying day.

The boat was farther off now, its oars catching the dying sunlight. Above, a stray whisper of wind sang a sad dirge through the rigging and made the flag still there at the gaff snap once, twice, in the breeze.

The flag.

Nobody had ever taken down the Union Jack.

Quietly, Brendan went to the halyard, lowered the flag, and ran up the Stars and Stripes until the huge, bold American colors waved proudly in the afternoon sun. There. All was as it should be, now. He stood there for a moment, then went to the tiller, empty now of any hand to guide it. The light wind had pushed the schooner around to face the breeze, her fore and main luffing.

A course to nowhere.

He pushed the tiller hard over, and slowly, sluggishly, *Kestrel*'s nose began to come around. Water was now slicing up and over her bowsprit. Her jib-boom. Beginning to spill over her foredeck with each long, ancient swell.

A glance at the compass. Just a little more, now.

Kestrel continued her slow, anguished turn, trying her best, until the very end, to answer her captain.

There. North-by-northwest.

Pointed toward home.

Brendan lashed the tiller for the little schooner's final course, looked up at the set of the sails, and watched the boat, now tiny with distance, fading into the coming twilight. He took off the old black tricorne, held it in his hands for a long moment, and then placed it on the compass box, over the needle that now pointed steadily north-by-northwest.

He looked around the empty deck for the last time. Looked up at the valiant Stars and Stripes, the white bars glowing orange in the last of the setting sun, and touched his fingers to his temple in a tight and wordless salute.

When he went below, he found Mira unresponsive.

He shook her. He called brokenly to her, trying to rouse her. She lay unmoving.

I will never leave you.

He got up and shut the cabin door, knowing the water would be coming soon, and got into bed with his beloved wife. He wrapped his arms around her and lay there in the gathering gloom, trying to hold the life in her, telling himself that the coolness of her skin was only because the fever had finally broke.

I will never leave you.

Kestrel gave a last sigh of anguish and her bowsprit slipped beneath the waves.

The water came.

Dawn.

Pastel pink skies, purple, salmon and gold, and a sea that was empty in all directions for as far as the eye could see.

A solitary gull skimmed over the waves, the light catching its feathers and painting them with the colors of morning. The bird wheeled as its sharp eye saw something drifting on the sea's surface, and changing its course, went to investigate.

It was only an old black hat from another time and place, floating alone on a sea of emptiness.

The gull moved on.

Eventually, the hat became saturated, and finally sank beneath the waves.

CHAPTER 31

He heard groaning.

The sound of someone in deep pain, coming from far, far away.

Eventually, the groans grew louder, and Connor realized they were his own.

"He's coming to," someone murmured.

He struggled toward consciousness, clawing through waves of pain in his head, and dragged open eyes that felt weighted with lead. The room, if that's what he was in, was spinning and Connor, weak and unable to do more than raise himself up on an elbow, turned and vomited over the side of the bed before shutting his eyes and falling back down against the hot, damp sheets beneath him.

Someone was bathing his chin, his mouth, his cheeks with cold water. He heard a rag being squeezed out and with all his strength, lifted his hand and caught the small, feminine one that now held the linen cloth to his aching, pounding skull.

"Rhiannon," he murmured.

"I'm here. You're going to be all right."

"I'm going to be sick again," he said, and just in time, she had a bowl for him.

The bed was moving, and opening his eyes once more he saw that they were not in a room at all, but aboard a ship, and a big one at that. High, gracefully arched deck beams above, painted white and sparkling in sunlight reflected off the water. Panoramic stern windows, most of which had the curtains drawn against the blazing Caribbean sun. A black and white diamond-checkered floor mat, elegant furniture, a feeling of grandeur, comfort and space.

"Where am I?" he asked, greatly confused.

"Sir Graham's flagship, *Orion*."

". . . What?"

It was too much for Connor's head and he lay back against the pillow, trying not to be sick again. He felt Rhiannon's soft touch upon his forearm and tried to focus on it as he shut his eyes and lay there, trying to get his bearings, to make sense of things. Somewhere nearby, a door opened and he heard footsteps, authoritative and steady, coming toward him.

"How is he?"

A familiar English voice: "Awake, sir. Finally."

Connor opened his eyes once more and turning his head on the pillow, saw his cousin's curly black hair, its unruliness tamed with a short bit of leather at his nape. He'd been sitting there all along.

"Delmore?" He tried to grin, but it hurt too much. "Your shirt, man . . . it's unbuttoned, you slacker. . . ."

"Yes, well, it's hot in here. And I have you to thank for my new lax standards."

Connor smiled, but Delmore was getting to his feet as his admiral approached. The flag captain looked warily at Sir Graham and shook his head and the admiral, who looked like he'd been about to say something, snapped his mouth shut in irritation.

Connor felt alarm sweep through him. "What is it?"

Sir Graham turned on him. "Go to sleep, Connor. You took a hit that nearly bashed the brains out of your damned skull. What little ones you have, in any case."

But Connor wasn't listening. There was a chapter of his life missing, something to do with *Kestrel* and the stolen, well-armed merchantman full of pirates, and he tried desperately to fill it in.

"Why am I here?"

"You're here because your sister had a dream, and thanks to your damned foolhardiness, you—"

"Not now," Rhiannon said firmly, locking her gaze with the admiral's and shaking her head. "*Not now.*"

"If not now, when? Tomorrow? Next year? He's got a lot to answer for, and he's going to start immediately!"

"No, Sir Graham. You will let him rest. I forbid this conversation."

Listen to her, standing up to one of the king's most decorated admirals. And I'd once thought her timid?

"I have questions for him." Sir Graham's fist hit a table. "I want answers."

"Then go ask Liam Doherty. Or Nathan Ashton. My husband has been badly hurt, he only just woke up, and you will *not* speak of what happened. *Not. Now.*"

"What *did* happen?" Connor managed, wishing he could put a gun to his head and make the pain stop. "I'm no callow youth . . . for God's sake, don't treat me like one."

"I'll tell you what happened, you reckless, proud, and utterly useless piece of—"

"Sir Graham, *enough*!" Rhiannon said sharply. "If you can't drop this, then I must ask you to leave!"

Connor pushed himself backward in the bed and tried to sit up, but his head spun, and his stomach spun with it, and he shut his eyes against a renewed wave of pain that felt as if someone was pounding the sharp end of an axe blade into his skull. He felt Rhiannon's hand supporting him. Sir Graham, it seemed, was furious. Not just furious but extremely upset, as though this was personal and not just about the fact that he, Connor, had only done what he, as an American privateer, was supposed to be doing by picking that convoy clean.

But maybe it wasn't about the convoy.

Maybe there was something more.

He opened his mouth to ask, but the admiral had already turned his back and was stalking angrily toward the door. A moment later it slammed, and the great cabin was quiet once more.

"Well?" he asked, looking from his proper, stern-faced English cousin to the beautiful woman he had married. She, who had just set an admiral firmly in his place, protecting him, shielding him from something that they all seemed to know but which, for him, belonged in that strange and empty lost chunk of time between when he'd realized, too late, that he'd been fooled by the pirate ship's disguise, and waking up aboard a British admiral's flagship.

His wife and cousin exchanged glances. Something unspoken passed between them, and Connor was suddenly afraid.

"Tell me," he said, gripping her hand. "I deserve to know."

She glanced again at Delmore Lord, a look full of unspoken meaning, and the flag captain stood up, his mouth pained and his gray eyes almost purple with sorrow. "I'll leave you to it," he said quietly, and with a bow to Rhiannon, strode quietly from the cabin.

Silence.

Just the sunlight, sparkling like needles against the bulkhead, the inside of his skull, painting his wife's classic profile in white. Sunlight that seemed serene and peaceful, but Connor knew in his suddenly fearful heart that there was a place where that sunlight would never reach, and he was about to be cast down into that place and that place was called hell.

"You took a terrible blow to the head," Rhiannon said quietly. "You've been unconscious for almost two days. There is time enough, Connor, to talk about what happened and why you're here. But I think you should rest first."

"You know I can't. You know I *won't*."

She took his hand. "Yes. I know that." She lifted his hand to her cheek, pressed his knuckles to her mouth and closed her eyes, and it was then that he saw the sparkle of tears on her lashes, and a single, shimmering droplet beginning to track from out of the corner of her eye.

Hell beckoned, and he sensed its deep, yawning blackness, widening, waiting for him.

"I have . . . I have some terrible news for you, Connor. I don't know how to tell you this—" the tear was sliding down her cheek now, and her eyes looked glassy and wet as she looked down at him, her bottom lip beginning to quiver.

"Tell me," he said firmly, and took another step closer to that black, unending chasm.

"*Kestrel* is gone," she choked out. "And your parents, with her."

Connor just stared at her.

He could do no more.

And beneath his feet, hell opened.

Hell was hearing what had happened after he'd been thrown twenty feet, only to slam into the iron breech of a gun so that his father, his father whom he had belittled, insulted, and hurt, was left to clean up his mess. Hell was hearing how his mother had actually been dying of the fever down in *Kestrel*'s cabin and knowing that his father, probably coming topside that last time to tell him the awful truth, had nobody to share his anguish with. Hell was hearing how his father had taken command of *Kestrel* when they were about to get pounded to sawdust and instead of running upwind, as Connor had tried to do, had instead turned the valiant little ship straight toward her massive enemy and managed to cripple her enough that the fight was decided before it had ever begun. Except, the fight hadn't been decided, then. It had been decided when he, Connor, had scoffed at his father's wise advice to leave the bigger ship be. It had been decided when he, Connor, desperate to prove himself to his crew, to himself, and especially to his father, had sent a challenging shot across her bows. It had been decided long before that first deadly broadside, and *Kestrel* had not come out the winner.

Kestrel, gone.

"Just a ship," he'd said offhandedly, hurtfully, to his father.

His father. His father, whom, Rhiannon choked out through her tears, had picked him up in his arms and carried him like a baby to the rail, handed him into Liam Doherty's care, and given up the place in the boat that might have been his. His father, who had quietly borne his derision, and those last, oh, God, those last terrible, terrible words that could never be taken back.

You're an old man, a fake, and worst of all, you're a damned coward.

And as his wife told him of those final moments when he, Connor, had been spared the agony of watching his father's final sacrifice, something that seemed tragically unfair in itself, Connor felt the numbness that had wrapped itself around his heart, his soul, begin to dissipate, and a pain that was more intense than anything in his head pierced his heart, made its way up into his sinuses, and he began to weep.

You're an old man, a fake, and worst of all, you're a damned coward.

Words, hurtful, hateful words, that could never be taken back.

The last words he had said to his beloved *Dadaí.*

"Oh, God," he cried brokenly, and then his head was in his hands and he was sobbing such that he couldn't draw breath, rocking back and forth and crying great, unmanly tears and bawling like he hadn't done since old Preble had slammed the cane across his fingers and Mother had taken him in her arms and wrapped and kissed his little finger and told him how special he was, and now Mother was dead, and *Dadaí* too, dead and drowned and forever entombed upon the ship that he, Connor, had sent to her death.

But he hadn't sent just *Kestrel* to her death.

"I killed them, Rhiannon," he choked out, feeling her arms go around his quaking shoulders. "By my need to prove myself, *I killed my parents.*"

"You did not kill them, Connor. Your mother was dying. Your father made the decision he did because he didn't want to leave her."

"No, you don't understand, Rhiannon, you don't know what was in my head, what drove me, why I insisted, *insisted*, that we hail that ship when I knew deep in my gut that I was making a mistake, but oh, no, I had to do it, and now I can never take it back and now they're dead, *dead*, and it's all b-because . . . of *me-e-e-e.* . . ."

He broke down into terrible keening sobs, and Rhiannon, holding his rocking, anguished body in her arms, cried right along with him.

"Connor, don't do this to yourself," she sobbed, trying to contain his pain within her own tight, unyielding embrace. "You didn't make your mother get sick, you didn't make her decide to go home when she did, this is not your fault. Please, *please*, don't do this."

"I told my father he was a . . . he was a *coward*." The keening sobs were the most piercing sounds of anguish that Rhiannon had ever heard. "A coward. My l-last w-w-words to him. . . . Oh, oh, *God*."

Rhiannon remembered that final, endearing image she had of Brendan Merrick. Of him standing on the schooner's deck above them, the ship already listing beneath his feet, the last one still aboard, with his son, his beloved son, cradled in his arms in a final embrace. The kiss the father had left on the son's forehead. A father's forgiveness. A father's love.

Unbreakable.

Infinite.

Forever.

"Fate was with us, Connor," she was saying, feeling his hot tears soaking against her bosom, his fist, with its sad little broken finger, curling like a cold claw in the soft muslin of her sleeve. "We drifted in the boat all night . . . if there had been any sort of a sea, it would have swamped us. But it was glassy and calm . . . no waves to swamp us . . . as though someone was looking out for us. The following morning, when the sun came up, we saw Sir Graham's flagship far, far in the distance, coming toward us. . . Your sister had had a dream . . . begged him to go and look for us. She knew. She *knew*."

"*Kestrel*—" His voice broke on a sob. "Was she gone by then?"

Rhiannon held him tightly. "The sea was empty, Connor. I'm sorry."

Hell yawned open yet farther, tormenting him with what it must have been like aboard the little schooner in her final moments, tormenting him with what his father's last thoughts must have been as *Kestrel* slid, forever, beneath the waves, and he wondered if drowning hurt and if they had suffered and how dark and cold and lonely and terrible it must have been as the schooner slipped down, down, down, heading for a final resting place so deep that no man had ever been able to chart it.

You're an old man, a fake, and worst of all, you're a damned coward.

"You were no coward, Da," he choked out, on a fresh wave of tears. "Oh, God, you were no coward. . . ."

Rhiannon held him until he could cry no more, until the strange, keening wails coming from the back of his throat ceased, only for him to wake over and over again and start the bitter weeping all over. She stroked his hair, avoiding the crusted blood high above his ear, held him tightly to her breast and tried to absolve him of his sins.

But she was no priest, no savior, just his wife.

And for Connor, there was no salvation from hell.

And no absolution.

CHAPTER 32

She stayed with him the rest of the morning, watching over him as he slept, restlessly, fitfully, the tears running down his face even in sleep until he woke, screaming in terror about drowning before his panicked green stare found her own and the gentle, soothing, motions of her hand on his shoulders, the back of his head as she folded him to her heart, finally managed to calm his frantic shaking.

Sir Graham came in a short time later and found his brother-in-law sitting up in bed and staring vacantly out the stern windows, Rhiannon in a chair beside him and holding his hand.

"Connor," he said.

Connor blinked, and slowly turned his head to look at the admiral.

Or rather, through him.

"I trust that Rhiannon told you."

It was a moment before Connor answered. "She did."

"I need to know about this ship. The one you attacked."

"Nothing to tell," Connor said dully. "She won, we lost."

"You made a stupid decision."

"Aye, I did."

"And you attacked that convoy and cut out numerous ships from it, too, didn't you?"

Connor was back to staring without seeing out the stern windows. "Yes."

"I'm taking you back to Barbados as my prisoner of war. You'll be exchanged in due course, just like any other American."

Connor said nothing, only continued to gaze dully out the window.

"I didn't want to do this, you know, but you forced my hand."

Rhiannon had heard enough. "Sir Graham, have you no pity?"

"Pity? *Pity?!* After his recklessness and stupidity cost him not only his own ship, but the lives of his mother and father?" Now, Sir Graham's eyes were strangely moist and he turned angrily away, unwilling to allow this show of emotion. "They weren't my parents, but I loved them just the same. And Brendan Merrick was one of the finest men that God ever created. A man who *was my friend.*"

"I think, Sir Graham, that Connor is suffering enough," Rhiannon said coldly. "Ask him what you will about what happened, but I won't let you stand there and hurt him, and make him feel any worse than he already does just to assuage your own pain."

The admiral's blue eyes hardened. A muscle twitched in his jaw. "Do you realize how hard this is going to be, to have to tell my *wife*? What do you think she's going to do when she learns that her own brother was responsible for the death of her parents?!"

"*Stop it!* And if Maeve had a dream that sent you out looking for us, don't you think she probably already knows what happened? You are cruel and unfeeling to stand there as you are and say the things you do! And while you might condemn my husband for his recklessness, *I* see it as a blessing and a gift. A *gift*! Because what is a flaw in one person's eyes is something to admire in another's, and some day, maybe you'll appreciate the gifts that God gave my husband instead of condemning him for them!"

There was a knock on the door.

"What is it?" roared the admiral.

A Royal Marine poked his head in. "Liam Doherty to see you, sir. And the Ashton brothers."

"Good. Maybe between the four of you, I'll finally get a true picture of what the hell happened out there."

Between the three of you, Rhiannon thought, still holding Connor's hand. He had not said a word throughout Sir Graham's tirade, only lying there with his eyes staring unseeingly out the great windows, and Rhiannon wondered if he'd even heard anything the admiral had said.

"Hey, Con," said Nathan, coming up to the bed while Toby stood mutely behind him. "Glad to see you awake. You had us all worried."

Connor heard his cousin's words as if from a long distance away. They skated over him like the breeze off the ocean, passing him by, meaning little, if anything. He couldn't think of anything to say. The constant buzzing in his blood that kept him ever-moving, the ceaseless racing of his thoughts, had dulled to a nothingness that he couldn't access. But through it, he was aware of an awkwardness in his cousin's demeanor, a resentment, even, and Connor was sensitive enough that that didn't escape him. He turned dull eyes from his idle perusal of the stern windows and looked at his cousin and there, in Nathan's steady brown eyes, he saw his suspicions confirmed.

You blame me, too. I know you do. His gaze shifted to Toby, and the boy who had idolized him, who had thought he walked on water, looked away, unable to meet his eyes. *You both do.*

He could not blame them.

And Liam Doherty, who was like an uncle to him . . . his father's best and beloved friend, as faithful and true a friend as one could ever have wished—

Liam would not even look at him. Instead, he walked over to the stern windows and stood there gazing out over the sea behind them.

You too, then.

He shut his eyes and thought about what it would be like to be dead, and found himself yearning for it. Longing for it. Wishing he could trade places with his father. Anything to escape this awful, unrelenting pain.

"So you encountered this so-called merchant ship north of Puerto Rico," Sir Graham was saying. "Flying minimal canvas, poorly handled, from a distance, unarmed. What was her tonnage? What flag was she flying?'

Nathan's quiet voice. Liam's. Connor shut his eyes again and let his mind ride its inevitable, self-directed course, taking him far away, as it had once done so many times in a long-ago schoolroom as his teacher had tried to make him understand that no, the letter P was not made like that, and it faced this way and not that, and that it was hard to believe he was the son of the famous Captain Brendan Merrick when he was so stupid he couldn't even tell the difference between this letter and that letter . . . .

Connor's head drooped on the pillow and he dozed, content only with the gentle, loving stroke of his wife's hand against his arm. He heard, in bits and pieces, the admiral sharply questioning the actions that had led up to the attack . . . Nathan's responses about the course they'd been on . . . Toby filling in details as he remembered them . . . Liam Doherty still standing by the window. Once, when Connor dragged open his eyes, he saw his father's old friend raise his hand and surreptitiously pass a knuckle beneath his eye before taking out a handkerchief and quietly raising it to his turned-away face.

After that, Connor let his unreinable, untrainable mind take him where it would, and as the voices around him faded into a low, pleasant drone and then the bliss of nothingness, he found escape in sleep that was, this time, deep, dark, and dreamless.

And Rhiannon, still sitting by his bedside and holding his hand, never left him.

They dropped anchor in Carlisle Bay a day and a half later where Connor, finally able to stand shakily on his feet, was hustled out of the great cabin by two Royal Marines and brought topside.

He had not eaten a thing since he'd woken, and had only accepted a few sips of water. Nothing more.

Rhiannon was indignant.

"You don't have to make a spectacle of him," she said savagely, as Sir Graham directed his men to take her husband to the local gaol. "There's no reason he can't stay here aboard your flagship. Or with his brother on *Sandpiper*. You're doing this just to be cruel!"

"I'm doing this because if I don't, my wife is likely to murder him in cold blood," the admiral snapped, and when Maeve came aboard, eyes blazing, her beautiful hair falling down over her knuckles as she collapsed, crying, on her husband's quarterdeck at being told the news, Rhiannon understood. Crazed with grief, Maeve howled out her anguish to the sky, and then, as her brother was being led off the ship, she snatched up a cutlass and charged him.

Sir Graham had anticipated it and easily caught her.

"You stupid, unthinking, selfish, murdering *bastard*!" she screamed after her brother. "*How could you?!*"

Connor stiffened, but was made to keep walking, and Rhiannon ran to be beside him.

"Where he goes, I go," she said firmly, taking his hand.

Sir Graham just shrugged. There was Kieran, standing on the deck of the sloop that his father had designed and built for him, his eyes huge and haunted.

"He went and did it just as I told you all along that he would!" Maeve was screaming in her hysteria. "Never listened to anyone but himself, always thought he knew more than everybody else, had to go and show off in front of everyone, didn't he? And now he's lost *Kestrel*! He's gone and killed *Dadaí*, and Mother, too!"

Connor, still very weak, tripped over a ring bolt on the big ship's deck and fell to one knee. There he remained, bent over and defeated, his head lowered, his thick, tousled curls, still encrusted with blood, hanging dejectedly around his face.

His shoulders were quietly shaking.

Rhiannon went up to him and laid a hand on his back. A body couldn't take much more.

And suddenly she knew what she must do.

There was one sibling that looked to have inherited their father's thoughtful sensitivity and cooler head, and he was the one whose solemn, wide-set amber eyes were gazing quietly out at them from across the water.

It was unthinkable for Connor to be held prisoner in the Falconer household, not with his sister almost insane with grief. Liam Doherty, Nathan and Toby Ashton, Sir Graham, Maeve, all of them . . . their resentment toward him was palpable. They had rejected him. Every last one of them.

And there was no way in hell that Rhiannon was going to allow Sir Graham to throw her husband in a Bajan gaol.

She marched up to the admiral.

"Let him remain with his brother aboard his sloop," she demanded. "It's not like he's going to go anywhere. Or, can."

In the end the admiral capitulated, a dull and lifeless Connor was sent to stay aboard *Sandpiper* with Kieran, and *Sandpiper* was ordered to stay right where she was anchored in Carlisle Bay until Sir Graham Falconer decided what the hell he was going to do.

CHAPTER 33

Three days later, Ned began to complain that his muscles ached. He stopped eating, said he was tired, and pleaded to go to bed early, much to the surprise of his father and numb, hollow-eyed mother.

By the time he wandered, hot, shaking, and sweaty, into his parents' bedroom in the wee hours of the morning, Sir Graham knew that the same fever that his mother-in-law had contracted had now fallen on his one and only son.

And he felt everything inside of him still.

Sir Graham Falconer had been in fierce, bloody battles and was about the finest that England could offer when it came to raw, unquenchable, sheer, pig-headed courage. But when his little boy came staggering into his bedroom in the middle of the night, crying that he didn't feel well and his brow hot with sweat beneath his father's hand, the admiral knew a fear such as he'd never known before.

Outside, the wind gusted once, twice, shaking the coconut palms and whistling a bit as it pushed through their stiff and shaky leaves, and Sir Graham knew that dirty weather was on its way.

Maybe not tomorrow. Maybe not the next day.

But coming.

"Papa . . . I don't feel well," little Ned said weakly, and the blood went cold in his father's veins.

At sunrise, that same ominous wind was pulling at *Sandpiper*'s pennant some seventy feet above her deck and Kieran, studying it, looked to the east and then up at the sky above.

Clouds. Sheep's wool, they were. High, meticulously patterned tufts of thin white cotton, all arranged as though by a giant hand, hundreds of them piling into each other and stretching from high overhead to the distant horizon. He was a mariner. He knew what those clouds meant. When the sky looked like sheep's wool, it foretold an incoming storm.

The wind moved uneasily through the rigging.

Or something worse.

Kieran looked down at the sea and wondered if, on the other side of the island that faced the open Atlantic, the swells were already building in from the west. Time, perhaps, to think about seeking deeper water. Or to lash the sloop nine ways from sideways at the pier and hope that whatever monstrous work of nature was on its way might spare them.

He wished his father were here. He would advise him what to do.

Kieran's solemn amber eyes darkened a shade, and he turned and walked aft. Tragedy, it seemed, was never content to wrap its dire net over a few chosen, unlucky few, but instead took great delight in rippling out and making the lives of as many people as it could, unbearably miserable.

He did not have the hot nature of his sister and brother. They had grown up tempestuous, irrepressible, difficult, with Connor getting in constant trouble for brawling, disrespect and making trouble, and Maeve running away from home when she was just sixteen. They had visited more than their share of worry and heartache on their beleaguered parents.

But Kieran was of a more thoughtful, measured nature. When Maeve and Connor had been fist-fighting, he had been sitting out in the stable reading Shakespeare and composing, clandestinely and in terror of being found out, a love sonnet to a girl down in Market Square who probably didn't even know he existed. He'd hidden it beneath the hay when his mother had come looking for him and then, fearful of it being discovered, he'd torn it into bits and thrown it to the wind.

Maeve—fiery, beautiful, and a force of nature in herself, would never forgive Connor for what he had done. Nathan and Toby would be quicker to come around, and then there was poor Liam Doherty, suffering, perhaps, more than any of them . . . the old Irishman couldn't bear to even look at Connor, but Kieran knew that it had nothing to do with resentment over his older brother's decision and what had come of it.

It was because it was impossible to behold Connor without seeing a younger image of their father.

Poor Liam. Poor Sir Graham, who had to manage their wild and willful sister.

But most of all, Kieran's heart went out to Connor.

He looked up at the pennant once more, and then let his gaze move forward to the sloop's long, upswept head-rig pointing far out over the water. There, lying prone on his belly along the jib-boom was his older brother, framed against the sheep's wool clouds beyond.

He had been out there all night.

Kieran stood there watching the motionless figure for a long time.

Then, his eyes troubled, he went below.

Connor, lying far out and above the water, his cheek pressed against the sun-warmed spar and his arms hanging down on either side, was unaware of his brother's presence.

He didn't have the strength to move. He, who had spent his life dealing with restless energy, didn't have the will to move, either. Food didn't appeal to him, though Rhiannon, bless her sweet heart, had tried to get him to eat some turtle soup last night. He had taken a mouthful or two then word-lessly pushed the bowl aside, got up from the table and had come out here, far away from everyone and everything, to be alone with his agony.

Beneath him the sea had picked up a bit of chop, and the wind made a brief, gusting howl through the rigging far above deck.

Connor noted these facts with a part of his brain that no longer seemed to belong to him. Was it possible for a body to be dead inside, dead all over, really, with only one's mind still functioning? Or was it that his mind was dead, and his body was the one thing that still had any feeling? He could no longer tell the difference. He felt numb. Detached from himself. As though he were being dragged through time and space in a body that belonged to a stranger.

Something warm tickled his cheek, and he realized he was weeping.

Please, God, give me relief from this pain.

His neck was stiff, and he turned his head toward the east, laying his other cheek, now stubbled with several day's growth, against the spar. There, far off, the horizon was a riotous collage of red and crimson, the blushing, fiery light just touching a bank of distant clouds. He could feel the weather changing. He didn't need a barometer to know that far to the east, a storm was coming in.

He could feel it in his bones.

And he didn't care.

He shut his eyes, seeing the blood-red light against the back of his eyelids, trying to shut his mind to what his sister had screamed, what Nathan's and Toby's and Sir Graham's eyes had said, what his own heart knew:

You killed them.

The tears leaked from his eyes.

You're an old man, a fake, and worst of all, you're a damned coward.

His flat, haunted gaze fell on the place where *Kestrel* had been anchored, and he shut his eyes, unable to look at the empty place on the water. Dear God, was there no place to get away from this gnawing guilt, this anguish and self-loathing that made every breath he took one that he wished would be his last? Unable to stand it any longer, he pushed himself up and, swaying weakly for want of food, made his way back along the jib-boom, the bowsprit, and back to the sloop's decks.

Do it now. Do it now, before anyone else is up, and make the pain finally stop.

His mouth grim, he strode to the shrouds, hooked a hand through the tarred rope, and began to climb. High. Higher. So high that at last he was in the crosstrees where the mast ended and the topmast began, and there, ignoring the dizziness in his head, the nausea in his belly, and the trembling weakness in his body, he thought about leaping from the rigging.

Not to dive.

But to die.

Rhiannon awoke with a start.

Something wasn't right. Her eyes flew open in the darkness, and she immediately realized she was in the bunk in the main cabin of Kieran Merrick's little sloop.

Connor needs you.

She sat up, looking for him in the heavy gloom. She was alone. Fear gnawed at the base of her spine. She found the old pantaloons that Toby had lent her, yanked them on under her night shift, grabbed Connor's sleeveless waistcoat and hurriedly left the cabin.

Topside, the fresh, heady saltiness of the night air still lay over everything, though dawn had broken in a riotous display of color and cloud to the east. Waves lapped against the sloop's hull. Rhiannon, concerned, looked around, but the deck was deserted. And yet, with that part of herself that was so intimately connected to her husband, that had woken her in his absence and told her that he needed her, that made her increasingly fearful for reasons she did not yet understand, Rhiannon knew that he was here.

A strange sound was coming from aloft.

Weeping. The kind of raw, anguished sobbing that comes from a soul that has been ripped asunder in grief, horrible to bear and even more horrible to behold.

Rhiannon felt her own eyes well up with tears. She would give up everything she had in this world, if only it would relieve his suffering.

She walked to the base of the mast and looked up. There, silhouetted against the slowly-lightening sky high, high above, she could see her husband's form, his dangling feet. His forehead rested against the mast, and he appeared oblivious to her presence.

"Connor."

The weeping abruptly ceased.

"Connor, please come down. I'm . . . frightened for you."

"Go away, Rhiannon," he said brokenly. "There is nothing you or anyone can do for me."

Rhiannon had seen her husband aloft in the rigging as often as she'd seen him swaggering across a deck. She had seen him take absurd risks with his life and his safety, she had seen him do things that would have had most men quaking in terror. But never, never, had she been as afraid for him as she was at this moment.

You need to go to him.

Now.

Her mouth went suddenly dry and her palms broke out in a hot, clammy sweat as she contemplated what she was about to do.

Best *not* to contemplate it.

If she contemplated it, she might not do it.

And if she didn't do it, she did not want to think of what Connor was up there contemplating, himself.

She walked to the larboard side and there, swallowed hard and took a deep, steadying breath. The shrouds, that tarred, crosshatched network of roping that supported the mast on either side of the ship, pinnacled upward and inward like an ever narrowing ladder, finally ending at the crosstrees so high above. She had seen the crew climb them to go aloft. If they could do it, then surely, so could she.

I am young. I am strong.

She put a hand on the ropes, climbed gingerly up on a nearby gun, and then put a foot on the rail as she prepared her ascent. Her body was quaking with terror.

I can do this. I will *do this. And I will do it, Connor, because I love you.*

She took her foot off the rail, gripped the rough, hard, roping, and slowly began to climb.

Don't look down. Put your head up and look at your knuckles in front of you and just keep moving. You have to do this. He needs you like he's never needed anyone before. Climb, Rhiannon. Just climb.

Because Rhiannon knew that if he chose to give up, it really wouldn't matter whether she fell to her own death. Life, she knew with a sudden, gripping certainty, was not worth living without him. This man who had taught her that fear was not necessarily a bad thing, that life was too short not to leap, shouting with joy, out into space, that life was meant to be *lived*.

In her mind she saw him grinning, as he had done so often in happier times. *Go ahead, Rhiannon. Live a little.*

She kept climbing, fiercely determined, trembling hands pulling her upward, flattening herself against the roping as the shrouds narrowed and the deck grew smaller and smaller beneath her.

You taught me how to live, Connor. You taught me how to live, and I'm not *going to let you die.*

She could feel the slow rock of the ship all the more up here, the sway of the mast itself in these hard, taut ratlines that supported it. Nausea swam in her stomach and she fought against a sudden feeling of hysteria. Of fear so paralyzing she was afraid she was going to faint. Her hands were now shaking, sweating, and numb. Terror clenched her belly, and she took several deep gulps, forcing herself to continue on, her fear coming in tiny little whimpers from the back of her throat.

Courage, he'd once told her, wasn't about doing things you weren't afraid to do, no matter how terrifying anyone else found them. Courage was doing the things you *were* terrified to do, no matter how un-terrifying anyone else found them.

The whimpering in the back of her throat began to sound like an animal caught in a trap, and Rhiannon bit savagely down on her lip and continued moving ever upward. The shrouds had narrowed considerably now, making her all the more aware of the nothingness of space all around her, the distance between herself and the deck so far below, the very tenuous, perilous, aloneness of her position as she realized the height she had attained.

But every terrifying step brought her closer to her husband.

To any hope of saving him.

The whimpering in the back of her throat stopped, and wrapping both hands firmly around the rough roping, her knuckles white as bone, she looked up. There he was, just a few feet above, his bare foot dangling several inches from her eyes.

"Connor."

He did not respond, and remained unmoving with his forehead leaning against the topmast. She did not know if he was asleep, or so far gone in grief that the world had ceased to matter to him. Her paralyzing fear as she'd ascended the mast was nothing compared to the stark terror she felt now as she realized there was nothing keeping him from tumbling to his death.

"Connor!"

This time he raised his head, though the movement seemed to cost him all of his strength, and he looked dully down at her.

"Connor, you have to come down. Please."

"There is nothing for me to come down for, Rhiannon." His eyes were huge wells of pain behind a forced, unhappy smile. "Y'know, I've always been told that hell was a place we go after we die, but now . . . now I know that that was all a lie. Hell is right here. Right now."

"Things will get better."

"They are only getting worse."

"They're getting worse because every time you relive what happened, your mind embellishes it a little more, putting in details that weren't there originally, piling more and more guilt up on you. The decision you made was not such a bad one, Connor. You did the very thing that has made you such a successful privateer in the first place. You acted with certainty and decision. With faith in that decision, and in yourself. Making yourself feel guilty will not change what happened, it will not bring them back, and there are too many people right here, now, who love you very much, Connor. People who would be hurt for the rest of their lives if you do what I think you came up here to do."

"You don't know what I came up here to do."

"I *do* know. I see it in your eyes."

"You see nothing."

"Yes, you are correct. I see nothing. Nothing at all, and that frightens me, that nothingness. I see a man who has given up. A man who has stopped believing in himself, who believes the worst of himself, because he thinks that punishing himself as harshly as possible will somehow make the pain go away or change the outcome of what happened. But I'll tell you this, Connor. It's not going to make the pain go away. It's only going to make it worse."

He turned his face away from her, laying his cheek against the mast.

"When I was a little girl, I lost my parents, Connor. I know what it feels to grieve."

"Aye, well, I'm sure you didn't kill them. As I did, mine."

"*You didn't kill them.* Your mother was gravely ill, Connor. Probably dying. Her last wish was to go home to Newburyport, and you tried to make that happen for her. You did not cause her to get sick."

"I went after that ship against my father's advice."

"Any privateer worth his salt would have done the same. It was a big, lumbering merchant ship."

"My father knew, long before I did, that it was anything but."

"And what makes you think that ship wouldn't have attacked *us*, no matter whether you initiated it or not?"

"If we'd fled to windward, it could never have caught us. Nothing, absolutely nothing, could have caught *Kestrel* heading to windward."

"Liam told me her guns were heavier than *Kestrel*'s, and capable of much longer range. She could have fired into us long before we got as close as we did, and the outcome would have been the same."

"You are very sweet, Rhiannon, but you are no naval tactician."

"I'm no sailor, either. And my arms are getting very, very tired."

He lifted his head and turned, and for the first time seemed to realize just what she had done. That she, so fearful of heights, of the things that he enjoyed and took comfort in, had climbed the shrouds and was here, high, high above the deck and terrified for her life.

"Oh, my God," he said. "Rhiannon—"

She had been biting her lip so hard that it had gone numb.

"I love you, Connor Merrick. I love you in all your recklessness and daring and ability to live life to the fullest. I love you for the risks you have taught me to take, for giving me the courage to take those risks, and for showing me what it's like to live, to really *live*." She felt a sob building in her own throat and said fiercely, "I want to spend the rest of my life exploring all the wonderful and exciting things you have to show me, and I want to do it with you, at your side."

Something fell on her knuckles, and looking up, she saw that the tears were running freely down his face.

"I love you, Connor."

He wiped at his eyes.

"I love you. Please. Come down."

He looked fully at her then, his eyes green, glassy orbs of pain, and pushed himself back from the mast.

"I love you, too, Rhiannon."

And then, very carefully, because his own body was so weak, depleted and shaky, he moved to the starboard side and, matching his progress to hers, slowly descended, his haunted gaze holding hers all the way down.

She had said she loved him.

Pushed through the most terrifying thing she could have done in order to throw him a lifeline.

And in his heart, Connor felt the floodgates open.

CHAPTER 34

Her legs were trembling, her knees like custard when her feet finally touched the deck.

She had done it.

On the other side of the ship, her husband also reached the deck and sobbing, she ran to him and threw herself into his arms. He wrapped them fiercely around her, his own choking sobs buried in her hair, and clung to her as if he would never let her go.

"I love you, Rhiannon," he said brokenly. "Oh, God, you don't know how close I came to giving up. . . ."

She clung to him, rocking with him, her own tears coming hard and fast because oh, dear heavens, she *did* know. His lips claimed hers in hard desperation, in fierce gratitude, and she melted against him, shaking with relief.

"I love you, Rhiannon. Oh, God, I love you. You are the bravest, dearest, most incredible and generous woman that I have ever met—"

She slid her hands up the sides of his rough, stubbled cheeks and cradled his face in her palms. "Let's go below, Connor." She looked deeply up into his eyes and touched a thumb to his upper lip. "I just want to be alone with you."

"We are alone."

"No . . . your brother just came up from below, and he's pretending not to notice us."

He nodded, and she saw the hollows beneath his cheeks and the sunken look to his eyes. The swagger and confidence that was so much a part of him was gone, and it broke her heart. She had not seen him eat since the morning that *Kestrel* had come up on the pirate ship. He was weak, and he'd been hurt badly, both physically and emotionally. And while she might have saved his life today, Rhiannon knew in her heart that he needed far more than what she was able to give him.

He needed forgiveness from his sister.

He needed forgiveness from his cousins, Liam, and Sir Graham.

But most of all, he needed forgiveness from himself.

She took his hand and led him toward the hatch, and once below in the stern cabin, she coaxed him down into the narrow bunk, slid in beside him, and pulled the light blanket up to their waists. They did not waste time in words, but came together with a quiet, gentle sweetness borne of desperation and relief. And when it was over, she wrapped her arms around him, held him tightly to herself, and felt the little sloop moving restlessly beneath them as the wind began to pick up.

By the time she realized that a storm was building, her husband was asleep.

Moments later, Rhiannon, still holding him tightly in her arms, was too.

Kieran, polishing a bit of brasswork and casting a thoughtful eye at the darkening sky above, saw movement out of the corner of his eye and putting down the rag, looked up to see a Royal Navy boat cutting through the building chop and heading toward them.

He felt a quick surge of irritation. Couldn't they just leave his poor brother alone?

With a heavy sigh he tossed the rag down, strode across the deserted deck, and went to the rail. There he stood and watched as the boat, oars flashing in perfect rhythm, came up against *Sandpiper*'s sleek black hull and crisp commands were shouted out.

There was a blue-and-white clad officer in the stern; a gust of wind came up and pushed his hat askew and impatiently, he reached up and righted it.

"Hello, Delmore," Kieran called down to his English cousin. "I trust you're not here on a mere social call."

Delmore, too, was looking up at the sky. The high, patterned sheep's wool from the morning had given way to building gray cloud, and the sun was rapidly disappearing. "May I come aboard, Kieran?"

"By all means. But if you're here to add to Connor's burdens, I'm afraid I must ask you to return another time."

"I must speak with your brother."

Kieran took a deep, resigned sigh. "Very well, then. It's not like I have any authority or crew to deny you."

The English captain gave a tightly reined smile, but as he came aboard the sloop a few minutes later Kieran saw that his face was taut with worry, his gray eyes almost violet.

"What is it?" Kieran asked immediately.

"The admiral's son. Little Ned." Delmore took off his hat against a sudden gust of wind, smoothed his unruly black curls, and replaced it. His eyes were grave as he looked at Kieran. "He's got the fever, Kieran."

Kieran just stared at him.

"The same one, I think, that your mother had. Sir Graham and Lady Falconer are beside themselves. I thought you should know."

"Oh, Christ," Kieran said, turning away. "And you came here to lay even more despair on my brother's shoulders? For God's sake, Del, he's a strong man, but even he has a breaking point and he's about reached it. He adores that boy. This will send him right over the edge. What the devil would you have me do?"

"Let Connor come back with me."

"What?!"

"The boy is delirious with fever, Kieran. He's calling for his uncle."

"Oh, man," Kieran muttered.

Another gust of wind whistled through the rigging above, and Kieran felt the little sloop begin to move uneasily on the swells.

"What do you wish to do?" Delmore persisted. "Keep the information from your brother so as to protect him from even more grief? How do you think he'll feel if the boy, God forbid, dies, and he learns that it was he whom little Ned was calling for in his last moments but he wasn't there for him? You think he'll be able to live with *that*?"

Kieran looked away.

"Please, Kieran. Summon your brother. He needs to know."

Kieran nodded, turned, and headed aft. Oh, Lord save them all, when would the grief ever end? Hadn't they all been through enough? And now this?

He found the door to the stern cabin closed. Taking a deep breath, he raised a hand and knocked against it. It was a long moment before there was movement within and then Rhiannon, her eyes heavy with sleep and her beautiful hair tousled, opened the door just wide enough to peek out.

"What is it?" she asked quietly.

"I need to see Connor."

"He's sleeping, Kieran." She turned to look over her shoulder. "He *needs* to sleep. Please don't ask me to wake him."

"I must, Rhiannon. You know that I wouldn't ask it if it wasn't critical."

She looked at him with a mixture of concern and impatience. "I'll only wake him if it's a matter of life or death."

"It might be, Rhiannon. Please. Just do it."

She gave him a last, questioning look, then turned, leaving the door open for him to follow her into the gloom of the cabin. There in the bunk lay his brother, deeply asleep, still and unmoving.

The two of them stood looking down at him. "Life or death," Rhiannon warned. "Nothing less."

"Nothing less."

She leaned down and, smoothing back a thick auburn curl, kissed his brow. "Connor, love. Wake up," she whispered. "Kieran is here. He needs to speak with you."

She took his hand in her own and gently rubbed at his knuckles as his eyes opened, staring blankly up at the deckhead for a moment before he realized where he was and the heavy shadows fell over his eyes once more. He turned his head on the pillow and looked dully at his brother.

"What is it, Kieran?"

Kieran felt his own gut churn. His brother was weak. Battered. Depleted. Oh, dear God.

"It's Ned," he said quietly. "He's sick with the fever. Delmore came to get you."

Connor sat up in bed and rested the heels of his hands in his eye sockets, his thick chestnut hair falling down over his knuckles. He stayed there for a long, silent moment.

"Con?"

"I'm the last person anyone in that household wants to see right now."

"You're the *only* person that little Ned wants to see."

Connor shut his eyes. "This nightmare just won't end, will it?"

"Delmore is waiting topside to take you ashore. I think you should go."

Connor swung out of bed and stood up, swaying with weakness. Rhiannon exchanged worried glances with Kieran and together, they helped him to dress. All but the clothes on his back had gone down with *Kestrel*, but he and Kieran were of a similar height and build, and Kieran's green, double-breasted cutaway tailcoat and biscuit-colored pantaloons fit him perfectly. Then, tight-lipped and silent, Connor quietly walked toward the door, leaning heavily on them both as a wave of dizziness hit him. At the ladder that led up to the hatch, he paused to gather his composure and then, feigning a strength he didn't have, climbed wearily topside.

The weather had changed for the worse. Overhead, the clouds had built and lowered, heavy with rain and their own importance. Wind was picking up, and the beautiful turquoise hues of Carlisle Bay had turned to a deep, troubled blue-gray.

Delmore stood there waiting for him. He put a hand out to his cousin. "Thank you for coming, Connor. I know this isn't easy for you."

Connor said nothing, but just nodded. He felt dizzy from hunger and lack of sleep, and a deep, heavy weariness lay across his shoulders like a yoke.

"We shouldn't delay," Delmore said, moving to the rail.

"How bad is he?"

"Bad. Very bad."

Oh, dear God. Connor felt pain pierce his already battered heart. *I can't take much more,* he thought. *None of us can.*

His arms were shaking with weakness as he let himself down the side of the sloop, her black sides and white strake reminding him so much of *Kestrel*. He heard Kieran say something about staying behind and making preparations to anchor the sloop at both bow and stern against the incoming storm, that he would be along as soon as he could, and the rest of his brother's words were lost to a sudden gust of wind. Connor all but fell the last few feet into the boat. There, the Royal Navy tars waited, eyes straight ahead, all of them perfectly turned out and as rigid in their details as Delmore himself.

Connor took a seat and put his head and elbows on his knees, then locked his hands around the back of his neck. He felt as though he was going to pass out.

"Thank you, I'm quite all right," said a feminine voice beside him, and then *she* was there, gently offering her own strong, lithe body for him to lean against so nobody would see how weak he was, and Connor shut his eyes and gratefully accepted her quiet gift.

What a woman he had married.

She, who anticipated his every need, who sought to save his pride in front of his cousin and these Britons, who was going to go with him into the lion's den that was his sister's home, was right here with him.

There was nothing more that he needed.

He sat there with his elbows on his knees, his head down, aware of the silence around them as the seamen rowed hurriedly back toward shore under their coxswain's orders. Connor could feel the chop against the bow of the boat, and opening his eyes and looking down at the bit of water that had collected in the hull at his feet, he saw that the afternoon had gone even darker.

"Going t' be quite a blow, sir," said one of the tars, as though reading Connor's thoughts. "Don't think Oi've ever seen clouds quite that dark here in Paradise."

"Think it's an 'urricane?"

"Never saw one, but you can feel somethink in the air. This un's going t' be big. Really big."

"Shut up and row," Delmore snapped.

Connor shut his eyes. Rhiannon's arm was around his back now, and he leaned gratefully into her strength. Shortly after, the boat lurched against the sandy beach and his cousin leaped out.

He must have noted Connor's weakened condition, because he frowned and offered a hand.

"Much obliged," Connor said, and took it.

With Rhiannon at his side and Delmore in front of them, they moved quietly up the beach. Overhead, the coconut palms moved restlessly in the building wind, their tops beginning to bend and lean in the increasing gusts. A drop of rain splashed down from above, landing on Connor's nose. The color of the trees grew darker, and the chatter of birds went strangely quiet.

They reached the Falconer mansion just as the sky began to open up in earnest. Inside, a servant took Delmore's hat and coat, and Sir Graham himself came striding out of the long gallery where he had been quietly pacing, stopping to gaze out the windows every five minutes in anticipation of their arrival.

"Connor," he said, holding out his hand and frowning as he saw the pallor of his brother-in-law's skin, the haunted, sunken look in his eyes. "Thank you for coming."

Connor did not accept the offered hand. "Where is he?"

"In his bedroom. Follow me."

The awkwardness of the moment was past and Connor, steeling himself against his sister's condemnation and his dread over what state he would find his beloved little nephew in, summoned every bit of his strength and followed the admiral. Beside him Rhiannon walked, her hand in his. Only she knew how tightly he was clinging to that hand.

Only she knew that it was his lifeline.

Outside, an abrupt flash lit up the day as lightning crashed down from above, and suddenly wind and rain came sweeping in through open windows. Servants ran to close the hurricane shutters; others hurried to light candles against the sudden, thickening darkness that the storm had brought with it.

Alannah was waiting outside the boy's bedroom, her eyes tragic. "Go on in," she said. "He's been calling for you."

The door was ajar and Connor, with Rhiannon beside him, slipped quietly into the chamber. Like the day outside, the room was painted in a heavy gray light that even the candles in their hurricane lamps could not penetrate. Connor saw an unfamiliar man in black tails whom he assumed was the doctor, mixing something with mortar and pestle at a desk beneath the shuttered window. He saw Maeve sitting forlornly in a chair beside the bed, her dark red hair caught in a ribbon and hanging in neglected snarls down her back. Liam stood behind her, looking far older than Connor had ever seen him. The old man's eyes met his, and in their blue, blue depths, Connor saw the sudden gleam of tears.

Maeve looked up then, her gold eyes dominating her pale and anguished face.

"You came," she whispered.

He would not meet her gaze. "Did you think I would not?"

He walked up to the bed and finally, mustering every shred of his courage, looked down at the little boy.

"Oh, Ned," he breathed, and gently easing himself down beside the small body, reached out to take his nephew's hand. The skin was hot and dry, and felt like paper. The boy, his face flushed and damp with sweat, opened eyes that were glassy with fever.

"Uncle Connor . . . I don't feel well."

"I'm here, lad. I came as soon as I was told."

"My eyeballs ache . . . my head hurts . . . and I'm so hot . . . so . . . so . . . hot."

The doctor turned from where he'd been mixing his concoction and came back over to the bed. He was a stooped man with sad eyes and deep jowls that made him look a bit like an old hound. He looked up at Connor, then down, then suddenly back up again, frowning. "Are you ill, sir? You don't look much better than the boy does."

Connor ignored the question. "What ails him?"

"Malaria, I think."

"Can't you give him something for it?"

"Give him something? What? Prayers are about all I have left to give at this point."

Maeve let out a choking sob and quickly pushed her hand against her mouth, turning her face into her husband's embrace as he sat beside her.

The boy's breath whistled harsh and shallow through his lungs. He closed his glazed eyes, his long black lashes lying against flushed cheeks. "She's beautiful in the sunset, you know. . . All the colors of the sky are in her sails. . . . "

"It's the fever talking," the doctor continued. "I've made up a poultice. We'll pack it on his skin, perhaps it will bring the fever down."

"Reds and oranges and pinks. And light . . . so much light . . . her sails are made of it . . . it hurts my eyes to look at them. Grandma says I can fire the guns."

Maeve began rocking back and forth in her grief.

Connor reached for the sea sponge standing in a nearby bowl of water, and squeezing it out, gently bathed his little nephew's brow. "Why are you using a poultice, sir, when there's Peruvian bark to be had?"

"Peruvian bark? You mean Jesuit's bark? A proven cure for malaria, but where, sir, do you think I'm going to find any? It's not something I have in my possession, that's for certain."

"There's a doctor on St. Vincent who has a store of it."

"And how would you know such a thing? Are you a physician?"

"No, sir." Connor glanced at Sir Graham with a hint of his old defiance. "I am an American privateer. And a damned good one. Recently, I captured a ship that was carrying a store of the stuff back to England, sent by this doctor in St. Vincent to his colleague in London. It was part of the manifest."

"How do we know that doctor on St. Vincent even has any left?"

Connor looked at the older man flatly. "We don't."

Outside, the wind grew stronger, and the shutters rattled. Trees began to thrash against the house and the light through the slats of the shutters grew cold and ugly as the day went as dark a night.

Sir Graham let out a defeated breath. "St. Vincent is a hundred miles from here," he said bleakly. "We'll have to wait until the storm blows itself out. There's no way a ship can get out in this weather."

"That could be days," Maeve cried, her tears leaking through her fingers as she rocked, hunched over in anguish.

Little Ned, it was apparent, did not have days.

Connor shrugged. "It's due west."

"What are you saying?"

"Wind's blowing due west. And hard." He looked up at Sir Graham. "I could do it, you know."

Maeve looked up. "Do what?" she demanded.

"Go fetch the Peruvian bark."

Sir Graham shook his head. "Madness. Not in this storm, you couldn't."

"Give me something with a sail and a rudder and I tell you, I can."

"Even the heaviest ships in my fleet are double anchored at stem and stern to ride this thing out. To venture out in this weather is suicide, and you know it!"

"Aye, I do. But I don't think you have a choice, Admiral."

Maeve leaped to her feet. "Damn you, Connor! I won't let you do it, I won't suffer any more grief because of your damned recklessness and need for glory!"

Brother and sister faced each other, neither one willing to back down. And in the charged silence, the doctor put a hand on the boy's hot brow and frowned.

"I daresay, Lady Falconer, that if you *don't* let him do it, the one you'll be grieving, with all certainty, is your son."

Connor had heard enough. Let them all bicker and worry and waste time. He was not going to stand here and let his nephew die. Oh, no. Not on *his* watch. Ignoring the fatigue in his own body, the weakness of limb and the dull ache that still persisted in his skull, he strode angrily to the door and there, turned and faced them all with defiant eyes.

"The problem with all of you is that you don't know how to *live*," he muttered. "Well, I lost the two people who, beside my beloved wife, were dearer and more precious to me than anyone in the world, and I'm not going to stand here and watch someone else I love die when I can damn well do something about it. Send me off with or without your blessing, but damn you, damn all of you, I'm going."

"Wait," Sir Graham said. "*Wait.*"

Connor turned, his fists clenched, his eyes resolute. "Throw me back under arrest, Sir Graham. But don't put this death on my conscience. Oh, no. Don't you *dare.*"

The admiral faced him squarely. "I will go with you."

"No!" shouted Maeve. "No, I won't allow it! I need you here, *Ned* needs you here!"

But it was old Liam who stepped away from the bed and went to join Connor at the door. He looked up at the tall, charismatic young man who looked so much like the one he had spent his life devoted to, a man who couldn't be more different from his father . . . and yet, couldn't be more alike.

A man who had inherited Captain Brendan Jay Merrick's famous courage—and wasn't afraid to use it.

"I'll go with ye," he said quietly, and turned to face the others. "You're needed here, Sir Graham. Connor and I will go."

"I'll go, too."

In their anguish, everyone had forgotten Delmore Lord, standing quietly at the door. Now, the admiral's flag captain went to stand with the old Irishman and his American cousin whose eyes, for the first time in days, were beginning to show signs of purpose.

Of life.

"If Connor thinks he can do it, then I have faith in him and will do all I can to support him. You don't have a choice, Sir Graham."

Rhiannon, the tears springing to her eyes, stared at the three of them for a long, anguished moment. Old Liam, standing beside Connor as he must have spent his life standing beside Brendan. Delmore Lord, eyes steady as he bravely defied his admiral and chanced his own death for the sake of a little boy.

Oh, Connor, she thought. *I know why you have to do this. I know that it's more than just your love for your nephew that drives you. This is your chance for absolution. I understand that. But oh, dear God, I'm worried sick about you. Worried sick.*

Outside, thunder rolled, and the very ground seemed to shake beneath the house.

"I'll need a ship," Connor said, beginning to pace. "Something small. Fore and aft rigged. Easily managed with a minimal crew."

Sir Graham was still shaking his head, unable, in his own grief and worry for his only son, to make a decision.

Wind moaned under the eaves, and outside, something blew over and banged against a railing.

"Sir Graham!" Connor insisted sharply. "We don't have much time."

"Take the cutter, *Rapier*," the admiral said. "She's fast and seaworthy. Del will take you to her."

In moments the room was a swirl of activity as plans were hastily made and men began filing hurriedly out. At last only Connor remained, with Maeve still in her chair and numb with grief, and Rhiannon, who had sat down on the bed beside the little boy.

Maeve looked up at her brother with tragic eyes. "You don't have to do this," she said. "Not after what I said to you."

"I'm not doing it for you. I'm doing it for *him*."

"Thank you all the same. I know we haven't always seen eye to eye, Connor, but our differences arise from the fact we're so much alike."

Connor's foot was tapping against the floor, his energy building. "I know that."

"Godspeed, my brother."

"Farewell, Maeve."

Rhiannon got up and followed him to the door. Little Ned never moved as she left the bed. His condition had worsened in the hour that they'd been here and Rhiannon feared, deep in her heart, that no matter how fast *Rapier* was, she would never make it back in time with the medicine that the boy so desperately needed.

The wind howled outside, gathering in strength and fury.

If she made it back at all.

One-Eye, Jacques, and the scanty remains of *Kestrel's* crew were there waiting for Connor when he, accompanied by Rhiannon, Liam and Delmore, arrived at the dock. Connor didn't stop to question how they must have found out about his mission. "I don't need to tell you about the risks," he shouted to them over the howl of the wind as he looked gravely at each face in turn. "There are no guarantees we're going to make it."

"If anyone can get a ship from here to St. Vincent in this weather, sir, it's you."

"Aye, Captain. We didn't desert you before, and we ain't gonna desert you now."

The wind was roaring straight out of the east now, and long threads of foam streamed along the choppy, restless waters of Carlisle Bay. Nobody said what was obvious.

It was going to be a lot, lot worse out at sea, beyond the protection of the harbor.

Footsteps echoed on the dock. Looking over his shoulder, Connor saw two figures approaching, bent against the wind but unmistakable in their familiarity.

His heart warmed. Nathan and Toby.

It wasn't forgiveness, but it was trust, and that was close enough.

It had to be.

One of the Royal Navy tars yelled up from below. "Boat's ready, sir!"

There was no time to delay.

Connor glanced down, seeing the boat leaping and bucking in the rising seas as her crew tried to keep her fended away from the poles supporting the pier. One by one, the brave men who had volunteered to accompany him climbed down into the little vessel that looked so fragile against the elements and now, more than ever before, Connor was aware of the huge weight of his responsibility to them.

And what their loyalty, their faith in him, meant to him.

Shielding their faces against the rain and huddled under tarpaulin coats, they looked up at the man whom they trusted to lead them into hell and back.

I am my father's son. And I can do this. I will do this.

He turned to the woman in his arms, using his back to shelter her from the wind and rain as he threaded his fingers into her hair and, holding her head steady, touched his forehead to hers.

"It's time for me to go, Rhiannon."

"I know." She bravely held back her tears.

"I love you," he said. "No matter what happens, never forget that."

She nodded jerkily. "I love you too, Connor. You are a better man than any I've ever met. God bless you. And keep you."

He enfolded her in his arms, silently transmitting his thoughts to her even though he knew in his heart that she already knew what he would say if he could put them to voice. *I know this is hard for you. I know the sacrifice you're making, Rhiannon. Thank you for giving me your blessing on this. Thank you for understanding that it is something I must do, not just for little Ned, not just for my family . . . but for myself.*

Absolution.

He claimed her lips in a long, desperate kiss and then, turning his back, followed the others down into the waiting boat.

He looked up, seeing her tragic, terrified face.

"Live a little!" he yelled up to her, flashing that old reckless smile. "See you when we get back!"

The boat pushed off. Rhiannon stood there, her skirts whipping around her legs as she clung to a post so as not to be blown off her feet. Even in the few minutes she'd been here, the wind had increased in force and fury. She watched the boat's struggles to reach the long, low cutter anchored near the rest of the fleet, saw its few inhabitants going up and over the vessel's sides, and moments later, sail began to bloom at its long, rakish nose.

Above, the clouds made a huge, sky-wide vortex of grey and purple and black.

The cutter was moving now, heeling hard over in the wind and already showing a bone in her teeth as she gathered speed.

And Rhiannon feared, with everything in her heart, that she was never coming back.

CHAPTER 35

The afternoon grew darker yet, so dark that it was impossible to tell when the day ended and nightfall began.

Five o' clock. Seven o' clock. Midnight. Ned tossed fitfully in the bed, flinging aside the damp sheets and mumbling in his delirium while his anguished mother bathed his brow, his father paced the gallery with a cold cup of coffee and stared out into the wind-torn darkness, and somewhere, a small vessel rode the fury of the worst storm to hit the Caribbean in over a decade.

In her own bedroom Rhiannon, her long, red-gold hair caught in a thick braid and hanging down her back, opened the shutters and sat by the window, looking out into a night as black as Hades. Wind screamed around the corners of the house and she could see the coconut palms bent nearly double under the onslaught.

Connor was out there somewhere.

How long would it take the cutter to reach St. Vincent, a hundred miles away? Probably not long with the wind howling out of the east as it was, though Sir Graham had told her earlier that it had begun to veer to the southeast. At least, if it continued on that pattern, the cutter wouldn't have to beat back against it on her return to Barbados.

Provided she would be returning.

Rain was blowing into the room, and Rhiannon closed the shutters once more.

She got into bed but lay there in the darkness, listening to the roar of the wind outside, the slash of rain against the shutters, her mind conjuring up things she did not want to think about. Her own restlessness got the better of her, and some time in the wee hours of the morning she finally got up and, the hurricane lamp in her hand, went to check on Maeve and little Ned.

The room was bathed in candlelight, painting a soft golden glow over the rich mahogany furniture, the high walls, the damp white sheets that lay twisted around the boy's small body. Maeve had not moved, and for a moment, Rhiannon stood watching her sister-in-law as she tenderly bathed the child's brow with the sponge. She looked up then, and saw Rhiannon.

"How is he?"

Maeve's eyes were haunted. "I don't want to say he's worse, Rhiannon, because if I do, that will make it true."

But it was clear that the child's condition had deteriorated. His black hair was damp with sweat, and his breathing had grown shallow and faint.

"I tried to rouse him a little while ago so that he could take something to drink," Maeve whispered. "But I couldn't.

At least . . . at least, he'll be with Mother and Da." Her voice caught on a sob. "They'll take care of him in heaven."

Rhiannon pulled up a chair on the opposite side of the bed. "Your brother will get that medicine, Maeve. He's going to save Ned's life. I know it in my very bones."

"Reckless idiot," Maeve said, not unkindly.

"Reckless, yes."

"That very trait of his that caused him so much trouble . . . never did I think I'd be grateful for it. That the very thing we always condemned him for, and thought of as his greatest fault, would end up being a blessing. Nobody else would have even considered going out in this weather . . . Nobody. If he makes it back, I have much to apologize for."

"He's suffering terribly, Maeve."

"I know . . . and I'm sorry for that. I said things, did things, in my grief that were wrong. That were cruel. And perhaps, if I was there, I would have made the same decisions."

The two women sat in the candlelit silence, and it occurred to Rhiannon that the howling roar of the wind outside had diminished. Somewhere downstairs, a clock chimed.

Ned moaned and turned his head to the side. His lips had gone dry and chapped.

"I'm happy he found you, you know," Maeve said. "My brother was always a carefree spirit, happy in nature but quick to anger, but deep down inside, I don't think he ever thought very highly of himself. Yes, he projected an image he wanted the world to see and believe, but underneath it all, he didn't believe it himself. But I've seen the change in him since he met you, Rhiannon. He's more . . . relaxed. Anchored. More sure of himself, now, in a way that is no longer false, but genuine."

"He has been good for me, too. He taught me how to swim. And to dive from the rail of a ship. And on that last day, he let me take *Kestrel*'s tiller." She smiled in remembrance. "It was one of the most memorable, incredible moments of my life." She looked down, picking at a thread in her sleeve. "She had a soul, didn't she?"

"Aye. She sure did."

Maeve's eyes grew distant, and she looked up as Sir Graham entered the room.

"How is he?" he asked.

"I think you should stay, Gray." She took her little boy's hand. "I don't think he has long, now."

Rhiannon saw the tears gathering in the admiral's eyes. She would leave this little family with their pain, and their privacy. She got up, and quietly left the room.

Outside, the wind had abated yet further, and as she walked through the long, dark gallery Rhiannon saw that a servant had already come through and opened the shutters, allowing the breeze, gusty now and indeed coming in from the southeast, to sweep through the long room. A dull grey light hung over everything and noting it, Rhiannon went to the great double doors, pushed them open, and stepped out onto the verandah.

Above, the stars were reappearing, revealed in all their cold, sparkling beauty as the great bands of cloud slid silently off to the north. Far off to the east, over the hills themselves, a faint blush of pale light heralded the coming dawn.

Rhiannon got down on her knees and prayed.

For little Ned.

For the Falconers.

For Liam and Nathan and Toby and Delmore and One-Eye and Jacques and for the cutter, *Rapier*.

But mostly, she prayed for Connor.

And as the dawn grew brighter, the sun rising triumphantly up through high, striated remnants of the storm to paint the harbor orange, red, and gold, Rhiannon turned her head to the west and the open sea.

There, in the distance, was the cutter *Rapier*.

Tears slipped silently down Rhiannon's cheeks.

He had done it.

The doctor was summoned before the cutter could even reach the anchorage, the medicine was administered, and Connor Merrick's brave and selfless act saved the little boy's life.

Absolution.

On a beautiful morning two weeks later the American privateer stood at the pier, his lean, handsome form shown off by a snug-fitting black tailcoat cut away at the waist, buff pantaloons tucked into Hessian boots, and a smart new round hat that would offer him little protection from the tropical sun. But that didn't really matter. Where they were headed, it was likely to be a lot colder.

"Please give Gwyneth my love," Maeve said, holding newborn Grace in her arms while the twins, Mary and Anne, tugged at her skirts. Standing between her and his father stood Ned, still pale, still recovering, but alive. He was looking worshipfully up at his uncle as Connor hugged his sister, shook hands with the admiral, and gave Delmore Lord a quick thump on the back before embracing him.

"Have a care, sir, you'll muss the lace on my coat," the British captain said with a little smile. "I have an image to keep up, you know."

"Live a little," Connor said, playfully punching his cousin's shoulder. "And come visit, Del, when you bring the admiral and his family back across the Atlantic. If he can spare you."

Connor and Rhiannon knelt down and hugged the twins, and then Connor came to Ned.

"Take care of my sister, young man. I expect nothing less of you."

"I will, Uncle Connor." The boy's throat worked, and he tried, manfully, to keep his emotions at bay. "Thank you for saving my life. For risking yours so that I would be okay. Were you awfully scared, Uncle Connor?"

"Terrified," his uncle said softly, smiling down at the child. "But not as frightened as I would have been had I not gone."

"When I was sick . . . I had a dream. *They* told me you would go. That you'd be the only one crazy enough to do it and that because of you, I'd be all right. After that, I wasn't scared of dying anymore. He let me take the tiller. And she let me fire a cannon that had its own name."

Connor's indulgent smile froze. "What are you saying, lad?"

The boy shrugged, and suddenly self-conscious, looked down at his feet. "It was just a dream, Uncle Connor."

Connor looked at the boy for a long moment, and a sudden shaft of light speared through high cloud and sparkled peacefully on the waves.

"Just a dream," he said softly, exchanging a glance with his sister, and then his wife. "And what was the cannon's name, Ned?"

"Freedom."

Freedom.

Connor looked up at Maeve, and the words lay unspoken between them. But his sister gave a tremulous smile, and tears stood in her eyes—happy ones, of relief and gratitude—and the sunlight brightened yet further.

They were going home. First to England, to make good on Connor's promise to get his wife to Morninghall Abbey in time for the birth of her sister's baby. Then, on to Newburyport.

"Just behave yourself in my waters," Sir Graham said with false gruffness. "No privateering until you're well north of the Indies. I beg of you." He cast a sideways glance at Kieran, who stood with his hands clasped behind his back, smiling fondly. "Bad enough that I'm stuck with one Merrick brother to have to watch like a hawk. Don't make me come after you."

Connor laughed, and wrapped his arm around Rhiannon. "Given that I've got a ship like *Rapier* to command, that's a tall order, Sir Graham. But I promise not to make you regret such a generous gift."

"It's the least I could do, Connor, for all that you did for my family." He reached out and firmly shook his brother-in-law's hand. "Be well. And thank you."

The cutter lay waiting atop her reflection in the turquoise water, Nathan, Toby, One-Eye and Jacques already aboard.

"Guess it's time to say good-bye, then," Connor said.

He embraced his young brother, who thought to stay here in the tropics for a while longer, though the twinkle in his eye suggested that Sir Graham's worries about yet another Merrick privateer were well-founded. Then he and Rhiannon hugged each of his family one last time, his heart freed from its guilt, his fingers worrying one of the bright brass buttons of his new double-breasted coat in his eagerness to get underway.

There was one last person to say farewell to.

Liam Doherty would not be heading north with them.

"My old bones rather like it down here, lad," he said, holding out his hand to Connor after embracing Rhiannon in a great bear hug. "Maybe there's no cure for the rheumatism, but this is about as close as I think I'll ever get."

"Come visit us, Liam." Connor smiled. "Barbados in the winter might be good for your rheumatism, but Newburyport in the summertime will be good for your soul."

"I'll do that, lad." Liam looked down for a moment, then reached deeply into his pocket and drew out a folded piece of vellum. "Here. Read this when . . . when you're ready."

Connor laughed, because Liam knew as well as anyone, now, that he couldn't read. At least, not very well. But still, it was kind of the old man whom he loved like an uncle to pen a few words to him when, perhaps, uttering them might be too emotional for them both.

They went back a long way, he and Liam.

Connor put the paper deep in his pocket, his mind went off in the many unchaseable directions it was wont to go, and he forgot about it.

An hour later they had weighed anchor, and *Rapier*, her long jib-boom pointing the way, was steering a course for England.

EPILOGUE

Damon de Wolfe, the Marquess of Morninghall and one-time holder of the Black Wolf persona himself, was pacing the floors of his great Cotswolds home as his wife, screaming in agony as the pains of labor seized her once again, struggled upstairs to deliver his firstborn.

"If I didn't have you to thank for saving my life, Connor, after that whole Black Wolf business, I swear I'd have more than a little to say to you for compromising my ward in Barbados. Is the world not safe from you?"

"No, my lord. I'm afraid not."

"Got the paper this morning. The *Times*. Some damned American privateer was harrying and harassing our shipping in the Channel right under the noses of the fleet as recently as last Sunday. Took a few prizes and made off with them, and in broad daylight as well. But you wouldn't know anything about that, I suppose."

Connor's grin was completely innocent. "I suppose I wouldn't, my lord."

"Stop with the my lord nonsense. I'm Damon to you, and you know it."

"Yes." Connor's grin spread. "My lord."

Upstairs, there was another loud cry from Gwyneth, and Damon got up and resumed his pacing. "It was good of you to get Rhiannon back here so she could be with her sister during this. And that dog of hers was howling for her constantly. You'll have to take him back with you, my nerves are shot. Shot. I thought that having a baby was supposed to be the most blessed event in the entire damned world. All rainbows, bliss and light. By God, I'm a wreck. I'll be damned if I ever put myself through this kind of hell ever again."

Connor, smirking, poured a measure of the rum he had brought from Barbados into his brother-in-law's glass. "Here. Drink this. I thought I was restless, but you give new meaning to the word."

The marquess snatched up the glass and downed it on one gulp.

"What's taking that baby so long to arrive?" he snapped. "For God's sake, you'd think the women would let a man into the room if only to ease his own suffering. This worry is bloody well killing me."

"I think, Damon, that they are managing very well without you." He refilled his brother-in-law's glass. "Here. A toast to your coming heir."

"A toast," the marquess said, and drank.

Connor looked out over the beautiful English countryside, alive now with the bright virginal greens of early spring. He was thinking about a certain several ships in the English Channel. Ships that were, at this very moment, being sailed as prizes back to Newburyport. . . .

". . . Don't ever get your wife pregnant," Morninghall was saying, beginning to pace once more. "Oh, she'll tell you how her back hurts and her stomach's upset and that she can't get comfortable at night and that her shoes no longer fit, but I tell you, Connor, her grievances are nothing, *nothing*, compared to the absolute *hell* that I'm in right now. Absolute hell, I tell you!"

"Everything will be fine, Damon. Here, have some more rum."

The marquess grabbed the glass, but at that moment Rhiannon suddenly appeared at the doorway. She was smiling, unable to contain her own delight.

"Come upstairs, Damon," she said. "You have a baby son."

The child was named Philip Edward Antony de Wolfe, given some English courtesy title that Connor couldn't remember and which meant little to him anyhow, and *oohed* and *aahed* over by the entire household: the ancient butler, the housekeeper, the servants, the staff, even Rhiannon's elderly dog Mattie, who sniffed at the newborn in curiosity then gave his red, wrinkled little cheek a swipe with his tongue.

"I hope you like dogs, Connor," Rhiannon said as afterward, they skirted a newly-planted field bordered by trees, new in leaf, whose branches waved in the breeze. "It was good of Gwyneth and Damon to take care of him for me while I was away, but I think they're going to have their hands full for a time."

"Well, since we're starting our own zoo, why not?" Connor said, thinking of the two cats that his father, he'd been told, had handed down into the boat as *Kestrel* was foundering and which, of course, had ended up on *Rapier*.

His mind tracked back to the marquess' uncharacteristic angst as Gwyneth had been in labor and he wondered if he, when and if the time came, would handle the event with at least a little more calm.

His wife reached out and put her hand in his, and together, the two moved toward the beautiful Cotswold hills that commanded a view for miles around, the fields newly tilled and planted and divided by ancient hedgerows. There was a decided nip in the air today, a last little reminder that spring was still in its infancy, and Connor was glad that he'd remembered to bring the black cutaway coat he'd bought in Barbados.

Not that he, far more comfortable in more casual wear, had bothered to wear it since he'd stuffed the thing in a trunk and promptly forgotten about it several hours out of Carlisle Bay.

"How are you feeling today, Rhiannon?" he asked, as he watched her elderly bird dog, Mattie, trotting far ahead of them, nose to the ground.

"I feel fine. Why wouldn't I?"

"Well, maybe you're carrying a baby, yourself."

"Well, if I am, it's early days yet, Connor. And when the time comes, I'm sure you'll give me much to smile about and take my mind off my own discomfort when things start to get a little uncomfortable."

The memory of Gwyneth's screams came suddenly back to him. *A little uncomfortable?*

He had a feeling she wouldn't be smiling.

Mattie, far ahead, was waiting at the top of the grassy knoll, tongue hanging out, the wind blowing his long, floppy ears back as he turned his face into the breeze.

Hand-in-hand, they continued their walk and eventually caught up to the dog, who, with a groan, lay down and let the early spring sunshine soak into his fur.

"Pretty up here," Connor said, sitting down. "You can see for miles." His smile was a little rueful as the wind came up and played with his tousled curls. "Though I confess, it's a bit constraining, even so."

"And why is that?"

"Because we're too far inland. I can't see the ocean. I *need* to see the ocean."

"It's in your blood, isn't it?"

"Aye, my love. I guess it is."

Rhiannon sat down beside him and happily leaned into the warm strength of his shoulder as his arm curled around her. "Lord of the sea," she murmured.

"Hmm?"

"Oh, nothing. Just thinking out loud. About Gwyneth and me . . . how we each married noblemen, in our own way. She, the lord of Morninghall . . . me, the lord of the sea."

Connor's green eyes glinted, and he laughed, a rich, all-encompassing sound that warmed her very soul.

"I love you, Rhiannon," he said, touching his forehead to hers and then letting his lips drift down until they lingered at the side of her mouth. "You're the best thing that ever happened to me."

"I love you, too, Connor. You're the best thing that ever happened to *me*."

He shifted position in order to kiss her better, and as he drew back, anticipating spending the afternoon, perhaps, back in bed with her, he felt something in his coat pocket. Frowning, he dug a hand inside and felt it close on a folded piece of vellum.

"What's this?" He pulled it out. "Oh, right, of course. I'd forgotten it, all this time."

He started to put it back into his pocket, thinking, only, of pulling his lovely young wife to her feet and finding some place a little less exposed in which to make love to her.

"What is it?"

"Oh, just a letter from Liam. Probably full of sentimental Irish balderdash or some such thing."

"You haven't read it?"

He just raised a brow and looked at her.

"Here," she said. "Give it to me. I'll read it for you." She looked up at him. "If you want."

"Aye, sure." He handed her the letter, grinning. "Go ahead."

Rhiannon opened the paper, and immediately, her heart seemed to stop in her throat. She looked up at Connor. "It's not from Liam," she whispered. "It's . . . it's from your father."

The carefree smile faded, and he took the letter from her. Yes, it was his Da's beloved, familiar hand. Sudden anguish welled up behind his eyes, and swallowing hard, he began to put the letter back in his pocket. "I . . . I'll look at it some other time," he said, turning away to hide the sudden gleam of tears.

"I understand."

She took his hand, but the letter, like the person himself who had written it, was now a presence there with them, between them, demanding to be heard, unwilling to let itself be forgotten or laid aside for another day.

His hand went back into his pocket.

Emerged with the carefully folded vellum.

"Go ahead," he finally said, and gave her the letter. She slowly opened it, and a shaft of sunlight came down through the drifting clouds above and made the paper seem to glow in her hand.

My dear and beloved son,

As I write this, it is late in the afternoon and time weighs heavily on my hands, though perhaps, for others, it is passing faster than it should be. By the time you read this, the inevitable events that I foresee happening will have transpired and, because of that, I know that this letter will bring you a sadness that I certainly do not intend for you to feel.

Your mother is dying, Connor. I pen these words from Kestrel's cabin, a place where she and I spent many a happy moment, a place that brought us together, a place where so much of our early lives transpired. I did not tell you just how ill your mother is, perhaps because I knew you needed every resource at your command to deal with the demands of running a ship, perhaps because I did not want to upset you, but more so, if I am to be truthful, because confessing it in writing or in the spoken word only confirms what I know in my heart to be true, and that has been something I have been unwilling, and unable, to face.

Aside from my beloved children, your mother—along with Kestrel herself—has been the great love of my life, and I will not leave either of them. There is not enough room in the boat for us, but even if there were I would not take that seat, and your mother, I know, would not survive hours out on an open craft, waiting for rescue. I know where she would wish to spend her last moments, and I know where I wish to spend mine. God knows I never wanted to spend eternity confined to a plot in the dirt behind St. Paul's Church back in Newburyport, and neither, I daresay, did your mother. I am where I want to be, with the two women I loved most in this world, and the three of us are together as, I believe in my heart, we were always meant to be.

Do not grieve for me, my son. I have lived a rich, full, blessed and wonderful life. I have seen and done things that most people only dream about, watched my three beautiful children grow into strong, loving adults that any parent would be proud of, welcomed that greatest treasure of all, grandchildren, into the world and known that through them, a part of me will always remain. I do not welcome death, but nor do I fear it, and never have; I know, with the certainty of my heart, that life goes on in ways that remain forever mysterious to us all.

I am proud of you, Connor. As proud of a son as it's possible for a father to be. You are so much like I was at your age, and I see you struggling to find acceptance and acclaim while doubting everything that you are. (You should know that had I been the young man I once was, I, too, would have attacked that ship. Stop blaming yourself, as I know you've been doing. She would have caught us, anyhow.) Your mother and I have never doubted you, and I know that through your trials, you will become stronger. Keep your beautiful and loving Rhiannon close by your side, and nourish each other with your respective strengths. Comfort each other through life's sorrows, love each other through all of it. You could not have found a better woman to stand at your side as you walk through your life, and I could not be prouder, and happier, to call her my daughter.

In closing, I leave you with this. When you get back home to Newburyport you will find, in my office at the shipyard, a set of drafts that I drew up for you. They were originally meant to replace Merrimack, *but this war won't go on forever, lad, and I foresee, in this coming new age, American-built ships, Newburyport-built ships, becoming the reigning queens of ocean trade—there will be great fortunes to be had there, and the ship whose design awaits you will be the first of this new breed to ply the seas, ships that are going to be bigger, longer, leaner, and most of all, faster, than anything that has come before. The world is changing, my dear son, and you are on the verge of an exciting new era. Take the drafts, and have Uncle Matt build her for you.*

I have no regrets and neither, my beloved son, should you. Live your life to the fullest, as you already know how to do, and leave guilt, self-recrimination, and grief behind you. You have made me proud. You have made me happy. You have given me the greatest blessings that it's possible for a son to give his father.

I love you.
Until we meet again,
— Dadaí

Rhiannon slowly looked up and handed the letter to her husband, who sat gazing far out over the English countryside, his eyes distant. He took the letter, looked at the words that his father had written, and pressed the paper to his lips for a long, long moment.

And then he folded it, carefully, and slid it back down into his pocket.

"Grandchildren," he murmured, with a watery smile.

"It's what they always wanted."

He stood up, pulling her to her feet, watching the sun play through the high, fluffy clouds as the earth thrust its adoring, seeking face skyward in this yearly ritual, this timeless resurrection of life.

"Guess we'd better go work on giving them some," Connor said, and hand in hand, the two of them headed steadily back toward the house.

the end

AUTHOR'S NOTE

Though *Lord Of The Sea* was written in 2013, it actually had its origins many years before when, as a young woman, I headed over to nearby Newburyport during my lunch break to see the "tall ship" that was visiting. Aside from that grand old lady *USS Constitution* in Boston, I had never seen a "tall ship" before, and I was unprepared for the visual impact of driving into the waterside parking lot and seeing, rising above the trees with her pennants flying from their highest reaches, two tall, sharply raked masts. Though the ship herself wasn't all that big, these proud, distinctive masts towered over our little city, and the name of the ship to whom they belonged was *Pride of Baltimore.*

Pride was a faithfully replicated Baltimore privateer, built in 1977 to celebrate Maryland's maritime heritage and to act as a goodwill ambassador for the city of Baltimore. Sailing to many ports around the world, the sleek black topsail schooner captured the hearts of all who saw her. Sadly, just

Danelle Harmon

a year or two after she took our collective breath away here in Newburyport, the magnificent *Pride* was lost at sea to a freak squall in the Caribbean, taking her captain, three crewmembers and her two cats with her. Her loss brought unmeasurable grief and pain to all who loved and admired the "wild black mare" for she was arguably the most beautiful ship in the world, and while eventually Baltimore pulled from the ashes of its grief a replacement ship which was christened *Pride of Baltimore II*, there would never be another like her.

A few short years after *Pride's* tragic loss, I found myself under contract with Avon Books and committed to writing a second seafaring romance (*Captain Of My Heart*) to follow up my bestselling debut book, *Pirate In My Arms*. I knew I wanted the book to be set in my hometown city of Newburyport, knew that it would feature a unique and magnificent ship, and knew that it would be my memories of *Pride of Baltimore* that would step up to fill the role. *Pride* was *Kestrel*. Or maybe *Kestrel* was *Pride*. In any case they were, with very slight modifications, pretty much the same ship, and though *Kestrel* was a New England-built schooner of 1778 (and I confess to taking certain anachronistic liberties with her), she was never anything but what she actually was and what I always meant her to be: a Baltimore privateer.

Those who know the story of *Pride's* unforgettable nine years and her tragic and untimely loss will recognize many similarities between her story and *Kestrel's*—similarities that go far beyond the simple things like identical specifications of depth, draft, beam and hull length, and pet names that their respective captains had for each ship. These similarities are deliberate and intentional, and are my way of paying homage to a ship I only knew for a short time, but which left me with a lifetime of awe and admiration, and dare I say, love.

I hope I've done her justice.

— Danelle Harmon,
near Newburyport, Massachusetts
December 21, 2013

ABOUT THE AUTHOR

*N*ew York Times and *USA Today* bestselling author Danelle Harmon has written twelve critically acclaimed and award-winning books, with many being published all over the world. A Massachusetts native, she has lived in Great Britain, though these days she and her English husband make their home in New England with their daughter Emma and numerous animals including three dogs, an Egyptian Arabian horse, and a flock of pet chickens. Danelle enjoys reading, spending time with family, friends and her animals, and sailing her Melonseed skiff, *Kestrel II*. She welcomes email from her readers and can be reached at Danelle@danelleharmon.com or through any of the means listed below:

Connect with me online!
www.facebook.com/DanelleHarmon
Website: Danelleharmon.com
Twitter: @DanelleHarmon
Pinterest: http://www.pinterest.com/danelleharmon/

READ BELOW FOR MORE BOOKS FROM DANELLE HARMON, including a special sneak-peak from her # 1 Kindle Store download, THE WILD ONE!

The *Kestrel* Books include, in order:
Captain Of My Heart (Captain Brendan Merrick and Mira Ashton)
My Lady Pirate (Sir Graham Falconer and Maeve Merrick)
Wicked At Heart (the Marquess of Morninghall and Gwyneth Evans Simms)
Lord Of The Sea (Connor Merrick and Rhiannon Evans)
(see below for more information)

Discover more titles from Danelle Harmon's popular and bestselling

HEROS OF THE SEA SERIES

MASTER OF MY DREAMS
(Heroes of the Sea Series, Book # 1)

The emotional and unforgettable story of a tough Royal Navy captain and the beautiful Irish stowaway who teaches him how to love once again. (Featuring Captain Christian Lord and Deirdre O' Devir, parents of Delmore Lord and Colin Lord)

An Amazon KINDLE Top Ten Bestselling Historical Romance!
An Amazon KINDLE #1 Bestseller (Sea Adventures)!

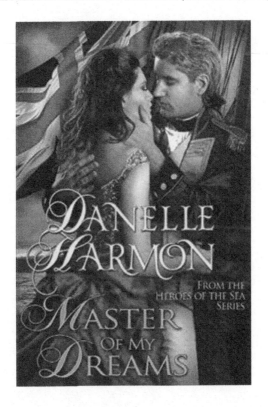

CAPTAIN OF MY HEART
(Heroes Of The Sea Series, Book # 2)

Thrilling romantic adventures abound on board the 1778 Yankee privateer schooner *Kestrel*, captained by dashing Irishman Brendan Merrick — who meets his match in the outrageous shipbuilder's daughter, Mira Ashton!

An Amazon KINDLE Top Ten Bestselling Historical Romance!
An Amazon KINDLE #1 Bestseller in Sea Adventures!
 # 8 on the *New York Times* Bestseller list as part of FOUR IRRESISTIBLE ROGUES!
 # 11 on the *USA TODAY* Bestseller list as part of FOUR IRRESISTIBLE ROGUES!

MY LADY PIRATE
(Heroes Of The Sea Series, Book # 3)

The sexy, swashbuckling tale of Pirate Queen of the Caribbean Maeve Merrick, and the powerful English hero who is determined to win her heart at all costs.

Winner of *Romantic Times* Magazine's Reviewers Choice Certificate of Excellence!
Winner of *Romantic Times* K.I.S.S. Hero Award!
An Amazon KINDLE Bestseller!

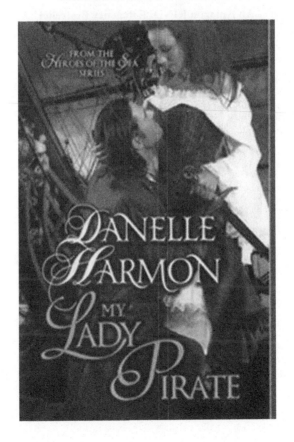

TAKEN BY STORM
(Heroes Of The Sea Series, Book # 4)

Disgraced naval hero Colin Lord wants only to pursue his new career as a London veterinarian and put his tragic past behind him. But when fugitive heiress Lady Ariadne St. Aubyn convinces him to help get her prized racehorse to Norfolk before every reward hunter in England can catch her, Colin finds himself swept up into an adventure he could never have imagined. A treat for animal lovers everywhere!

An Amazon KINDLE Regency Bestseller!

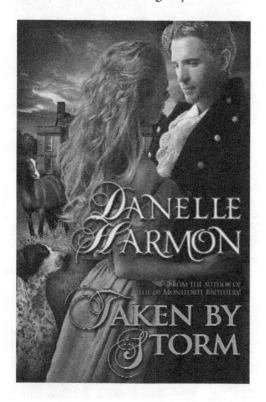

WICKED AT HEART

(Heroes Of The Sea Series, Book # 5)

A Beauty-and-the-Beast tale of love and redemption between the dark and brooding Marquess of Morninghall and Lady Gwyneth Evans Simms, the woman who is determined to heal his tortured heart.

Winner of a *Romantic Times* Magazine K.I.S.S. Hero Award!
Nominated for *Romantic Times* Magazine's K.I.S.S. Hero of the Year!
An Amazon KINDLE Bestseller in Historical Romance!

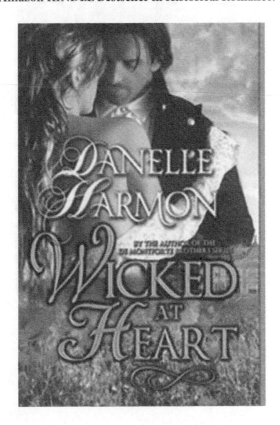

THE ADMIRAL'S HEART

A sweet and sexy short story/novella about second chances, with appearances by Captain Brendan Jay Merrick, Captain Christian Lord, and the de Montforte Brothers!

An Amazon KINDLE bestseller in Short Stories!
An Amazon KINDLE bestseller in Anthologies!

and:

THE INTERNATIONALLY BESTSELLING, AWARD-
WINNING, CRITICALLY ACCLAIMED

DE MONTFORTE BROTHERS SERIES

"The bluest of blood; the boldest of hearts;
the de Montforte brothers will take your breath away."
Meet the dashing and aristocratic De Montforte
Brothers by Danelle Harmon:

THE WILD ONE (try it free on Kindle!) - read on for a
special sneak peek
THE BELOVED ONE
THE DEFIANT ONE
THE WICKED ONE

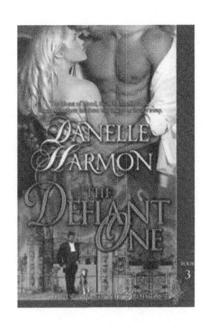

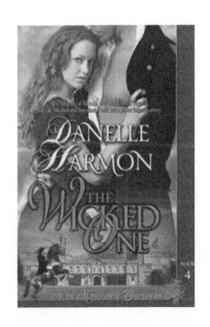

And now, for a special "sneak peek" from the first book in Danelle Harmon's bestselling de Montforte brothers series!

FREE ON AMAZON!
** A Number One in Kindle Store Bestseller **

THE WILD ONE

By Danelle Harmon
Book 1 of the De Montforte Brothers Series

---

*P*ROLOGUE

Newman House, 18 April, 1775

> *My dear brother, Lucien,*
>
> *It has just gone dark and as I pen these words to you, an air of rising tension hangs above this troubled town. Tonight, several regiments — including mine, the King's Own — have been ordered by General Gage, commander in chief of our forces here in Boston, out to Concord to seize and destroy a significant store of arms and munitions that the rebels have secreted there. Due to the clandestine nature of this assignment, I have ordered my batman, Billingshurst, to withhold the posting of this letter until the morrow, when the mission will have been completed and secrecy will no longer be of concern.*

Although it is my most ardent hope that no blood will be shed on either side during this endeavour, I find that my heart, in these final moments before I must leave, is restless and uneasy. It is not for myself that I am afraid, but another. As you know from my previous letters home, I have met a young woman here with whom I have become attached in a warm friendship. I suspect you do not approve of my becoming so enamoured of a storekeeper's daughter, but things are different in this place, and when a fellow is three thousand miles away from home, love makes a far more desirable companion than loneliness. My dear Miss Paige has made me happy, Lucien, and earlier tonight, she accepted my plea for her hand in marriage; I beg you to understand, and forgive, for I know that someday when you meet her, you will love her as I do.

My brother, I have but one thing to ask of you, and knowing that you will see to my wishes is the only thing that calms my troubled soul during these last few moments before we depart. If anything should happen to me — tonight, tomorrow, or at any time whilst I am here in Boston — I beg of you to find it in your heart to show charity and kindness to my angel, my Juliet, for she means the world to me. I know you will take care of her if ever I cannot. Do this for me and I shall be happy, Lucien.

I must close now, as the others are gathered downstairs in the parlour, and we are all ready to move. May God bless and keep you, my dear brother, and Gareth, Andrew, and sweet Nerissa, too.

Charles

Sometime during the last hour, it had begun to grow dark.

Lucien de Montforte turned the letter over in his hands, his gaze shuttered, his mind far away as he stared out the window over the downs that stood like sentinels against the fading twilight. A breath of pink still glowed in the western sky, but it would soon be gone. He hated this time of night, this still and lonely hour just after sunset when old ghosts were near, and distant memories welled up in the heart with the poignant nearness of yesterday, close enough to see yet always too elusive to touch.

But the letter was real. Too real.

He ran a thumb over the heavy vellum, the bold, elegant script that had been so distinctive of Charles's style — both on paper, in thought, and on the field — still looking as fresh as if it had been written yesterday, not last April. His own name was there on the front: *To His Grace the Duke of Blackheath, Blackheath Castle, nr. Ravenscombe, Berkshire, England.*

They were probably the last words Charles had ever written.

Carefully, he folded the letter along creases that had become fragile and well-worn. The blob of red wax with which his brother had sealed the letter came together at the edges like a wound that had never healed, and try as he might to avoid seeing them, his gaze caught the words that someone, probably Billingshurst, had written on the back....

Found on the desk of Captain Lord Charles Adair de Montforte on the 19th of April 1775, the day on which his lordship was killed in the fighting at Concord. Please deliver to addressee.

A pang went through him. Dead, gone, and all but forgotten, just like that.

The Duke of Blackheath carefully laid the letter inside the drawer, which he shut and locked. He gazed once more out the window, lord of all he surveyed but unable to master his own bitter emptiness. A mile away, at the foot of the downs, he could just see the twinkling lights of Ravenscombe village, could envision its ancient church with its Norman tower and tombs of de Montforte dead. And there, inside, high on the stone wall of the chancel, was the simple bronze plaque that was all they had to tell posterity that his brother had ever even lived.

Charles, the second son.

God help them all if anything happened to him, Lucien, and the dukedom passed to the third.

No. God would not be so cruel.

He snuffed the single candle and with the darkness enclosing him, the sky still glowing beyond the window, moved from the room.

CHAPTER 1

Berkshire, England, 1776

The Flying White was bound for Oxford, and it was running late. Now, trying to make up time lost to a broken axle, the driver had whipped up the team, and the coach careered through the night in a cacophony of shouts, thundering hooves, and cries from the passengers who were clinging for their lives on the roof above.

Strong lanterns cut through the rainy darkness, picking out ditches, trees, and hedgerows as the vehicle hurtled through the Lambourn Downs at a pace that had Juliet Paige's heart in her throat. Because of Charlotte, her six-month-old daughter, Juliet had been lucky enough to get a seat inside the coach, but even so, her head banged against the leather squabs on the right, her shoulder against an elderly gent on her left, and her neck ached with the constant side to side movement. On the seat across from her, another young mother clung to her two frightened children, one huddled under each arm. It had been a dreadful run up from Southampton indeed, and Juliet was feeling almost as ill as she had during the long sea voyage over from Boston.

The coach hit a bump, became airborne for a split second, and landed hard, snapping her neck, throwing her violently against the man on her left, and causing the passengers clinging to the roof above to cry out in terror. Someone's trunk went flying off the coach, but the driver never slowed the galloping team.

"God help us!" murmured the young mother across from Juliet as her children cringed fearfully against her.

Juliet grasped the strap and hung her head, fighting nausea as she hugged her own child. Her lips touched the baby's downy gold curls. "Almost there," she whispered, for Charlotte's ears alone. "Almost there—to your papa's home."

Suddenly without warning, there were shouts, a horse's frightened whinny, and violent curses from the driver. Someone on the roof screamed. The coach careened madly, the inhabitants both inside and out shrieking in terror as the vehicle hurtled along on two wheels for another forty or fifty feet before finally crashing heavily down on its axles with another neck-snapping jolt, shattering a window with the impact and spilling the elderly gent to the floor. Outside, someone was sobbing in fear and pain.

And inside, the atmosphere of the coach went as still as death.

"We're being robbed!" cried the old man, getting to his knees to peer out the rain-spattered window.

Shots rang out. There was a heavy thud from above, then movement just beyond the ominous black pane. And then suddenly, without warning it imploded, showering the inside passengers in a hail of glass.

Gasping, they looked up to see a heavy pistol—and a masked face just beyond it.

"Yer money or yer life. *Now!*"

It was the very devil of a night. No moon, no stars, and a light rain stinging his face as Lord Gareth Francis de Montforte sent his horse, Crusader, flying down the Wantage road at a speed approaching suicide. Stands of beech and oak shot past, there then gone. Pounding hooves splashed through puddles and echoed against the hedgerows that bracketed the road. Gareth glanced over his shoulder, saw nothing but a long empty stretch of road behind him, and shouted with glee. Another race won—Perry, Chilcot, and the rest of the Den of Debauchery would never catch him now!

Laughing, he patted Crusader's neck as the hunter pounded through the night. "Well done, good fellow! Well done—"

And pulled him up sharply at he passed Wether Down.

It took him only a moment to assess the situation.

Highwaymen. And by the looks of it, they were helping themselves to the pickings—and passengers—of the Flying White from Southampton.

The Flying White? The young gentleman reached inside his coat pocket and pulled out his watch, squinting to see its face in the darkness. Damned late for the Flying White . . .

He dropped the timepiece back into his pocket, steadied Crusader, and considered what to do. No gentlemen of the road, this lot, but a trio of desperate, hardened killers. The driver and guard lay on the ground beside the coach, both presumably dead. Somewhere a child was crying, and now one of the bandits, with a face that made a hatchet look kind, smashed in the windows of the coach with the butt end of his gun. Gareth reached for his pistol. The thought of quietly turning around and going back the way he'd come never occurred to him. The thought of waiting for his friends, probably a mile behind thanks to Crusader's blistering speed, didn't occur to him, either. Especially when he saw one of the bandits yank open the door of the coach and haul out a struggling young woman.

He had just the briefest glimpse of her face—scared, pale, beautiful—before one of the highwaymen shot out the lanterns of the coach and darkness fell over the entire scene. Someone screamed. Another shot rang out, silencing the frightened cry abruptly.

His face grim, the young gentleman knotted his horse's reins and removed his gloves, pulling each one carefully off by the fingertips. With a watchful eye on the highwaymen, he slipped his feet from the irons and vaulted lightly down from the thoroughbred's tall back, his glossy top boots of Spanish leather landing in chalk mud up to his ankles. The horse never moved. He doffed his fine new surtout and laid it over the saddle along with his tricorne and gloves. He tucked the lace at his wrist safely inside his sleeve to protect it from any soot or sparks his pistol might emit. Then he crept through the knee-high weeds and nettles that grew thick at the side of the road, priming and loading the pistol as he moved stealthily toward the stricken coach. He would have time to squeeze off only one shot before they were upon him, and that one shot had to count.

"Everybo'y out. *Now!*"

Holding Charlotte tightly against her, Juliet managed to remain calm as the robber snared her wrist and jerked her violently from the vehicle. She landed awkwardly in the sticky white mud and would have gone down if not for the huge, bearlike hand that yanked her to her feet. Perhaps, she thought numbly, it was the very fact that it *was* bearlike that she was able to keep her head—and her wits—about her, for Juliet had been born and raised in the woods of Maine, and she was no stranger to bears, Indians, and a host of other threats that made these English highwaymen look benign by comparison.

But they were certainly not benign. The slain driver lay face-down in the mud. The bodies of one of the guards and a passenger were sprawled in the weeds nearby. A shudder went through her. She was glad of the darkness. Glad that the poor little children still inside the coach were spared the horrors that daylight would have revealed.

Cuddling Charlotte, she stood beside the other passengers as the robbers yanked people down from the roof and lined them up in front of the coach. A woman was sobbing. A girl clung pitifully to the old man, perhaps her grandfather. One fellow, finely dressed and obviously a gentleman, angrily protested the treatment of the women and without a word, one of the highwayman stuck his pistol into his belly and shot him dead. As he fell, the wretched group gasped in dismay and horror. Then the last passengers were dragged from the coach, the two children clinging to their mother's skirts and crying piteously.

They all huddled together in the rainy darkness, too terrified to speak as, one by one, they were relieved of their money, their jewels, their watches, and their pride.

And then the bandits came to Juliet.

"Gimme yer money, girl, all of it. Now!"

Juliet complied. Without a sound, she handed over her reticule.

"The necklace, too."

Her hand went to her throat. Hesitated. The robber cuffed it away in impatience, ripping the thin gold chain from her neck and dropping the miniature of Charlotte's dead father into his leather bag.

"Any jewels?"

She was still staring at the bag. "No."

"Any rings?"

"No."

But he grabbed her hand, held it up, and saw it: a promise made but broken by death. It was Charles's signet ring—her engagement ring—the last thing her beloved fiancé had given her before he had died in the fighting at Concord.

"Filthy lyin' bitch, give it to me!"

Juliet stood her ground. She looked him straight in the eye and firmly, quietly, repeated the single word.

"*No.*"

Without warning he backhanded her across the cheek, and she fell to her knees in the mud, cutting her palm on a stone as she tried to prevent injury to the baby. Her hair tumbled down around her face. Charlotte began screaming. And Juliet looked up, only to see the black hole of a pistol's mouth two inches away, the robber behind it snarling with rage.

Her life passed before her eyes.

And at that moment a shot rang out from somewhere off to her right, a dark rose exploded on the highwayman's chest, and with a look of surprise, he pitched forward, dead.

Only one shot, but by God, I made it count.

The other two highwaymen jerked around at the bark of Gareth's pistol. Their faces mirrored disbelief as they took in his fine shirt and lace at throat and sleeve, his silk waistcoat, expensive boots, expensive breeches, expensive everything. They saw him as a plum ripe for the picking, and Gareth knew it. He went for his sword.

"Get on your horses and go, and neither of you shall be hurt."

For a moment, neither the highwaymen nor the passengers moved. Then, slowly, one of the highwayman began to smile. The other, to sneer.

"Now!" Gareth commanded, still moving forward and trying to bluff them with his display of cool authority.

And then all hell broke loose.

Tongues of flame cracked from the highwaymen's pistols and Gareth heard the low whine of a ball passing at close range. Passengers screamed and dived for cover. The coach horses reared, whinnying in fear. Gareth, his sword raised, charged through the tangle of nettle that grew dense at the side of the road, trying to get to the robbers before they could reload and fire. His foot hit a patch of mud and he went down, his cheek slamming into the stinging nettles.

One of the highwayman came racing toward him, spewing a torrent of foul language and intent only on finishing him off. Gareth lay gasping, then flung himself hard to the left as the bandit's pistol coughed another spear of flame. Where his shoulder had been, a plume of mud shot several inches into the air.

The brigand was still coming, roaring at the top of his lungs, already bringing up a second pistol.

Gamely, Gareth tried to get to his feet and reach his sword. He slipped in the wet weeds, his cheek on fire as though he'd been stung by a hundred bees. He was outnumbered, his pistol spent, his sword just out of reach. But he wasn't done for. Not yet. Not by any stretch of the imagination. He lunged for his sword, rolled onto his back, and sitting up, flung the weapon at the oncoming highwayman with all his strength.

The blade caught the robber just beneath the jaw and nearly took his head off. He went over backward, clawing at his throat, his dying breath a terrible, rasping gurgle.

And then Gareth saw one of the two children running toward him, obviously thinking he was the only safety left in this world gone mad.

"*Billy!*" the mother was screaming. "Billy, no, *get back!*"

The last highwayman spun around. Wild-eyed and desperate, he saw the fleeing child, saw that his two friends were dead, and, as though to avenge a night gone wrong, brought his pistol up, training it on the little boy's back.

"*Billeeeeeeee!*"

Gareth lunged to his feet, threw himself at the child, and tumbled him to the ground, shielding him with his body. The pistol exploded at close range, deafening him, a white-hot lance of fire ripping through his ribs as he rolled over and over through grass and weeds and nettles, the child still in his arms.

He came to rest upon his back, the wet weeds beneath him, blood gushing hotly from his side. He lay still, blinking up at the trees, the rain falling gently upon his throbbing cheek.

His fading mind echoed his earlier words. *Well done, good fellow! Well done . . .*

The child sprang up and ran, sobbing, back to his mother.

And for Lord Gareth de Montforte, all went dark . . .

If you enjoyed this excerpt, download your free copy of THE WILD ONE!

Made in United States
North Haven, CT
30 January 2024

48116104R00286